The Iron Cursed

Book Seven of the Iron Soul Series

J.M. Briggs

Contents

For you the readers.
You aren't why I write,
but you certainly help.

1

The Dead

Magic couldn't restore the dead to life: Alex Adams was living proof of that. Many times over. There was no spell that could fix this. Had it gone differently maybe there would have been time to use the Iron Chalice to save them from their injuries, but their deaths had been almost instant.

The funeral hall was still, the soft murmur of voices behind her seeming very far away. Two dark wooden caskets were laid out side by side with smiling photographs of Doctor Elizabeth Adams née Kilmer and Michael Adams in front of them. They were nice photos, Alex decided as she studied them, even if they were from a few years ago. There had been more gray hairs on both of their heads and more wrinkles on their faces, but in the photos, they were smiling with eyes full of life.

A phantom warmth slid over her hand as Alex allowed herself to remember the last time she'd been to a funeral, and her mom had held her hand. She couldn't remember who had died, but something about funerals always made her cry. Almost always. Right now, there were no tears. The churning of different emotions in her chest stretched at her skin. Her eyes landed on the two coffins again. Somehow it hit her at that moment that they contained her parents. Her mom and her dad were in those things, and this was it. She wasn't ever going to see them again.

Alex shivered as the cold tangle in her chest tightened and tried to knot further. Images of a truck flashed in front of her eyes. Vertigo hit Alex and she gripped the bottom of the chair she was seated on. Someone was talking at the podium now. He was vaguely familiar and Alex thought that her father probably worked with him. Across the aisle, her mom's best friend since college was crying. She blinked away the tears that had started to gather and pushed down the wave of grief. Soon enough the emotions were swallowed up by the thick ocean in her chest. It all dulled and she allowed herself to pay attention to the goings on around her.

More people came up to speak. Many of them offered sad but supportive smiles to her. Alex nodded each time but didn't try to smile or say anything. Next to her, Matt said something once or twice as people shook his hand. Ed on Matt's far side stayed silent and completely still, looking like some sort of reaper in his all-black suit.

Lots of people had come. The funeral hall they'd gotten for the service was almost filled with the rows of chairs containing coworkers and friends of her late parents. However, there were faces that Alex recognized much more clearly. Several of her old high school friends who had remained local for college filled one row near some of Matt's friends and a larger group of people from Ed's own grade. Michelle, who she'd been with on the track team during junior year of high school, caught her eye and offered her a weak smile.

Alex tried not to stare. In truth she didn't pay much attention to the people in high school she'd been so certain would always be her friends. Not being physically close had taken its toll, but Alex knew that much of the distance was her own fault. She never called anymore and rarely responded to online messages. What was there to talk about? They weren't mages and couldn't know about magic.

Holding back a grimace, Alex glanced over at Matt. In his black suit, he looked older than his twenty-three years. Guilt and pride mixed strangely in her chest as it occurred to her how proud their parents would have been. He was already transferring to a local law school and had left his part-time job. Matt had been the one taking care of the arrangements and was progressing through the custody process for Ed. She would be returning to Ravenslake to a different set of responsibilities and leaving Matt to bear it all alone. The guilt overtook the pride and Alex's hands trembled as she fought down the rush of emotion. In her chest, the tight, painful knot threatened to take over and Alex squeezed her eyes shut.

A tear slipped out from her right eye. Pulling on her magic, Alex let the warm energy spread through her chest and limbs. It wrapped around the little knot and soothed the sharp ache that was trying to make itself known. She breathed easier and opened her eyes to focus on the faces moving in front of her. Alex knew that she'd never remember all of them, but she wanted to at least make some effort to recognize the people who came.

"How horrible for the kids," someone said behind them. Alex tensed up and tried to ignore them. "Matt's seeking custody I understand."

"Will they be alright?" a male voice whispered.

"Elizabeth and Michael had life insurance," a third voice explained. "Apparently a larger policy until all the children were through school, so at least their educations won't suffer."

"Still... the poor things."

Glancing towards Matt, Alex watched her brother's jaw tighten. The line of speakers ended and the man from the funeral home whose name escaped Alex stood up to close the ceremony. Standing up, Alex brushed off her black skirt and carefully got her balance in the black heels. The comforting weight of an iron dagger tucked away in her purse rested against her hip as she followed Matt to the front of the room. Ed fell into step behind her and she stayed quiet as the others in the room came up towards them.

There were soft words of well-wishing and a few more religious remarks that made Alex want to roll her eyes. Some people had nice things to say about her parents and others told them to call if they needed anything. It all seemed too rehearsed to Alex; inorganic and stiff. She didn't try to smile and was very aware of the coffins just behind her. The knot started to ache again, but the magic and mess of emotions swallowed it up quickly.

Time slipped away and Alex just kept shaking hands and nodding. Next to her Ed made small grunts and sounds in response to questions. People gave her and Matt worried looks and moved off into small groups.

The tone of the room changed. Alex frowned and looked around, bracing herself for something bad to happen. At the back of the room, she caught sight of Morgana who met her eyes and shook her head. Not magic then. Ed moved away from her side as the last of the line headed for the main hall and the food.

Matt frowned at her, his eyes dark and angry. There were furrows much like their father's forming between his eyebrows, but then he shook his head and tightened his jaw. Alex waited, giving him a moment to collect himself and said nothing. Matt licked his lips and looked over his shoulder at Edward. Their younger brother was sitting in one of the chairs with a splotchy face and red eyes. The sight made the knot twinge again.

"How can you be so distant?" Matt's voice was low and Alex's eyes jumped back to him. The anger in her brother's eyes was turning to fury, and for the first time ever Alex thought he might hit her. "Mom and Dad are dead!"

She waited for him to say it was her fault. In truth it was, and she almost wanted him to say it. The car crash had been caused by Arthur out of some sort of petty revenge for breaking his mother's spell over the Fae. Magic fluttered around Alex, soothing her as it washed over her skin. Death wasn't the end. She almost said as much, but her lips didn't want to move.

"Alex?" Matt sounded sadder now. "What happened? You're so…" he trailed off. Her brother took a physical step back, his whole posture and expression suddenly changed. Silence filled the space between them. A desire to say something, maybe hug him hit Alex in the chest, but she didn't move. "I need to check on Ed," Matt finally said. "Just try to…" He shook his head again. "Just make sure you're available. A lot of people came to support us."

He moved away and Alex swallowed. Suddenly alone, she turned and looked at the photographs of her parents. Something shifted in her chest again, but she viciously forced it down as her knees tried to tremble. She folded her hands awkwardly in front of herself and glanced around the room. Some of her old friends were gathered together near the doorway. Morgana was seated in a chair near the back watching everyone calmly. Alex nodded to her and walked over to her old high school friends.

"Alex," Michelle greeted. She stepped forward and hugged Alex. "I'm so sorry."

"Thanks for coming," Alex replied. Michelle nodded vaguely, a few strands of her brown hair falling into her face.

"It's just horrible," Emily added. The blonde tugged at the bottom of her black skirt that was probably too short for a funeral before giving Alex a hug. The contact felt strange and it was all Alex could do not to jump away. "If you need anything..." The sentence trailed off and they stood in silence.

"We'll be fine," Alex forced out.

"Are you going back to school or staying in Spokane?" Michelle asked. "You could transfer for the next semester."

"I'm going back to Ravenslake," Alex answered. "Matt is moving back to Spokane. He's transferring into Gonzaga law school for the fall."

"Well, that's good then," Emily agreed. Then she looked around nervously. "Good turnout, I suppose."

"Yeah, I guess so." Alex shrugged a little and looked out into the front hall. People were sitting in the more comfortable chairs and chatting in small groups. Some looked more relaxed now as they pointed at photos that had been put on one wall. "It's nice to see so many people wanting to honor Mom and Dad."

"I just can't imagine," Michelle told her. "When my mom heard-" Michelle stopped herself and shook her head. "I'm really very sorry, Alex. This is terrible."

"We'll be okay."

Those words were the best that Alex could manage. Yet they were weak and too vague. Michelle and Emily both frowned at her, looking torn between wanting to say something and fear that they'd say the wrong thing. Bad situation overall and Alex didn't try to reassure them. The three of them tried not to just stare awkwardly at each other, and Alex wondered just when things had changed so much. She couldn't remember any moment when their friendships fell away, but she couldn't remember the last time she'd called them or they'd called her. It had gone both ways and it wasn't something she could blame on magic. That was almost reassuring.

"Alex," Matt called. She turned with a mix of relief and dread to find her brother standing behind her. "The cremation."

Matt put a hand on her back and gently pushed her towards the front of the room again. Two men from the funeral home in well-worn black suits were waiting for them. Ed was lingering by an impressive flower arrangement from the newspaper their father had worked at and eyeing it dangerously. Guilt tried to take over again. Ed had been the one most excited to learn that she was a mage. He'd also been the least frightened when Alex had explained that it was the mixing of multiple worlds that generated magic. She and her fellow mages were in a way just glorified white blood cells meant to get rid of beings from other worlds and from different sets of physical rules. Her parents had been scared for her, but Ed had just wanted to see her use magic. Now it had cost him his parents.

The men said a few words to them and Alex heard the attendees file back in. There were a few moments of silence and then the funeral directors closed the caskets and hit a switch. There was a soft thrum of a machine and the coffins began to slide away. Alex wasn't sure if they were going straight into the fire or into another room. She supposed it didn't really matter, and she forced herself to watch solemnly. Her gray eyes jumped back to the photographs of her parents and she swallowed thickly.

"Why did you want them cremated?" Matt asked. He crossed his arms in front of him. "It was the only thing you actually seemed to care about."

Alex ignored the thinly veiled insult. He didn't understand. This wasn't his fault or the result of what he'd been born carrying. If she let the grief have any power there'd be nothing left. Soft voices filled her head and Alex kept her eyes open and locked on the coffins as they rolled out of sight. If she didn't close her eyes, then maybe she wouldn't see all the other funerals that she'd dreamed of in the last few days.

"Cremation helps release all of a soul," Alex answered. "Part of my soul got stuck in my first body."

The words were honest, but Matt gasped sharply. Something in his eyes flickered. He looked angry and then heartbroken before resignation overtook his features. The expression was all wrong for him, but Alex said nothing. Her eyes moved to the screens that now covered the dark tunnels her parents' coffins had vanished into. Next to her, Matt made some sort of abortive sound before he stepped away and said something to Ed. Behind Alex, their footfalls managed to echo against the carpeted floor as the sound of voices faded away.

"Alex?" Morgana's voice said behind her a few moments later. Then there was a hand on her shoulder. "The others are outside if you want to..."

"No," Alex replied. She didn't turn around to look at Morgana. "I know they're here." Where else would they be? It was a Saturday and they'd driven up to Spokane the night before. Merlin was guarding Ravenslake, but her friends had wanted to be with her. "I'm fine, Morgana." Alex was still staring at the screens. "Just remembering."

2

The Nonmagical

It wasn't easy for Lance to keep his focus on the road as they drove through the darkness. In front of him the highway stretched out towards Ravenslake and his bed, but his mind was bristling with apprehension and ideas. He couldn't help but worry about Alex. All through the funeral she'd been like a statue. They'd stayed in the back of the hall and watched, unable to do anything, but there just in case. Ahead of them, Lance could see the lights of Morgana's car as it followed the curves of the road. Time ticked by slowly as the pop music played at a low volume.

"I don't know about you guys, but all I want to see now is my bed," Bran said. "Any idea how much longer?"

"We're close now," Lance promised. "Maybe another twenty minutes."

"Good, I need sleep," Jenny said. She was in the passenger seat next to him and the three mages Aiden, Bran, and Nicki were in the back of his truck cab. "I have a meeting first thing tomorrow with one of my TAs. I'm going to need so much coffee."

"Can you skip it?" Nicki asked, leaning forward a bit.

"No, this is about my final project. I really need some help and it's one of my major classes."

"Well with how crazy things have been this year I'd be impressed if any of us got decent grades," Aiden said. "At least my parents know about the whole magic thing and won't kill me. Still, a professor's son flunking out; embarrassing."

"You aren't going to flunk out," Nicki sighed. "Stop being so dramatic."

"We're going into our junior years and school hasn't exactly been our priority," Aiden said. "Not to mention what happens after we graduate. Do we find jobs in Ravenslake and hope that they give us enough time off to travel and fight monsters?"

Maybe he didn't mean it to, but Aiden's question came out dark and foreboding. Lance suppressed a shiver. It was a cold reminder of the life the mages were dealing with. He looked towards Jenny and even in the dim light he could see that she was uneasy. Silence filled the truck again, with the low pop music seeming to fade away in the tense atmosphere.

"At least there was no sign of Arthur," Jenny said softly. "That's what I was worried about most at the funeral."

"Yeah, all that work to put down the blood protection spells and he just..." Bran shuddered, and the truck fell silent again.

Lance shifted nervously in the driver's seat and glanced up towards his visor. There was a photo of his family stashed up there, and while he couldn't see it, Lance knew it well enough. His mom was smiling and his step-father had an arm around her while his younger siblings stood in the front. The relief he'd enjoyed when Alex had made a point of casting the blood spell on Portland to keep his family safe was now twisting into dread. Part of him knew that he wouldn't be Arthur's primary target, but then again, he and Jenny had thrown their lot in with the mages. He might not have any magic himself, but he hadn't stopped trying to help where he could.

"I can't believe she's going to classes tomorrow," Bran said. His voice was sad and distant. "Seems too soon."

"Yeah, but I don't think she wants to have time to think about it," Nicki replied. She sounded just as sad and Lance risked a glance back at her in the rearview mirror. The redhead was collapsed in her seat with a deep frown that made her look much older. "Alex has already decided that she's going to class tomorrow. She's insisting that she's alright every time that I talk to her."

"But Morgana hinted that Alex saw it happen." Aiden shuddered and pressed his lips together. Lance was afraid that he might just get sick. "That's just horrible."

"Alex hasn't told me." Nicki's frown somehow deepened. "I'm not sure if she's coming back to the dorm. Morgana made some noises that she's going to ask Alex to stay with her."

"That might be for the best," Lance heard himself say.

"Yeah, but living with a professor might draw attention," Bran countered. His jaw was tense and Lance recognized that Bran was mulling something over. "Still, we probably already spend too much time around the professors by most people's standards. Our outside social lives have been slowly vanishing."

"I'm not sure Alex cares," Nicki sighed. "I'm worried about her."

"When my mom first died, I didn't react too much at first," Jenny said. His girlfriend twisted around in the passenger seat to look back at the others. "I didn't want to talk about it or acknowledge it. Mom had been ill for a while. We just need to be here for Alex and let her try to process everything on her own terms." Lance nodded in agreement at the statement but couldn't help but notice that Bran didn't look convinced when he looked back at the others.

Aiden straightened up and forced a smile. "Well, when she gets back to school, we'll all support her." His expression turned more serious. "Hopefully Arthur won't try anything else like that."

"I don't like knowing there's a way around the blood protection," Nicki said. "Sure, in Ravenslake my Gran is probably safe since Arthur probably won't try anything so close by, but we haven't even gone to California-" Nicki cut herself off quickly.

"I know," Jenny said. "Hopefully Alex will be willing to go down there soon. Maybe the blood protection spell isn't perfect, but I'd rather have it near my dad. Besides, it couldn't hurt to mess with the Pendreds a bit." There was an icy bite to that last part and Lance smiled a little. Jenny caught his eye and gave him a smirk. "We need to utilize every weapon we have against Arthur."

"The issue is, how do we deal with Arthur?" Aiden asked. "He's proven many times that murder is an option for him."

"We have to kill him," Nicki said bluntly. "He almost killed Alex, and when you saved her, it nearly killed you. He and the Queen enslaved all the creatures from the Sídhe branch of the Tree of Reality and now he's murdered Alex's parents. We have to kill him."

"I won't argue with that," Aiden replied. "But we need a plan of attack. He's good at slipping away in water tunnels. He escaped last time and then killed Alex's parents. We need a better plan than just kill him."

"He's half Sídhe like Merlin and Morgana," Nicki said. "Honestly I'm not sure if normal weapons would work on him. The professors have never been very frank about the extent of their immortality."

"I'm pretty sure they can be hurt," Bran offered. "The issue is that Arthur is at least some kind of mage, thanks to being made with the Iron

Chain." They all shuddered at the mention of the dangerous artifact. "So, he probably has the same boost to his durability that we do. That said, we know that we can be injured."

"Yeah, he shoved a sword through Alex's gut," Nicki said bluntly. Jenny suddenly twisted next to him and looked back at her. "It won't do us any good to sugarcoat what Arthur is capable of. He can hurt us and we can hurt him."

Silence gripped the truck once more. Lance debated turning up the music, but this was the first time they'd really talked about all this. He didn't like it, but his gut said that the mages needed a chance to verbally work through this. A car passed them on the highway, its headlights illuminating Jenny's features. She glanced his way, catching his brown eyes with her own.

"So have you two thought about next year?" Aiden asked. It thankfully provided a new topic. "I know that things are weird at university. Are you coming back next year?"

Lance barely kept himself from looking at Jenny as she tensed. They hadn't talked about it. Originally when everything had come out, that they were reincarnations and that the others were mages, she'd wanted to transfer. Lance had just wanted her to give them a chance. Now that she had, he'd been guilty of not even thinking about the future.

"Things have changed," Jenny said carefully. Her voice was strong despite her caution. "When I originally expressed my intention to transfer, we still thought Arthur was on our side and that he was the Iron Soul. Now we know that Alex is the real Iron Soul. I'm not sure I'm comfortable leaving her. I know that she has all of you, but with the death of her parents..." Jenny's confidence faltered. "It doesn't seem right to leave now."

Letting out a breath, Lance nodded in agreement. He hadn't been aware of how much he didn't want to leave Ravenslake until Aiden had asked. In truth, he probably needed to examine that. Alex wasn't Arto: he'd never betrayed her and had tried to be a friend, so it wasn't like he actually owed her for anything. Not in this life anyway, and Alex hadn't expressed much interest in rehashing out hurts from prior lives. In fact, she'd been happy when he and Jenny got together properly and openly in this life.

"I know we're not mages," Jenny added. "But I'd like to help. Anyway, if we leave, Arthur might decide that we're good targets."

"He still might," Bran said. He leaned forward from the back and put a hand on Jenny's shoulder. "You don't have magic to protect yourselves."

"Then I'll have to practice with that dagger Alex gave me," Jenny replied. Lance smiled at the tone of her voice. She was sexy when she was like this. "I'm not going to let Arthur drive me off."

"There's a lot to think about for next year," Nicki said. Her voice radiated approval and a bit of excitement. "We're planning to rent a house so that we're together. It may or might not be a good idea for you to join us."

"There's a lot to sort out," Bran agreed. "But no point in trying to do so now. We have to see what happens with Alex first."

"Yeah, what happens with Alex," Nicki sighed.

And they were back to the darker and more depressing topic. Lance wanted to say something, to try and soothe the tense emotions in the truck but wasn't sure what he could say. It was late and they were tired. Up ahead Morgana's car suddenly slammed on the brakes and swerved in the road. Lance hit the brakes, shouting for the others to hold on as something silvery rushed out into the road. Lance steered the truck as calmly as he could as more silver shapes leapt out of the darkness. Gripping the wheel tightly, he pulled the truck over.

Behind him the mages were shouting and his eyes jumped past the silver figures to Morgana's car. Two figures had come out of the car and were rushing towards the silver shapes. Lance's heart was racing as the back doors of his truck opened. One of the figures turned to them, revealing golden armor that gleamed in the light of his headlights. Long horns curved out of its forehead and he could see pointed ears where its long translucent hair parted. It was a Síd. Not one of the modern descendants that had lived in this world for years, but one of the originals. They were back.

"Stay in the truck!" Nicki ordered.

Nodding, Lance blinked as a fireball collided with the chest of the Síd he'd been staring at. It shouted something even as it stumbled back. A large silvery hound, the first thing that had run out into the road, jumped forward only to be hit with another fireball. The hound fell and the Síd drew a long golden sword. A lance made of ice lodged itself in the creature's chest and it dissolved into golden dust.

Lance forced himself to breathe and scanned what he could see in the light of the headlights. There were several Sídhe, but they were all on foot with hounds circling around the mages. Bran moved his right hand as yellow magic flared around him, and several of the hounds were thrown back into the darkness. Aiden shouted something and a wave of fire erupted from his hands, blasting forward like a flamethrower. Another of the Sídhe and a hound vanished in the flames, but more kept coming down the hill.

He wasn't sure how many there were. Jenny made a small sound of fear and pressed against him. Suddenly her door was pulled open and a hand in a golden gauntlet reached in to grab Jenny. She shrieked and began to kick frantically. Lance leaned forward in the driver's seat and fumbled for the iron dagger he kept strapped to the back of his jeans. Jenny ripped hers from her purse with an angry cry.

Lance couldn't breathe as his girlfriend stabbed at the Síd's hands with the dagger. An odd mix of pride and relief filled him as the creature shrieked and let go. Jenny shifted faster than he'd ever seen before and shoved the dagger into the Síd's neck. The Síd froze in place, agony on all of its features for a moment before it began to crumble into dust. With a huff, Jenny grabbed the door and pulled it closed. Lance hit the lock button. He reached over to wrap an arm around her even as Jenny panted for air.

"That was a bit scary." Jenny looked down at her dagger. Already the thin layer of silver blood was disappearing. "Maybe I'm better with it than I thought."

Nodding, Lance glanced outside where whips of silver light were lashing through the air. He remembered that silver was the color of Morgana's magic. Lightning hit another Síd approaching the truck and Jenny gave a small cheer at the sight of Alex's magic.

"We must still be outside the blood protection," Lance said softly. He looked around at the side of the road. "If you see a mile marker let me know."

"Right; the mages need to build a new gate," Jenny agreed.

She made a small sound of alarm as a Síd hit her side of the truck and began to dissolve. Outside, Bran nodded to them before shoving a wave of magic at a lunging hound. Lance nodded vaguely in return, knowing that the mages weren't really paying attention to them, but grateful that they were looking out for them. He tightened his fingers around the hilt of his dagger and grit his teeth. Irritation and frustration were building up in his chest as he watched Alex scream something and blast another Síd with her lightning.

Alex's movements were fast and smooth, almost practiced in a way that he didn't think they'd been before. After each strike, her face was going almost completely blank. Something about it added to his unease. Three Sídhe rushed for her. A wave of dark gray magic rolled out from Alex, slicing into all three of them and filling the air with a sharp ozone smell.

"I wish we could help," Jenny said softly.

Another Síd ran out of the shadows, a golden sword in hand. A soft gasp escaped Jenny, but yellow magic picked it up and held it in the air. Seconds later, a fireball collided with it. The golden armor dissolved and the being fell apart into golden dust.

"Me too," Lance agreed. "But us running out there right now would only be a distraction."

"Yeah," Jenny sighed.

They were quiet for another few moments. One of the Sídhe hit the front of the truck, making the whole thing jolt before a lightning bolt struck it down. A hound rushed Alex only for a whip of silver light to catch the thing and rip it apart.

"Will you stay, Lance?" Jenny asked. "Even with all of this?" She gestured out the window with a weak chuckle.

"I will if you do."

"It's not that I have any lingering feelings for Alex," Jenny said. Her voice was soft and she sounded embarrassed. "It just seems wrong to leave, and I do care about her, but not like that."

"I know," Lance assured her. He chuckled a little despite the seriousness of the conversation and the strangeness of having it while the mages battled outside his truck. "And I do get it. After everything that's happened walking away just seems wrong. Even if there isn't much we can do to help."

"Yeah," Jenny agreed. She sighed loudly, the sound filling the truck cab. "Still, we've been able to help here and there. And depending on what's going on with Alex she might need some non-magical friends."

"Even with our history?" Lance asked. He wasn't so sure about that. "We might not be mages, Jenny, but it's still messy."

"We're the good thing that came from all of this," Jenny reminded him. "Maybe seeing that will help Alex with everything she's dealing with."

Lance wasn't sure about Jenny's theory, but Alex did seem fine with seeing them together. She'd just lost her parents and was still reeling from the ugly discovery of one of her prior lives being a slave ship captain and creating the Iron Chain. They might not remember everything, but he and Jenny did know a thing or two about coping with the reality of being a reincarnation. Maybe, just maybe they could help.

Someone knocked on the window, making them both jump. Aiden was just outside, a bit sweaty, but smiling. Lance unlocked the truck doors and leaned forward to check on the others. Morgana was speaking to Alex, both of them standing in the headlights of his truck. The expression on Alex's face was that same vacant one she'd been wearing all through the funeral. Even as Aiden, Bran, and Nicki climbed into the back safe and sound, Lance couldn't help but worry.

3

Irish Morning

4 65 B.C.E. The Golden Vale, Ireland

The long grasses of the rolling hills caught the wind and swayed before him. Overhead the sky was clear and bright blue with only a few stray wisps of clouds. The sun had only just risen and was spreading a warm golden glow across the landscape. A small group of trees cast long twisting shadows over the edge of the pasture. Earthen walls marked the boundaries and made him wonder, not for the first time, why they insisted he stand guard.

His eyes traced the landscape absentmindedly from his seat on a lower section of the overgrown earthen wall. A short distance away, the sheep were grazing peacefully with a few baas being exchanged from time to time. It was a quiet and utterly dull day. Holding back a sigh, he pushed some loose strands of brown hair from his eyes and scanned the horizon again. He could just see the small artificial hill looming beyond the fields.

He tilted his head as he tied back his hair and considered it thoughtfully. According to the stories, it was a home of the Sídhe. The Fair Folk lived down below the Earth in their realm of gold and magic. He wasn't sure he believed it, but he'd never gone poking around. Another sheep bleated and moved closer to him as it grazed. A soft laugh escaped him and three of the sheep looked up at him.

The summer heat was rolling over his skin. Even at night, it stayed warm enough that mornings were pleasant. He bent down to the simple hide sack and pulled out a rough biscuit wrapped in woven reeds. Taking a bite, he watched the sheep. It didn't take long for boredom to set in. The sheep were all in good health and moving well, if slowly, as they grazed. The only reason he was here was to be on alert for predators or a rival tribe coming after the sheep. Neither seemed likely this morning and he quickly finished his biscuit.

Picking up his cruit, he gently plucked one of the horsehair strings. A soft note hung in the air and made him smile. The triangular frame wasn't very solid, but it kept the horsehairs strung tightly enough that even the softest brush released a musical note. There were small carvings in the wood, nothing fancy of course, but little things he'd done when bored. His favorite was a deer with long curving antlers. He plucked the strings in the beginning of a song and let his mind wander.

"Leugio!"

The voice pulled him out of his thoughts and he straightened up. Looking around, Leugio caught sight of a man waving to him and rushing through the fields. It took him only a moment to recognize the figure in his green tunic. Standing up, Leugio frowned and set his bag and the cruit down gently. He gave a warning look to the nearest sheep and strode across the pasture as the other young man collapsed against the far wall.

Galvyn was a bit younger than him, having been born in the winter while he'd come along in the summer before. Galvyn had always been stockier and stronger than him, but also heavier and slower. If Galvyn hadn't been so pleasant, Leugio might have been afraid of him when they were boys.

"What is it, Galvyn?" He frowned as he took in the face that was pale despite his run. Galvyn was panting and looked ready to fall over. Holding out his waterskin, Leugio was surprised when Galvyn waved it off. Galvyn opened his mouth a few times, but nothing came out. "What's wrong?"

"It's your sister," he panted. "Keelia's missing."

"Missing?" Leugio repeated. He closed the remaining distance to Galvyn, looming over the other boy. "What do you mean? What happened?"

"I'm not sure," Galvyn said, still panting for air. "Your mother sent me to find you. She isn't with you, is she?"

"No, I haven't seen her since last night," Leugio shook his head, forcing back the worry growing in his chest. "I think she was in bed this morning when I left. Did Mother say anything else?"

"No, not really. She came out of her roundhouse and asked me if I'd seen Keelia this morning. I asked around the village, but no one has seen her."

"What about Kent?" Leugio asked quickly. "She doesn't go anywhere without that dog."

"He's missing too," Galvyn said. He took another gasping breath and then straightened up. "Go back to the village. I'll watch the flock."

Leugio nodded and rushed back to his things. He grabbed his bag and slung it over his shoulder. Picking up his cruit, he found his eyes being drawn towards the distant hill of the Sídhe. There was a bad feeling growing in his gut that made his whole body heavy and off balance. Galvyn caught his gaze and swallowed nervously.

"Do you think they took her?"

"I don't know…" Leugio shook himself. "I'll go and speak with my mother. Maybe Keelia and Kent just woke up early and went out before the sun rose."

"That's when it's most dangerous," Galvyn said. He was all but falling over himself now and eyed the hill fearfully. "If they took her-"

"They didn't," Leugio snapped. He leaned against the earthen wall and leveraged himself over it. "Stay here, Galvyn: I'll find Keelia."

The words were confident, but something was twisting in his stomach. Some instinct made him look back at the Sídhe mound. Part of him itched to run towards it. Part of him was certain that his sister was in that direction, but the sensible part won out. His feet rushed him down the well-worn pathway back to the village. Around him, the green landscape and lush trees flashed by. His nostrils filled with the smells of the livestock and cooking food. The noise of the day was already rolling out down around him. Houses were clustered together on the hill up ahead and surrounded by a thick wooden wall. Guards stood at the ready by the gate and eyed him as he approached.

He ignored them and passed through the open gate. Leugio looked around for any sign of his mother, but she wasn't waiting for him. His mother's roundhouse was old and starting to fall apart. As he stepped inside, his eyes jumped over to his sister's bed. Her blankets were a mess, as if she'd kicked them away in a hurry. Everything else was in place. The pots at the center of the house by the firepit were still here. A loom in the corner had the start of a new blanket. A basket of reeds for making more baskets was at the foot of his sister's bed. None of the family valuables were gone. There were no clues.

"Mother!"

His mother was frantically digging through one of his sister's bags. She looked up at him with wide, frightened brown eyes. Jumping to her feet, she rushed over to him. Leugio stepped forward to catch her hand, fearful that in her state she'd trip and fall into the fire. Tears were streaming down her cheeks and she was quivering. However, she collected herself quickly and looked up at him imploringly.

"Leugio, was she here this morning when you left?"

"I think so," he said. "But it was dark, Mother. I was trying not to wake either of you." Leugio looked back at the bed, frowning. "You didn't see her? You didn't hear her say anything?"

"I don't know," his mother cried. "Her bed was empty this morning, but I woke a little late. I didn't think much of it. You know what she's like, and Kent was gone so I knew they must be together. But then I started making breakfast and called her so she could take some to you, but there was no answer. Galvyn couldn't find her in the village and Perth didn't see her out on the paths."

"Where else would she go?" Leugio asked helplessly. "She knows better than to enter the forests alone: Keelia may like to be by herself, but she wouldn't put herself in danger."

"Oh, Leugio, what if the Sídhe took her?" His mother was nearly hysterical now, her whole body shaking. "If she went before sunrise-"

"Mother, the Sídhe didn't kidnap her from the village," Leugio said. He grabbed her arm and tried to calm her down. "We have iron tools and weapons all over the place."

"If it was too early... too dark and she strayed too far then maybe-"

The sound of barking made her fall silent. Other dogs began barking in response, and despite knowing there were any number of dogs in the village, Leugio headed outside with his mother on his heels. A large dog with a reddish tint to his dark fur was running up the path towards him.

"Kent!"

Dropping to a knee, he pet the dog automatically. There were no wounds on the dog, but there was some kind of residue around his mouth. Leugio eyed it carefully as his mother started calling for his sister.

"Why is Kent back?" she demanded. "Where is Keelia?"

"I'm not sure," Leugio said gently. He stood up and tried to grab her arm. "Mother, calm down, please." His plea was soft, but his mother took a shaky breath and nodded. Her eyes dropped back to Kent, almost suspiciously. "Why don't you go and check with the guards again. Maybe someone ran into Keelia on their way out to the pastures."

His mother looked back at him, biting her bottom lip. Then she slowly nodded, and he released her arm. With slow steps, she moved away and went to the corner of their yard where a few others were gathering. One of the other local women wrapped an arm around her and spoke in hushed tones. Leugio exhaled slowly, trying to ignore the sick feeling growing in his gut. Kent was looking up at him and whimpering softly. Leugio reached down and patted the dog on the head.

"Easy boy," he said. "I wish you could talk."

Whimpering, the dog shifted down the eastern path. It seemed worried and torn but determined. Leugio nodded to himself. Kent had always been a smart dog. If Keelia had gone out early with him and crossed paths with a Síd.... He stopped that line of thought.

"Sit, Kent," he ordered. "I'll be right back."

He looked towards his mother again. She was still down the path and was now speaking with one of the guards. Hesitating, Leugio looked between her and the roundhouse. She'd be worried if he left, but then again, she'd wanted him to go out looking for his sister. That's all he was really doing. With that justification firmly in mind, he slipped back into the roundhouse. Leugio grabbed his bag and cruit from the bed and latched his cloak around his shoulders. On impulse, his free hand touched the iron brooch that clasped his cloak. It had a simple, curving design and a long, sharp needle that went from one side of the circular form to the other which held it in place. There wasn't much left of the original knot design as his fingers had long since worn the metal smooth. His father had given it to him shortly before he'd been killed in battle. Today it was warm and gave him strength.

He got a few looks as he stepped back outside, but no one said anything. Kent looked up at him hopefully. Peering over his shoulder, Leugio watched his mother in the corner. She was still crying, and he started walking. With his left hand, he gestured for Kent to come. The dog leapt after him and ran a little ahead of him, heading straight for the second gate. That gate led out towards the Sídhe Mound, he realized darkly. His stomach twisted, but Leugio kept putting one foot in front of the other. He didn't let himself look back at the village.

With each step, Leugio's fear increased. A sense of worry and wrong-ness churned in his chest. He was close to the mound now, and there was something in the air that he didn't trust. The scent of the grass and the animals was fading away, yet it wasn't really being replaced, there just wasn't anything else. Leugio wasn't sure if it was all his imagination, but something just seemed wrong.

Kent whimpered softly, but the dog didn't stop walking beside him. Leugio choked on a wave of gratitude for the dog's loyalty. Reaching down, he stroked the dog's rough fur. His fingers twisted in the longer strands on Kent's back and he forced himself to take a deep breath. As he did, his chest twanged in dull pain while a shiver went down his spine.

The mound loomed up ahead. Grass had long since grown over the top and if you didn't know what it was it wouldn't have drawn attention. There were other small mounds scattered across the landscape, but those were graves. This was different. Leugio was close to it now and could see a small black opening lined with rocks.

He looked around for any sign of his sister. There were a few human footprints and pawprints in the mud off the path. Swallowing, Leugio stepped off the path and studied them. A few feet further were thick patches of herbs and he realized that his sister truly had gone too far while gathering. Kent whined again and Leugio licked at his suddenly bone-dry lips. Something shifted in the shadows ahead of him, catching his attention in the corner of his eye.

Leugio froze, standing completely still even as a low growl escaped Kent. The figure was leaning against the side of the mound, hidden in a long shadow cast by the hillside. It was tall and slim, wearing a long white robe with delicate embroidery. Long, pale, almost translucent hair was bound back simply, revealing an almost human face, but it was too pale and violet eyes stared at him. There were a pair of horns curling up from the being's forehead, but they were smaller than he had always envisioned. The sense of wrongness was somehow worse around the creature, and yet better without any reason.

"A mortal comes to the Sídhe Mound," the Síd said. Its voice was soft and musical, but there was an edge to it. Violet eyes swept over him. "The question is, why?"

"I'm looking for a young girl," Leugio managed. His words tried to catch in his throat and weighed heavily on his tongue. "About this tall." He held his hand up to his mid-chest. "Brown hair and brown eyes, slight freckling around her nose." The Síd wasn't reacting to him. "Did one of your kind take her?"

There was a moment of silence as the Síd studied him. There was a hint of amusement in its eyes that set Leugio on edge. The Síd glanced in the direction of the path and the village.

"Yes. Faridon brought a young girl in early this morning," the Síd said. "The sun was on his heels. It was foolish." Then the Síd leaned forward and looked him over. "Coming here was foolish on your part, mortal."

"She's my sister."

"Ah, family loyalty." The Síd sounded almost sad and its eyes lingered on the dagger on his belt. "Iron?"

"Your weakness," Leugio agreed. He rested his hand on the hilt. "How do I get my sister back?"

"You don't," the Sid answered. It shook its head and looked out towards the green fields. "It is no longer our custom to take your children, but sometimes one of us does. But once we take something, we do not return it."

"She's my sister!" Leugio pulled the dagger free and watched the Síd squirm at the sight of the metal shining in the sunlight. "She's just a girl. She belongs with her family! Not underground in your realm."

Something flared in his chest: a rush of warmth that sparked through his feet and blasted up through his legs. The Síd brought up a hand and drummed its chin thoughtfully. A heavy looking golden bracelet was on its wrist, but Leugio remembered the tales of magic gold. It would vanish once it was separated from the Síd. Still, it made no move to attack him or block his path.

"I suppose you make a fair argument," the Síd said.

Leugio didn't like his tone- at least, he thought it was a he- and something about the way it was eying him made Leugio nervous. His mind raced, trying to remember the different stories. He wasn't sure what he was supposed to do.

"So where is my sister?" Leugio asked. His voice wavered slightly, but he kept meeting the Síd's gaze. "How do I find her?"

"I suppose that I could give you some advice," the Síd said slowly. Leugio frowned, realizing now that the Síd was eying his cruit curiously. "In exchange for something, of course."

"I didn't think we mere mortals would have anything you Sídhe wanted." Leugio's frown deepened as he watched the creature. It shifted slightly and sat up straighter.

"Usually not, but we are not quite what you believe us to be," the Síd said. It almost sounded sad. "I suspect that Faridon was attempting to prove something to himself or the others."

"What about you?"

"We are not what we once were. Denying that is the path of fools." The Síd shrugged, but somehow still seemed powerful and graceful to Leugio. "I can give you advice and the path through the mound tunnels in exchange for your cruit."

"My cruit?" Leugio looked down at the simple instrument and then back at the Sid suspiciously. "Why?"

"I like the look of the carvings, lad, nothing more. An item made by mortal hands and willingly traded has a certain appeal to me."

Leugio eyed the dark entrance into the small hill and then looked back at the Síd. "Are you in exile?"

"Me? No. If I was, I would be much further away. No, I just tire of hiding beneath the earth when the hill provides a safe spot to watch your world."

Nothing about the creature felt right or made sense, but Leugio found himself nodding. Stepping forward, he held out the cruit nervously. He wondered if the being had some power to use it against him, or if since he'd made it himself the Síd could cast magic on him through it. But the Síd gently took the cruit. It smiled a little and then strummed a finger over the tight strings. Then it sang a few words that rolled past his ears.

They were unfamiliar, but something about them seemed off, like they were trying to twist themselves into a shape he knew. Leugio frowned in a mix of confusion and irritation, only for the Síd to stop a moment later. It held the cruit protectively in its lap and nodded to him. Then it pointed into the darkness.

"Go straight until you reach the first fork in the path. One is illuminated by light, but the other is much darker. Follow the darker path. It will be difficult with your eyes, but you will find another branch. You must take the right path until you find a staircase leading down and to the right. Continue to stay to the right until you find a golden set of armor on display. There is a small passage hidden behind it. Follow the passage to a set of three doors. Take the middle one and that will lead you into the prison. If your sister is still alive and has not been handed off to someone, that is where she will be."

"And if she's been handed off?"

"Then she will already be in the home of a Síd somewhere in the village. You will not be able to reach her then." The Síd gave him a dark look, its violet eyes fixed coldly on him. "If that is the case all you can do is try to escape. Even with that dagger, you will find that a great challenge." The Síd's lips twisted into a smirk. "My best advice, boy, is to run home now."

Leugio tensed at the warning but forced himself to nod. Kent was still growling lowly and he looked towards the entrance. He swung his pack off his back. The Síd watched him silently and plucked a few more strings as he dug out a torch. It was merely a stick, but one end was wrapped in old cloth. He dug into one of his pouches and pulled out his flint. The torch caught easily enough and he pulled his pack back on.

With one more glance towards the strange Síd, Leugio stepped forward with the torch in his left hand and the iron dagger in his right. A cold wind seemed to blow out of the mound entrance and he hesitated once more. There were a few stories about people recovering taken children, but he suddenly wasn't sure if he believed them. Licking his lips, Leugio found himself considering heading back home, but then Kent sniffed at the air and took a hesitant step forward. Leugio nodded to himself and followed the dog's lead.

4

Through the Fog

Alex groaned softly. She was asleep; at least, she thought she was. Everything was hazy around her and she could sort of remember going to bed after taking a long run. Yet she was standing in a thick field of fog in her normal clothes. Alex frowned and looked around, the lull of sleep beginning to fade as her mind took in her surroundings. For a moment she resisted: dreams that started out with this kind of awareness usually weren't pleasant.

Bracing herself, Alex waited to fall. She waited for the floor to collapse and to descend into another time and place. Instead, the fog just churned and began to take on strange shapes. It curled and spun without even a hint of a breeze. Soft, barely there and distant sounds reached her ears and Alex peered harder into the fog, waiting for whatever was coming.

There were faces. They appeared only in brief glimpses as the fog wafted and cleared, but then they were gone. People were laughing around her, their voices echoing. Someone touched her shoulder and kissed her neck. She spun around, but there was no one there. A shiver consumed her body as her heart pounded. Turning in a circle, Alex tried to find something solid and constant, but there was nothing. It was a blur of twisting fog. She saw smiles, bright happy eyes, and glimpses of hair.

Nothing stayed still long enough for her to see the details properly. There was a flicker of fear, but another warm laugh drove it away.

Stepping forward, Alex held her hands out in front of her. The faces faded away into mist. It surrounded her, drifting lazily through the air. She looked down nervously. Mist was thick around her feet, blocking any sign of a floor or void. Alex inhaled sharply, unsure if she was relieved by that or not. Everything was muted, from sounds to the physical sensations.

Walking in the mist, Alex held out a hand and watched the air brush over her fingertips. There was no chill to it and she only barely felt a sensation of the coolness wash over her flesh. Shifting her hand, Alex waved at the mist and watched it part, but it revealed nothing new. Just more of the expanse. This was a dream: it might go on forever, but Alex started walking again. There was no sound from her footfalls, not even a muffled one. Nothing to indicate she was really moving. Opening her mouth, Alex tried to call out, but the air seemed too heavy as she breathed it in.

Then something shifted in front of her. Alex froze in place, her body swaying as the mist closed in around her. Raising a hand, she waved it around in an attempt to see something. More voices were echoing around her. Someone called the name Arto. Her eyes searched the mist, but she couldn't see anything. Another voice called Gottfried. Then the voices rose in a cacophony of names and noise so Alex could no longer tell any of them apart.

The mist swept together into a thick cloud. Before Alex could shift back a figure emerged and started moving towards her. She was pretty with large eyes, a broad nose, and a welcoming smile. Her clothing was vaguely familiar and made of woven red cloth, but Alex couldn't place the time period for the life of her. The figure's skin was a deep olive tone that made the golden bangles she wore stand out. Something about her made Alex's stomach drop.

"Who are you?" Alex asked. Her voice echoed in the mist.

The woman just laughed at her. Leaning forward, she caught Alex's chin and kissed her hard on the mouth. Alex's eyes widened, but her body froze. A laugh built up in her chest and the kiss tugged at her memory. With a smile, the woman stepped away and ran one finger down her cheek. Then the woman vanished, turning back into mist. Shaking her head, Alex licked her lips only to sputter at her own action and turned around frantically. There was no sign of the woman, but the fog was gathering once more.

Now an older woman with long silver hair in a braid over her shoulder stepped forth but didn't stop. Alex moved out of her way and heard her humming softly as she passed. She said nothing, but just glanced at Alex and offered her a toothless smile. The woman's eyes wrinkled up and she laughed before the fog swooped in around her. Then she too was gone.

Farther away was a tall man with broad shoulders and a thick brown beard with hints of gray and beads woven into it. He wore a rough tunic and a long cloak clasped at the shoulder. Sad eyes looked towards her for a moment before he stepped into the mist once more. As soon as he was gone another figure emerged. This one was younger with blond hair and dressed in more modern if slightly old-fashioned clothes. Alex tensed as she realized he was in a uniform with a Nazi band around his arm. But then he too was gone without even a glance her way.

This time it was a pair of girls who came running out of the mist. They had darker skin and shining black hair pulled back in braids. Alex stepped forward, her right hand coming up to reach for them, but they didn't see her. As quickly as they'd appeared they vanished back into the mists.

Now there were more figures moving around her. Some said a few words before fading away, some smiled while others never even looked at her. There were men and women, children and the elderly in a mix of ethnicities. Sometimes their clothes gave her clues, but others were unknowable. They all moved past her and faded back into the fog. Alex turned and tried to look at all of them.

Her whole body froze as she spotted a very familiar face. Gottfried's wife Ilse walking with a young girl beside her. Air rushed from Alex's lungs as she recognized the little girl as her-his daughter Elsa. She took a step towards them, but they vanished from sight as another figure moved in front of her. This one looked Asian and was dressed in what looked like a red robe. He offered her a smile and said a name, but it meant nothing to her.

Alex stopped in place and shook her head. They were too many now. Their faces tugged at memories, but the names wouldn't come. Names danced on the tip of her tongue but refused to be voiced. Her chest tightened painfully with each new face. Pained whimpers and gasps for air escaped Alex. She wrapped her arms around herself and lowered her eyes, trying to ignore them.

"Alex," her mother's voice called.

Looking up quickly, Alex held back a sob. Her own parents had appeared only a few feet in front of her. They were staring at each other; her father's hand on her mother's cheek and her mother giving him a familiar half smile. Alex tried to call to them, but nothing came out. Tears gathered in her eyes and the tangle in her chest turned icy. Trembling hands reached towards them before Alex could stop herself. They didn't notice her even as a whimper escaped her.

"Mommy." Her voice was weak and cracking, but she could finally make words form. Alex's eyes drank in her parents. The knot in her chest expanded, sending shivers racing down her limbs. "Daddy?"

This time they turned. Her mom smiled brightly and said her name again. It rolled over the mist and Alex tried to move. Tears were beginning to escape her eyes and trickle over her cheeks. Sniffing, she opened her mouth to speak again, but nothing came out. Her parents were watching her with sad little smiles. Her mom rested her head against her dad's shoulder.

Something broke.

"I'm sorry," Alex sobbed. "I'm so sorry. I didn't mean for it to happen. I tried to protect you and Spokane and-"

The other voices were back. From the mist, there were calls of many names: Thor, Arto, Leugio, Lokpal, Gofiben, Cuthbert, Gottfried and others that were too unfamiliar for her to even understand.

"Shut up!" Alex shouted. Her voice echoed away in the mist but didn't stop the voices. "Shut up! Not now!"

Stumbling forward, Alex reached a hand out to her mom. Her dad's smile remained sad and they said nothing. Alex's throat closed up, but she managed another step. Around them, the voices were louder than ever. People were calling her. Sorrow, anger, joy, and a hundred other emotions were tugging her in different directions. It took all of Alex's focus to keep her eyes on her parents and not answer another voice. She could feel pulls to each voice and name. Something in her wanted to go to them, but if Alex gave in to them, she knew that she'd never find the way back to her parents.

"Mommy?" She begged her mother with her eyes to say something. "Please... I'm sorry."

Then they began to turn to mist. With a scream of terror, Alex leapt forward and tried to grab her mom's arm, but all she caught was air. It slipped through her fingers and the last image of her mom and dad burned itself into her eyes. The knot slipped. Grief crashed down and Alex's knees fell out beneath her. A shriek, a sob tore out of her throat. The sound drowned out all the other voices. It rang through the mist, promising pain to anything that got too close. And as the scream died down, so did the voices.

She was alone now in the mist, on her knees and defeated. Slowly, it began to lift. There was nothing around her, just an endless black. A faint light surrounded her, but there was nothing else in the void. Alex didn't care. She didn't stand or start moving. Instead, she sat down and pulled her knees to her chest. Lowering her head down, tears ran down Alex's cheeks and the shudders consumed her body. She gripped her legs and began to rock. A soft hum escaped her and wafted through the air. Alex didn't even recognize it as her mom's lullaby, but she kept humming it.

A chill swept in, sinking into her skin and down to her bones. The emotions were pulling again and voices began to call once more. Shaking her head, Alex refused to look up. She blocked out the voices as best she could. She would not answer any of them: she would not even acknowledge them. Her chest grew hot and Alex tightened her grip on her legs. Hot, sharp pains radiated from her left leg, and she flinched. The jolts traveled farther and Alex tried to move, but the pain only got worse. The voices were fading away and the chill eased, just a little.

Opening her eyes, Alex wasn't surprised to find herself looking at the plain ceiling of her dorm room. She twisted her fingers into the fabric of her sheets and comforter. One hand came up to wipe away the tears rolling down the sides of her face. She bit her lip to keep the sob building up in her chest from escaping. A painful jolt in her leg made her flinch. A cramp. Alex groaned and tried to flex her leg. She was actually grateful for the pain. Inhaling slowly, Alex willed the muscles to relax and gradually it did.

She still didn't move. As the pain faded the lingering ache in her chest became stronger. Alex tightened her grip on the comforter as the knot threatened to completely unravel. Her magic gathered in her chest slowly, sluggishly, as if resisting what she wanted it to do. Closing her eyes, Alex focused on the point of pain. That knot of emotions that was tangled up in a mess right below her heart. In a flutter of warm sparks, her magic wrapped itself around the knot, hiding it away from the world. Exhaling slowly, Alex let her whole body relax into the bed. The slightly worn-out spring poked into her back and Alex eased her death grip on the linens.

Licking her lips, Alex told herself to stay calm, but the faces were burned onto the backs of her eyelids. With a groan, she swung her legs out of the bed and sat up. Her feet touched down on the thin carpet of her dorm room and Alex sat still, staring into the darkness as her eyes adjusted. The faint blue glow from her laptop cable illuminated part of her desk, and after a moment Alex stood up and reached over to turn on the lamp.

Warm yellow light filled the corner and Alex rubbed at her eyes. The faces were finally fading, but something still ached in her chest. Leaning on the edge of her desk, Alex rolled her stiff shoulders and pulled on more of her magic. It coiled tighter around the knot of emotions. Alex rubbed at the middle of her chest through her pajamas top. The ache remained, dulled, but it was still there.

Picking up her phone, Alex grimaced as she checked the time. It was too early to be up but too late to really think she'd get back to sleep. Outside the sky was dark and there was no sign of anyone on the lit sidewalks. She pulled out her desk chair and sat down. Alex didn't even bother turning on her computer, but instead just set her hands on the edge of the wooden desk. Looking down at her fingers, she focused on the tiny details of them, and what made them different from the other hands she'd had.

The most obvious was that she was the only known female Iron Soul incarnation. They still didn't know why the sudden change after three thousand years, and Alex sometimes wondered if Merlin and Morgana had just missed one. Her fingers were smaller than most men's would be, but not very delicate, if she was honest. They were modern hands too: they'd benefitted from a lack of hard labor and access to lotion. There was a small scar on her left middle knuckle from a bad scrape when she was seven or eight, but otherwise they were blemish free.

She turned her hands and flexed her fingers. Arto's hands had been rough thanks to a life on the move and smithing. Thor's had been the same way. Gottfried's hands had been more like hers due to the life of a professor. Alex rubbed her forefinger and thumb together, feeling the brush of the ridges of her fingerprints together. At least those were different in each life.

Alex reached for her glass of water and took long, greedy gulps. The flush of warmth in her chest had sealed off the last of the chilly ache. Alex looked down at her hands one more time and then turned on her computer. Straightening up in her desk chair, she placed her hand over the mouse and got started on her next essay.

5

Another Gateway

Making a Gate was not how Alex wanted to spend her afternoon. The week so far had been long enough, with everyone who knew about the death of her parents tiptoeing around her, and it wasn't even over yet. At least it wasn't high school and most people didn't have a clue. Gossip just wasn't as powerful a steamroller on a college campus. Yet the week had still managed to be a long haul of avoiding anything that made her think too much of her parents.

Even now the knot in her chest tightened and Alex could feel magic pulsing up through her boots to reinforce the magical barrier. Some part of her knew this was dangerous, but the rest didn't care. It kept the pain away and dimmed the voices. It was all too loud.

The game trail provided them with something of a route, but the hillside was still steep and the packs of iron on their backs ensured it wasn't an easy climb. This wasn't a recreational area and honestly, Alex was more than a little worried about Merlin's SUV and Aiden's truck being towed from their places just off the road. There was nothing for it though; this is where those Sídhe had come from, so it was where they had to go.

Her mind kept jumping around as they hiked. No one was in a talkative mood. Alex wanted to enjoy the scent of the pine and the fresh air, but she just couldn't. Too much was trying to barge in and make itself heard. She didn't want to hear any of it. Alex grabbed onto a tree as her feet began to slip back. Behind her, Bran asked if she was okay and Alex assured him that she was before moving again. It was slow going, but as they climbed something tugged at her magic. She stopped and looked around. Ahead of her, Merlin and Morgana were talking and pointing in different directions.

"They don't know where the tunnel is, do they?" Bran asked. "Lovely."

"There wasn't time to scout it out," Morgana called down to them. "Really, Ambrose, judging from the lay of the land, it is this way." She gestured to the right of the game trail. "That would let them get down the hill without too much effort."

"Yes, but the hillside would better fit a tunnel this way," Merlin replied. "They did need to construct the tunnel first. They wouldn't know the best place for access to a town or a road."

"Actually," Alex started to say. The tug on her magic was becoming stronger and she found her eyes drawn to the left of the trail. Everyone was looking at her. "I think it might be this way."

"There's a ravine down there," Merlin said with a slight frown.

"Oh, well maybe, but I sense something that way," Alex explained weakly. "I don't know how to explain it but-"

"You lead the way, Alex," Morgana said. The dark-haired woman smiled at her reassuringly. "If that's what you feel then it is probably right."

A few months ago, Alex would have preened under the praise. At least, she thought so. It was all confusing now. Morgana was important to her:

always had been. In her own odd way, the older female mage was kind, warm, and supportive. She'd had faith in Alex gaining control over her magic, but now Alex thought there was more to her emotions than just the affection of a student towards a mentor. Arto, the first Iron Soul, had been the younger half-brother of Morgana, and she was fiercely loyal to his memory. Alex feared that he was creeping into her own thoughts and emotions now. Or had he always been there in the background but she was just unaware?

"Alex?" Nicki was looking at her. "Is there something more?"

"What? No," Alex said, recovering quickly. "I was just trying to see if I could feel anything else."

That wasn't a bad idea, but the others were already waiting for her. Alex could tell that Nicki didn't really believe her. Was she losing herself in thought more than she used to? There were whispers in the back of her mind all the time now. They were quiet yet distracting, so she must be more distracted, right? Shaking herself, she took the lead down the side of the hill.

There was another tug. Beneath her feet, the ground seemed to thrum with building magic. That was a bit new; or was it? Alex frowned, uncertain of the answer. In her head, the voices got a little louder and the knot in her chest tightened. Exhaling slowly, she did her best to ignore it. She wasn't going to break down. Not now.

Merlin hadn't been wrong about the ravine. Ahead of them, the small creeks joined together in a rocky low area. Yet at the far end of the ravine and half hidden by low tree branches was an opening in the rocks of the hillside. Alex froze as she caught sight of a pair of violet eyes peering out at them from the darkness.

"Guards!" Morgana shouted. "Spread out!"

Alex brought her hands up in front of her. Gray magic appeared around her fingertips, giving her skin a strange glow. The thrum of the earth beneath her feet responded to the danger as the spark in her chest exploded into life.

Three Sídhe dressed in golden armor drew their swords and marched towards them. The horns curling out of their heads were covered in ornate golden plating that matched their armor and gauntlets. White hair was twisted around the horns and their pale skin shimmered in the low sun. Alex noticed that their eyes squinted in pain from the light, but they still didn't retreat into the darkness. It was surprising, but this wasn't the time to question it. The Sídhe stayed close together for half the distance before suddenly spreading out. An attempt to flank, one of the voices in Alex's head noted.

With each step the Sídhe took forward out of the tunnel, the pulse of the magic around her became stronger. Every second they were here caused the Iron Realm, Earth itself, to push back at them through Alex and her fellow mages. Alex focused her thoughts on her magic. It was easy now to 'see' the bolt of lightning, and her magic made it so. She struck down the first Síd as a blast of yellow magic from Bran hit another one. A red bolt from Aiden, sailed through where Bran's had been. There were more guards coming out now: they'd clearly learned from her escape and having their earlier entrance sealed.

She released a wave of dark gray magic, watching it ripple through the air. It struck the Sídhe, but didn't destroy any of them, rather making them all stumble. Her fellow mages took advantage and released a volley of spells at them. Silver magic from Morgana killed one and green bolts from Merlin struck down another. It was almost easy now. A familiar dance as none of these Sídhe were able to return fire. There were enough of them though that they were closing quickly.

One headed straight for her. The Síd bore down at her, swinging a golden sword. Around them, the ravine flickered in her vision, replaced with a tunnel made of tightly fitted stones. Alex blinked back the vision and threw herself away from the sword just in time. There was a shout of alarm behind her. Silver magic flashed past Alex, striking the Síd in the chest. It fought against the magic for a moment, trying to move, but its armor crumbled and it screamed before dissolving into golden dust.

Shaking her head, Alex rolled to her feet and threw her hand forward. Lightning blasted forth from her fingertips and exploded across the ravine to strike a Síd. It vanished in a rush of gold. In the corner of her eye, Alex saw a Hound destroyed in a flash of fire. Another Síd was pinned to the side of the ravine by ice spikes and began to dissolve a moment later when Bran thrust an iron dagger into its neck.

Then as quickly as the noise and fighting had begun it was over. All the guards were dead, and the only noise was the water babbling along in the small creek. Alex looked towards Morgana. The older mage was eyeing the tunnel suspiciously.

"There will be more down there. I'm sure they heard the fight," Morgana said. "Ambrose and I will stand guard, but you start working on the gate."

Merlin nodded in agreement and the pair marched closer to the opening in the hillside. Their hands were glowing with their magic, and Alex could faintly see wisps of it hanging in the air at the edge of the vision. It was distracting, but she forced herself to turn towards Bran, Aiden, and Nicki.

Aiden was already shrugging out of his backpack and pulling out the iron bars that he'd been charged with carrying. Alex pulled off her own backpack and moved to join him as Nicki and Bran added their iron to the pile. Dumping the iron out of the bag, Alex looked it over carefully and told herself to breathe. This wasn't the first time they'd made a Gate, but this was different. She looked down at her hands for a moment before drawing her dagger from its sheath on her belt. With a grimace, she carefully cut her left index finger. Blood seeped out of the wound and Alex brushed her finger over the first of the iron bars, leaving a soft red mark. She squeezed her finger and repeated the process on the next two bars.

"Are you going to do that with all of them?" Nicki asked with a hint of worry.

"No," Alex replied. She forced a small smile. "I don't think that's necessary. I just thought I'd give myself a handicap on this one." She looked towards Merlin and Morgana. "Uh, how do you want to do this? I mean making the Gate and standing guard?"

"Arto was able to make Iron Gates himself," Merlin said calmly. Alex bit her lip despite the fact that there was no judgment in Merlin's tone. "I'd like us to start easing Alex into making them with less outside help. That way she can create Gates even if the rest of us have to fight. Make this Gate with the others; Morgana and I will be here, but only if you really need us."

Nodding her understanding, Alex had to admit that it was a valid point. This tunnel had guards and they'd been willing to come out into the sunlight even though it half blinded them. If the Sídhe were that desperate to get human slaves again then they might end up with big fights on their hands. It wasn't a pleasant thought, but Alex couldn't ignore the possibility.

Taking Nicki's hand, Alex gave it a soft squeeze of thanks and then took Aiden's hand. The magic crept over her skin, licking up her arms and feeling both familiar and alien at the same time. Nicki and Aiden's magic were familiar and that of allies, but her body knew it wasn't her own. The reaction was stronger than it ever had been before and was a sharp reminder of why healing magic was so difficult.

Alex tried to calm down. They were safe, she told herself, and there was time to focus. Pulling on the power her friends were offering, Alex felt the alien magic brush over her skin as her own magic reached out for it. They twisted together and Alex didn't need to look down to know that their magic was turning gray to match her own. Slowly, bit by bit, she took control over it all and pushed it towards the iron bars. Gray magic swept forward and spun into them as a thin gray stream.

The spots of her blood on the iron flashed bright red. There was a shout from Merlin, but it was hazy to her mind. Alex's eyes jumped up from the iron to the hole in the hillside. Distantly she remembered the crying of the children she'd saved, but something else was poking at her memory. There was another face now: a young preteen girl with brown hair and defiant eyes. The ravine rippled in the corners of her vision, the rocky ground becoming a grassy plain for a moment. Then it was gone, and the iron bars were floating in front of her.

Everything tensed. The magic built, thrumming in the air like a string about to break. There were voices from inside the tunnel that echoed up into the ravine. They were horrible to Alex's ears, too high and unnatural. She knew them as the enemy, and the magic reacted. Everything snapped. Alex released the hands of her friends, feeling the magic rush out of her and into the metal.

Flying through the air, the iron bars twisted and struck the stone sides of the opening with a deafening clang. In her chest, Alex's heart started to race. She could see the patches of her red blood glittering brighter than the rest of the iron. The bars forced themselves into the stone, causing it to crack and crumble. A Síd appeared and swung a gold sword at an iron bar that was narrowing and stretching across the opening. The golden sword shattered, sending flakes of Sídhe gold through the air. It glinted in the sunlight and vanished.

A blast of green from Merlin struck the Síd in the chest. It stumbled back into the darkness, but its screams could still be heard. In the limbo that the tunnels formed between Earth and the Sídhe empire, Alex wasn't sure how long it would take the magic to kill it. She turned her hands and pulled on more magic. It rushed forth at her command.

There were faint strings of gray linking her fingertips and the iron bars like marionette puppets. With the turn of her hand, the iron bars stretched out across the opening and crisscrossed to form the barrier. Deep in the tunnel there were now howls of rage, but they meant nothing to Alex. There were shimmers of magic hanging in the air, faint little wisps of color. It was different, and beautiful. Slowly the connections between her fingers and the iron began to fade. It lingered briefly in the air, but the magic slipped into the new Iron Gate and settled there.

The Gate shimmered in the sunlight and Alex's eyes could see the magic sinking into the stone. Like a gray haze, it was spreading through the rocks and hillside, carving itself and its intention into and around the stones. She watched it, completely unaware of the others. A soft breeze tickled the back of her neck and alerted her to the sweat trickling down her back.

"Marvelous, Alex!" Morgana cheered. The older mage rushed to the twisting iron bars that crisscrossed over each other in the opening of rock. Running a finger over the iron, Morgana's smile widened, and even from her position Alex could see a shimmer of magic rising through the metal to meet the mage's finger. "You were able to put a great deal of magic into the metal. And so quickly too!"

"It felt... well, it wasn't too hard actually. Not compared to last time-" Alex cut herself off, not wanting to remember that the last, and only Iron

Gate they'd made. It had been with Arthur. "Maybe his magic actually made it harder."

"That's very possible," Merlin said kindly. He stepped over to her and placed a hand on her shoulder. It was comforting and kept her swaying body steady. "It's likely that by using your blood he was pulling magic from you."

"Yeah." Alex licked her lips. The world was blurry and the whispers were getting louder. Shaking her head in an attempt to clear them, Alex let her exhaustion show. "But still... not super easy."

"Indeed," Morgana agreed. She quickly returned to Alex's side and put a warm hand on her other shoulder. "I think that's enough for today, Ambrose. Alex needs rest."

The urge to insist she was fine rose up sharply in Alex, but she kept it in. The bundle of magic and grief in her chest throbbed, but she stayed silent. Morgana gave her another smile and joined Merlin in examining the Gate. They both seemed pleased and the whispers calmed a little. Then she exhaled and closed her eyes for a moment. Someone took her arm and Alex looked over at them. It was Aiden, and Alex quickly forced a reassuring smile. Everything was just fine.

6

Stirrings of Magic

465 B.C.E. The Golden Vale, Ireland

Leugio sensed the world change as he moved into the Sídhe mound. The smells all vanished. Darkness washed over him and the torch cast no light. Leugio froze in the entrance, but as quickly as the world had flickered away it returned. Then a sweet floral scent filled his nostrils, unlike anything he'd smelled before. He brushed his fingers across the iron clasp of his cloak. It centered him and he managed another step.

A nagging voice in the back of his mind urged him to hurry. Vaguely he thought he heard crying echoing down the tunnel. It spurred him to take another step. There were no guards. He was alone as he went further, leaving the Síd behind him. The low light from the outside world faded more and more with each step. His torchlight surrounded him and Kent. The cries were louder now. It was Keelia: certainty set into his bones and Kent perked up. Leugio tightened his grip on his dagger and made himself walk faster.

Up ahead the path split: one way was lit by glowing torches at regular intervals and the other was darker with only an occasional torch. Remembering the Síd's words, and hoping he was true to their deal, he turned and walked down the dark tunnel. Kent trotted along beside him as the tunnel gradually sloped down. A cold breeze hit his face and Leugio shifted the torch. There was an opening to the right.

"So far so good," he said.

His voice echoed in the tunnel and he grimaced. There was the soft muted sound of voices from far away, and also the faint sound of crying. He kept moving and came to the staircase. There were only two torches fixed to the wall, providing little light. Pausing at the top, he listened, but there were no new noises. He took the first few steps quickly, mindful of his footing while Kent climbed down beside him.

The bottom was in sight when a sound in the hallway below made him freeze. In the light of the torches, Leugio saw another Síd appear at the bottom of the stairs. It looked up at him with wide violet eyes that then narrowed. Then it drew a golden sword from its belt which flashed in the light of the torches. Like the Síd outside it was dressed in an elegant tunic rather than armor. Still, the sword looked dangerous enough as the Síd began charging up the stairs.

Snarling, Kent leapt forward. The Síd tried to move, but the large dog caught its arm in his teeth. Shock fogged Leugio's mind, but only for a moment. He raced down the stairs with his iron dagger at the ready. The Síd looked up in alarm and opened its mouth to shout. Before he could change his mind, Leugio shoved the dagger forward into the creature's chest. Its eyes widened and Leugio's heart stuttered. They were frozen. Then a low groan escaped the Síd.

He released the dagger and the creature slumped to the ground. Kent released the arm. For a moment nothing happened. The Síd shook slightly on the stairs and silvery blood seeped out of its mouth. A wave of illness hit Leugio as the adrenaline rush ended. His knees quivered and he fell against the wall, turning his eyes away from the Síd. Kent made a small sound and growled. There were voices in the distance.

The urge to turn back hit Leugio, but his feet didn't move. A soft cry echoed towards him, somehow louder than the voices. His mind narrowed on that sound and Kent whimpered. The dog looked up at him and then down the tunnel. Swallowing, Leugio nodded and knelt by the dying creature. He gripped the hilt of his iron dagger and pulled it out. It slid free without any resistance as the flesh around it turned gray and began to fall away. Like ash; like a collapsing log in the fire, he thought.

Then it was gone, leaving only a few pieces of clothing. Some instinct told him to pick them up and hide them, but Leugio's hands trembled. Kent took a few more steps and then looked back at him. Nodding, Leugio stood and forced his feet forward. The darkness ahead seemed thicker now. It was far too quiet. While he could hear distant voices there were no familiar sounds of life to be heard. No livestock, no clanging of workmen or people moving around. Just distant musical voices.

This world was alien to him. It hit Leugio all at once that he had willingly entered the Sídhe domain. Taking a deep breath, Leugio focused on his sister. He forced himself to think of poor Keelia being grabbed by one of them and brought down here. At his side, Kent was nudging his leg with faint traces of silver blood around his mouth that were slowly fading.

"Alright, boy," Leugio said. His voice echoed around them. "Let's keep moving."

Leugio repeated the directions that he'd gotten from the Síd, hoping once more that their trade meant that the Síd had been honest. His stomach turned and Leugio swallowed a rush of bile. His legs shook as the initial desperation and insane courage that had compelled him forward began to wear off. The hallway was lit by torches all the way down, all of them a few feet apart creating areas of shadow. Every time he passed through a darker area; his heart jumped painfully.

The air was stale and smelt a bit of ash over the flowery smell. Some small part of Leugio wondered just how the Sídhe managed to survive underground. The stories said it was magic and that the mounds connected to a special magical realm, but so far there were just tunnels and darkness. Just as Kent was beginning to whimper again and doubts once more crept into his mind something glittered in the light of the torch.

It was a series of small golden plates expertly molded together. There were small designs scattered on the edge of the plates for decoration, and on the whole it seemed far more like a work of art than any true warrior gear. Yet this was what he'd been told to look for. The golden armor was supported by a wooden frame. Small carvings all across the wood beckoned Leugio forward and he peered at the whole display in surprise and confusion. Sídhe gold was well known to him; known to practically everyone. They were cautioned against ever accepting it from one of the creatures, as it would vanish. He wasn't sure how or why, but something about the displayed armor seemed wrong to him. It was like it shouldn't have been able to be there at all.

Shaking his head, Leugio carefully stepped around the display. If he hadn't known to look for it, he might have walked right past the small tunnel. Kent sniffed at the air and sneezed lightly. Leugio shifted the iron dagger still clutched in his right hand just enough to pet the dog with two fingers. The rough texture of the fur was earthy and familiar. With that, he headed down the narrow tunnel.

Leugio searched his mind for any stories that might reveal something. He knew that the king kept prisoners, but he wasn't sure about the Sídhe. Then again, his strange guide had directed him this way, so maybe it was some kind of holding area. The idea settled coldly in his stomach.

Shivering, he made his feet move forward. His footfalls were too loud on the stone and he wished that he had Kent's softer paws.

Another guard stepped out of the shadows. Its violet eyes widened in surprise. Leugio jumped at it with a grunt, swinging his dagger as Kent rushed forward. The dog bit its leg and he slashed at its chest. The Síd twisted out of the way even as it shouted in pain from Kent's attack. Down the tunnel, there was a sudden sound of more footfalls. Terror surged in his chest. He swung his dagger again, this time slicing the Sid across its arm. The Síd stumbled back, shaking its leg in an attempt to get Kent off. Falling against the wall, it struggled to pull its sword. Leugio stepped forward and used the distraction to push the dagger into its neck. The Síd squirmed helplessly, clawing at its throat. Leugio ripped the dagger free and looked down the tunnel.

Three Sídhe were running forward. Rather than tunics, they were wearing heavier clothing like leather. Their swords were already drawn. Kent snarled, and in the corner of his eye Leugio saw the Síd he'd stabbed falling apart. There was no wind, and his eyes dropped unbidden to the small pile of dust on the stones. Shaking himself, he focused on the nearest Sídhe and waved his dagger in front of him. They slowed and eyed him with sharp violet gazes. His heartbeat echoed in his ears. He was breathing more heavily now, his limbs feeling stronger and yet ready to shake at any moment.

One of the Sídhe pushed forward. He ducked the sword and slashed the dagger forward, leaving a cut across the thick armor to his shock. Something sliced his arm and blood trickled from the wound. A noise of frustration escaped the Síd and his eyes narrowed on a reddish tint seeping across the golden blade. Kent had grabbed its arm, but the other two were advancing. Leugio jabbed the dagger forward, trying to catch the Sid in the neck. It brought up its free arm and grabbed his hand.

A tight grip squeezed the sides of his hand. Pain rippled down his arm and his legs trembled as the Síd forced him back. Shrieking reached his ears as the Síd's long nails began to dig into his flesh. Leugio realized it was him. Kent barked and then the Síd twisted away. The dagger fell from his fingers even as he was freed and the Síd retreated from Kent's teeth.

As the iron dagger hit the floor of the tunnel, the metallic clatter echoed around him and the Sídhe closed in. One kicked fearfully at the dagger, sending it sliding across the stone floor. Leugio stumbled back to retrieve his weapon while Kent yelped and hit the wall as a Síd kicked him. Teeth flashed in the low torchlight as Kent whirled and ripped at another Sídhe's leg. A sword flashed through the air and Leugio ducked frantically. He heard the blade ring against the wall. Leugio jabbed the dagger forward, catching a Síd's hand. It hissed in pain and dropped its sword.

Victory was short lived. Kent's target fell back and frantically shook off the dog. The tunnel became a mess of whines, snarls, and blades striking stone. Leugio frantically dodged another attack. He waved the dagger around in front of himself, trying to catch another Síd. They were eyeing the iron blade carefully, but it wasn't stopping them. He swung around and waved the blade at another pair of Sídhe coming up behind him. His left hand trembled and the torch slipped from his fingers.

They were closing in around him. There were more than three now, coming in behind him and down the corridor. Terror gripped at his chest. A pained yelp from Kent cut through the noise in his ears. His eyes found a Síd on his right with a dagger raised to finish him. Something hummed through his feet, mixing with the terror and twisting around his heart. Fire burst forth in his chest, flooding through his entire body. Leugio was sure he was dying, knew a final blow was coming. Yet all he wanted, all he could focus, on was throwing these things back. He needed to find Keelia. A cry echoed up through the corridors and another snarl and cry from Kent sent it all tumbling over a strange new edge.

The fire burst out. Bright white sparks flew off his hands, illuminating the whole of the passage. A scream from a Síd was all the warning any got as a ring of white exploded around him. The Sídhe were shoved into the wall, their backs and heads cracking against the stone. Some managed to yell, some to scream, and others only managed small gurgles before their bodies began to turn to dust. Turning around, Leugio found the two Sídhe behind him dissolving. Suddenly they were all gone.

Looking down at his hand, Leugio gasped as white sparks glittered around his fingers. A sharp tingling jolted up his arm. The air was forced from his lungs, but a dull whimper pulled his attention away. Kent was whining in pain and limping forward. Dropping to his knees beside the dog, Leugio held back tears as he took in the matted, bloody fur. Kent turned and looked at him, his dark brown eyes dull with pain, but then Kent limped forward another step. Another pained whimper escaped him.

Ignoring the white sparks, Leugio grabbed at Kent's neck to keep him from moving forward. His chest ached even as his mind pushed away logic and the rational knowledge that the poor creature was done for. His fingers were glowing as he patted the dog fondly. Yet even the strange glow wasn't enough to distract him from the grief coiling in his chest.

"I'm sorry, boy," he said. "I- stay here, I'll find Keelia." Breathing was harder now and Leugio shivered. His energy was draining away, but he didn't understand it. "I'll find her," he promised. "Really, boy, just lay down for a while. When I find her, I can carry you out."

The words sounded hollow. The ache in his chest was growing and a white spark jumped off his fingers. His eyes moved to his hand, but he didn't understand. Now the ache was in his head and his eyes were burning. Closing his eyes, Leugio shook his head as chills swept up his spine.

Kent whined; the sound more surprised than pained. Leugio swayed, weakness rolling over him. Forcing open his eyes, he looked down the tunnel first, but they were still alone. A growing light caught his attention and he looked down at his hands. The white sparks had turned into soft waves of light that washed across Kent's side. The dog shuddered and tried to move away, but Leugio's right hand tightened on the scuff of his neck on impulse. His eyes were drawn to the sparks as the misshapen side of Kent began to glow. It shifted; there was a sharp, strange grinding sound. The sparks began to vanish into Kent's side.

"Heal," Leugio whispered. He licked his lips and swallowed; his mouth painfully dry. "Heal." The sparks shimmered brightly and Kent stopped shifting away. "Easy, boy." He brushed over the dog's thick fur. The strange burning in his chest was getting stronger again, but this time fueled by hope and a hint of desperation. "Easy, boy."

Kent barked and jumped away, shaking his whole body. The magic snapped back against Leugio's chest, knocking him lower on his knees. Leugio tried to stand, but his legs trembled and he panted for air. He raised his eyes and looked at Kent. The dog came back to him and licked his face. Leaning back, Leugio laughed a little, but the exhaustion was weighing on him. His back hit the wall and the shock of cold woke him up a bit, but it wasn't enough. The ache in his head was worse and there was a dull burn in his chest. At the edge of his vision shadows were dancing.

"Just... give me a second, Kent," he panted. Rubbing Kent's fur, Leugio gently touched the dog's side, but Kent made no sounds. The dog shifted slightly, stepping forward and then looking back at him. There was no limping and no open wounds in the skin, even if the drying blood remained. "How did I...?" He shook his head and looked at his hands. There was a thin layer of blood and marks from the Síd's nails, but also a faint glow that was quickly dimming. "Magic. I have magic."

Kent whined and turned away from him, heading down the tunnel. Leugio grabbed his dagger from the ground, noting the large chip in the blade. After a moment of hesitation, he slid it into the sheath on his belt and picked the torch back up. Inhaling deeply, Leugio stumbled forward. He had to use his right hand to support himself against the wall.

He wasn't injured, but his body ached. Leugio could only remember a few days in his life when he'd been left so tired, but that had always involved heavy labor. Kent stayed close to him, sniffing the air. Panting, Leugio slumped against the wall. His vision was blurring, with only the points of light from the torches being clear. His mind was still tripping over Kent's sudden recovery and how he'd stopped all those Sídhe. Looking down at his hands, Leugio tried to smile, but the ache was too much. Instead, he groaned and shuffled forward.

7

Advisor Meeting

Monday was a drearier day than normal. Students were moving around the campus like zombies, even those with espressos and caffeine drinks in hand. There was a hint of rain and ozone in the air that warned of a storm, but so far it had rolled over the mountains and just parked. Every so often there was a rumble from the sky, but the rain had yet to fall. Alex hated it.

She hated all of it. She hated the look Nicki had given her when she had arrived late last night. She hated the final words her brothers had said to her and the fact that Ed wouldn't even hug her. Alex hated the distance between her and her brothers now even as she was grateful for it. Most of all she hated the dreams and voices and hated that she needed them. They were the only things keeping the knot contained and holding her grief back.

Classes were an exercise in patience. She was done with most of her general education classes which meant that she didn't have to feel the others watching her through class, but instead it meant that the teachers were. Alex was beginning to hate university policy too. She hadn't paid it much mind before. It certainly hadn't been a point of concern when she'd chosen the University of Ravenslake as her university of choice.

Then again, magic had apparently taken a role in that. Policy dictated that her teachers were all treating her with kid gloves. Her deadlines for upcoming papers were being extended without her having to ask and they were leaving her alone during class. One day back and frustration was already growing in her gut.

None of her fellow students paid her much mind. While the teachers had been informed, Alex supposed that there would be no reason for the other students to know. A car crash with three fatalities in Spokane, Washington had no reason to be news in Ravenslake, Oregon. Instead, the rest of the world was just going on with their normal lives, completely unaware of her loss or the dangerous magical war brewing beneath the surface.

Anger towards Arthur ached in her chest, right below the knot of grief Alex was holding at bay. She didn't mind the anger: it was the simplest and most straightforward thing in her life right now. So, she focused on that, took her notes in class and tried to ignore the looks she got from the professors. Her phone beeped with an email halfway through lunch. It was an official looking email from the English department requesting that she meet with her advisor. Alex knew that it really wasn't much of a request. Not for the first time she had serious doubts about her English with a literature focus major.

The English department offices were the same as most other department offices. A receptionist with a full inbox sat near the main door and there were a few chairs for waiting students. On the walls were framed book covers and notices of upcoming meetings. There was a rather battered bookshelf tucked next to a small table in one corner with reference books and old paperback copies of classics. One of the students waiting glanced her way before looking back at the documents in their hand. Alex peered at the receptionist who didn't even look up at her from the file he was working on and kept walking towards Merlin's office. The door was open and he was waiting for her.

Nothing about Merlin indicated that he was thousands of years old. He had the appearance of an older man with deep laugh lines around his eyes. His brown eyes were intense and almost glowed with wisdom, but most people would chalk that up to him being a literature professor. The only sign of his ancient past in Bronze Age Britain was a small triskelion pin that he wore on the lapel of his jacket. It was made of iron and had small tool marks on it, but even it was very modern. There was no staff, no cloak, and no talismans around his neck, and something about that seemed wrong to Alex all of a sudden. Still, she forced a slight smile and stepped into the office.

Merlin's office hadn't changed much. There were some new books on the shelves and he'd replaced one of the art prints on his wall. On his desk were an electric kettle and two tea cups. Alex hadn't been much of one for tea before meeting the professors, but despite them not actually originating from the period of time where British people drank tea, they seemed to have adopted it. Maybe it was an odd form of national pride they still carried.

From his chair, Merlin offered her a wide smile and gestured to the armchair by his desk. Alex pulled off her messenger bag and set it on the ground. Merlin eyed the door she'd left open with a slight frown. Then he raised his fingers and green sparks appeared for a moment. He moved his fingers and the door swung shut.

"There was no one in the hallway," Merlin said. He gave her a warm smile that brightened his brown eyes. "Now, Alex, how are you?"

"I'm fine," Alex replied. She shrugged slightly. "It's a bit weird being back in classes, but the structure is good." Brushing a strand of hair behind her ear, Alex cleared her throat slightly and pulled a small notebook out of her bag. "Honestly I've not finished my course schedule for next year, but I'm looking at mostly English classes with a couple-"

"Alex," Merlin interrupted. He held up his hand. "That's not what this meeting is about." He seemed adrift for a moment. "I'm glad that you're already planning for next year's classes, especially in light of recent events, but..." Merlin seemed to be struggling for the right words. There was a flush of satisfaction and even amusement through Alex that almost made her smile. "This is about the loss of your parents. You've suffered a deep loss."

"I'm doing alright, Professor Yates," Alex said. It was strange calling him by his formal name, but she hoped it would warn him not to push. "Like I said, the structure of being back in school is helping. I got up this morning and knew what I needed to do and went to class."

Merlin seemed surprised and even a little distressed at her answer. Nonetheless, he nodded slowly and then reached for the kettle. Without a word, he poured her some tea and the scent of Earl Grey filled Alex's nostrils. She accepted the offered tea with a nod and then took a slow sip. That seemed to relax Merlin a little.

"I'm worried about you, Alex," Merlin finally said. He held his own mug of tea and watched her sadly. "You've lost your parents, but don't seem to be grieving."

"Everyone grieves in their own way." She didn't meet his eyes and looked towards the window. For a change, Alex found herself actually wishing for an attack, but with the Queen's spell broken and the Iron Gate holding that was very unlikely. "I'm done crying."

"Yes, but..." Merlin sighed and shook his head. He was silent for a moment and just watched her. "I can't help but feel that something is wrong." Smiling gently at her, Merlin leaned forward. "You've always been such a bright, cheerful girl."

"Not really."

"To me you are," Merlin countered. "While yes, you've never really given yourself enough credit for what you're capable of, you've also never been so... distant." He paused and frowned, a hint of alarm in his eyes. "Except when you were aware that Jenny and Lance were cheating. You were withdrawn then. Has something happened?"

"No, Lance and Jenny are fine and it doesn't bother me," Alex assured him. She really just wanted to get up and leave. "I'm glad they're together and happy. I'm not sure if I believe in soul mates or anything like that, but those two deserve a chance to be happy on their own terms."

Several whispers of agreement echoed in her head, and the sense of solidarity sank into Alex's bones. She relaxed a little and took a sip of the tea. It was bitterer than she usually liked her drinks, but Alex suspected that she could get used to it. Merlin was still watching her. Looking outside, Alex noted the brightness of the green she could already see in the trees and the lawn. She could hear the muffled sounds of campus life beyond the glass. A ray of sun hit the window, telling Alex that the cloud cover was breaking. Something shifted in her chest a little, but she didn't dare try to figure out what it was.

"Alex, I know we aren't close, and I regret that," Merlin said. His features were mournful. "In addition to being your magical mentor, well, one of them, I am also your academic advisor. Yet I focused more on Arthur than you. Under the circumstances, it seemed appropriate, but I still should have been there more when you needed me, when you were frustrated by using your magic."

"I was fine," Alex said. She looked down into the softly swirling tea. "Morgana helped me. And when you think about it, that makes sense. She was my sister in another life."

"Yes, but in that same life I was…" Merlin trailed off, grief appearing on his face. Something in Alex twisted. It was like the knot of grief, but this one wasn't for her parents. She hissed in alarm, surprise, and pain as it flooded her whole body with an aching sensation. "Anyway," Merlin said. "I want you to know that if you need anything or ever wish to talk, I will listen. If there's ever something you don't want to talk to Morgana about, of course." Merlin forced a smile. "I don't wish to disrupt your relationship with her. I'm grateful that she's been able to be there for you."

"You were a good father," Alex said. The words just slipped out as tears gathered in her eyes. Merlin's brown eyes widened and he stuttered.

Dropping her eyes, Alex leaned forward and rested her elbows on her knees. Her whole body was heavy and yet there was a charge of nervous energy she didn't know how to deal with pulsing in her veins. Something was loud in her head and the soft flow of magic in her chest wavered. Then there was a hand on the top of her head, putting gentle pressure on her scalp. It was familiar, and comforting, and… Alex inhaled slowly on some long-trained instinct.

"That's it," Merlin's voice said. It was gentle but thick with emotion. A hand took the teacup from her and set it on the desk with a soft clink. "Just breathe, Alex."

She obeyed and took another breath. Her magic responded and evened out, wrapping around the knot in her chest protectively. The ache eased and Alex blinked her eyes to clear the tears. She could hear Merlin making soft comforting sounds as if she was a child. Yet something about it was very familiar. Embarrassment hit her and she didn't dare move. She rolled her lips together and nervously waited for Merlin to say something, anything.

"I'm sorry," Merlin finally said. "I'm not sure how to help you with the memories, Alex." There was a heavy silence and Alex heard a door outside open and then close. The distant sounds of voices could be heard, but neither of them spoke for several minutes. She closed her eyes and let some part of her draw comfort from the weight of Merlin's hand on her head. "Are the memories difficult?"

"I'm not sure." Alex swallowed and twisted her hands together even as she kept her eyes down. "They're just... there.". It was a terrible explanation. "There's just an awareness that wasn't there before. I... I can hear them sometimes," Alex said. The declaration was met with a soft gasp. "They aren't loud, but... they're there."

Alex grimaced at her own words, but she had no idea how to explain it. Dread was quickly replacing embarrassment as certainty set in that she shouldn't have told Merlin. She waited for him to say or do something, but he was silent. Alex almost looked up at him but couldn't deal with the thought of his expression at this revelation. Instead, they were both silent and Alex focused on the sounds of people in the hallway and outside on the lawn. The ticking of the wall clock became louder with each passing moment until it was almost unbearable.

"Do you think that's why you're having difficulty coping with your parents' death?"

The question sent an icy wave down Alex's spine. She straightened up sharply and shifted away from Merlin's hand. Before she could think better of it or Merlin could move, Alex grabbed her bag and stood up. She made it to the door with Merlin only a few steps behind her. Alex didn't stop. She couldn't stop moving. The whispers were silent as her own panicked thoughts raged.

Walking out of the office, Alex ignored the surprised look she got from the receptionist near the department door. She didn't even bother smiling or looking pleasant. Alex pulled open the door and stepped out into the main hallway. There were students moving about alone or in small groups, all of them minding their own business. A few glanced her way as she stepped into the flow of traffic and then they backed off. Alex clenched her hand around the strap of her bag as the other formed a fist. Someone brushed against her shoulder and Alex turned her head to give them a dark look. Their eyes widened and they scampered away.

She quickly took the stairs down to the main floor and pushed her way out into the fresh air. A warm breeze tickled her face and sent her long blonde hair into her eyes. Alex didn't care. She stepped off to the side and inhaled deeply. There was the smell of the lake and the mountain evergreens on the wind. It seeped into her skin and Alex's fingers relaxed.

Closing her eyes, Alex hissed as the truck appeared once more. Her chest tightened and the air rushed out of her as her knees trembled. She couldn't make her eyes open. One of her hands found the brick wall behind her and grabbed onto a small rough edge. It was solid and real. The scraping of her fingertips against it took over and the truck vanished. Opening her eyes, Alex swallowed and pushed herself off the wall, walking away from the building as quickly as she could. She'd be hearing about this soon enough.

8

The Outsider

He was never going to get used to this. At least that's what Lance thought now, even as a little voice nagged at him that if it kept up, he probably would. In his seat at the side of the room, Lance did his best to sit still and not disturb the mages. It wasn't easy. His mind was still reeling from even being welcomed to the meeting again and not being given research to do as soon as he entered. On the other side of the small table by Merlin's window sat Jenny, who at least managed to look much calmer than him.

Yet he'd gotten the text like all the others. When he'd pulled up with Jenny in his truck Morgana had opened the door for them. The older mage had even said hello without any underlying irritation in her voice. Merlin had greeted them with nods and provided them with glasses of iced tea. He was even confident that they hadn't been poisoned. While Lance was aware that he'd been seated at the side of the room; he couldn't ignore the fact that he was here with the mages once more.

Alex was of course near the center of the room in one of Merlin's large plush armchairs with Morgana hovering just behind her. Merlin was seated across from Alex on the sofa with Nicki and Aiden on either side of him. Bran was in the second armchair and they were all watching the Brownie Timothy as he bounced up onto the coffee table beside the plate of sandwiches. Lance rubbed the leg of his jeans as nervous sweat built up on his palm. There was something hanging in the air that put him on edge; something he couldn't put his finger on.

"Does anyone need anything?" Morgana asked. She even looked over towards him and Jenny. The woman's green eyes locked on his own and Lance found it difficult to speak. Warming up to them, or not the woman still terrified him. He shook his head and touched the glass of iced tea on the table beside him. "Very well. Timothy wanted a chance to speak with everyone."

"Yes, yes," Timothy said quickly. The Brownie rubbed its hands nervously on the front of his small doll coat. Its small eyes turned towards Alex. "I'm leaving to find my kin. Mages need to know more of what is happening since the spell was broken. My family can help us learn what has happened."

"Will you be safe?" Alex asked. She leaned forward and Lance almost smiled at the obvious concern on her face. Even after everything, she still just wanted to protect others. It was reassuring. "I mean, they won't hurt you for having been around us?"

"No no," Timothy assured them. "In old days Brownies always lived with humans and helped them. Only stopped when humans didn't want to know about magic anymore." He paused and tilted his head. "Even now most still don't."

"But we're mages," Alex said. "Doesn't that change anything? I mean, they won't see it as helping the enemy or anything like that will they?"

It took Timothy too long to answer. The Brownie looked uncomfortable and unsure. With each passing moment, the expression on Alex's face darkened. Then she looked over at Merlin with cold gray eyes.

"He's not going then!"

"Alex, we don't know what will happen," Merlin said. He held up his hands in a calming gesture, but Lance could tell it wouldn't help. "We haven't asked him to go."

"Mages need to know," Timothy said. Then he scuffed his foot on the top of the table. "And I need to know what has happened to my kin. I need to know if they are alive or not."

The mages all flinched, except for Merlin and Morgana, but even they looked slightly distressed. A long exhale escaped Lance as he waited for some sort of explosion. It didn't come. Alex slumped back in her chair. All emotion was gone from her face; she just looked thoughtful or maybe bored. There wasn't a trace of her rage from a moment ago, or guilt, or sadness. Just nothing, and that made a cold weight settle in his stomach.

"It wasn't our fault," Morgana said. Her voice was thinner than usual. "None of us cast that spell, and we did not actively go out looking for Faeries to fight. Scáthbás cast the spell and sent those Faeries after us. With our magic, she must have known that she was sending them to their deaths. She was just gambling on one of them getting lucky at some point." Morgana's voice was stronger now and she looked at all the younger mages in turn. "We had to defend ourselves, and you found the solution as quickly as you could. There was nothing more you could have done."

"We still killed a lot of them," Alex murmured.

"Alex," Merlin called. "In the last attack, you freed as many as you could. Even before breaking the spell, you freed those you could nearby and protected them from the rising blood spell. The only reason Timothy is even standing safely in the bounds of Ravenslake is because you built an exception into the spell." Something about Merlin's voice was soothing and it seemed to roll down Lance's spine. There was a faint hum to the voices and a hint of something in the air. Lance vaguely wondered if he was using some sort of magic. "Release your guilt," Merlin urged. "You and the others did everything that you could."

"And now I want to help," Timothy said. He was smiling up at Alex again with that slightly adoring look. "Mages need to know how Faeries are reacting."

"What do you think you'll find?" Nicki asked. She was toying with the end of her braid of red hair, looking almost as nervous as Alex had been. "Do you think they'll be angry with you?"

"Most will be happy to be freed," Timothy assured her. He nodded determinedly. "Some may be angry, but I'll tell them to spread the word that Scáthbás did it, not the Iron Soul."

Opening her mouth, Alex seemed ready to argue for a moment, but then nodded and pressed her lips together. Lance saw Morgana's shoulders relax in relief as his own frown deepened. Timothy was looking up at Alex nervously, clearly picking up on the tension in the room.

"Thank you for helping us," Alex said. "Just be careful, okay?"

"I'll be careful," Timothy promised. He glanced around at all of them. "Mages and friends be careful as well. I'm not sure how the other Faery creatures will respond to all these changes."

Then Timothy jumped off the table and bounced towards the kitchen. Leaning forward, Lance tried to catch sight of the small creature, but he was gone from view too quickly. He glanced towards Jenny, who shrugged. Lance wondered if Timothy was leaving now and grabbing supplies. Though, maybe Timothy could teleport or was waiting until nightfall. His head ached a little at the thoughts, and Lance nearly groaned at the reminder of how poorly he understood what was happening around him.

"He's more confident than I would be," Bran said. He was turned in his chair and peering into Merlin's kitchen. Shaking his head, he smiled at all of them. "But maybe he's right to be. This is a strange situation: I assume there isn't a precedent for it."

"Not as such," Merlin agreed. "In the past we have formed alliances with beings from other worlds that live here." Merlin leaned forward to rest his elbows on his knees and tented his fingers in front of him. "But yes, this is a bit more than anything that has ever happened before. Sadly, the creatures do seem to have recognized that it wasn't just the Queen's magic affecting them, which isn't good for us."

"It is not Alex's fault," Morgana said. Her voice rang with authority.

"Of course not," Merlin agreed. He gave Alex a soft smile, but her expression remained blank. "It just highlights the danger of our enemies gaining control of the Iron Artifacts that the Iron Soul has made in the past."

"Still, it is connected to me," Alex said. She almost managed to sound nonchalant, but her fingers tightened against the armrests. "Let's face it: Arthur probably has magic because of how he was made. Piggybacking on the Iron Chain's magic or something." Her jaw tightened, and Lance glanced towards a visibly worried Bran. "'Course he still has magic now; the breaking of the Iron Chain didn't change that. He was able to scramble that driver's head and use him to kill my parents."

The thick awkward silence was back. In the corner of his eye Lance saw Jenny grimace and make an abortive move to stand. Guilt mixed with understanding filled her face and Lance was reminded once more that Jenny understood what it was like to lose a parent. His eyes moved across the mages quickly. Nicki was watching Alex with worry, and he noted for the first time how tired she looked. Wondering if Alex was keeping her awake at night, Lance looked toward Aiden, but he just seemed at a loss. Bran was watching Alex thoughtfully and his fingers were toying with something in his hand. Lance caught a flash of metal. His throat tightened in response.

"Speaking of which, Alex, how are you today?" Merlin asked. He coughed a bit as if speaking was a chore. There was something heavy in his brown eyes that made Lance feel like he was falling, and the look wasn't even directed towards him. "How are you sleeping? Any nightmares?"

Alex tensed at the question and the temperature in the room seemed to drop. Lance noted Bran straightening up his chair and Nicki grimacing. Morgana shifted and put a hand on Alex's shoulder. For a moment no one said anything.

"I have some nightmares." Alex's voice was almost dismissive. "It isn't pleasant, but I'm okay." She nodded and forced a painful looking smile. "One day at a time." Then she shook her head. "And honestly I'm not the priority. Hopefully, Timothy can bring us back some information, because we need to know what the Queen is up to now. Arthur hinted that they're still interested in trying to locate Cathanáil. Do you think there's any chance they'll find it?"

The deflection was painfully obvious and Merlin looked unhappy, but to Lance's surprise he didn't push. Instead, the eldest of the mages shook his head sadly and picked up his iced tea. He took a sip while the rest of the room waited. Lance looked over at Morgana. She was staring down at Alex with a soft and sad expression, her hand still resting on Alex's shoulder.

"We still have the issue of waking Old Ones," Merlin said. He turned his gaze around the room, eying each of them in turn. "Some like Sif are allies, but there are others who, like Chernobog, have gone mad over the years. Hopefully, most of those that wake will be on our side or at least willing to stay neutral, but I fear we should be prepared for some new enemies."

"What does that have to do with the Sword?" Bran asked.

"These Old Ones have been sleeping in water. They have an affinity for it, and that may help them to find the Sword. When Arthur lost his grip on it, the Sword was carried through the waters of the world. That tunnel doesn't last forever, so the Sword was released somewhere. It will be in a place with water, but that could be anywhere from the oceans to a swimming pool. Obviously, an ocean is the most likely place and an Old One could get lucky enough to stumble upon it."

"Have you had any thoughts on how we might find it?" Aiden asked. He looked uneasy and a touch embarrassed. In any other setting, Lance would have reminded him that what he'd done had been for the best. Arthur with Cathanáil would have been worse than just losing the Sword. Lance knew that in his gut and he wasn't even sure of the extent of the Sword's power. "Do you think Alex could find it if she worked with Bran?"

"There is still the issue of retrieving it even if they could focus in on it," Merlin said. The mage pressed his lips and hummed to himself for a moment. "But I suppose with Alex gaining more control, it might work if she gathers up some magic to help her. Even if we can't get to the Sword, perhaps we can at least confirm that no enemies have it."

Alex shifted in her chair, an odd look of excitement and dread on her face. She tilted her head and seemed to be listening to something as her eyes went vacant. Frowning, Lance leaned forward to try and get a better look at her face, but it was gone as quickly as it had come. Alex nodded in agreement and shuddered a little, earning her another worried glance from Morgana.

"It's worth a try," Alex agreed. "Have you heard anything from Sif?" Her voice went a little higher at the mention of Sif's name.

"Nothing yet, but I'm sure Sif will be in touch soon."

"Hopefully she'll stay safe," Alex said. There was something in her voice, something distant and yet deeply invested. "We wouldn't have been able to break the spell if she hadn't found the potion."

"Yes," Merlin agreed. "We were fortunate that she tracked down Cyrridven's last home. With some luck, she'll be able to tell us more soon."

A long sigh escaped Alex and her fingers dug into the armrests of the chair for a moment. Then she straightened up and forced a little smile. "Okay," Alex said breaking the silence. "We have the start of a plan, or at least a way to gather some information." She gave them all a wide smile that failed to reach her gray eyes. They remained too dark and too shadowed for Lance's nerves. "Anyone have anything else to report?"

The conversation shifted slowly to a discussion about new spells to try. Nicki wanted to work on telekinesis with Bran while Aiden had plans to go through his RPG books again for new ideas. Lance took advantage of his placement off to the side and studied the mages. Part of him disliked the separation that was apparent by where Merlin had placed him and Jenny, but it gave him the ability to really look at all of them. Alex was toying with her hands and staring off into space. Her head tilted a tiny bit and Lance got the impression she was listening to something he couldn't hear.

Nicki kept sending glances towards Aiden. Her worry and fear for his recovery still hadn't completely faded, even after a couple of months and their trip to Paris. Aiden was looking between Merlin and Morgana uneasily and they were both sporting fixed little smiles. Those two had practice at looking calm even when they weren't, but Lance thought he saw a glimmer of apprehension in their eyes.

Bran was the calmest. He was seated in his armchair and watching Alex. Then he turned and met Lance's gaze. Neither of them said anything nor made any gestures. Lance relaxed a little. At least there was one other sane person in the mix of all this. Bran nodded to him: a tiny little nod, but it got his agreement across. Holding back a sigh, Lance returned the gesture.

Something brushed against his hand and Lance turned to find Jenny looking at him. There was a sad smile on her face and the pressure on his hand increased. Smiling, Lance turned his hand to thread their fingers together. There was more than one other sane person. He was silent as Jenny turned her head and watched Alex. He could see the worry for their friend on her face, and Lance wondered just how long it would be before something fell apart.

9

The Rescued

465 B.C.E. The Golden Vale, Ireland

Everything ached. Leugio made himself slowly keep moving, using the wall to support himself. Kent kept pausing and looking back at him, a silent plea for him to hurry shining in his eyes. Leugio hoped that meant he could smell Keelia. Taking another step, he bit back a groan. A dark thought formed in the back of his mind, that even if he found Keelia, now he was in no condition to get her out.

He didn't stop. It wouldn't really matter now anyway. He couldn't leave. Even with his heart racing and the fear closing in, Leugio knew that he wasn't going to leave. His sister was in the dark somewhere. The Sídhe had taken his sister, and some instinct fought hard against that. There was another fearful cry that echoed up the dark pathway and Kent snarled. The dog's whole body tensed, torn between running forward and staying with him.

Inhaling slowly, Leugio gave himself a moment. The ache in his muscles eased a little, but the taste of the air seemed wrong. It bothered him more now and he wondered if that was the magic he'd used. Had it changed something here? Or something in him? Kent whimpered and trotted ahead, looking back at him imploringly. It was enough to get him moving again and he kept following the tunnel.

The stone was cool and smooth beneath his hand. Every so often he caught a whiff of a more natural, earthy smell that reassured him that he hadn't strayed too far from home. Stories blurred together in his head as he tried to remember the way out and any advice he could gather from the tales he'd been told. There were fewer torches now, or at least it seemed that way with shadows creeping in.

Kent kept moving and somehow Leugio mostly kept up with his pace. His hand gripping the torch was sweaty and even the rough wood was trying to slide out of his grasp. Keeping one hand against the wall, he kept leveraging himself along. The magic was still pulsing in his chest, and he recognized it now. It had always been there, just faint and unnoticed. He'd had no idea what it was or what it could do. Now he could only be grateful for whatever instincts his fear had given him.

The tunnel opened ahead, widening into a circular room with a few doorways leading off it. Dark stone was barely illuminated by torches, but the scene was clear. There were three Sídhe standing around his sister. Keelia was on her knees in the center of the room, bound by some sort of thin chain with her mouth gagged. To Leugio's horror, one of the Sídhe was running its long fingers through her brown hair thoughtfully. She was glaring up at them and trying to move away. There was a darkening patch on her right cheek.

Kent snarled, the sound resonating through the room. The Sídhe spun around in surprise, their violet eyes widening in shock. Keelia's eyes met his and he could see her worry for him, her relief, and her anger all welling up in her dark eyes. There was a heartbeat of stillness. Then everything happened at once.

Only one of the Sídhe had a sword which it quickly pulled. Kent jumped forward to put himself between Keelia and the Síd nearest to her. The creature looked at the dog in surprise and a touch of fear. It and the other unarmed Síd fled, vanishing through one of the doors with frantic shouts.

Leugio pushed himself off the wall. His right hand jumped to his dagger, and he pulled the weapon forth in one quick movement. The guard spun around and lashed at him with its sword. Ducking away from it, he slashed the dagger forward. Kent distracted the guard, trying to bite its leg. The Síd dodged his first wild swipe, but his second swing caught its arm. Leugio stumbled, his foot slipping on the stone, and he fell against the wall.

Grunting, Leugio twisted away from the wall. In the distance there was yelling. He stepped back, his heart pounding, and slashed with the dagger again. The gold sword of the guard hit the stone beside his head with a sharp metallic ring. Metal fragments cracked off and he backed away. Kent's snarling was suddenly louder and there was another choked scream. The guard tried to twist away from the dog that now had a firm grip on its leg. Leugio jabbed his dagger forward, catching the Síd in the hand. It roared in pain and pulled back as its skin began to darken. Leugio didn't wait. He shoved the dagger forward, closing his eyes as the metal slid into the Síd's unprotected neck.

The Síd collapsed on the ground. Leugio forced his eyes open but didn't linger to watch its death. He nearly tripped over it as he reached frantically for his sister. Two more Sídhe came rushing in through the door the other two had fled through, both of them armed. Panic was clamoring through his system. Blood was seeping down his arm. He wasn't sure when that had happened.

Suddenly, Keelia rolled forward, knocking into the legs of the nearest Síd and sending it stumbling. Kent took advantage as it fell to the floor and jumped at its neck. His stomach turned and bile filled Leugio's mouth. Once again, he feared that his legs were going to collapse, but somehow, he stayed upright as the second Síd headed straight for him.

In the corner of his eye Leugio saw his sister struggling against her bonds. Twisting around, she freed one hand and tore off her gag. She climbed to her feet and tackled the remaining guard from behind. It hit the ground with a grunt of pain and Keelia's fingers reached for the sword in its hand. The Síd struggled and Leugio stumbled forward to help her. He had to jump against the wall as the sword slashed wildly. Holding out his dagger, Leugio made a move to attack, but his knees quaked. The dagger dropped to the floor with a clatter, but Keelia made a grab for it. The Síd was crawling away from her when Keelia got the dagger and slashed at its throat.

There was a gurgle of pain and the Síd collapsed. Silvery blood spilled out onto the floor and the body started to slowly dissolve. Behind him, there was yet more shouting. Looking towards Keelia, he found his sister climbing to her feet, Kent growling at her side. He turned around, panting at the effort, and found three more Sídhe coming towards them.

A fearful sound escaped Keelia. Anger, fear, and most of all an absolute desire to save Keelia filled Leugio's chest. The spark flared back to life, and he pulled on it, wishing, telling, begging it to push them back. White sparks exploded from his hands. The wave of magic rolled across the Sídhe guards, knocking them back into the walls. He tried to count them, but everything was on fire. His eyes hurt, his muscles convulsed, and his lungs burned.

Two of the Sídhe scrambled to their feet and advanced. Keelia's eyes widened and she jumped between the Sídhe and her brother. Leugio collapsed against the wall. The strength he'd mustered was spent. His chest ached and his legs were burning. Every muscle quivered and threatened to give out beneath him. Kent snarled, putting himself between the Sídhe guards and his humans. Leugio almost smiled at the show of loyalty but couldn't manage it.

The third guard had recovered and was on his feet, but all of them seemed uncertain as to what they should do. They were all nearly identical with the same golden swords and leather armor. None wore anything like the elegant golden armor he'd seen on display. His head pounded. His knees quaked and Keelia stepped back next to him.

Straightening up, Keelia waved the dagger threateningly in front of her. Looking at his sister in surprise, Leugio found her brown eyes bright with an internal fire and her features calm and cold. He'd never seen her like that. Keelia had always been sweet and playful. None of that was here now.

"Back off," she growled. She stepped closer to him, shifting her body next to his and carefully took on some of his weight. "My brother has magic, and I will fight with this iron, my teeth, and my nails to leave here." Her tone was sharp and low. She meant every word and Leugio looked at her in shock. "I will take as many of you as I can with me. Stand aside and you live."

One Síd started to step forward. Kent lunged at him, biting into its leg and Keelia jabbed the dagger forward. It twisted away frantically, but she sliced into its arm. Silvery blood oozed forth even as the white flesh around the wound began to glimmer and turn dark. Another Síd grabbed him and tried to pull him back, but Kent did not release his target until Keelia ordered him to. In the corner of his eye, Leugio saw another Síd moving towards him.

He pulled on the faint flare of power lingering in his chest. The ache spread, but he didn't relent. Magic rushed down his arm and he flexed his fingers, releasing tiny white sparks that encircled his fingertips. The Síd stopped and then backed away.

"Stand aside," Keelia ordered.

Her voice was louder this time and Kent barked. The sound echoed in the stone hall, and the Sídhe drew back. Several of them glared at them, but one huffed and outright turned and walked away. It vanished through one of the side doors, grumbling something. Leugio watched him go uncertainly. Then the other two began to move back. The way out was open to them and Leugio nodded towards the tunnel he'd come through.

Keelia didn't have to be told out loud. She took on more of his weight and they started walking. The adrenaline was burned away. Fear remained however and Leugio's ears were straining for even the slightest sound of them being followed. Kent was fixed to Keelia's side but kept glancing back. He guessed the dog didn't like knowing there was danger behind, but Leugio was in no shape to summon more magic.

"Don't follow us," Keelia said. "We may be tired, but if you make us fight for our lives, you'll discover how much damage we can do."

Grinning, Leugio felt a jolt of pride and outright admiration for his little sister. While she'd needed help, it was clear that she could take care of herself. The thought made him smile a little, even if it didn't banish all his worries. They passed the golden armor and he gently shifted to guide her towards the stairs. Keelia nodded, and he swallowed back the blood he could taste in his mouth. His tongue found a small wound in the side of his mouth. When it had happened, he wasn't sure.

Leugio grew stronger as they climbed the stairs. It was odd because he would have thought that the climb would have weakened him. Yet there was something in the air that helped as he inhaled it. The musty scent of the ground was growing stronger while the strange flowery scent of the Sídhe's domain was fading away. The ache was still present in his muscles though, and while he could feel that faint fluttering of power in his chest, he knew it wasn't safe to touch. He'd been burned on the inside by it. That was the only way he could understand it.

He managed to point Keelia towards the entrance, tracing their steps back. Behind them he could hear low voices, but they were fading. The Sídhe had gambled and lost. He hoped that they'd keep to themselves for a while after this. Nothing was worse than hearing the tales of young children taken, or worse, traded away by their parents. His grip around Keelia's shoulder tightened for a moment.

"Easy, Leugio," his sister said. Kent kept climbing up the stairs ahead of them, sniffing at the air. "I've got you."

They seemed to be alone. Distantly he could hear voices and sounds that were familiar from his own village, his own home. He wondered where down here the rest of the Sídhe lived. Wondered if they had families like his own, if they married and lived in houses built underground or if they just had little rooms off the tunnels. The stories didn't say, but then again people who crossed their threshold weren't usually supposed to return.

"Thank you for coming to help me," Keelia said. Her voice was soft and low, almost a whisper.

"Always: you're my sister." He grunted a little and shifted his weight off her a bit. "I'm feeling a bit better now."

"Let me help." She glanced his way and then looked down at Kent. "So... you have magic. I thought those were just stories."

"I did too. Never noticed it before today, but when I was surrounded, it just happened and then when Kent was hurt-"

"Kent was hurt?"

"Uh, yes, just a bit," he assured her. "The magic healed him, but it was... really exhausting. I'm not sure how I even stood up after it."

"I'm sorry. I wasn't careful this morning. I slipped in some mud and twisted my ankle. Kent stayed with me, but two of the Sídhe found me."

"Kent came running back to the village. We'd noticed you were missing already, but that was what told me you were probably hurt or that the Sídhe had gotten you."

"Yeah, Kent attacked one of the Sídhe while the other dragged me off. I guess he killed it, but I was already gone." Keelia shook her head. "I'm not sure; it all happened so fast." Her breathing suddenly became faster and ragged.

"It's alright," Leugio whispered. "Let's just get home. We're not out of danger yet." He swallowed thickly as fear clawed its way up his chest. "I'm not sure how many more guards there are. I... I killed the ones we came across on our way down to you."

"Understood."

They were silent, listening to the distant sounds of the Sídhe and bracing for another attack. The spark in his chest was gone now, snuffed out and leaving a smoldering sore spot below his heart. It wasn't hard to find their way out. The air became fresher and fresher with each step. Keelia was pulling him along faster and faster. Kent's stride had changed as the dog's excitement for the open sky grew.

Inhaling the air greedily, Leugio almost collapsed. Almost all his weight was on Keelia's narrow shoulders, but his little sister kept pulling him forward. Her grip was tight on his shoulder, silently promising that she wasn't going to let him go any more than he'd let her go. It bolstered him and he made those last few steps into the sunshine.

He closed his eyes against the bright light and tilted up his face. A soft cry of relief escaped Keelia. Kent barked happily and Leugio opened his eyes. Trying to speak, he found his mouth too dry and looked at Keelia. Tears were shining in her eyes, but she was smiling at him.

"So, you found her then," the Síd said. It was still sitting in the shadows and plucking at the cruit's strings. Looking back into the tunnel, it hummed to itself and then smiled. "I hope that Faridon at least is dead." That smile made Leugio's stomach turn and Keelia tugged him further into the sunlight. His sister brandished the iron dagger once more, but the Síd didn't react at all. Instead, its eyes stayed on Leugio and he nodded slightly to itself. "Interesting." Then it rose from its lounging position and stepped into the darkness of the tunnel. "You best be getting home, little Iron Children."

Keelia took a few steps back, pulling him away from the Síd. It calmly plucked at the tight strings of the cruit and seemed to pay them no mind. Kent growled a little, but Keelia ordered him to hush. The dog looked back at her and slowly, very slowly, Keelia turned them around. Before them, the faint path headed over the rolling hills. Leugio thought that maybe he could see their village, and it gave him some strength. It would take some time for them to get home, but he looked down at the top of Keelia's head and placed a quick kiss on the hairline. His sister looked up at him and the fear and anger in her eyes finally eased. She smiled at him, and Leugio grinned in response. They'd get home, of that he was certain. They were both safe now.

10

Dreams of Dying

Alex could hear the whispers. They were distant, but in her sleep they came closer and closer. One voice stood out to her. It was higher pitched, almost feminine, but with a chill to it that inspired fear. Some part of her knew that she was sleeping, and she willed herself to wake up, wanting to escape that strange voice.

"No no no," the voice said. It was suddenly louder than all the others. "No no no, Iron Soul; time to sleep. Time to dream: so many memories, so much just beneath the surface. Time to dream and let it all out." The voice faded away and sleep pulled her down, harder and deeper than before.

The truck was bearing down. There was a shocked gasp. Everything lurched to the side. There was a cut off scream, metal crunched, and a crash shook the whole world. All the noises collapsed into one long shattering sound. Her mother was thrown into her father. There was red, so much red and more crunching.

The coffins sat on the matching tables amongst flowers and photographs. It was a poor substitute. No photo had ever properly captured her mom's smile or the twinkle in her dad's eye. Matt and Ed were barely holding it together, and in privacy, they cried. She didn't. The tangle in her chest tightened. There was a soft, whispering voice, taunting her, and laughing at the nightmare. The other voices rose up, becoming louder and louder in an attempt to drown out the cold voice. Yet it only laughed louder.

The world was blurry, but they could see the hillside and the dark black opening. Everything was getting cold. Fingers dug into the ground. It was moist. Blood, they released darkly, pouring out of their own wound. The ache of magic filled their chest: it burned and yet they weren't done. A few feet away, Medraut was gloating, watching them struggle with a small smile. So this was how it ended. Betrayed on three sides: wife, friend, and kin. The first two seemed insignificant now. Had they been able to see Gwenyvar they would have wished her well, begged Luegáed to take care of her.

The pain was getting worse, but they struggled to their knees. They could sense the pulse of the magic in the ground beneath them, they could smell it in the air. It rippled across their flesh, providing a small comfort. Yet it had also been a burden. Merlin had taken them from their family long ago and while it had always been their destiny, their purpose to serve the realm, they allowed themselves a flicker of anger. Still, it changed nothing, and they pushed on the magic, urging it towards the iron on the ground.

The iron bent and twisted in the air, taking the shape they wanted; the shape they needed. All the weapons were transformed by the white sparks of their magic. They pushed it. The metal was flung into the opening in the hill, into the tunnel the Sídhe had carved into their world. In a flurry of magic, the iron stretched into bars, covering the entrance, and locking the remaining Sídhe inside the tunnels. Out of their world. Satisfaction was short lived. Their thirst was worse, and the cold was consuming them.

Everything changed, and yet nothing did. They were in a bed with a beautiful blonde woman beside them holding their hand. Her green eyes were full of tears, her features resigned and sad. Nevertheless, she forced a small smile for them and reached out. Her skin was smooth against their own face, brushing tenderly over wrinkles. There were faces beyond hers that all looked sad and worried. Above them the rough rafters of the long house were hazy, and the distant sounds of the community were muffled. The pain was already past. The woman said something soothing, but the words no longer meant anything. Their heart was slowing, and their eyelids were heavy. It was time to sleep.

The voices were louder, washing over them as the darkness took over. Restless and worried as a thousand images flashed before their eyes. They didn't know what to focus on. Understanding eluded them. Confusion took over and the darkness churned. A strange high-pitched voice taunted them from beyond their reach. Around them the darkness shifted.

Fighting to stay above the water, their limbs were already heavy. The current kept pushing them faster and faster. Water splashed over their head. They'd been trying to breathe only to fill their mouth with the foul water. Coughing, they flailed, but it was becoming harder and harder. Another wave crashed over them, knocking what little air they had out of their lungs. They scrambled, grasping at the surface, trying to hold themselves above the river's surface. Then they were pulled down. Everything blurred; the last air was gone. Blackness crept in; they couldn't move their arms, and then the black won.

It swirled around them, thicker than before, taking on a life of its own. They were drowning again, but not in water. The laughing was louder. The voices were shouting to fight. Some swore, some shouted advice and it all turned into a deafening dim. Yet the darkness was winning, closing in as that strange voice urged it on. In the darkness, shapes were forming, but monstrous ones. They were familiar, strange, and frightening.

Rocks were falling. The cliff was collapsing right above them. The ground shook, sending them falling to their knees. Grasping at the ground, their heart raced, but they couldn't move. They looked up. Rocks were falling. They were too close. The first pebbles hit, and they managed to stand. A few steps were all they managed before the quivering ground sent them falling once more. The rocks hit the ground with thunderous crashes. Everything was falling. A rock hit, they screamed. Another rock hit and another and another. In the distance, the screams of the village echoed. They couldn't run away. The rocks were falling. Another hit and the world went dark.

They didn't stay long in the dark this time. It changed too quickly, but something was closer now. That strange voice, the one that didn't belong at all was closer. So close they could feel it behind them. It was creeping up, giggling even as they tried to understand. What was happening? Where were they? What had happened to them? Only the darkness won and pulled them under again, deeper and deeper into terrible memories.

Coughing, they tried to gasp, but it was no use. The ache filled their body. Their muscles were all but gone. They couldn't stand from the bed even if they tried. They coughed again and tried to call for help, but there was no one there anymore. Everyone was hiding, running. They didn't blame them. Moving their head, they examined the sores on their chest. Sweat and dirt were caked around the black bubbles of skin and pus. All hope was lost; there was no way back. With quivering limbs, they tried to move again. Hunger was gnawing at their stomach, and they were desperate for a drink: anything would have done, but it was all gone. There was nothing left but to die. Muscles quivered and they coughed again. Black spots danced across their vision, and they collapsed back on the bed.

The prairie stretched out before them. Rolling hills golden with the native grasses and sunbaked dirt. A bison herd was moving slowly and grazing peacefully in the distance. It should have been serene, but their heart was pounding and they kept moving. Behind them, they could hear war cries and shouting. They ran faster, urging their aching legs to keep moving. Their lungs burned, but they kept running. A sharp pain in the back made them slow. It radiated outward, sending ripples of agony down their body. They slowed, stumbling over the rocks. An arrow. They fell to the ground, meeting it with a hard thump. The darkness claimed them once again.

They'd almost become used to the dark. It was comforting in its own way down here below the streets of Paris. There was a perfect stillness around them. Even knowing that the city was busy above did nothing to diminish it. They could hear nothing of the city now, but every so often they thought there was a vibration that made it down through the rocks. Flexing their fingers, they hissed in pain as the dozens of tiny scrapes pulled too far and dirt dug deeper into their flesh. The ache through their body was beginning to ease.

It was too hot though. Reaching up they loosened the collar of their uniform; it was meaningless to them after all now. Across their fingertips, they thought they could still hear an echo of the Hammer's power, but it was gone now. Buried beneath ancient bones in another tunnel far from where they'd come to die. Even if they'd wanted to, they could never find the Hammer again, or a way out of the catacombs. There was a hint of temptation to try. A desire to get out and somehow convince the Gestapo and the rest of the SS that they'd been innocent in the theft of the Hammer. Dietrich was most certainly dead already, but the reasons hadn't changed. Sighing, they leaned back against the wall.

Time had lost meaning. Their fingers went up and found the small carving they'd made. A last little message, one of loyalty to Germany: the real Germany of families, and not the twisted form it now held. Their arm fell and they exhaled slowly. There was no point in delaying it. Starvation would take time. While peaceful, they didn't wish to sit in the darkness alone for so long. Too much time to think and miss their family. Dear Ilse and their children. Their hand found the service firearm and brought it up to their temple. Placing their finger on the trigger, they inhaled one more time and then squeezed.

The cold was unbearable. They were shivering and stumbling through the snow. There was just too much of it. They weren't going to make it back. Slipping in the snow, they tried to adjust their leg, but it was too stiff. The muscles were exhausted. Another step. They almost fell again but staggered forward. Around them, the wind howled, and the white veil thickened. Another step.

The shivering stopped. They stopped moving. A thought tried to form, but they couldn't grasp it. They knew something but couldn't remember what. The cold was too much. Their eyes were heavy. Their muscles ached, but the cold kept coming. Another step. The cold was digging in, deeper and deeper now. They inhaled, but even with the knitted hood it was too cold. Another step: their legs wouldn't bend. They fell into the snow. Cold all around them. There was no heat left in the ground. They couldn't feel their legs anymore. They tried to move, but it didn't work. Thoughts wouldn't form properly, but one tiny fear pushed forward. They were dying.

Falling back into the darkness, they sensed someone right behind them. They tried to turn, but the form gripped their neck. Icy fingers dug into their skin. Every hair on their arms rose and goosebumps erupted all the way down their body. A faint blue glow coming from behind them lit the darkness. They didn't move, didn't breathe. Around them the darkness was full of their voices, whispering advice, but none of it helped.

"Iron Soul." The cold form leaned closer. "Iron Soul, so many bad dreams."

They tried to speak, but no words would form. Too many voices, too many languages and questions all fighting. They couldn't choose the one to say. No unity, no agreement. Only confusion and the cold.

"I am Brekszta," the form said. "And this is only the beginning."

It struck them. Cold blasted through their body, making their legs collapse. They tried to fight, but the darkness was thick. The shapes in the dark were reaching for them. More dreams, more deaths were waiting. They could sense them, almost remember them. Almost touch each of the times they'd been pulled under.

The sheets tangled about their legs: they were trapped and even a fast kick did not dislodge them. There was knocking nearby, almost frantic. Someone called a name, but it was unfamiliar. There was darkness around them, but they were on a soft surface. It smelled safe and familiar, but they couldn't remember. Another kick sent a heavy blanket and the sheets to the floor.

They sat up and looked around. In the corner of their eye, there was a flare of magic. Blue sparks appeared and the knocking stopped. The sparks spun around a strange latch on the door, and it swung open. A young woman with long red hair dashed into the room with wide blue eyes. Lights suddenly came on, blinding them for a moment.

The redhead stopped as suddenly as she'd come in, studying them with fear being replaced by confusion on her face. The woman was waiting for something, but what they weren't sure. Opening their mouth, they tried to find some words, but the mess of voices was too much. There were too many words and so there was only silence.

"Alex?" the woman called. She took a step closer, bending slightly to better look at them. "Are you okay?"

They understood the words, and yet something about the question was alien. Something throbbed in their chest at the gentle and worried tone. Opening their mouth, they started to say something, but the words died. They didn't know what to say. The woman sat on the edge of the bed next to them. Surprisingly there was no rush of irritation or worry at the very familiar action. Yet they couldn't summon up a name.

"Alex?"

"Who are you?" The question spilled forth and the woman drew back as if she'd been slapped.

"Alex? That- that isn't funny." A pained sort of laugh escaped the woman and her eyes darted over to the desk where a laptop and a phone sat. "Uh, should I call Morgana?"

That name was familiar. Their chest twisted as fondness, aggravation, and sadness hit all at once. The woman reached over and caught their face, turning them so their eyes met hers. The woman's eyes were bright blue and intense as they searched for something. It was familiar. Another voice, a softer one in the background, was growing louder.

"Alex, I need you to focus on my face," the woman said. "My name is Nicki. Nicole Russell. I'm a mage like you and a student in Ravenslake, Oregon." The words were familiar to them. Something must have reflected that in their eyes because Nicki straightened up and smiled a little. "That's it, focus on me. Your name is Alexandra Adams. You're a student of English Literature, remember?"

Closing their eyes, they shook their head. The voices were clamoring and arguing now. That softer voice was louder than ever and pushing forward. The knot in their chest was twisting. Nicki grabbed their arms and held them steady.

The softer voice was winning. Alex. That name echoed. Groaning, they shook their head and things cleared. Bringing up their hands, they rubbed at the side of their head. Nicki lowered her hands and smiled at them. She nodded encouragingly and the fog began to clear.

"Alex?"

"I'm fine, Nicki," Alex said. Releasing a slow breath, she dropped her hands and shuddered. "Sorry... got lost in a nightmare, I guess."

"You guess?" Nicki raised a doubtful eyebrow. "Alex, that isn't normal."

"I'm fine." Alex forced a smile and scooted back on the bed. "It was weird though."

"Do you want to talk about it?"

"It was just memories of my other lives," Alex replied. She looked towards her desk, frowning a little at the faint blue glow from her computer. It was familiar. "Except at the end."

"What happened at the end, Alex?" Nicki asked. She jumped up and grabbed the small notebook from Alex's desk, holding a pencil over the page. "It may be important."

"I doubt it." Alex shook her head again but couldn't help but remember the cold. "Like I said it was just a nightmare."

"You couldn't remember me or your own name!"

"Yes, I could! It just got... shuffled to the side for a moment," Alex protested. She could see the worry in Nicki's eyes and knew an argument was coming. "Brekszta," she said quickly. "There was this being in the darkness between the nightmare segments, I guess. It called itself Brekszta."

"Brekszta," Nicki repeated. She sounded out the name again and wrote it down. "That sounds familiar. What else?"

"Nothing else," Alex grumbled. "Look, Nicki, it was a nightmare."

"You were tossing and turning and shouting in your sleep." Nicki fixed her with a look. "We should call Merlin and Morgana."

"No," Alex's hand brushed across the soft plush fur of her stuffed dog. Picking up Galahad, Alex brought him to her chest and hugged him tightly. Nicki's gaze softened. "Look, Nicki, we'll see them tomorrow. It was just a nightmare and maybe some kind of warning."

"What did you dream about?" Nicki asked. Her voice was gentler this time.

Laying back on her bed, Alex looked up at the ceiling of her dorm room. For a moment she didn't say anything and hoped that Nicki would leave it alone. Of course, it was Nicki, so she just pulled out the desk chair and sat down. A sigh escaped Alex and she turned her head to look at her friend and fellow mage.

"Dying." Nicki's eyes widened and Alex rolled over to face the wall, pulling Galahad to her chest. "There's a lot of old bad memories in my head now, Nicki; sometimes they're going to come out. I need some sleep, so don't forget to turn the light off."

Nothing happened for a few minutes. Nicki didn't move, but thankfully she didn't try to talk either. Then there was a sigh of defeat and the tear of a page being removed from a notebook. Alex listened to the paper flutter as Nicki folded it up and eased her death grip on Galahad. A moment later the lights were turned off leaving her in the dark room alone. However, Nicki didn't shut the door when she left.

11

The Old Wife and Ally

Morgana's living room was bright with natural sunlight pouring through the windows. A pitcher of iced tea, a plate of cookies, and a bowl of mixed nuts were waiting on the coffee table amongst the sofas and armchairs. Alex gave Morgana a smile but was aware of the older woman checking her over with her eyes. Somehow Alex doubted there was enough under-eye concealer in the world to fool Morgana.

Nevertheless, Alex gave Morgana a warm smile and on impulse leaned down to press a kiss to her cheek. Morgana raised an eyebrow, but Alex caught her lips twitching into a smile. Alex nodded to Merlin, who was watching her with sharp brown eyes. Nervousness twisted in her gut. He hadn't tried to talk to her about her reaction in his office yet, but Alex was sure it was coming.

She sat down in the armchair and poured a glass of iced tea. Nicki sat on the end of the sofa closest to her and Alex offered her the glass. Her roommate took it, giving her a small nod in return. There was another knock on the door and Morgana moved to open it. A few moments later Bran and Aiden strolled in with Lance and Jenny only a few steps behind them. Alex gave them all a wide smile, noting that Bran and Jenny both looked at her a bit funny and started pouring iced teas for everyone. She considered standing up to hug Jenny, but her legs quivered uneasily at the mere thought of getting up. Holding back a yawn, she focused on her task and keeping her hand steady.

Alex knew Nicki was watching her. That had been the case all day and Alex was left to wonder if Nicki had gotten any sleep this morning after the incident. She hadn't managed to fall asleep but had stayed curled up in the bed for a few more hours. The weight of the other mage's eyes was beginning to itch a bit. Everyone settled down and the plate of cookies was eagerly attacked. They might have had breakfast only an hour ago, but that really didn't matter.

"So, what's on the agenda for today?" Aiden asked. He leaned his head over the sofa's back to look up at Morgana. "Training? Research? Anything special?"

"Actually, we received some news," Morgana said. "A guest will be joining us shortly."

Blinking in surprise, Alex glanced towards Merlin, but his face gave nothing away. Neither he nor Morgana looked worried so Alex guessed it was probably okay. Aiden grabbed another cookie and looked her way, but Alex could only shrug in silent response.

"Does anyone have anything else to report first?" Merlin asked.

"I've made some progress with telekinesis," Aiden said. He grinned and Bran fist bumped with him. In the corner of her eye, Alex saw Lance shake his head fondly at the pair. "And I've got a list of a couple other things I want to try."

A knock on the front door made Alex look towards Morgana. The older woman walked back to the entry hall, her boots tapping against the wooden floor. Leaning forward, Alex tried to get a glimpse of the visitor. A suspicion formed in her head and her heart thudded a little harder.

"Hello, Sif," Morgana said. Her tone was civil, if a touch guarded. Alex felt a rush of irritation that she couldn't fully explain.

"Hello, Morgana," Sif replied.

Sif stepped into view and Alex straightened up. The Old One looked completely human now wearing jeans, a reddish turtleneck shirt, and a light jacket. With a smile, she shrugged out of her coat and hung it up on the hooks. She nodded to Morgana and walked into the living room to join them.

Alex found her eyes locked onto Sif. Part of her wanted to look away, but she couldn't. One of the dream memories pushed its way forward. She'd been laying on a bed dying and it had been Sif holding her hand. Her long golden hair was the same and her fine features softened as she looked at Alex. Comfort built in her chest even as tears began to gather in her eyes. Alex licked her lips and swallowed; her mouth suddenly dry. The memory brought dozens of emotions to the forefront and they battled for dominance. There was an urge to hug Sif, thank her, and cry all at once. Reaching down, Alex picked up her glass of iced tea and gulped it down. The cool liquid helped ease whatever hold Sif's presence had on her, and she was able to breathe again.

Bran caught her eye. He was frowning slightly and Alex inwardly cursed his remarkable perception. Turning her attention back to Sif, Alex's mouth went dry again and she downed the rest of her drink. The knot of emotions in her chest was shaking a little and even tugging on her magic didn't do much to help. She studied the glass in her hand, wondering if she could somehow get away with not looking at Sif.

That thought made her chest tighten again. Something raged at not seeing her. It was sharp, sad, and angry all at once. Alex was looking up at Sif again before she could stop herself. The shimmer of her golden hair was so familiar. For a split second, her fingers itched to touch it. Alex tightened her grip on her glass, fighting back the urge.

"Greetings, Sif," Merlin said. He stood up and smiled at the Old One, actually looking pleased to see her. "I am relieved to see you safely returned."

"Thank you, Merlin." Sif nodded in greeting to him, but her eyes quickly moved over to Alex. For a moment their gazes held and Alex felt like she was floating. Sif turned her attention back to Morgana. "I have good news and bad news. More and more Old Ones are stirring, though some are choosing to go back to sleep as they don't feel right."

"Take a seat," Merlin offered.

Sif walked further into the room and sat down in the empty armchair gracefully. Crossing her ankles, she sat delicately and gave the sense of complete ease. Alex glanced towards the iced tea pitcher, but Aiden beat her to it. He poured a glass and offered it to Sif with a kind smile.

"Thank you," Sif said. She took a sip of the iced tea. "Well, I'm afraid that I can't provide you with a complete list yet of who might be plotting against you. Most of the worst are dead at this point. Baldr agreed to go and see if he could keep some of the others asleep for a bit longer."

"That would be nice," Merlin said. He leaned against the back of the sofa as Morgana walked over to stand behind Alex's chair. "But I doubt it will give us much more time."

"True, but it can take time for an Old One to fully wake," Sif said. "It took me almost two years to fully regain awareness. Not to mention the modern world can be... disorienting."

"Who do you think will be the most urgent threat?" Morgana asked. "Things with the Sídhe are such that we can't afford risks."

"Have you learned anything on that front?" Sif asked.

"Not yet I'm afraid," Merlin said. He shook his head and drummed his fingers on the armchair. "The Brownie, Timothy, went to open contact between us and the Fae, but he has yet to return."

"Our plan still is to have Alex create a few more Iron Gates in the area," Morgana explained. She reached over and touched Alex's shoulder. "If you're up to it, then perhaps we should go out of town a little way tomorrow."

"Shouldn't we do it on an alignment day?" Alex managed to ask. Tearing her eyes away from Sif, she looked up at Morgana. The tension in her chest eased a little. "For the power I mean?"

"I think you have enough control now that you don't need the boost from an alignment day," Morgana said. Her voice was proud, but there was underlying worry in her eyes as she studied Alex. "We can't keep putting it off."

"Yeah, uh, okay then. I'll do my homework tonight," Alex said. "Any thoughts on where you want to put it?"

"Morgana and I will check over some maps tonight," Merlin said. He offered Alex a small reassuring smile. "Will the rest of you be able to help?"

"I can," Bran said. "Just let us know where to meet you."

"Sure," Aiden replied. "I can finish stuff up tonight."

"That's not a problem," Nicki agreed. She was looking at her phone. "Though I am having dinner with Gran at seven tomorrow."

"That shouldn't be a problem," Merlin assured her. "You've all done this before, but we do need to make an effort on that front."

Sif smiled, though Alex caught a hint of discomfort in her eyes. "I'm glad to see that you and the current mages have things so well organized," Sif said. Alex couldn't tell if she meant it or not: it didn't seem like they were organized to her. "How are you doing with all of this, Alex?" Sif asked. Her green eyes were kind and Alex knew they saw far too much. "Given the recent events?"

"Uh, I'm alright." The words were hard to say; Alex's mouth was far too dry and rough. "Not great, but I'm doing okay."

"Alex had a pretty bad nightmare last night," Nicki said. Alex held back a grimace as everyone turned to look at her. "I woke her up when I heard her tossing and turning."

"Your parents?" Morgana asked. Her hand came up to pat her head gently, running fingers down the back of her hair. "Are you sure you're alright?"

"It wasn't..." Alex trailed off. "I wasn't good, but I'm alright." She hesitated for a moment and made sure that she didn't look at Nicki. Alex all but prayed that her roommate didn't say anything more. "There was this darkness and something was behind me."

"Alex said the name of the being was Brekszta," Nicki said. Alex glared at her, resisting the urge to kick her only because Merlin and Morgana were watching. "She wasn't in good shape when she woke up."

Thankfully Nicki stopped there. She caught Alex's gaze and Alex could see the conflict in Nicki's blue eyes. Giving her a small nod, Alex silently thanked her for not revealing that she hadn't been able to remember her.

"Brekszta," Sif repeated. Her shoulders slumped and her green eyes dulled. "Yes, I suppose that fits. She is an Old One that seems to have gone mad. I encountered her briefly while I was searching for Cyrridven's home."

"What happened?"

"Nothing much: she made her insanity clear and made some threats against the Iron Realm and the Iron Soul," Sif answered. At Merlin's wide eyes, Sif shook her head. "There's nothing that unusual about that,

Merlin. Some Old Ones say things like that only to go back into the water."

"Is there a limit to the cleansing?" Nicki asked. "I mean, if they go mad can they be cured by going back into the water?"

"To a point," Sif said. There was a cautious note to her voice and she glanced towards Alex. "But only a few have ever returned to sanity after they begin their fall. The most notable one that I know of was Shiva." Sif frowned thoughtfully for a moment and then shook her head. "I'm afraid I don't know the details, but from what I've heard he was aided by the Iron Soul."

"Yes," Merlin said. "That's one of the reasons why we have an alliance with Shiva. Lokpal even entrusted the Iron Trishula to Shiva, who swore to keep an eye on the demons who dwell in the Indian subcontinent." Merlin sighed loudly and tented his fingers in front of him. "It's one of the reasons why India isn't a priority right now."

"But back to the issue," Bran interrupted. "Who is Brekszta? Did you know her, Sif?"

"Not well," Sif answered. "Like I said, I briefly encountered her and she was already in poor condition."

In the corner of her eye, Alex saw Jenny pulling out her cellphone. She was seated with Lance over by the living room window, and a look of concentration took over Jenny's features as she did something on her phone. Lance leaned over slightly to see what she was doing.

"You won't find much on Brekszta online, Jenny," Morgana said. She looked a touch amused. "The Old Ones who were worshiped as deities from that part of the world have largely been forgotten. Christian monks did a great deal to destroy those stories."

"It says here that she was a goddess of night and dreams," Jenny said. Holding up her phone, she shifted a bit nervously. "But not much else: no myths or legends connected with her are listed."

"That's not surprising," Sif replied. She was watching Jenny with a hint of curiosity. Alex suddenly realized that Sif might be able to tell that Jenny and Lance weren't mages: she'd be wondering about their being there. "As Morgana said, much of that folklore was lost."

Alex shivered. There may not be much, but the mere description of Brekszta as a deity of night and dreams was a little too on the nose. Holding back a frown, she looked back towards Sif whose attention was now on Merlin. He nodded slightly to her and Alex tightened her fist at the silent conversation happening. There was irritation, a touch of real anger, and other emotions that came and went too quickly for her to identify. She forced her fist open and shivered as she flexed her fingers.

"Alex," Morgana said. Her grip on her shoulder tightened. "We'll review what we know of Brekszta. Write down anything you remember from dreams. This may have been a warning from your magic."

She really doubted that. Alex almost snorted. Last night's dreams had not been from the Iron Realm or her magical connection to the world, or anything else positive that Morgana might imagine. But she nodded. Nicki opened her mouth to say something but shut it slowly as Alex looked her way.

"I think that's enough for today," Merlin said. His voice resonated through the room, drawing everyone's attention. "Morgana and I will go over the details with Sif and build a list of things we may need to study. You children complete your work and we'll have details for tomorrow's task. Don't practice your magic tonight: we'll need as much power as possible for creating another Iron Gate."

The dismissal hung in the air. Alex blinked and glanced towards the others. They appeared just as confused and even Aiden was frowning thoughtfully. Nothing had really been discussed and Alex had the feeling that tomorrow wouldn't see any real information about Brekszta given to them either. Bran stood up first and nodded to Merlin. He caught her eye and Alex forced herself out of the chair. Aiden snagged the last cookie and put it in his mouth as he tugged Nicki off the sofa. They walked past Alex to join Lance and Jenny near the doorway.

Alex lingered for a moment uneasily. Bran brushed his hand against hers as he walked by. With slow steps, she left the living room. The others were already out the front door and through the screen door she could see Nicki, Aiden, and Bran all talking. As she picked up her bag and checked the position of her dagger, Alex heard and sensed someone behind her.

"Alex." Sif reached out and caught her hand. Their fingers slipped against each other and Alex had to swallow. She turned to look at Sif and her chest tightened. "I'm so sorry about your parents," Sif said kindly. "I didn't even consider how losing them might be affecting you." Sif sighed sadly. "I'm afraid that in many ways I still don't understand humans."

"You married one," Alex said, the words slipping out. She snapped her jaw shut, a mix of horror and embarrassment flaring in her chest.

Chuckling, Sif shook her head fondly. "Thor was... boisterous and very convincing. I knew that I shouldn't have become involved with him, but he won me over in the end." Her expression changed. "I'm not sure how much I'll be able to help. I don't have Cyrridven's connection to the Iron Realm. She was something of a legend and a mystery even amongst Old Ones, but I'll try. This is the only home I've ever known, and from what Merlin and Morgana tell me of Arthur he could be very dangerous to us all."

"Yeah." It was a bit easier to speak now and the rush of emotion was easing. "I'm more worried about my brothers at this point. Arthur killed my parents despite the blood protection so…" Alex stopped talking. She didn't want to think about it.

"I'll check in on them," Sif offered. "There are a few protections that we Old Ones can manage. Maybe they'll help."

"I'd appreciate that." Alex managed a small smile but was aware of how sad she probably looked. "They're all I have now… even if they are angry at me."

"It is difficult for mortals to understand," Sif replied. "Thor and I lived in a lodge between my people and his; the distance helped."

"Well, they're in Spokane and I'm here, so maybe the distance will help this time." Alex shifted uneasily. "Uh, are you sticking around?"

"Only for a little while. I suspect that Merlin and Morgana will ask me to look into Brekszta."

"Thank you for helping." Alex found that she truly meant the words. "Given what happened to Cyrridven."

"This realm is the only home I have ever had." Sif's eyes were soft and understanding. Then she leaned forward and kissed Alex's forehead. "Go on; your friends are probably worried." Winking at her, Sif's smile became more mischievous. "And I wouldn't want your other former wife to get jealous."

Stunned, Alex just gaped at Sif, but the Old One shook her head fondly. Releasing Alex's hand, she brought a hand up to touch her cheek. "You're not Thor, Alexandra Adams. Don't worry, I know that, but I'd like to think he'd have been grateful to know that I'd look after you."

"I doubt that." The words slipped out and carried a hint of jealousy.

Sif raised an eyebrow and chuckled. "You may be right. Thor never did like knowing he'd be reborn. I love him deeply, but he was more than a touch arrogant. The stories that were spread about him didn't help matters at all."

"Sif… Thor died of old age, didn't he?"

"Yes," Sif answered. She studied Alex for a long moment. "Yes, he did. I was with him, as were some of his human relatives and members of my family." Stepping back, Sif nodded towards the door. "Don't worry, I'll do what I can to help Merlin and Morgana ensure that you have the chance to die an old woman."

"Right," Alex said. "See you soon."

Sif kissed her cheek and opened the screen door for her. Alex stepped out onto the porch. A sense of dread was settling at the base of her spine. Some painful certainty that nothing Sif, Merlin, or even Morgana could do would see her live to old age. The thought had crossed her mind before: it had been the reason why she'd told her parents the truth about magic. Yet this was different, and she all but stumbled down the stairs.

Sif's lips burned against her cheek, waring with the cold dread. Alex's knees trembled and Alex swallowed, licking her lips. Nicki caught her hand and squeezed it. The sensation pulled Alex back to the present and her stomach dropped. Heat rushed up through her face and in the corner of her eye, she caught Nicki watching her. Embarrassment warred with uneasy and even frightened emotions.

"I don't like girls that way," Alex muttered.

"I didn't think that," Nicki said gently. "I was just thinking that your other lives have a nasty way of pushing through at the worst moments, don't they?"

Alex thought back to her uncomfortable meeting with Merlin. Just thinking about it inspired the same mixture of worry and embarrassment. "Yeah," she agreed. "They do."

"And you're the only known girl," Nicki added. "It's a good thing you haven't got the testosterone to complicate that."

Holding back a groan, Alex snorted and gave Nicki a dark look. The redhead just grinned and squeezed her hand again. They walked down the gravel driveway to Alex's car. Alex noted the others getting into their cars to leave. She knew she should say something, but exhaustion clung to her bones and a headache was forming behind her eyes. Too many things were going through her head.

Alex unlocked her driver's side door while Nicki called out to the others. She trusted Nicki to say their goodbyes; she'd need what energy she did have for getting her homework done. Alex was about to climb into the driver's side when Nicki snatched the keys from her hand and firmly pointed to the passenger's side. She blinked at her roommate for a moment as Lance's truck pulled out of the drive, but then Alex obediently moved around the car. If Nicki wanted to drive them home, Alex was happy to let her.

12

Life After the Mound

64 B.C.E. The Golden Vale, Ireland

The sheep baaed softly as they moved slowly to graze. Above Leugio a bright blue sky with only a few scattered clouds put him at ease. The air was thick with the smell of earth and the musk of the sheep. A playful breeze brushed across his face and made the long grasses of the hillside sing. This was not a day to be concerned about the Sídhe. Yet Leugio always was now. He was always aware of them. The passing of autumn and winter had not changed that. Ever since he returned Keelia to the surface there was a strange awareness in his chest.

Checking on the sheep, he quickly counted them, but all were present. There was nothing unusual on the horizon. The suspicion remained a nagging little voice at the back of his mind. It wouldn't go away and he began to whistle to distract himself. Walking along the earthen wall that separated the pasture from the rest of the fields, Leugio kicked lightly at a tuft of grass. One of the sheep looked up at him but quickly lost interest. An odd worry had been following him all day, like he'd forgotten or misplaced something. His fingers toyed with the brooch on his tunic, feeling it warm beneath his skin.

Nearby the song of birds echoed down from a tree. Leugio sighed to himself, shook his head and returned to watching the sheep. This was nothing more than lingering worries about the Sídhe, he told himself. Worrying would do him no good. Instead, he turned his focus back to the wood bow he was shaping into a new cruit. It wouldn't be as fancy as his old one, but he could add decoration later.

His eyes landed on the Sídhe mound, where a thick layer of green was growing over the artificial hillside. It was greening up along with the rest of the world as spring advanced. Even now there was no sign of the Sídhe. While the village had been fearful and braced for some act of vengeance, there had been nothing. Leugio wasn't even sure how many of them he'd killed, and yet there had been no retribution. He didn't understand it. Perhaps there was some sort of silent understanding that if you rescued a child, you were left alone. Perhaps that odd Síd that had given him advice had kept the others from attacking. Maybe there weren't enough of them now.

A sheep looked up at him and baaed. Glaring back at it, Leugio grumbled to himself. He wondered how long it would take for this paranoia to fade. Plucking at the first of the strings, Leugio grimaced at the sour note. He shook his head and gently adjusted it as best he could, pulling it a little tighter in the small notch. When he tried again a slightly smoother note chimed in the air. He moved on to the next and repeated the process with each string. Glancing back towards the Sídhe hill, he vaguely wondered what the Sídhe were doing with his first cruit. The notion that they might be able to use some kind of magic on it worried him.

This time he just sighed. Today it seemed wasn't going to be a calm one for his thoughts. He played on the cruit for a while, routinely adjusting the tightness of the hairs. Slowly the sounds coming from the cruit smoothed out and he didn't hate every other one. Staring again at the mound, Leugio felt that odd stirring in his chest.

Leugio was always aware of it now. There was a flicker beneath his heart that he carried with him every day. Sometimes, when he closed his eyes and focused on the smell of the world around him, it would brighten like a low flame suddenly fed dry moss. Quiet moments were the easiest and when he was in the pasture with the sheep, he was most aware of it. The problem was he still had no real idea of what to do with it.

In the past seasons, he'd often thought about what had happened in the mound, but never... Leugio looked down at his hands. They looked the same as ever. Flexing his fingers, Leugio forced himself to take slow deep breaths. Rather than dimming the sensation, it was enhanced. There were no sparks, no sign of magic, but it was there. Just out of reach.

Maybe it was foolish, maybe it was a mistake, but he could feel it there. Stronger today than it had been for more than a season. He had to try. Leugio closed his eyes and tried to think of something. He wasn't being attacked and didn't want to hurt the sheep. That wouldn't be pleasant to explain. The magic hummed beneath his skin and Leugio settled on the idea of making a small light, like a torch.

Something flared brightly enough for him to see it through his eyelids. Opening his eyes, he gasped and then grinned. There was a glowing white orb in his hand, floating just above the skin of his palm. Excitement crashed through his chest only to turn to nervousness a moment later. The orb shimmered and tiny sparks of white flew off of it. They vanished into the air like cooling embers into the night. Leugio was transfixed even as the flare in his chest began to thin. His arms were heavy and the orb slowly vanished.

"Leugio!"

He turned to see his mother coming up the path. Her long cloak was draped over her shoulders and wisps of brown hair hung in her face. He turned around on the earthen wall so he was facing her. It took her only a few more moments to reach him.

"Some lunch," his mother said. She smiled at him and held out a clay bowl and a wrapped package of jerky.

"Uh, thank you." He moved over and accepted the clay bowl with a slight frown. "I brought something with me mother."

"I just- I just wanted to make sure you were here and alright."

Freezing, Leugio almost lost his grip on the bowl. He recovered quickly and nodded in understanding. Smiling, he carefully set the items down on the wall and leaned forward to kiss her cheek.

"I'm fine, Mother. Nothing unusual has happened today. Please try not to worry."

The wrinkles around her eyes were more pronounced than they used to be, making her look older. Her hands came up and rested against his cheeks. They were shaking slightly, and Leugio just stayed still. Slowly, his mother recovered and smiled. Patting his cheek, she turned and began moving back towards the village. His mother's discomfort was understandable. It would take time for the fear to fade. It would take time for him to stop dreaming of the mound tunnels.

Keelia was safe. The Sídhe hadn't left their mound for the past season and in the village, the whispers and stunned looks had mostly stopped. Keelia had spoken of his rescue and his magic, but no one knew what to make of it. He never knew what to say; what to do about all of it. How could he explain? Closing his eyes, he rolled his shoulders and eyed the sheep once again. There was still a hint of the magic against his skin and Leugio knew in his gut that he could call the orb forth again if he wished.

He ate his lunch quickly and used the grass and some water to clean his hands. Rinsing out the bowl, he hummed softly along with the uneven baaing of the sheep. In the distance, he could just smell some cooking over the musk of the sheep and hear the sounds of village life. Leugio settled down against the wall with his pack against his hip.

The day dragged on. Nothing happened in the pasture. He adjusted his cruit again for a while. Then he turned his attention to sharpening his dagger. Leugio wished he'd brought some reeds to work on a basket. In truth, it probably wasn't really necessary for him to be here.

"What do you think?" Leugio asked the nearest sheep. It didn't even have the decency to look at him. "At least the Sídhe don't seem interested in wool or mutton: you should be grateful for that."

One of the other sheep baaed at him. He picked up his cruit and strummed the strings. Sweet sounds reverberated through the air around him. His fingers began to move on their own, finding the strings and learning just where to pluck on the new instrument. Inside his chest, the little spark of magic hummed in tune. The sensation was strange, and yet oddly comforting.

He reached up and rubbed his brooch. There was a spark against his fingers and Leugio gasped. Looking down at his hands, he found a faint white glow surrounding them. Then it flickered away. He studied his fingers. That had not been expected. First magic and now some odd reaction to iron. Leugio considered that thought carefully. The Sídhe were weak to iron and his magic had first appeared to fight them. Even now, his magic felt stronger than it did in the village thanks to the mound being closer. Maybe it was all connected.

Leugio's eyes shifted up, drawn towards the mound. A strange and terrible thought occurred to him. His mother had just checked on him and wasn't likely to return anytime soon. Standing up, Leugio kept a tight hold of his cruit and glanced at the sheep one more time. They wouldn't miss him. He picked up his pack and before he could change his mind, he started walking.

The mound grew larger with each step. He knew that it really wasn't that large, but the knowledge of what it was and it having loomed over his home his whole life made it seem that way. Somehow the memory of the tunnels lit by torches made it even more frightening. Knowing made it all so much worse. But he kept walking. The flutter in his chest and the hum beneath his skin was growing stronger.

There was a Síd in the shadow of the mound entrance. It was playing a cruit and wore heavy gold bracelets glittering in the low light. The figure raised its face, revealing the pale features of its kind, and while they mostly looked the same to him, Leugio was sure that it was the one he'd spoken to when Keelia was taken. His eyes jumped to the cruit and he almost smiled. The wood had been polished a bit more and had a soft gleam to it, but it was definitely his carving work.

"I see the cruit serves you well," Leugio said in greeting. His voice was higher pitched than usual, but he didn't stutter.

"I see time has made you bolder," the Síd replied. "But there has been no child brought here this day."

"Yes, I mean, that isn't why I've come." Leugio paused and frantically tried to gather his thoughts. "I was actually hoping that you would be outside the mound."

"Ah, you were looking for me then."

"I never got your name when we last met," Leugio said cautiously.

"Nor I yours," the Síd countered.

Forcing a small smile, Leugio tried to stay relaxed. "I am Leugio."

"I am Iúdás." He nodded to Leugio and lowered his violet eyes back to the cruit. "What brings you back to the mound then, Leugio?"

"I am surprised that you still sit outside, Iúdás." He tripped over the name a little, but the Síd merely smiled enigmatically.

"Perhaps it is my responsibility," Iúdás suggested. "Or perhaps I enjoy the smell of the sunlight, though it burns my eyes."

They were dancing around the real topic. Leugio knew it, but he didn't trust himself. He didn't know the right words to use or how to lure the Síd into giving information. Iúdás just kept playing the cruit and watching him. There was a sword strapped to his belt and Leugio used the chance to examine what Iúdás wore. It was loose and fine fabric; not armor like the others who came to the surface wore.

"So, what does bring you outside, Iúdás?" Leugio finally asked. His palms were sweaty and he gripped his new cruit tightly. "You carry a sword, but do not have armor like the others."

"I am not a raider," Iúdás replied. "It is not my talent nor my desire to seek out conflict."

"Which is why you gave me directions rather than try to stop me."

"Indeed," Iúdás agreed. "Though I shall confess that I did not expect you to come out. I could smell the magic trying to come forth, but did not think it would be enough to keep you alive."

"And yet you didn't stop me when I did come out. Why?"

"You had won back your sister," Iúdás answered. "And I knew that meant you had used the magic. I have no interest in fighting a mage if I do not have to." Iúdás' eyes were lingering on his brooch. "There is little magic in the world right now, but what there is obeys you."

There was something in the words, something that sounded familiar. Perhaps from a dream, or maybe it just made sense. Swallowing, Leugio tried to find the words for the questions churning in his chest. The magic was humming beneath his skin so strongly that it was almost hot. He tore a hand off his cruit and touched his brooch. Iúdás followed the movement with his eyes.

"What brings you back here, young mage?"

"Mage," Leugio repeated. "I wanted to know why I used magic in the tunnels. It is stronger now."

"It would be."

Silence filled the space between them. Iúdás watched him with sharp, violet eyes and Leugio tried to muster enough courage to ask his questions. Already he was worried that this was a mistake and eyed the tunnel entrance. There were more Sídhe down there, maybe just waiting for a moment to strike.

"We don't like the sunlight," Iúdás said. "Our ancestors came from a much darker world. Your sunlight is too harsh for us. Even I remain in the shade of the entrance." Iúdás plucked at another string and the smooth, sweet sound eased Leugio a tiny bit. "You have magic. It rises when your world is invaded by those from another. Or when someone with the potential for magic goes too close to elements from another world." Iúdás gestured to the entrance. "You saw it down there: one of the only suits of armor from our world. It has been carefully protected and preserved."

"How did you come here?"

"I know little of the process used by the ancients to enter your world," Iúdás said slowly. "It was a strange form of magic. I believe that there must have been some kind of magic on the home world that they first used to travel to new worlds. When they reached yours, the Iron Realm fought back. Mages like you were born who reacted to their presence and gained powers."

"Oh." Leugio had more questions, but it sank in that he was asking a being that was his enemy by his own explanation. He gripped his brooch again, and once more Iúdás watched the motion. "Thank you for the explanation."

"I have no craving for war, Leugio," Iúdás said. "I will counsel the others to be more peaceful in the future. Though I have no power over other colonies, so do not hold their actions against me and mine."

Somehow the words were both pleading and an order at the same time. Nodding, Leugio stepped back. The sunlight warmed his skin and he focused on the feeling of the magic just beneath his skin. On impulse, he flexed his fingers and envisioned another orb of light. White sparks flowed out of his hand and swirled together to form the small sphere just above his palm. Iúdás made a small sound and squinted his eyes.

"Uh, thank you, Iúdás." Leugio dropped his hand and let the magic flicker away. "For the information."

Backing away, Leugio minded his footing and didn't turn all the way around until he was a good thirty feet from the mound. There was a nervous tension in his chest, and even more questions in his head. Something about Iúdás' words about having no power over the other mounds set him on edge. Maybe there were more raids than they'd heard about. Was he supposed to seek out violent Sídhe and stop them? Was that what being a mage meant?

He hurried back towards the pasture. The sun had moved a good distance and the worried cries his mother would make if he vanished again danced through his mind. One hand went up to rub his brooch once more, but this time he was aware of the action. It was warm and re-assuring. A wider figure was pacing alongside the pasture. Remembering the last time Galvyn had come seeking him at the pasture, Leugio sped up his pace.

"Galvyn!" he called when he was close. His friend spun to face him. "What brings you here?"

"Where were you?!" Galvyn demanded. "I was about to go back to the village and alert your mother!" His friend's eyes widened. "The Sídhe didn't take you, did they?" Galvyn almost tripped dashing closer to him.

"No," Leugio promised. "Nothing like that." He almost said that he'd gone to the mound, but stopped himself. "No, I just needed to stretch my legs."

"Needed to stretch your legs," Galvyn repeated slowly. He gave Leugio a doubtful look but shook his head. "As you say."

"Why did you come looking for me anyway?" Leugio asked. "Is Keelia alright?"

"Oh, she's fine," Galvyn said quickly. His eyes lit up even as he shifted between his feet nervously. "There's a messenger in the village. He wants to see you. He's come on behalf of Eochu Finn!"

Leugio paused at the name. "Eochu Finn?" he repeated. "The king?"

"Exactly!" Galvyn gestured towards the village. "You're being summoned to see the king!"

13

Whispers of Lives Past

The smell of pine, earth, and grass was comforting. It was reassuring to Alex in a way that she wasn't ready to take a look at. When she was young, she'd enjoyed the smell of grass and liked it when the yard grew high because her father was too busy to mow. She'd laid back in the grass and let it hide her from the world. Just her in a grass nest and the blue sky overhead. But this was more than that, it went deeper than her childhood. The presence of the others tickled at the back of her head.

"This is the area where the hikers reported they saw wolves," Merlin said from ahead of her. "Stay alert and keep your eyes open for Sídhe, Hounds, or a tunnel."

"Any chance they actually just saw wolves?" Aiden asked.

"The report described them as large, thin, and silver," Morgana replied. "It is possible but given that the Sídhe have begun to break through the protection of the first Iron Gate we should assume the worst. Hopefully, putting another Iron Gate into place will slow them down."

"How many Iron Gates will it take to stop them?" Bran asked. "How many were there in the British Isles?"

Merlin and Morgana both looked a little surprised at the question and Alex's lips twitched up. Leave it to Bran to ask the obvious question that they've forgotten the answer to.

"I'm not sure," Merlin replied slowly. "Over a dozen by the end of the war."

"It's impossible to say how many it will take at this juncture," Morgana added. "We will monitor the situation, of course."

And that was the end of that conversation. Alex held back a sigh as they spread out a bit more on the rough game trail. Nothing clearly indicated that the Sídhe had been in the area yet. There weren't any footprints in the dirt or signs of a large creature like a horse moving through the area. Then again, the Sídhe didn't always bother with making the tunnels large enough for their steeds. They were too eager for more slaves. The thought sent a jolt of rage through Alex's chest that vibrated against the tight, cold bundle of grief locked up under her heart.

Alex strained her ears, but there were no unusual sounds in the distance. There were birds chirping and the sound of the wind in the trees, but nothing that gave away the position of this latest tunnel. Everyone stopped moving when Merlin did except for her. Alex almost walked into Aiden's back, but Nicki's hand caught her arm. Then they were all looking at her expectantly.

"What?" Alex looked between her friends and the professors. "Did I miss something?"

"Do you sense anything?" Morgana asked gently. "You sensed the last Sídhe tunnel. Anything from this one?"

"It would make sense that you would know where to find it," Merlin added. "Your ability with energy is remarkable, and the tunnel would allow their magical energy to seep into Earth."

"Uh, right," Alex said.

She nodded and Nicki let go of her hand. Closing her eyes, Alex tried to ignore the others staring at her. Alex focused on her magic and pulled on it gently. Beneath her heart, the small bundle of grief wrapped in magic sparked for a moment before the magic streamed around it. Alex opened her fists and let the magic flow out through her fingers. It was still a bit strange, but as she kept her eyes closed, she willed the magic to let her see through it. There was a mist spreading out around her, slowly creeping across the hillside.

There was something. The magic wavered to the left and further up the hill. Alex pushed all her senses in that direction. There was a dark goldish hue there, pressing against her magic. On instinct, she grabbed at the foreign magic and pulled. It resisted for a moment but began to shift. Her ability to see expanded and there was a vague outline of a hole in the hillside, rough and torn open like an explosion had rocked the mountain. Something pushed against her magic and there was a flash of violet eyes.

Alex gasped. The magic fluttered painfully in her chest, threatening to snap back violently into her body. Instead, she pushed it out with a frantic command to stay there and wait. Like an obedient dog, the magic backed off and curled up. Her eyes opened and Alex brought a hand up to rub her sore chest.

"That way," she choked out. Pointing up ahead of them, she nodded and swallowed. "Up there."

Merlin moved first with Aiden on his heels. Nicki touched her shoulder for a moment before heading up after them. Morgana's green eyes were fixed on her and Alex offered the older mage a shaky smile. Bran stepped up next to her and offered his hand. Taking it with a small smile, Alex let him support her shaky legs as they followed the others up the hillside.

Magic flared gently around the hands of Merlin and Morgana, brushing against her own magic lingering in the air. It flared to Alex's gaze like bright lights, but she made herself keep moving. They pushed through the underbrush quickly and Alex gasped. An orb of dark gray magic was hanging in the air, just waiting for her. There was a slight shimmer around it as the energy slowly dissipated from the surface but there it was. A small laugh of victory escaped her as it sunk in that she was about to turn the Sídhe's own world energy against them. Beyond the orb, just as she had seen through the magic, was a rough opening in the hillside.

"Well done!" Merlin cheered. His eyes were on the waiting magic.

"There's one in the tunnel!" Alex called out in warning.

Morgana moved first. She shoved her hand forward and released a beam of silver magic. It shot through the air into the tunnel, illuminating the rough, rocky sides and glinted off the golden armor of the Síd. The armor began to dissolve, but the Síd remained intact. There was a grunt of pain and the Síd stumbled back. It reached for a horn on its side that Alex recognized. Yellow magic flared in the corner of her eye and the horn was suddenly ripped from the Síd's hand. It flew out into the sunlight and the Síd pulled its sword with a sharp, smooth motion. The Síd never had a chance to do anything else. A green bolt hit it in the neck and Síd began to dissolve.

"Nicely done," Alex said softly to Bran. "Grabbing the horn like that."

"Glad to help," Bran replied. "Though I know how much Morgana likes to kill Sídhe."

That earned him a look from Morgana. Despite the woman's stern look, Alex could tell she was amused. Merlin was still staring into the tunnel, but slowly lowered his hand.

"I don't think the others heard," Merlin said. "There may have been only one guard."

"Then we might as well get started," Alex said. "What first?"

"We have the iron." Merlin gestured towards the bags. "Last time you all joined hands in order to share magic but given Alex's ability to convert the magic of others to her own, I'd like to try something different this time."

An internal uh oh in Alex's head made her freeze. In the back of her mind, there was a curious buzz of voices that Alex desperately ignored. She glanced towards her friends and found them looking at her with reassuring smiles. At least they were confident that this would work. Merlin said something, but Alex missed it. Morgana caught her eye and frowned slightly.

"We're going to release some magic," Morgana said calmly. "See if it is enough for you to guide the creation of a gate." Morgana stepped towards her and put a hand on her shoulder. "Will you be alright trying this, Alex?" Her voice was lower now, keeping the question just between the pair of them.

"Yeah, it'll be fine," Alex replied. "A good exercise for me too." Speaking a bit louder now, she looked at Aiden. "Just don't set anything on fire. Let's start slow so I can gather up the magic."

There were traded looks. Alex couldn't blame them for that. Those weren't the best instructions. Eyeing the opening where she was supposed to put the gate, Alex nibbled at her lower lip and fought to keep her hands still. She glanced towards the orb of gray magic still hanging in the air and shrugged off her bag. Alex took a few steps away from the others and watched as Bran and Aiden shifted the bags of iron rods closer. They set the bags on the ground between her and the other mages with a soft thump.

"You've got this, Alex." Nicki gave her a wide smile and Aiden nodded in agreement.

Unsure of what to say, Alex looked expectantly towards Merlin and Morgana. The whispers grew louder and Alex inhaled slowly. She focused on the wind cascading over the leaves and the sway of the pine tree branches. They were alone, and the spring sun was streaming down through the treetops.

Flashes of color drew her attention back to the others. Sparks of their differently colored magics were swirling around their hands. In their little semi-circle, they looked a bit like some sort of performance art display. Aiden released a flare of fire that shot into the air. It exploded in a rush of little, colored sparks like a firework. Laughing, Alex watched the sparks fall to the earth, content with the knowledge that Nicki was ready with her water magic. Aiden grinned at her and winked.

Bran raised a hand and yellow magic flashed through the air for a moment before all but vanishing. Overhead the rustling of the leaves intensified and Alex looked up as branches were pushed away by an unseen hand to let in more sunlight. There was a rush of blue from Nicki as she conjured the shimmering shape of a dragon. It flew into the air amongst them and opened its mouth in a silent roar. Bran and Aiden clapped and Nicki dropped into a grand bow.

There was a noise from the tunnel and green magic flashed around Merlin's hand. Alex looked at the orb of gray magic. It shimmered in response to her attention. Despite the playful release of magic, she was well aware of the iron waiting for her. Closing her eyes for a moment, she inhaled slowly and flexed her fingers. Alex released a soft wave of her own magic, concentrating on it spreading out around her, filling the air unseen. Then she opened her eyes.

Her vision shifted. The normal colors of the world muted and darkened while the lines of magic turned neon. There was vibrant red, cool blue, bright silver, leaf green, and sunshine yellow sparks spinning lazily through the air. Mere traces of magic left by the others, but Alex extended a hand. There was a flicker of resistance, but then the sparks turned into streams of color, racing towards her. In a flash of light, the orb dissolved into a river of sparks and rushed towards her. The colors began to blend together.

Dark gray magic spun off of her fingertips. It reached out through the air, meeting the stream of magic. Alex's gray magic twisted around the different colors, and as it all coiled into her hands. Alex watched as the red of Aiden's magic dulled and shifted to the metallic gray of her magic. Nicki's blue faded as did Merlin's green. Bran's yellow turned gray and she gathered it all together around her hands.

Alex concentrated on keeping all the magic together. Already she could feel it tingling across her skin and slipping away. She willed it to condense so she could use it later. The magic hummed in response and the gray mass spun tighter and tighter. Within moments it had formed a large gray orb that hung in the air before Alex. Flexing her fingers, Alex allowed herself a small sigh of relief, but said nothing. Instead, she turned her attention to the open bags and the pieces of iron glittering in the low light through the treetops.

She closed her eyes and ignored the others and the iron for a moment. Just at the edge of her senses was a vibration. It sang in the air like a low constant rumble of thunder. Her hair was rising as if a storm was building around her. In Alex's chest, her magic flared in response, surging down to her fingertips. Alex opened her eyes, pushed out her magic, and called the magic stored in the orb.

Dark gray sparks of magic blasted through the air, encircling the bags in a mass of gray. As it churned, Alex almost thought she saw a jolt of lightning which only enhanced the storm effect. Alex twitched her fingers towards the iron and pictured the magic entering the metal. The air rippled. Gray sparks poured into the waiting metal bars.

Swallowing, Alex turned her hands palm up and raised them. Slowly the first of the iron bars rose out of the bag and hovered in the air. Alex's eyes narrowed on the thick pieces of wrought metal. She could still see hammer marks in places where they'd been pounded into shape. Hints of Merlin's magic were just beneath the surface of the iron in faint flashes of green. In other pieces Alex sensed her own stored magic rising to blend with the gray storm.

The iron bands twisted in the air, shimmering with Alex's dark gray magic. With a flick of her wrist, she sent them hurtling into the opening. There was a roar that echoed out to her, but it was too late. The Sídhe had come. Their guard had fallen and they hadn't defended this entrance properly. Whispers turned to a mess of voices, some suspicious and some triumphant.

With a shuddering crack, the metal embedded itself into the stone. The hillside groaned and the glowing iron rods twisted around each other. Magic sparks flew off her fingertips, but Alex kept her gaze firmly on the metal. Around her the air was humming, faster and faster. Beneath her feet, the pulse of the Earth was accelerating. More magic climbed through her legs and passed through her chest before sweeping down her arms. It gathered around the metal, settled into the iron, and into the rock.

Magic pulled sharply, stretching out in the air between her and the iron. The gate was now formed, pulling in all the magic she could give it. In her chest, the familiar spark that connected Alex with the Iron Realm turned hot. One of the kinder voices was whispering to her. The words weren't clear, but it was urging her on. More magic— more magic will protect the Iron Realm. Arto. The name sprang to mind and Alex tugged on the connection, ignoring the ache beginning to spread down her limbs. More sparks erupted from her fingertips and followed the shimmering threads to the gate.

Then the threads snapped. Alex's knees quivered. Bran caught her arm and kept her upright. Panting for air, Alex fought back the darkness creeping in at the edges of her vision. Yet the gleaming of the Gate kept her focus. Pride swelled in her chest, easing the ache. Already, magic was radiating out from the Gate. It was settling like a mist over the area, soothing the knot in her chest. The pain didn't vanish, but for a moment Alex was able to forget that it was there. Several of the voices quieted in the back of her head. For a moment there was no pain and soft silence.

"Alex?" Aiden called.

"You okay?" Bran asked.

The forest shifted. Alex blinked as the colors at the edge of her vision changed for a moment. Through the soles of her shoes, the pulse of the magic grew stronger. The trees vanished and she was on a grassy hill looking at a gleaming metal gate in the hillside. Morgana was next to it, but younger and wearing a long blue cloak that fluttered in the wind.

Then it was gone. Alex was back in an Oregon forest, smelling the pine trees and fighting to stay upright. The wisps of magic still hanging in the air rushed towards her. Alex felt them slipping into her palm and closed her hand into a fist. They seeped into her skin and she grew a little stronger. She looked over towards Nicki who was watching her with a deepening frown. Morgana was still studying the Gate, but Merlin took a hesitant step forward.

The world swayed. The greens of the trees blurred together. One of the voices grew louder all of a sudden, calling her name and shouting words that made no sense. The others joined in, no longer whispering. Pushing them away, Alex found herself stumbling across the terrain. Morgana's voice cut through the haze as she called to her, alarm ringing in her voice. Some of the voices quieted for a moment.

Alex uselessly brought her hands to her ears, trying to block out the noise. It echoed, rattled, and rumbled in her head. All of them, all at once, all straining to be heard. A sob ripped from her throat. Dropping to the ground, she lowered her head to the cool surface of the rocks. The sharp edge of one dug into her skin, but Alex welcomed the distraction. There were hands on her shoulders, someone was hugging her, rocking her, but the voices wouldn't stop.

Some were more comforting, but others were unfamiliar and sharp. One cut through the others in a storm of curses and bile surged up in her throat at Cuthbert's voice. She remembered the ship and the vacant eyes of the slaves. Then he was drowned out by the others shouting. A whimper escaped Alex; she shook her head, trying to shake them out. The grip on her shoulder tightened and a pained cry echoed through her. Forcing open her eyes, Alex tried to turn her head. She could see some of the trees and tried to focus on them. The noises didn't stop. Hands gripped her face and turned it further.

Morgana's green eyes were shining with fearful tears. Merlin was right beside her, one hand holding Alex's shoulder in a tight, unforgiving grip. One voice rose above the others. There was a crack and a rumble like thunder through her mind. Everything went still and silent for one blissful moment. Then it all went dark.

14

Spring Unpleasantness

It was a bright, sunny spring day in Ravenslake. Downtown was full of students and locals enjoying the chance to visit the shops and restaurants along Central and Main without having to worry about slush and snow. There were small banners and baskets of flowers hanging from the lampposts and chalkboard sidewalk signs in front of almost every door. It was an almost perfect atmosphere, and Lance was loving every moment.

Something about having Jenny next to him made Lance feel taller. He was already a tall young man and knew it, but with her arm resting in the crook of his own his back was straighter, his shoulders were broader and he was stronger. It was a very cliché sentiment, but one that he was happy to acknowledge. Maybe it was because he was in love with her, or maybe it was some sort of happiness caused by there being no problem in being seen with her. Either one was valid, but he didn't care which.

In the last couple of weeks, the rumors had finally begun to die down and while the other members of the football team and spirit squad still weren't happy with either of them, there was nothing for it. Still, Lance wasn't sure if he'd even be bothering with football next year. Now that he knew the truth of the strange happenings in Ravenslake a sport seemed like a poor time investment.

"Penny for your thoughts?"

Smiling down at Jenny, Lance just shrugged. "Nothing important; just thinking about some random things."

"Such as?"

"Well football for one," Lance said. "I don't know. With how weird things got and everything else happening, I probably won't bother with the team next year."

"You're not on a scholarship, are you?" Jenny asked, her brow furrowed a little in concern.

"Only for my first two years, and I've done that now," Lance said. "I don't think I'll be offered another one. The coaches liked Arthur best of the younger players."

There was a flicker in Jenny's eye at the mention of her ex-boyfriend, but irritation quickly took its place. "If they knew the truth," she growled. "If they even knew a fraction of the truth about him, they'd be grateful he was gone."

"Well evil and twisted or not, he was a good quarterback," Lance said. He smiled and tried to lighten her mood, but Jenny wasn't having it. "Hell of an arm."

"Probably cheated using magic just to make sure he fit all the stereotypes and expectations."

"Maybe." Lance didn't want to argue about Arthur. "But... uh, we haven't really talked about it. Are you staying next year?"

Jenny's steps faltered for a moment and her expression softened. Heart racing, Lance found himself struggling to breathe as he waited for an answer. He braced for the bad news and started planning his own transfer.

"I think so," Jenny said. "Maybe it's silly and if we were smart, we'd transfer out of here together." Lance couldn't help but grin at Jenny's assumption that they'd go together. "But if you're okay with it I'd like to stay." She dropped her eyes to the sidewalk and shuffled a little. "I just... I don't feel right leaving Alex." Then Jenny looked up at him, her eyes nearly frantic. "It's not that I have romantic-"

"I know." Lance reached over with his left hand to squeeze hers still cradled in his arm. "I know that's not the reason, Jenny, and I have no problem with trying to be loyal to a friend." Licking his lips, he took in Jenny's grateful smile and gathered his own thoughts. "I'm glad you want to stay. I do too, but I would have left and followed you."

"You would have?"

"In a heartbeat."

He smiled down at her, hoping that Jenny could see how sincere he was. She must have. The beaming smile she gave him brightened up the whole world. Jenny brought them to a stop and leaned up on her toes, curling a hand around his neck, and tugging him down. Their lips met in a soft kiss that made his heart speed up. Her fingers brushed over the skin of his neck before she pulled back. Winking at him, Jenny gave him a sly smile and started walking, pulling him gently along.

"We can't block traffic," she said. Her eyes were bright with mirth and behind them, there was a whistle of approval from someone on the street. "Besides, we have an audience," Jenny added. He could see a blush creeping up her features.

"Right, sorry." Lance grinned as Jenny's blush worsened, remembering that she was the one who had kissed him. "But that's on you."

"I know." Jenny cleared her throat. "Uh, so how your family doing?"

Chuckling slightly, Lance humored her and recited some of the more recent news from his family. Jenny for her part listened with a small smile and giggled in the right places about Chris and Kelly.

"How about you?" he asked. "Anything new with your dad?"

"Nothing as interesting as getting himself tangled up in a net while skateboarding," Jenny replied. She giggled again. "I don't think something like that would inspire much confidence in clients. And I hate to say it, but Dad really tries to play up the stern no-nonsense lawyer thing at the office and the courtroom. Even most of the partners I've met don't think he has a sense of humor."

"But he does, right?"

"Of course!" Jenny paused and glanced around cautiously. "I'll tell you something, but you can never reveal this to the lawyers of San Francisco." Lance snorted a bit at that. "Dad has a serious fondness for really bad old B movies."

"What, like monster films?"

"Exactly: the stupider and worse the science, the better."

"So, he's a geek like Aiden and Nicki?"

"I'm not sure," Jenny said. She looked thoughtful for a second. "Nah, I don't think so. Personally, I think he just enjoys the ridiculousness of them. I've never seen him really watch anything else geeky per se."

"Well, everyone needs something simple to take their mind off things. What about you? Do you watch them with him?"

"Sometimes." Jenny made a disgusted face. "But the women in them are so poorly written." Shuddering, her expression became even funnier. "I mean they can start off the film intelligent and confident, but by the end they're screaming and fainting."

"None of the women I know are like that," Lance said. He chuckled at the truth of it. Most of his female friends were mages who could cause a lot of damage when they thought it necessary. And Jenny? He glanced back towards her and tried not to smile too widely. "Magic or no, you aren't a damsel in distress."

"Yeah, well, screaming doesn't solve anything," Jenny said. "Though I wouldn't mind being able to do a bit more to help."

"I understand."

He did understand, and he bent over to drop a quick kiss to her forehead. They fell into silence, but Lance didn't mind. It wasn't an uncomfortable silence. In fact, it was pleasant not suffering the need to keep talking, though the calmer conversation about nothing important had been nice. However, the idea of someone needing something simple made him think of Alex. Maybe he and Jenny needed to meet with the others and discuss some stress relief ideas for her. The loss of her parents and the dreams she didn't want to talk about were taking their toll.

A strange giggle echoed up the alley they were passing, breaking into his thoughts. Jenny didn't react and Lance hoped that he'd imagined it. Yet he found himself looking down the shadowed alley. Something in the air was off, at least it seemed that way to Lance. Tightening his grip on Jenny's hand, he glanced around the main street of Ravenslake. The tightly packed small buildings were bright with spring decorations meant to lure students and locals into the various stores. By all merits it should be a beautiful spring day and he was spending it with his girlfriend. Instead, something was coming after them. He knew it in his gut.

"Lance?" Jenny's voice was soft and told him that she was now on high alert. "Did you see something?"

"No," Lance said. "Uh, not exactly." Shaking his head, he glanced into a nearby alley. It was dark thanks to the angle of the sun, but seemingly clear of danger. "I'm not sure. Thought I heard... something in the air just seems... off."

It was a bad answer, but thankfully Jenny didn't push for him to explain it. Her grip on his hand loosened as her right hand dug into her purse. Lance knew from experience that she was probably making sure that her iron dagger was close at hand. He could feel the weight of his own dagger in the small back holster tucked under his shirt. Lance tensed: he thought he heard something running in the back streets of the block.

"Should we head to Professor Yates'?" Jenny asked. "We parked the truck a few blocks back."

"It may be nothing."

"The mages were going to make another Gate today," Jenny reminded him. She didn't need to. They'd gone out for the day to distract themselves from that. "Something might have-"

"Don't say it, Jenny." Lance squeezed her hand tighter and they stopped in front of a small boutique window. "Don't even think it."

"Too late," Jenny replied. They began to walk in the direction they'd come from. "I'm thinking about it and worrying."

"The professors are with them," Lance said. He wasn't sure who he was trying to reassure. His brown eyes kept searching the area. "I'm not... I may just be overreacting."

"Paranoia in our lives isn't a bad thing."

"Maybe."

They passed the Central Diner which was full to the brim with students enjoying lunch. The noise spilled out into the street and Lance looked in through the large windows. He wasn't sure what he was looking for, but a sudden terrifying thought that Arthur was back in town suddenly hit him. Nothing was out of place. One of the other guys on the football team spotted him and waved. Lance forced a smile and nodded in return but kept moving.

Bookend Coffee was only a few blocks away, and they'd parked right at the end of the block. In some respects, it had been a waste to even drive, but with the threat of Faeries, Old Ones, and Arthur hanging over their heads Lance hated to be too far from transportation. A couple of people from his and Jenny's classes greeted them. Jenny smiled but didn't wave back, keeping her hand in her purse.

Around them, all the other people were completely unaware of the murderous creatures sneaking up on them. A crash down another alley made him grimace. Jenny pulled on his hand as they reached the opening of the small side street between two stores. Small figures were darting around in the shadows. Lance and Jenny stepped back from the alley, standing firmly in the sunlight.

"They can't go far." Jenny sounded more confident than he felt. "It's a sunny day and they don't see well in bright light."

"Sunglasses," Lance said. "Hats. Let's not make assumptions."

"Thanks for pointing that out," Jenny muttered. "I feel a lot better." She tugged lightly on his hand. "Come on; they may not be violent. Let's keep going."

"They shouldn't be able to be in town," Lance reminded her.

"If they are the peaceful ones like Timothy then they're fine," Jenny said. "Alex adjusted the spell to only repel those meaning harm."

"Yeah." Lance let out a soft sigh of relief and willed himself to relax. Jenny was right about the blood protection spell. "Okay, yeah, let's go. We'll let the others know that there are more Faeries in town."

"Good plan."

They were moving away when another crash in the alley drew their attention. A dumpster had been knocked away from the wall and small purplish eyes were looking out at them. Lance pulled Jenny further away from the opening. A rotting smell hit his nostrils and he checked the street. Someone passed them, holding their nose and complaining about alley cats without stopping to look.

Then four little figures stepped out from behind the dumpster. Lance knew what they were on sight. Red Caps. The ugly little creatures had been a problem before, and at this point the mythology surrounding them was well known to him. They were small and vaguely misshapen, with sharp corners and gangly limbs. Dressed in cast-off rags that in only a few cases had been tailored at all, they might have been dismissed as a pile of trash. But the worst part of their appearance wasn't the sharp vicious eyes or long pointed teeth: it was the blood red hats they wore.

One had a beret, two wore a simple cloth caps and another had a ripped-up ski mask. Tightening his fingers around the hilt of his dagger, Lance told himself to stay calm. A Red Cap smiled at them nastily, baring long needle-like teeth. Their dark eyes glinted and Lance's heart dropped to his stomach.

"Not friendly!" Jenny pulled on his arm. "Not friendly, come on!"

He didn't move fast enough. Two Red Caps lunged forward, swinging some sort of chain over their heads. Confusion hit Lance first, but then the chain wrapped around his leg. Jenny cried out in alarm, but his feet were suddenly pulled out from under him. Throwing the top of his body forward, Lance adjusted his fall just enough to keep his head from hitting the ground. The Red Caps giggled loudly and dragged him into the shadows.

Jenny was right behind him, pulling out her dagger. Lance struggled to roll on his side and get his own dagger out as the Red Caps surged forward. Stabbing down, Jenny caught one of the Red Caps in the arm, but the drastic height difference put her at a disadvantage. Lashing out with his unbound leg, Lance kicked one of the Red Caps away and swung his dagger at another one. He slashed through the light clothing and silver blood spurted over his hand. There was noise behind them in the street and Lance feared that more people were about to show up. One of the Red Caps looked towards the street before Jenny kicked it across the alley.

Lance grabbed the odd chain around his leg and ankle. It had small weights attached like a bola, which explained how he'd been caught. Jenny's small hands joined his in untangling it. Then they were on their feet just as the remaining Red Caps dashed deeper into the shadows. A couple of students were at the mouth of the alley looking confused. Their expressions changed when they looked down at him and Jenny.

"Someone tried to mug us," Jenny said sharply. She pulled off the last links of the chain and tossed it to the side.

Lance grabbed her hand and they climbed to their feet. The students look confused, but Lance didn't want to wait around. They started to run. Lance managed to slip his dagger back into its sheath and dug out his keys without releasing Jenny's hand. Behind them, the giggling grew louder, making a dark suspicion that there were more than four Red Caps in town form in Lance's brain. People jumped out of their way and a couple shouted at them for almost knocking them over. Someone called their names, but they didn't stop until they reached his truck. Lance unlocked Jenny's side first, finally releasing her hand so she could climb in.

"They aren't following us," Jenny said.

"At least not where we can see." Lance glanced around the sunny street, but then his eyes dropped to a nearby manhole. "Uh... Jenny, do you know anything about sewers?"

"No," she answered. "And this isn't the time to find out. Let's just go."

Lance climbed in and started up the truck, locking the doors. Slamming his foot on the gas, Lance became aware of his hands shaking.

The last traces of silvery blood were gone. The Faery creatures left no traces, no evidence of their existence in the world, but the memories remained. He began to slow down as they merged into traffic alongside the University and eased his death grip on the wheel.

"You okay?"

"I'm fine," Jenny said. She was panting and shaking. "Little shaken up, but I'm fine."

"They attacked us even though the spell is broken," Lance said. It was obvious, but his mind was a mess of worry, fear, and adrenaline. "They don't have to attack us anymore."

"The spell only made them attack the mages." Jenny shifted her purse and dug out her cellphone. "So, attacking us was a strategic choice." Lance watched as she took a fortifying breath. He almost smiled. Even a touch sweaty and with her long dark hair messy, she was stunning. "Anyway, those were Red Caps, and according to the books they have always been the most violent of the Faery creatures."

"I'm not sure," Lance muttered. Forcing his eyes back to the road, he shook his head. "A lot of them seemed to only exist to kill humans by dragging us into water or something else horrible."

"I don't even want to think about it." Jenny's phone beeped as she brought up her contacts. "I know the others are making a Gate, but they need to know about those Red Caps."

"Yeah," Lance agreed. "Alex won't be happy."

"I know." Jenny sighed loudly. "She'll be angry that they came after us."

As the phone rang, Lance glanced towards Jenny again. Her features were set with determination and he could see the anger burning in her eyes. He didn't blame her. Part of him wanted to turn around and find those Red Caps. Knowing that you'd only been attacked as a way of hurting a friend was a bitter pill to swallow.

"No answer," Jenny said.

"They may still be making the Gate, or hiking in and out of wherever they were," Lance said. "Phones can end up at the bottom of bags pretty easily."

"I guess so." She shook her head a little. "Let's just head for Professor Yates' house. That's where they left from this morning. If nothing else we can sit on that iron furniture on the patio."

"Right." Lance looked in the rearview mirror. "No signs of them following us."

"Hopefully the sun will keep them in that alley." Jenny shivered on the seat next to him. "Blood protection in place and the spell broken, but they still attack us. What is it going to take to stop these things?"

"I don't know."

"God, I hope Alex is okay." Jenny was holding the phone to her ear and nibbling nervously at her bottom lip. "Come on, Alex, pick up."

Something was wrong. He listened with one ear and kept his eyes on the road as Jenny tried calling the others again and again. No one was answering. Turning off the main road, he steered his truck towards Merlin's house. Sadly, when they pulled up, there were no familiar cars waiting for them.

15

King of Man

4 64 B.C.E. Cashel, Ireland

Clouds blocked out the sun and cast long shadows over the landscape as they came to the crest of the hill. Beneath Leugio his horse shifted and made a soft neighing sound that drew his attention for a moment. It was not enough to distract him from the fortified town less than a mile away. The town was built on a high hill of rock rising above the green plain. Leugio had never seen anything like it and remembered some of the strange stories he'd heard about how the massive stone pillar came to be there. A wooden wall surrounded the buildings, but from their vantage point Leugio could see some of the roundhouses.

In some ways, it wasn't too dissimilar from his home. The buildings were made of the same materials. There were workshops and animal pens. Beyond the wall he could make out the earthen walls of a few pastures and see the outline of the fields. It should have been familiar, but the way it stood above everything made him feel all too small.

Nudging his horse forward, he followed his escort Bradan towards the town. They kept to the worn road and passed by the fields. Several farmers looked up at them with only mild curiosity before returning to their work. Overhead the clouds moved on and warm sunlight poured over his arms. It didn't help against the nervous chill rolling up his spine. Leugio was struck with a sudden sense of having forgotten something and being unprepared.

How did one talk to a king? Was there something special he was supposed to say or do? Did he have to wait for the king to speak first or was that rude? He eyed the fortifications again and wondered if an attack was likely while he was here. That was the way of things, as he understood them. The kings ruled over areas of fertile land and controlled trade, but occasionally they also sent out raiding parties in an attempt to add more land to their domain. It wasn't a very good system, and it was just as well that his home village was in the heartland of the kingdom. He reached up and touched his brooch and tried to remember if his father had ever talked about meeting the king. The memories were too foggy and Leugio couldn't shake anything useful loose.

Holding back the desire to turn around and flee homeward, Leugio tried to relax. He didn't have any luck with that, but either Bradan didn't notice or he didn't care. Either one was possible based on the man's attitude over the last few days. Leugio's fingers tightened around the reins of his horse and he shifted on the beast's back. Scanning the horizon, Leugio noted several small hills, and he wondered if any of them were Sídhe mounds. It was a dark thought and he shivered.

They passed through the gate in the wall, and Leugio eyed the guards who were watching him curiously. Armed with swords and spears, they were dressed in some sort of leather armor that had small metal areas and wore helmets. It was impressive, but it only made him think back to the Sídhe and that golden set of armor.

The king's house was larger than any other roundhouse Leugio had ever seen. It filled the landscape with its sloped layered grass roof, and somehow gleamed in the sunlight. Parts of it were dry stone with fitted rocks making up the lower part of the house wall. Two men came over and took the reins of Bradan's horse. He climbed down calmly and adjusted his cloak, looking expectantly at Leugio. Thankfully one of the men grabbed the reins of his horse and Leugio carefully eased himself off the beast. It made a sound that might have been relief and Leugio patted its neck in silent thanks.

"Bradan, is there anything special that I need to do?" Leugio grabbed the bags hanging over the horse's back. "Anything I should say to the king?"

"No, nothing like that. Just be polite and answer any questions he has for you."

It wasn't much in the way of advice, but Bradan gave him no time to mull it over. Instead, a firm hand was put on his shoulder and he was pushed into the roundhouse. Leugio braced himself. He'd heard about kings; heard about their power and all the forces they could send out. After the strangeness of the Sídhe mound, he wasn't sure what to expect from this massive roundhouse. He regained his footing as he entered and straightened up, looking around nervously.

In truth the roundhouse was laid out much the same as others; it was just a lot bigger. There was a massive hearth in the center of the house with a few chairs around it and an impressive set of pots hung over the flickering flames. Smoke wafted up through the hole in the center of the roof, giving the roundhouse only a slightly smoky scent and a warm atmosphere. The other major difference was all the people. There were at least a dozen people in the roundhouse with room for those following them in. Leugio tried to keep his eyes from scanning the whole room, fearing that it might be rude, but he couldn't help it.

Parts of the roundhouse seemed very normal. Beds were tucked against one wall, there was a loom set up nearby and there were the small shelves for precious items. There was just more of everything. Old vases and bottles, bowls of beads, and finely carved items. Even the fact that there were just people waiting here in the middle of the day spoke of their affluence. Following Bradan towards the center of the roundhouse, Leugio let the warmth of the fire wash over his skin. It eased the cold nervousness a little.

There was a large carved wooden chair on the far side of the fire. In it sat a large man with thick muscular arms and a graying brown beard full of golden beads. His hair was receding and almost completely gray but pulled back in a braid. He instantly looked at Leugio, and appeared more surprised than anything, and a touch disappointed. Leugio suppressed a wave of hurt and anger. He was a shepherd who was a bit talented with music, not a warrior.

"Welcome, young man," Eochu Finn greeted. "So, you are the one who entered a Sídhe mound and returned. An impressive feat." The large man leaned forward in his chair, his fingers brushing over the hilt of a sword leaning against it. "Won't you tell us the tale? I've already heard many interesting things." His eyes took on an interested gleam that made Leugio's stomach tightened. "Including that you have magic."

Leugio loved Keelia, he truly did, but right now he was regretting not swearing her to secrecy about the strange power he'd managed to wield. Swallowing, he glanced around the crowd, but there were no familiar faces. A young woman caught his eye. She was pretty, with long dark hair pulled back in a series of braids. Golden jewelry decorated her wrists and neck. Her intelligent brown eyes were sizing him up in a way that made him feel very dirty and unimpressive. Then she offered him a tiny supportive smile.

"There is little to tell, sir," Leugio started carefully. "I was in the pasture when a friend alerted me that my sister had gone missing. I returned home to speak with my mother when our dog came rushing up. Kent, uh, the dog, sir, was agitated and I followed him back to the Sídhe Mound." He paused, uncertain as to how the next part would be taken.

"Go on."

"There was a Síd outside the mound in the shadows. I traded my cruit to it in exchange for information." His statement caused some murmurs in the crowd, but no outbursts. "It was able to tell me the right path to take in order to reach where my sister was being held."

"And it was truthful?" Eochu Finn's eyebrows shifted, shadowing his eyes, and his mouth tightened. There was something sharp in his gaze and Leugio was sure that there was a wrong way to answer.

"On the surface it was," he answered. "The directions did take me into the lower levels where my sister was." The king's look darkened and the murmurs grew louder. He was surrounded. Sweat gathered in his palms and his throat tightened. "But I can't say for certain that it ever meant for me to escape," he added urgently. "The location of my sister may have just aligned with where the most guards were."

Actually, that did make sense. Though Iúdás had been polite last time they met. Leugio decided against revealing that he'd been back to the mound to see the Síd. Eochu Finn's eyebrows went up a touch and he looked more interested now. Leugio wasn't relieved by that though; it actually made his gut turn slightly. There was too much happening here, too much that he didn't understand. Iúdás had provided a few answers that led to even more questions.

"But I was able to find my sister. Using my iron dagger, I fought a couple of the Sídhe before I found her."

"What of your magic?" someone in the crowd shouted. There were sounds of agreement and excitement, but Leugio kept his attention on Eochu Finn. The king did look curious.

"When the Sídhe were closing in around myself and my sister, some strange power did surround me and forced them back," Leugio explained carefully. Already people in the crowd were whispering amongst themselves. "But I was not able to control it: the magic reacted to me being in danger and to being in the territory of the Sídhe." Licking his lips, he tried to find the right words, but there weren't any. "I can't really explain it, sir."

Eochu Finn leaned back in his chair and kept staring at him. "There are tales of mages from long ago who battled the Sídhe," he said slowly. Leugio's chest tightened at the words and he braced himself. "And there are a few tales of those who have rescued children from the them, but they are rare. Your achievement is unusual, to say the least." The king's expression darkened and his gaze shifted. "I worry though what it might mean for the future."

"I don't understand," Leugio admitted. "I only know that one of the Sídhe took my sister. I traded my cruit to one of them for information, and it thought that the Síd who took my sister was trying to impress someone. It told me the way to find Keelia, and once we defeated the guards it didn't stand in our way. Beyond that, I have only the same understanding of the Sídhe as everyone else from those same stories."

His hands threatened to tremble. Everyone was staring at him. How was he supposed to react? What was he supposed to do? The king was watching him thoughtfully. Then the man sighed and shook his head.

"That is not what I was hoping to hear," Eochu Finn said. He straightened up in his chair. "But perhaps you know more than you realize. You have been into their accursed home and returned." He tapped the arms of the chair. "And you are sure that your sister was not switched with a Changeling?"

"Yes sir," he answered quickly. The thought had never occurred to him, but then he remembered Keelia grabbing the iron dagger and using it to defend them. "Absolutely certain. She handled an iron dagger after I found her."

"Then I have need of you to confirm that another of our people is, in fact, one of us!" Eochu Finn bellowed. He raised one of his large hands and gestured at the door. "I have another suspected Changeling for you to evaluate!"

Eyes widening, Leugio opened his mouth to protest, but his first words were lost in another roar from the crowd. In the corner of his eye, he saw the young woman he'd noticed earlier frown and spin around towards the doorway. Two men were striding inside with a small figure between them, bound by ropes.

The girl was small and frail. Her brown eyes were bloodshot and wide with terror, yet there was an exhausted air of resignation about her. The simple tunic and pants all but hung off of her and Leugio could see scaring from some kind of attack on the exposed part of her arm. Swallowing, he stayed still and said nothing, not trusting his own voice.

"This girl was found four days ago," Eochu Finn said. He cast a dark look at the girl. She didn't shrink back. There was only a soft whimper. "We believe she is a Changeling."

"Uh, have you tested her with iron?" Leugio asked. He glanced between the girl and Eochu Finn, his confusion building.

"Yes, but she hasn't fled from it. Perhaps some new immunity?"

"The Sídhe I fought against were all weak to iron," Leugio said carefully, keeping himself still. "Their bodies turned to dust after contact. My sister was even able to use it to keep them back as we left, just with the threat of attacking them with it. I don't think they are immune to it. There was true worry in their eyes."

The king made a thoughtful noise and the young woman he'd noticed earlier stepped out of the crowd to move closer to them. Those around her stepped back to give her space and the guards near the king made no move to stop her. Leugio noted Bradan rushing forward to the king's side, avoiding the child with a distasteful look on his face.

Leugio's eyes jumped back to the child. She looked terrified and struggled weakly against the guards like an animal trying to escape. It was all instinct. The young woman took a step towards her, a thunderous expression on her face, but a guard stopped her.

"Father, she isn't a Changeling," the young woman insisted. She glanced his way and moved closer to Eochu Finn. Leugio blinked in surprise but quickly absorbed in the information. "Look at her injuries and scars! Something terrible did happen to the girl, but it is clear she has just been wandering on her own! Perhaps a raid on a distant village, or maybe an animal attack."

"The Sídhe are becoming bolder," Eochu Finn said. "We cannot dismiss the threat of them putting a Changeling in our midst. That attack easily could have been the Sídhe now trying to play on our sympathies."

"I understand that, sir," Leugio said quickly. His heart was pounding too quickly now and he was sure everyone could hear it. "The Sídhe are dangerous." Exhaling slowly, he gave himself a moment to gather his thoughts. "I remember too clearly the fear I felt when I realized that my sister had been taken. When I found her and we made it out... I do understand."

"You're certain they are still weak to iron?"

"Yes, sir." Leugio nodded and saw the young woman smiling a little. "I am sure. They all reacted to it, keeping their eyes on it, and avoiding it the best they could." Hesitantly, he shifted his hand to his dagger. "May I?"

The king's daughter looked uneasy but didn't protest as her father nodded. There was no stirring of magic beneath his skin as he approached. Leugio knelt by the child who looked at him nervously. Yet she didn't pull back even as he took one of her bruised hands. He could more clearly see the scars now. They did look like claws from an animal, but he wasn't sure which predator had made them. Offering her a soft smile, he moved slowly and drew his dagger. The girl made a small noise of panic.

"I'm just going to prick you," he said gently.

Guilt rose in his chest: even a small prick would hurt and could become much worse. She'd clearly already been through a lot and he hesitated once again. His gaze went to the fire and he shifted on his knees to hold the blade into the flames for a moment. This earned him a small nod of approval from the king's daughter. Trying to smile for the girl, he carefully cut the tip of her thumb. She made a small whimper of pain and flinched, but there was no howl of pain. A red droplet gathered at the surface of the wound and Leugio sheathed the dagger. He touched the girl's head and looked up at the guards.

"She isn't a Changeling. The iron would have done much more harm and she would have retreated from it."

"Release the girl and take her to the old woman," Eochu Finn ordered.

The guards did as they were told and undid the knots in the rope. The girl rubbed at her wrists and looked around in confusion. When a guard reached for her again, she drew back with a small noise. The king's daughter moved forward quickly and knelt down between the girl and the fire before she could stumble into it. Leugio drew his hand back and made a soft noise, the sort he used to calm the animals.

"It's alright," the young woman said. She looked up at the guards. "I'll take over from here." She peered at him for a moment before carefully picking up the girl. The child tensed, but then all but collapsed against her. Leugio stood and helped the young woman stand, keeping a hand on her elbow.

"Forgive me," Eochu Finn said. He gestured to the young woman with an odd smile. "As you have no doubt gathered, this is my daughter, Flaitheas."

"A pleasure to meet you." Leugio tried to smile, but he had the feeling that it didn't turn out well. Nonetheless she smiled gently in return, her eyes a touch brighter.

"Father, I have no doubt you have things to discuss. I'll take care of the girl." Flaitheas smiled and looked at him once again. "And our guest must be tired after a full day of travel."

"Yes, yes." Eochu Finn waved a hand towards the door, already turning his attention towards Bradan who was stepping up beside the throne. "I leave them both to you, Flaitheas."

"Come with me," Flaitheas ordered.

Leugio nodded and didn't hesitate to follow her out of the round-house. As the cool air hit his skin, he gulped down a greedy breath. His knees shuddered and he was suddenly aware of what a long day it had been. Flaitheas lingered next to him, giving him a moment, which left him both grateful and embarrassed. Then she started walking down one of the trails, the little girl clinging tightly to her shoulders.

"Thank you for insisting that she wasn't a Síd," Flaitheas said. "I'm afraid that Father is becoming more paranoid every day about them."

"Does he have reason to be?"

"Well, the story we heard from your village wasn't the first," Flaitheas replied. "We know that the Sídhe occasionally take children from time to time, but there really does seem to be more activity from them recently."

"I-" Leugio stopped and shivered. Something about those words made his stomach turn. It reminded him too much of Iúdás' words about not being able to stop those outside of his own mound. Just thinking the name made Iúdás' face appear before him: it had been so calm, even detached when he and Keelia came out. Were they all truly like that? What did it mean? "That's not good to hear."

"I'm sorry," Flaitheas apologized as they kept walking. "You've had a long day, and Father didn't make it easier by springing his worries on you." She adjusted the little girl in her arms. "You must want to rest."

"I'll wait until the little one is alright," he answered. Flaitheas rewarded him with a bright smile.

16

Dead World

A landscape was forming around her. There were rolling hills, pastures, and a village made of wood and sod in the distance. Alex could see a larger, smooth hill that looked a bit out of place and inspired an odd desire to run in her. Around her, a voice whispered names that tugged at her memory, but Alex knew it was far too distant. The air was hot and heavy against her skin. She could smell ozone and looked up at a darkening sky. The voice grew louder, shouting a warning, but the other voices were returning. They had their own things to say.

Alex brought her hands up to cover her ears. It did no good, they were inside: they were always inside. She screamed. The sound surrounded her, echoed through her ears and reverberated in her skull. Suddenly the ozone smell was gone and her skin cooled off in an instant. She stopped screaming and opened her eyes.

She was back in the fog. That meant this was another dream, she realized with both relief and worry. Biting her lip, Alex tried to remember when she'd gone to sleep. Flickers of the last things she seen danced before her eyes, but nothing made much sense. It was difficult to remember, but Alex tried. They'd been making the new Gate. In truth, it was just a little thing in the rocks, but Merlin and Morgana had seemed pleased enough with it.

A laugh echoed in the fog around her. There was a low, but familiar glow of blue. Turning sharply, Alex searched for any sign of another person. She recalled that laugh from the last time she'd been here. Swallowing, Alex rubbed at her arms as a sudden chill crept up her spine. The laughter rippled through the fog once more. Figures were beginning to appear in the distance. Memories of the last time she'd been trapped here spilled forth and Alex frantically shook her head.

"Brekszta, stop this at once!" Alex shouted. Her words echoed in the vast darkness, bouncing back to her.

The distant blue glow faded into the fog, but there was another burst of laughter. Alex turned around, searching for any sign of the Old One, but all she could see were the humanoid figures in the fog moving towards her. She dropped her hands and pulled on her magic. Dream or not, real or not, she just wanted out. The flicker of magic in her gut exploded, sending magic flowing up her arms and down to her fingertips. Gray sparks erupted from her flesh and illuminated the fog, pushing it back.

"No," Alex shouted. "No! I'm not doing this again! They're dead! Their time is over! This is my lifetime and they don't get to have it!"

It had been the voices after she made the Gate. She remembered it now. They'd gotten so loud, so powerful that everything else had buckled beneath the weight of them. Even now she could hear growing whispers, both in her own head and out in the fog. They were pulling, teasing, and nagging her, trying to make her listen to them. But they weren't saying the same thing; it was just a mess of different voices.

Magic flashed out around her, swirling through the air and pushing back the dream. Alex slammed her eyes shut and let the magic flow. It was wild, barely controlled, with only her frantic wish to leave the dream to guide it. Maybe this was just another part of the dream: she didn't know. The voices were quieting and the laughter had stopped. A sharp voice screamed at her, but the words were lost in the pounding of Alex's own heart.

Distantly there were other voices. People calling her name; not one of the other names, but Alex. Nicki's voice and Morgana's voice. They were calling to her and she tried to reach for them. Alex tried to call to them, reassure them that she was okay. She wanted to wake up. But the weight of it all was too much. Her magic stretched out around her, but there was nothing. Just a dull chill in the air. Opening her eyes again, Alex exhaled slowly.

The darkness shifted. Gray magic rippled across an inky blackness that was sweeping in around her. It was a box, a cage, and yet the magic was changing it. Alex didn't move. The air changed, thinning, and taking on a smoky smell. Her feet began to sink into the ground or floor or whatever it was.

She'd used too much magic. The memory of making the Gate, the gathering of everyone's magic, and changing it to her own came back. Fear made Alex slam her eyes shut even as she tried to control it. This was just a dream, and the laughter was gone. None of it was real. Yet the pain wasn't waking her. Alex clenched her hands into fists, trying to hide and hold back the small quiver taking over her limbs. Confusion warred with fear and her determination that this was just a dream. It was all too blurred now.

Something brushed over her skin, leaving tingles in its wake. All the hairs on her arm were standing on end. In the distance, a dull sound was beginning to rise. The ache in her chest was spreading, but Alex didn't stop urging her magic to hold back the dark. It hurt. Part of her waited to wake up. That was how it was supposed to work, right?

The dull sound was growing louder. It was a howling, but not of any beast. Behind her eyelids, the darkness was fading. There was some sort of light now. Her feet quivered, the terrain changed, but Alex stood firm. This was familiar in a way, but she wasn't falling between dreams or memories this time. This was familiar and yet alien at once.

Her magic stopped. It just stopped like a vacuum cleaner with the plug suddenly pulled. That strange sound was louder now and Alex finally recognized it as the wind. Small things hit her face and Alex tentatively opened her eyes as she shielded her cheek with her hand. Ash filled her nostrils. Alex coughed and looked around in confusion. Beneath her feet the ground gave way, layers of ash and soot compressing as she moved. Alex stumbled forward, trying to see something through the billowing smoke. It was thick in the air, rising into a dark violet sky that was caught in twilight.

There was a small shrouded sun that was too far away. Debris circled it in a frightful ring, large enough for Alex to see the shadows passing over the deep reddish star. There were more massive fragments of rock closer to the planet, floating lazily across the sky like small jagged moons. The sun was low in the dark sky and sinking with every passing moment. Alex's eyes widened and she gasped in surprise, earning a mouthful of soot for the trouble. In response, her magic flickered back to life, though the ache intensified to a sharp pain running from her heart to her groin. Alex looked down at her hands. There was a faint gray glow around her skin, but as she rubbed her fingers together, she wasn't sure if it was real. This was some sort of dream: she may just be seeing her magic because she thought she should. Shaking her head, Alex pushed away the thought.

"Hello?" Alex called, shielding her mouth with her hand. Her voice wavered and Alex turned to examine the landscape. If this was some sort of new dream then at least she had full control over her body. "Brekszta, is this your doing?" There was no answer except for the wind, blowing more of the ashy dust. "I demand you release me at once!"

Nothing happened. The wind only howled and bits of ash hit her face. That alien red sun was setting, making the already violet color of the sky darken. Alex still didn't move. Her feet sunk into the sooty ground, but she couldn't muster the courage for that first step. Instead, she closed her eyes and listened. There was only the wind. Even the voices were gone. There were no whispers, no shouts or demands for her to do something. Just the wind. It was almost comforting, and yet it left Alex feeling like a boat off its mooring.

Slowly the ache in her chest eased. Alex opened her eyes. It was even darker now and there was a layer of ash over her skin, giving it a gray and faded appearance. She couldn't just stay here waiting to wake up. Shivering at the growing chill in the air, Alex made herself look around once more.

Overhead thousands of glittering stars illuminated a purplish line in the sky. It stretched out into the perfect blackness of space with the stars growing dimmer and more spread out. Alex just stared, eying the line of stars curiously. This wasn't Earth: none of the stars were familiar. It wasn't another life or memory then; this was something else. But somehow, she still had her magic so she was still connected to her body. Alex tried to smile, tried to convince herself that this was really just a dream, but she didn't completely believe it. There was a weight to the sky above her, heavy and vast while she was tiny. Fear bubbled up through her chest and Alex dropped her eyes, unable to keep looking.

Taking another step forward, Alex tripped when her foot sunk into the ash once more. The ground was too soft– there was nothing holding it together. No rocks were visible: just the layers of a burned-out world. Wind howled around her, icy and sharp. Shivering, Alex rubbed at her arms and kept moving. Climbing to the top of a slope, Alex peered out at a desolate landscape.

It was all black and gray. Small dunes of ash had been formed by the winds and up ahead she could see collapsed buildings. There was no movement and no sound except for the wind. She couldn't even see any kind of vegetation, dead or alive. Another gust of wind was so strong that it made Alex stumble. Gritting her teeth, she sped up even as her feet slipped in the ash and headed for the remains of the buildings.

They seemed to be made of dark stone, but Alex didn't trust that. There was too much ash and she wondered if there had been some sort of massive fire or eruption. The stars provided just enough light for her to stumble around as the last rays of the sun vanished. In her chest Alex's magic was pulsing in time with her heart.

Pushing the thought away, Alex focused on reaching the first of the buildings. A partially collapsed stone building formed an odd lean-to against another building. There wasn't much space underneath the shelter of a half wall leaning against another, but it was something. The architecture was made up of domes and arches with evidence of painted murals visible on the protected interior. Yet it wasn't familiar to her. She recognized the basics of the structure of course, but not the style from any history textbooks. The stone fitted together tightly even as it crumbled, without any sign of mortar or cement.

Ducking into the small area, Alex pulled on her magic. It rose slowly to her command, but gray sparks appeared around her hand. Alex flexed her fingers and drew the flickers of light together into a glowing orb. A soft, gray shine surrounded her and Alex studied the mural. There was a landscape scene with rolling hills and buildings. The vegetation seemed to be a pale sort of reddish green, but Alex thought that might be age. Sadly, there were no figures to be seen in what remained.

Alex grumbled under her breath. This was a strange dream, but dread was gathering in her stomach. Moving to the next collection of buildings, Alex stayed alert for any sounds other than the wind. She seemed to be alone, but a nervous tug in her gut made her worry. Why she was here was a mystery. Maybe this truly was just a dream: just a normal sort of dream brought on by magical exhaustion and Brekszta trying to meddle with her mind. She risked a look up towards the sky once more, noting the vague dark shapes of debris floating around the planet. Every so often more of the rocks blocked out the stars.

Her foot slipped again as she reached another collapsed building. This one was sunk further down into the ground. Alex grabbed at the wall, but her feet slid in the ash out from under her. Hitting the ground, Alex threw her arms up to protect her head. The light orb she'd created flickered but stayed intact.

Sitting up, she noted in surprise that there was an empty space which her feet had slid into beneath the half-collapsed walls. They were leaning against each other with only a small area exposed. She frowned and looked around, silently sending the light orb higher into the sky. It didn't reveal much, but as she stood up, Alex noticed that a few feet away the landscape changed. It was sunken in, roughly in the shape of a square. She turned her eyes back to the empty space she'd discovered and slowly worked her way forward. Her feet found a step and Alex brought the light orb back to her. Sending it forward, she peered down into the space and almost smiled as she found a staircase half buried by ash. While it was a mess, it looked intact, and as she shivered at another cold gust of wind, Alex made up her mind.

Staying low, she half walked and half crawled down the stairs, fearing slipping on the ash again. While she was sure that she was dreaming, Alex wasn't confident in what damage Brekszta could inflict on her. She made it to a flat landing that was almost free of ash and tried to dust herself off. It was a waste of time: her jeans were heavy with gray ash and she felt filthy.

Her light orb hung in the air, casting a soft gray glow over the walls. Alex inspected them thoughtfully, but there were no paintings here and nothing else that seemed of value. She walked forward slowly, using her feet to tap on the floor before she put her whole weight forward. Distantly she could still hear the wind. In her chest, Alex's magic was pulsing weakly, but still there. She stopped and inhaled slowly, focusing on her magic, but something about it was off. There was something wrong with it that she didn't understand. Other than the light orb she wasn't doing anything, and yet the magic was stretched out like she was doing multiple things.

The hallway opened into a large room. Over her head, the ceiling was making small groaning sounds. There was a faint cracking noise, a bit like glass, and Alex didn't dare think too long about that. Pulling on her protesting magic, Alex brightened the light orb to illuminate the whole room. It looked like a courtyard of some kind. Maybe a covered courtyard. There were several things that looked like planters, a toppled statue that was broken and a few collapsed hallways leading out of the courtyard.

Alex wasn't sure what to think. She'd been on the surface already, so this was below ground. Unless this was the original ground level... Shaking her head, Alex sighed. This was more Nicki's area of expertise than her own. She walked further into the courtyard and risked another look up. There was only a thick black layer over her head and a strange, faint shine. Maybe it was glass.

That didn't make her feel any better. She moved over by the walls and examined them. Here the murals had been better protected. The colors were a bit faded, but she could see strange beautiful flowers painted across the surface. There were tall buildings, alien trees, and symmetrical designs. Her foot hit one of the planters and she looked down. There was a shriveled plant devoid of any color. Reaching down, Alex gently touched what remained of a leaf, but the entire thing crumbled at the slight pressure, turning to dust in Alex's hand.

Everything here was dead.

She jumped away from the planter, nervously brushing her hands against each other in an attempt to clean them. Alex hesitated for a moment but went over to the statue. There was a small pedestal in the center of the courtyard where it had stood before it had fallen to the side. She could almost imagine a fleeing person knocking it over in their haste to escape.

Kneeling, Alex picked up the broken-off head of the statue and brushed away the faint layer of ash from the face. Parts of it were broken, but enough of the face remained that she gasped. There was a pair of cracked horns growing out of the forehead. The face was a little too narrow and fine for a human's, it had pointed ears, and while there was no color on the stone any longer, Alex knew that the eyes were supposed to be violet. She screamed and the head dropped from her hands, shattering on the old stone floor of the courtyard.

17

Her Screams

The day had been going so well. True, Lance was now sitting on a nice patio in an attractive iron chair with Jenny right across from him and their feet occasionally touched as they shifted, but the situation wasn't exactly relaxing. One, they were a pair of college students suddenly camped out on a professor's patio. Two, they each had iron daggers on the table by their right hands. And three, creatures bent on killing them could show up at any moment.

"We're in the sunlight," Jenny said, almost as if she read his mind. "We should be fine."

"Maybe there is a kind of Faery that is resistant to the harsh light of our sun."

"Maybe, but I'd rather not think about that," Jenny replied. She looked around nervously, her left hand toying with the pendant around her neck. "Probably wouldn't be resistant to iron though, and we're surrounded by that. If Arthur had any Faeries like that, he'd have already sent them."

"You think Arthur sent them?" Lance leaned forward over the table. "Even with the spell broken?"

"I.... yeah maybe." Jenny sighed and tugged on a strand of her long dark hair as she nibbled at her lower lip. At any other time, it would have made Lance lean forward to kiss her. "It's a bit naive, isn't it? To think that none of the Faeries would help him and the Queen? Surely some of them will want power or a chance to come out of the shadows."

"I guess you're right." Lance slumped in his chair and looked towards the house, wishing that Merlin and the others would hurry up and get back here. "I haven't thought much about it, but you're right. This isn't their world, and to avoid human panic and potential genocide they always have to hide."

"And with modern technology that's got to be getting harder and harder. I can't imagine many of them go above ground in crowded cities with a lot of cameras," Jenny said thoughtfully. "When you think about it, they probably live in smaller cities or in towns like this one."

"That's not very reassuring."

Swallowing, Lance wished they had something to drink. There were a couple of bottles of water stashed in his truck's emergency bag, but he doubted they'd be very refreshing. He rubbed the back of his neck and looked up towards the forested hills surrounding Ravenslake. Lance understood why Merlin and Morgana didn't live in the town proper, but did they really have to live so close to the forest with all those thick trees and long shadows?

Jenny pulled out her phone and sent out a group text but didn't look very hopeful. A gust of wind shook the distant trees and Lance grabbed for his dagger. Nothing came out of the tree line, but he was slow to relax. Jenny reached over and touched his arm, squeezing his muscles lightly. He was pleased to note a slight blush take over her cheeks and almost smiled. The weight room did have its rewards.

"Uh, so if we're staying next year, do you think we should try to move in with the mages?" Jenny suddenly asked.

It took Lance's brain a moment to catch up. "Yeah, maybe," he replied slowly. "Though we might put them in danger if they have to worry about us."

"Maybe, but those Red Caps attacked us. At least, I don't think they went after anyone else..." Jenny's face suddenly turned pale, and she was on the brink of panic. "Oh no! Lance, do you think-"

"No." He grabbed her hands and gave her a weak smile. "No, Jenny, I'm sure they were after us. We're connected to the mages, and if you're right about them helping Arthur, then going after us makes sense. Us being hurt would hurt Alex, and Arthur..." Lance trailed off– he couldn't bring himself to finish the sentence.

"He likes hurting Alex," Jenny finished. Her eyes were darker now, controlled rage simmering just beneath the surface. She exhaled slowly and the anger eased from her eyes, but Lance knew it was still there. "I just hope he leaves her brothers alone."

Lance nodded. He couldn't help but think about his siblings Chris and Kelly. His family was certainly vulnerable, even with the blood protection that Alex had placed around the house. Would Arthur go after them, or was he too unimportant in the grand scheme of things? Would Arthur actually kill anyone else, or was the fear he'd put into them all enough? There were too many questions, but Lance was very aware that he had the youngest siblings of all of them. It wasn't a reassuring thought. Nothing about Arthur's actions thus far gave him any reason to believe that Arthur had any moral limits, but maybe they would be pleasantly surprised.

"I still struggle with it all," Jenny said, her voice soft and resigned. "I close my eyes and think of Arthur, but all I see is that smiling boy from high school. Then I remember what he's done." She shivered and squeezed Lance's hands tightly. "It's like there are two people in my memories now, even when so many strange little things about him now make sense." A bitter laugh escaped Jenny, and Lance watched her blink away some tears. "I keep going over things, trying to see if there was anything important that he ever let slip."

"Have Merlin or Morgana asked you?"

"No: I don't think they trust me or have that much faith in me." Jenny's voice was matter of fact and accepting. Then she tilted her head cutely and smiled, short-circuiting his brain for a moment. "I guess it's something we need to think about: housing arrangements for next year, I mean."

"Uh, yeah." Lance was a bit disoriented now but pushed through. "If the mages don't want us there due to the danger, then we need to know soon."

"Exactly." Then Jenny bit her lower lip and dropped her eyes. "And we could always share. Become roommates, I mean, in that case."

Lance's brain wasn't able to fully process that thought. There were too many emotional reactions at her suggestion that left him dizzy. Before he could completely become a puddle at Jenny's feet, the sound of cars on the driveway made them both sit up straight. He released Jenny's hands as his heart started pounding for another reason. Lance's fingers twisted around the hilt of his dagger before he'd even thought about it. Then there were familiar voices and the slamming of car doors. He stood up from the table, making the chair drag across the cement patio with a squeal and sheathed his dagger.

It took them only moments to go around the house. Familiar cars and Merlin's SUV were now parked next to his truck and the mages were climbing out. There was extra activity at Merlin's SUV that made

Lance frown in worry. Aiden was carrying Alex in his arms, balancing her carefully as her head lay motionless against his shoulder. Lance started to step forward to both check on her and offer to help, but quickly stopped. At this point shifting her would be more troublesome than helpful.

Not wanting to surprise the mages, Lance called out in greeting. They all turned as one to look at him, Morgana's hand was raised and ready to summon magic. It inspired a jolt of fear in him, but he managed not to flinch back.

"Ah, Lance," Merlin greeted even as he frowned. "I was wondering about your truck. What brings you here?"

"Is Alex okay?" Jenny demanded as she rushed over next to Aiden. "What happened?"

"She's exhausted," Morgana replied calmly. "But we need to get her inside."

"There were Red Caps in town," Lance said. He didn't want the reason they were here to become lost in the worry over Alex. Nonetheless, his eyes jumped back to the unconscious young woman. Her face was deathly pale, and her eyelids were fluttering. "Not sure how many, but they attacked us."

"Red Caps?" Morgana repeated. "You're sure?"

"Small Faery creatures with blood red hats, so pretty sure."

"That isn't good." Morgana's brow furrowed and she rubbed the skin between her eyes, suddenly looking very tired. "I wouldn't have thought they could get through the blood protection spell, even with their high immunity to iron." Shaking her head, Morgana sighed softly. "Damn little psychopaths." Her expression softened and she looked at the pair of them. "You are uninjured?"

"Yeah, we just ran once we saw them," Jenny said.

"Good; once we know Alex is alright, I'll take a look. Where were they?"

"Right along Central," Lance answered.

"That's something at least," Morgana said.

Merlin got the front door open and held it so Aiden could step through it sideways. Alex's sneakers bumped against the doorframe, but she didn't wake or even react at all. Jenny made a small sound of worry and Nicki put an arm around her shoulders before he could. The redhead didn't say anything to his surprise and silently watched Alex vanish inside. Then she released Jenny and followed. Lance looked down at his girlfriend and without a word to each other they followed the mages inside.

The house was neat and tidy, but Lance noted that sheathed swords were tucked into various corners, against furniture, or behind chairs. He didn't have to study them to know that they'd all be iron. Alex was gently placed on the sofa, but her height was enough that her legs had to be bent and tucked.

Aiden wiped his forehead, looking a bit winded. "I'll move her to the guestroom in a minute," he said.

"I can use magic for that," Bran reminded him. He clapped Aiden's shoulder and added, "Now that the neighbors aren't at risk of seeing anything."

"Right, good." Aiden nodded, still panting. "Good. I thought I was in better shape than that."

"You could always join me in the weight room," Lance offered lightly. "I can make sure you don't kill yourself."

He meant it as a joke, but Aiden actually looked a little thoughtful. Then again, magic wasn't everything. Especially not in the daytime when others could see it. Judging from how much the mages ate nowadays their magic definitely had an impact on their metabolism, but it didn't add muscle tone.

"What happened?" Jenny asked again, her voice shifting to a higher pitch. "I thought you were making a Gate!"

"We were," Morgana answered. "And we did. To train Alex, we had her gather everyone's magic and use that to construct the Gate. It exhausted her. She's fine; just asleep for now."

"You're sure?"

"I checked her pulse, breathing, and eyes myself," Morgana assured her. "Pulse is a little high, but she seems to be dreaming."

Lance nodded in a little in understanding, but it didn't fully dispel his nervousness. "So, she'll wake up soon?"

"She should."

"What about..." Nicki started to ask but trailed off. She looked very worried and was watching Alex's face intently.

"What?" Merlin asked.

"Well... Brekszta," Nicki said. "What if she tries to get at Alex again?"

No one answered the question. No one even met each other's eyes. Morgana sighed, the sound filling the room, and brushed a hand over Alex's forehead. Merlin moved around the back of the sofa and put his hand on the crown of Alex's hand. Alex's eyes fluttered again, and a soft gasp escaped her. Alex's brow furrowed and Lance found himself stepping forward out of concern. Jenny caught his arm and pulled him back towards the loveseat. Nodding, he sat down next to her. The action spurred the others to sit down except for Merlin and Morgana who stayed with Alex.

"Should I take her back to the bedroom?" Bran asked. He raised his hand and warm yellow magic swirled around his fingertips. "Wouldn't take long, but she'd probably be more comfortable."

Morgana nodded, but Merlin was still staring thoughtfully at Alex. There was a hint of confusion in his brown eyes that worried Lance. After three thousand years the idea of anything confusing Merlin was unsettling. Glancing at Jenny, he found his girlfriend intensely watching Alex like she was trying to unravel all the secrets of how reincarnation worked and why.

Standing up, Bran gave them a reassuring smile and flicked his wrist. Yellow magic swept around Alex's prone form, shrouding her in a veil of shimmering sparks. It made him think of Arto's body wrapped in the mage's magic, and Lance fought back a shiver as Alex's body slowly lifted into the air. Memories teased at his brain. There were visions of strange fields and hills. Odd faces and smells tugged at him. The door had opened, and he struggled to shove it closed. He shook his head and shuddered, pushing away the memories.

They faded quickly like a dream, yet Lance was left with an icy sensation in his chest. If that was what Alex experienced from her other lives, then it was no wonder that she wasn't sleeping. Alex's body was floating gently above the sofa with her blonde hair drifting around her. It was a bit creepy honestly; like something out of a horror film. Bran moved closer to her and turned his hand, making the yellow magic shift.

Suddenly, Alex's body tensed. Her fingers clutched helplessly at the air, grasping for something that wasn't there. Bran froze as Alex's head tossed listlessly and she groaned. Everyone was still and waiting. Morgana started to step closer to Alex, extending a hand into the yellow sparks. Alex's head lashed and the fluttering of her eyelashes increased.

A blood-curdling scream filled the room. Alex's head was thrown back, her mouth open, and her eyes squeezed shut. Morgana pushed through the sparks and took Alex's hand. She spoke to Alex softly with comforting words and put a hand on her cheek. There was another cry and Lance pressed himself against the back of the loveseat.

Morgana said something, but it was lost in another scream. The magic around her rippled and the yellow darkened to gray. Morgana grunted as the gray sparks tried to push her back but didn't let go of Alex's hand. Bran made a strange sound of alarm and Jenny jumped off the loveseat. Alex's back arched and she cried out, the sound echoing through the house. It was a sharp, long, and unnatural sound.

Everyone drew back. Lance couldn't move. Around Alex, the gray magic swirled and tightened. The air hummed dangerously. The scent of ozone hit his nose. Reaching out, he grabbed Jenny and pulled her back onto the loveseat. Twisting his body, he cradled Jenny against his chest and turned his back on Alex. There was a crack. The smell of ozone filled his nose and his arm tightened around Jenny as she shrieked. Behind them there were shouts. Colors flashed around them. Then things went silent. He turned to look behind them.

Alex was back on the sofa, her eyes slowly opening as she groaned softly and stretched. There were strange dark marks across the walls of the room. The back of the sofa looked scorched. The other mages were spread out through the room, their hands in front of them surrounded by shades of their magic. Everything was very still. Then Alex shifted and began to sit up, blinking her eyes and rubbing her head. No one said anything.

18

Pookas and Sídhe

4 64 B.C.E. The Golden Vale, Ireland

There were traces of frost on the ground that crackled against the soles of his leather shoes. Leugio looked out across the landscape and exhaled slowly, watching his breath waft into the air. With a huff, he hoisted himself up onto the horse and gripped the rough reins. After years of rarely riding the things, Leugio was beginning to doubt he'd ever be comfortable on them. It wasn't enough that a year ago he'd entered a Sídhe mount to save his sister, but now he was subjected to frequent summons that forced him onto horses.

It was enough to almost make him laugh. Somehow his life had completely changed course. He'd been a shepherd who was good at woodworking and did the occasional artisan project to get his family something nice. He'd been the man of the family due to his father's death, but nothing special. Now he was called to aid his king and riding along with the king's daughter.

Flaitheas laughed, the sound ringing in the cool stiff air. It made Leugio smile automatically, and he glanced her way. Her long brown hair was piled in a complicated mess of braids on her head, with a few golden beads woven in for show.

"I'm sorry," Flaitheas said suddenly.

"Uh, for what?" Leugio looked around, worried that he'd missed something.

"Father keeps calling you back: that has to be difficult," Flaitheas explained. "Leaving your life over and over again. I was just thinking to myself about how odd it all must be for you."

"I don't mind so much," Leugio answered as his cheeks warmed. Flaitheas had been thinking about him. The very thought made his chest tighten. "My life isn't so interesting back home. My family is fine without me. There are plenty of others who can watch the sheep."

"It's strange still to think of you as a shepherd." Flaitheas shifted on her horse and studied him thoughtfully. "I suppose you lack the muscle of my father's soldiers, but none of them have ever entered a Sídhe mound."

Leugio wasn't sure how to take her remark. Was it meant to be some sort of compliment or was she mocking him? He didn't think she was mocking him; Flaitheas was many things, but he'd been around the king and his daughter often enough to know she wasn't cruel. Struggling for something to say, Leugio opened his mouth, but nothing came out.

"That sounded horrible, didn't it?" Flaitheas laughed nervously, the sound making Leugio's stomach twist. She was blushing a little and he stared at her in shock. He couldn't remember her ever being embarrassed. "Sorry, I just meant that you aren't a warrior by trade. That makes what you did for your sister all the braver. I'm not sure I could have gone into a Sídhe mound."

"Uh, thank you."

Leugio didn't know what else to say and they lapsed into silence. He glanced at the two warriors serving as their escort. Both of them were well armed while all he was carrying was an iron sword. Flaitheas' horse drew a little ahead of his as they came down into a small valley. A creek trickled along next to them, and the valley offered protection from the wind.

"We should stop and let the horses rest," one of their escorts said.

"A good idea, Aodh," Flaitheas agreed.

She stopped her horse and dismounted in one smooth, graceful movement. Leugio did not. He almost twisted his ankle when he finally hit the ground. Flaitheas glanced his way with concern, but he smiled in silent reassurance. Flaitheas shook her head and guided her horse to the water, where it began to drink.

Flaitheas, Aodh, and their other guard Nyle quickly pulled out some of their supplies for lunch as Leugio looked around. The valley was small, but there was a collection of boulders off to one side. Something here tickled at his senses and he wasn't sure what it was. He took a drink from his water skin and looked around one more time before joining the others. It was nothing fancy, but the dried meat and bread was welcome. Overhead clouds rolled over the sun and Flaitheas looked up with distaste.

"If it starts storming, we may not make it tonight," Flaitheas complained. "Eat quickly and let's hope the horses will make it."

"We'll make it," Nyle assured her. "You worry too much."

"If we run the horses too hard then we absolutely won't make the village." Aodh was much calmer. "We won't linger too long."

Then Leugio felt something. It was odd, like a whisper in the back of his mind or a hand just barely brushing against his skin. He sniffed at the air as the odd sensation grew and settled into his chest. It was familiar. Leugio froze. In his chest, the small flicker of magic was growing, like embers that had been suddenly fed dry moss. His fingers flexed and the magic started to gather. It was heady and exciting and frightening all at once. Holding back a smile, he struggled to keep the rush of magic away and focused on what was happening. He grasped the iron brooch on his cloak and blinked in surprise as the magic hummed against the metal.

Something moved in the corner of his eye. He heard Aodh make a sound of alarm and glanced towards the man. Something dark and quick passed through his vision too fast for him to see clearly. Leugio looked around, trying to spot whatever it was, but it was either too quick or there were multiples. Shadows were appearing and vanishing out of nothing every time his eyes settled on a spot. In his chest, the magic was dancing in response, but he didn't know what to do with it.

They were always in the corner of his eyes, even as he spun around trying to catch sight of them. An odd sound filled the air; caught between a growl and a laugh. It wasn't frightening exactly, but it made the hairs on the back of his neck stand on end. The shape in the corner of his eye stopped, but Leugio didn't turn to it. Instead, he stayed still and did his best to examine it. The shape was sort of like a dog, reminding him of Kent, but at the same time the shape was a little too fuzzy. It was almost like it wasn't there.

"Pookas," Flaitheas said softly. "Troublemakers. We haven't time for this."

Her words made the pitch of the noise change. It was deeper now, and Leugio's chest tightened with an odd sense of hurt. He wasn't sure what to make of it, but the impression was firmly in place now. Licking his lips, he listened to Flaitheas speak with their escorts in a sharp and clear voice.

"I'm sorry about that," Leugio said. His mouth was moving before he understood what was happening. "I know you don't mean any harm." The hurt was easing and he exhaled slowly. Flaitheas turned to look at him in confusion even as the odd blur of black continued to move behind her back. "We are in a hurry. I'm afraid that there are reports of the Sídhe taking children from a village a few miles from here. We need to get there by sundown and help them. Please, leave us be and let us help those who called for us."

There was another change in tone of the noise around them. Then the black shapes flickering in the corner of Leugio's eyes began to move away. Relaxing slowly, he watched the shapes until they hit the shadow of a tree and vanished. Leugio blinked and exhaled slowly. His eyes were dry and sore, but he couldn't deny a flutter of satisfaction in his chest.

"What just happened?" Flaitheas asked. She was looking around in confusion. "Did you use magic?"

"No," Leugio replied. "I just told them, well, you heard me. I guess they just wanted to play and then realized how serious we were."

"Pookas are trouble."

"Apparently they aren't unreasonable," Leugio said. He shrugged and almost took a step back from the look in Flaitheas' eyes. "I've never encountered them before now."

Then Flaitheas nodded. She still looked bemused; maybe a touch angry, but not at him. A soft chuckle escaped her. Then she sighed in relief and motioned towards the horses. She tossed him a packet of food and then hoisted herself up onto her horse. It seemed the break was already over. Then again, Leugio wasn't sure that he wanted the Pookas to think him a liar. He shoved some smoked meat into his mouth and clambered up onto his own horse. It made a sound of protest but thankfully stayed still long enough for him to balance.

"Hopefully they won't follow us," Aodh muttered. He led them out of the small valley, glancing around nervously. "You can never be sure with Pookas."

"They seemed to understand our situation," Leugio said. "They probably know when to stop."

"Pookas torment villages." Flaitheas turned around on her horse to look back past him. "There are plenty of reports of the bad luck they bring."

"Maybe it was deserved?" Leugio offered. "But let's keep moving and focus on the Sídhe."

Flaitheas' eyes met his and he saw what might have been respect glowing in them. It might have been silly, but he straightened up on the back of his horse. They didn't speak of the Pookas any longer, but Leugio found himself wondering just what they were really like. There'd never been Pookas in his own village, but he'd heard plenty of stories. It seemed at the very least that they disliked the Sídhe, or maybe they had sensed his magic building.

The spark was easing now that they were away from the Pookas. Leugio shifted his reins into his left hand and opened his right. Small white sparks danced out of his fingertips and hovered in the air like snowflakes. He flexed his fingers thoughtfully as the sparks dissipated. It seemed that the magic came more strongly when he was around the Faery creatures. He would have to remember that.

It started to rain and Leugio shuddered as the droplets rolled down his cheeks. His cloak was helping to keep the water off of him, but the wind was picking up. In the distance he could hear the rumble of thunder. Part of him wanted to stop, but the reports of the Sídhe and them taking children kept him going. He remembered all too clearly the terror when he'd realized that Keelia had been taken. That was not something he'd leave others helpless to.

"There it is," Flaitheas said, drawing Leugio's attention to her. Flaitheas was pointing to a collection of buildings on a nearby hill. "We'll be there soon. With any luck, they'll have more information for us. Father is very concerned about all the Sídhe activity."

"I'm in agreement with him," Leugio said darkly. "I don't like all this sudden activity on their part. There were always stories about an occasional sighting or them taking a child, but lately there's just so many."

"Father is worried it means they are planning something big," Flaitheas said. "Or that they have a new leader."

Leugio nodded slowly as he considered the idea. It would explain a great deal, but he had no idea if the different mounds scattered across the land could even communicate. Were they connected at all? Or were there mysterious messengers who had managed to stay hidden from them all? Both ideas made his uneasiness grow and he looked toward Flaitheas, waiting for her to say something more.

She stayed silent, looking out across the landscape with a sad expression. Then she shook her head and gently urged her horse forward. Their small band moved on, but Leugio tensed. In his chest, that odd sensation was building once again. He looked over his shoulder, wondering if the Pookas had followed them without him realizing it. There was nothing that he could see behind them. The dark clouds had blotted out the sun and his sight was limited. Yet there were no shadows in the corner of his eye. They kept moving towards the village, but the feeling didn't ease. It only grew worse.

"Leugio?" Flaitheas called. "Are you alright?"

"I..." He licked his lips. "We need to hurry. Something is coming."

Flaitheas straightened up and looked around them quickly. They seemed to be alone, but Leugio peered down at his hand. White sparks were beginning to gather around his right hand. Flaitheas gasped in surprise.

"There!" Aodh shouted. He gestured to their right.

Five Sídhe appeared on the rise of a small hill. They were all dressed in heavy leather armor and carried bronze swords. Magic rushed through his arms, expanding outward from his chest. It had a core, a center, Leugio realized with surprise. Unsure of what else to do, Leugio tugged at it and the magic came forth.

The Sídhe rushed them. Aodh shouted something, but it was lost in the roars of the Sídhe. White sparks flooded around his hands, illuminating the area around him. One of the Sídhe gaped at him with wide eyes. It lunged at his horse, swinging its bronze sword in an arc through the air. His horse screamed and Leugio tensed as the beast quivered beneath him. In a burst of adrenaline and fear, he jumped off its back and stumbled away. Magic flared in his hand and Leugio spun on his heel to face the Síd. His foot slid on the damp ground, but he stayed upright.

Frantically, he willed the magic into shape. He begged it to stop the Síd. White sparks rushed together and formed a bolt of magic like an arrow. It sped through the air and struck the Síd. The Síd's leather armor fell apart, dropping in pieces to the ground, and it staggered. More magic rushed through his arms and he threw it forward, commanding it to form another arrow. The magic hit again and the Síd vanished in a burst of golden dust.

More magic spilled out of his hands. His heart was racing and the sparks hovered in the air, waiting for him. Leugio's mind sputtered for a moment before grasping onto to the memory of the arrow. He turned to find Nyle fighting sword to sword with one of the Sídhe and Flaitheas dodging a blow from another. Throwing his hand forward, Leugio pushed the magic forth, willing it into another arrow.

The magic responded immediately. All the sparks rushed together and formed into a tight long bolt that sailed through the air. The bolt caught the Sid attacking Flaitheas right in the neck. With a sputter of pain, the creature began to dissolve into golden sparks. There were three left: one was fighting Nyle who was now on foot, and Aodh had two attacking him and his horse. The beast was rearing up and trying to escape the Sídhe, which only made it impossible for his rider to hit either of them. Aodh hit the ground with a groan, barely rolling away from the sharp hooves of his horse.

Leugio opened his hand and more white sparks appeared. Another bolt of white hit one of the Sídhe, which began to turn towards him as its armor collapsed. Leugio called forth the magic and, remembering what had happened in the tunnel, sent a wave of white sparks through the air. They rippled like a lake after a rock was tossed in, shoving the three Sídhe away from the humans. Nyle and Aodh's horses began to run away while the two men shouted.

The three Sídhe were all looking at him now with calculating eyes. Two of the Sídhe still had their weapons. They moved quickly, advancing on him. More white sparks illuminated the hillside. Thunder rolled in the distance and rain droplets hit his cheeks and arms. Panic was beginning to take over as the Sídhe lunged. A bolt of white hit one and he jumped to the side to avoid the other. The third growled at him as the one he'd hit dissolved into gold dust.

"A mage." The Síd glared at him. "The Lord will destroy you. He'll take the world and you'll have no power!"

"A lord?" Leugio repeated. "There's a new leader then?"

The Síd swung at him, and white magic flashed off his hands. A bolt of white slammed into the Síd, who screamed as the magic flickered across its body. Leugio's eyes swung to the third Síd that was running away. Nyle, on his horse, rushed over and struck it in the neck with his iron blade. It fell to the ground and began to dissolve. Exhaling, Leugio urged his heart to slow down and gasped for air. His knees trembled for a moment, but he managed to keep standing.

Flaitheas was still on her horse and the other two were finally coming back around on their steeds. She was staring down at him even as her eyes darted to the now empty space where the Sídhe had been. The awe radiating off her helped Leugio stay calm. The magic in his chest was dimming slightly, but he was aware of it. Ready and waiting.

"Your magic..." Flaitheas started to say. She shook her head. "It's amazing."

"Thank you," Leugio replied softly. He was looking down at his hands and smiled a little. "I'm getting better at using it." Then he looked over at his horse, it was moving badly, with a slash across one flank. "That's not good."

"You can ride with me," Flaitheas said quickly. "We should be able to get help in the village." She looked at him and nodded. "And now, perhaps we know what is happening."

"A new leader," Leugio agreed. "I don't like the sound of it."

"Neither do I and nor will father." Flaitheas seemed like she wanted to say more, but a flash of lightning made her grimace. The rain had yet to ease. "Come on, Leugio." She held a hand out to him and Leugio eyed the horse doubtfully. He looked back at his own horse, but Nyle had taken the reins and was leading it slowly. "I promise I won't laugh," Flaitheas promised. "You just killed three Sídhe. No one is going to judge you about being bad on horses."

Holding back a laugh, Leugio climbed on behind her. After a moment of hesitation, he rested his hands on her hips, not sure what else to do with them. Nyle caught his eye and grinned. Leugio knew his cheeks were heating up but pointedly ignored it as Flaitheas urged the horse forward.

19

News Comes

Alex's eyes struggled to adjust to the light. Her arms shuddered as she tried to lift herself up and then gave out, sending her sprawling back onto the soft surface again. In her chest her heart was racing so hard that her ribs were aching. The flutter of magic in her gut was hot and filled her limbs with a heavy hum. Every muscle was ready for a fight. Alex quickly took stock. She was on a soft surface, but it wasn't her bed. She was dressed in her jeans, and her shoes were still on. There was an ache spreading through her chest, different from the muscle ache and familiar. Too much magic, a voice supplied helpfully, but Alex pushed it away.

Sitting up a little, she turned her head and exhaled in relief. She was in Merlin's living room with the mages. The others were exchanging nervous looks that Alex didn't understand, but she didn't have the energy to ask. A slight smell of smoke reached her nose and she turned to inspect the sofa. There were small burn marks on it. She didn't remember those.

"Did I....?" she asked softly.

"You discharged some magic," Merlin said easily. He sounded very calm. "Don't worry about it. Simple enough to fix. Are you alright?"

Alex's mouth still tasted of ash. She could still hear that sharp wind. But she didn't want to reveal any of that. Instead, she pushed a little harder against her quivering arms and sat up. Morgana leaned forward and gripped her arm, helping her swing around so she could slump against the back of the sofa.

"Thanks," Alex said with a forced smile. Her throat hurt a bit; a dull, scratching sensation. "I'm okay."

Morgana looked at her with sharp, irritated green eyes that spoke volumes. Pushing herself into the back of the sofa, Alex tried to make herself smaller under that gaze. Then Nicki came over with a glass of water. Taking it with a soft smile, Alex sipped slowly at first and then started gulping down the cool liquid. It sent a small jolt of pain up through her skull but soothed the heat in her throat.

"You were screaming," Nicki told her unhelpfully. "What did you dream about? Was it Brekszta again?"

"Uh... yeah," Alex answered. She licked her lips and dropped her eyes to the glass of water. Taking another sip, she avoided Nicki's eyes. "It was weird."

"Alex?" Merlin called, a hint of warning in his voice. It rang through her head and some part of her was instantly cowed. "What happened?"

"I, uh..." Alex looked up at Merlin and then at Morgana. Then her eyes jumped over to the other mages, then to Lance and Jenny who were frowning deeply at her. "It's hard to explain... I did get pulled back into that nightmare. There was this fog and I could see some figures, but I didn't want to see those people again." She dropped her eyes, gripping the glass of water tightly. "So, I pulled on my magic and everything changed."

"Changed how?" Morgana asked gently. The older mage sat down on the sofa next to her, wrapping an arm around her shoulders. "Alex, what happened?"

"I'm not sure." Alex shuddered; the memory of that dark sky full of debris haunting her. "It was just some scary images," she said. "Brekszta was probably trying to scare me." She drained the last of the glass of water and smacked her lips together. "Wouldn't mind some more water."

Nicki's eyes narrowed, but she took the glass back. Something in her gaze warned Alex that this wasn't over. Then again, she wouldn't be able to hide her tossing and turning from her roommate. She forced her hands to stay still and inhaled slowly as she rolled her shoulders carefully. The ache was still there. Her skin was rough and raw like she'd truly been sandblasted on a strange world.

"What did she show you to scare you?" Merlin asked. He was watching her closely and Alex had no doubt both he and Morgana knew she was being evasive.

"It was the fog again like I said." The whispers in the back of Alex's mind grew louder now. A few were insisting that she tell them everything while others were mistrustful. Licking her lips, Alex blinked as Nicki returned with some more water for her. She gave her roommate a small smile and took a sip. "I used my magic to force it back."

"That must have been the reaction here," Morgana said. When Alex blinked in surprise, Morgana chuckled darkly and gestured to the walls. Alex's eyes widened as she took in the dark marks scattered across the room. "Bran was trying to move you back to the bedroom using magic when your power took over his and discharged. Don't worry, you didn't harm anyone."

"Oh." Alex dropped her eyes and took another long drink from the glass of water. "Well, I saw something new after I pushed back the fog.

I'm not sure where I was, but it was this strange dead place. There were ruins and debris everywhere. The ground was all ash and soot." Her hands trembled at the memory. "There was nothing alive there."

Morgana's hand rubbed her back again and the older mage pulled her a little closer. Soft lips pressed against Alex's forehead, surprising her for a moment. "Brekszta was just trying to frighten you," Morgana said gently. "It was just a nightmare."

"Most likely a vision of Earth destroyed," Merlin added. "As you said, she was just trying to frighten you. Remember that while Brekszta's ability to invade your dreams is disturbing, you cannot be harmed in them."

They were trying to comfort her, but they were wrong. It hadn't been some nightmare of Earth. That statue had been old: a remnant of the civilization that was destroyed by whatever had happened. The sun was too close, yet the sky too dark. Whatever she'd seen hadn't been Earth. Alex was certain that she'd forced back Brekszta's influence, so that vision had come from something else. There was a vague suspicion at the back of her mind amongst the whispers, but she couldn't fully form it. Couldn't explain or name it and it began to slip away.

"Anyway, I'm sorry I frightened all of you," Alex finally said. "Maybe I need to meditate more even though I have control over my magic. Maybe that will help with the dreams."

"You might even be able to put up some kind of barriers in your mind," Aiden suggested. "That's something you see in a lot of fantasy stuff."

"Not sure how I'd even start." Alex laughed a little and Aiden visibly relaxed at the sound. "But I'll give it a shot."

Suddenly something made Alex's magic flare in her chest. It sent a jolt of heat into her heart and made Alex look around in confusion. A small dark shape in the corner of her eye made Alex straighten up in alarm.

"Guys-"

The little shape ran across the floor and Jenny caught sight of it. She squealed and grabbed Lance's arm. "Mouse!"

"No, it's not!" Merlin shouted. He opened his palm and green magical sparks erupted around his fingers.

"No, Timothy!" A small voice called up. Merlin stopped and everyone was still for a moment. "I'm back!"

Alex released a sigh of relief as the small Brownie bounced up onto the coffee table. He was dressed in a cloak that looked like it had been made from a small cloth bag. He smiled up at her before looking around.

"Everyone's alright? Good!" Timothy cheered. He looked back at Alex and frowned a little. "I come with news from other Fairies."

"Is it about the Red Caps in town?" Jenny asked.

"There are Red Caps in town?" Alex's eyes widen and on impulse she started to stand only for Morgana to grip her shoulder to keep her in place. "When did that happen?"

"Jenny and I were attacked earlier today," Lance explained gently. "We're fine. We got away and came straight here to wait for all of you to come back from making the Gate."

"Red Caps are already here then," Timothy sighed. The creature's head dropped sadly and he shook his head. "I was hoping to get back before them."

"Then you knew they were coming?" There was a hint of anger and panic in Alex's voice. She bit her lower lip. "Are more coming?"

"I don't know," Timothy said. He looked up at Alex with watery dark eyes. "Some Faeries were friendly and glad to be free of spell, but Red Caps have always been..." Timothy shuddered. "Violent and nasty."

"And they seem to be immune to the blood spell," Morgana added. "Or at least some of them are. We can hope that they all haven't gotten through."

"Is it because I put in the exception?" Alex asked, looking up at Morgana. "Did I weaken the spell too much?"

"One, you didn't do that on purpose and two, I doubt your compassion is the problem," Morgana answered quickly. She gave Alex an almost stern look. "So don't put this on yourself, Alex."

"It may be a side effect from the power of the Chain," Merlin suggested. He hummed thoughtfully for a moment, drumming his fingers on the back of the sofa. "They were exposed to the magic of the Iron Realm for several months, and more correctly the power of the Iron Soul. While the Iron Chain was made by a darker life, his personality may have had some impact on how certain creatures reacted to the Chain."

Managing a nod, Alex kept her mouth tightly closed as her stomach turned. The memory of that slave ship was too clear in her mind. Those poor people that had been bound and their dead eyes were more vivid in her mind than some of her most precious childhood memories. Cuthbert's memories were getting sharper and stronger while her own were fading away. She held back a shudder and turned her attention to Timothy.

"Well, thank you for trying to warn us; at least no one was hurt."

"Still, we need to go and deal with these things," Morgana said. Merlin nodded in agreement and Jenny looked at them both in alarm. "Merlin and I can go hunting later tonight."

"But Faeries are coming to talk!" the Brownie shouted. Timothy's words drew everyone's attention. "That is other news," Timothy said. He looked embarrassed now. "Some of the Faeries I spoke to are coming to talk. They want to know what happened and help spread the information. Spell went far and was felt by all."

"Right," Nicki said. "That makes sense if you think about it. If I was taken over by a spell that made me violent and want to seek out mages I'd want to know how and why it happened."

"It's understandable," Bran agreed. "But what do we tell them?" Frowning, he glanced towards Alex and offered her an apologetic look before turning to Merlin. "I mean, it was done using an item made by the Iron Soul. That's not going to look good."

Merlin's eyes narrowed. Alex looked up at him and sighed. "They've got a point," Alex said. She scuffed her feet against the floor as her stomach churned painfully. "We probably need to be braced for some anger."

"It wasn't your fault," Aiden said. He was all but glowering. "You didn't cast the spell, the Queen did."

"Scáthbás' return frightens many." Timothy's voice trembled and Alex looked back at him sharply. "News is spreading. I answered what questions I could, but there will be more."

"That's to be expected." Morgana lowered her hand and rubbed Alex's back once more. "You said that the Faeries are coming to talk? What sort of representatives are we dealing with?"

"Volunteers from some of the colonies," Timothy answered quickly. "There are a few from further away who were drawn here by the spell and want to learn more before they return to their homes."

"How many are we talking about?" Lance asked. "And where?"

"Not sure how many, maybe a dozen. They're outside of town, on one of the trails," Timothy said.

"Is there a cave they're using?" Jenny asked.

"No, a few of the Sídhe have RVs."

It would have been funny under other circumstances, but right now it just reminded Alex of how the creatures lived on the outer edges of their world. They traveled at night, stayed underground or in shaded cities. She wondered how many there really were now, how organized they were, and if they had some sort of governments. Timothy used the term colonies, so were there democratic councils or a ruling prince? Did they organize markets in abandoned subway tunnels? It made her head hurt and her imagination spring into action.

"Is there a time they want to meet us?" Morgana asked. "Or were you to organize that?"

"Not so much." Timothy shifted uneasily again. "I came rushing because I overheard a group talking about the Red Caps they'd met on the way. They weren't with the others and I got worried."

"So, you aren't a spokesman for the others," Merlin said. His gaze narrowed and he looked towards the window. "How organized are they?"

"Not very," Timothy answered. "Staying in a large group now, but the different Faeries don't really trust each other. Everyone tends to stay with their own kind except for trading. Spell made everything worse and everyone is mad at each other."

"And those descended from the original Sídhe invaders?" Morgana leaned forward, her dark eyes glittering. "How are they being regarded?"

"Uh..." The Brownie seemed panicked, his eyes moving from mage to mage. Sympathy welled up in Alex's chest.

"Honestly everyone, Timothy isn't going to notice everything. Not when there is so much going on. He's a house Brownie, not a diplomat or a spy." Alex tried to keep her tone light but was afraid that her own nervousness crept through. Smiling down at the Brownie, Alex avoided thinking too much about the look of adoration Timothy was giving her. "Was there anything odd you noticed– anything that seemed out of place? Any strange behavior?"

"Well, a lot of them are together, which is strange," Timothy admitted. "The Sídhe seemed very quiet and thoughtful: they didn't talk much with any of the others, but they did let us on their RVs," Timothy said helpfully.

"And are they waiting for us now?" Alex asked. "Do you need to go back and let them know first or should we just go and see them?"

"Alex, now isn't a good idea," Morgana said quickly. "You're-"

"I'm fine," Alex said. "I can still use magic; besides, the longer we make them wait the tenser things could get. It just seems like a bad idea, especially if they don't usually stay together."

"If all the others are together, how did the Red Caps get here?" Jenny asked. "I mean they aren't tall enough to drive."

"The RVs did have to stop for gas at a truck stop," Timothy offered, turning to look at Jenny. "They could have gotten in a truck coming here."

"I hope we aren't going to find reports of a murdered truck driver," Lance said. He shuddered and pulled Jenny a bit closer.

"Yeah, thinking about that isn't helping." Alex slipped out of Morgana's grip and stood up, brushing off her jeans. "Anyway, we should probably head out to meet them."

"Alex, Morgana and I can go. There is no need for you to come with us," Merlin said. Standing up quickly, he gave her what he probably thought was a reassuring smile.

"You and Morgana don't have the best history with the Sídhe," Alex said bluntly. "I get that you want me safe, but the Iron Soul not coming with you could easily be taken the wrong way."

"She has a point," Bran agreed. "So, you three have to go, but the question is do you want Nicki, Aiden, and I to go with you or stay in Ravenslake?"

"We could follow you or head downtown and see if we can find the Red Caps," Aiden added. "I mean, we need to contain them before they hurt anyone."

Morgana frowned at them before her expression softened sadly. "Children... you do understand that you're talking about hunting them down? I know that you've killed Faeries in combat before, but they've always attacked you. Going looking for them is ... different."

Aiden, Nicki, and Bran exchanged a look. Their shoulders tightened and Alex could do nothing but watch a parade of emotions pass through their eyes. The idea of hunting made her own stomach turn, but then again, she knew so would a report of a murder in the morning. It was Bran who sighed first.

"I'll stay and patrol town," he said. "I don't like it and I get what you're saying, but what else can we do? I won't attack them unless they're going after someone or attack me." He shook his head. "That's the best I can offer."

"I'll go with you," Aiden said quickly. He straightened up a little and while he was a bit pale, his determination was clear.

Nicki nodded in agreement. "We'll look after town then."

"Lance and I could come to the meeting with iron swords," Jenny suddenly offered. "I know we aren't mage backup, but maybe having some baseline humans will be reassuring to the Faeries. We're on the same playing field as most of them."

Alex was silent as Jenny looked hopefully at Lance, who nodded. Without a word Merlin went to collect two of the swords. Timothy studied all of them, clearly picking up on the underlying tension. As

Merlin handed the swords to Lance and Jenny, he said something to them. They nodded in agreement, each taking a sword.

"Are we leaving now?" Timothy asked.

"I guess so," Alex said. "It isn't evening yet, but it will be soon enough."

"Twilight is better for us," Morgana said. "Lets us fall back if needed while letting the Faeries outside without harming their eyes. We are not going into the RVs, no matter what."

"Okay," Alex agreed.

Timothy bounced down from the coffee table and up onto the arm of the sofa next to Alex. "A moment, Timothy," Merlin called, walking over to them. "How did you get into the house without help? I understand that the blood protection spell doesn't repel you, but there is iron in all the door frames and windows."

"Oh, I found a mouse hole," Timothy answered. The Brownie smiled up at the professor who blinked in poorly contained horror. "Don't worry. Too small for anything other than mice and Brownies to squeeze through."

"Wow," Nicki laughed, biting her lower lip. "You must be very flexible."

"Brownie magic helps too," Timothy said. He waved his hand merrily. "Can't do much, but it helps get jobs done."

"Someday I'm going to have to study Brownie magic," Merlin muttered. "It has never made sense to me at all. They're one of the only Sídhe relative species that have hung on to their magic. I know their world is close to ours, but really!"

The blend of irritation, frustration, and curiosity in his voice made Alex smile. In the back of her head, she heard a couple of other voices chuckling warmly at the old mage's antics. Alex wasn't sure how many there were; the amused sounds all blurred together, but it provided a brief sense of comradery. Merlin shook his head and said something under his breath. Alex glanced around to find her shoulder bag and opened the front pocket for Timothy. The Brownie jumped inside and smiled at her before ducking down into the protective shade. They were off to meet with the Faeries. It was turning into one hell of a day.

20

Meeting the Faeries

Alex was all too aware of the heavy silence in the SUV as they drove out of town. Her muscles still ached, but the burning pain from using too much magic had dulled and she was confident that she could use more if needed. She drummed her fingers on her knees and watched the trees rush by her window.

Merlin turned the wheel of the SUV and they pulled off the highway. A worn gravel road headed into the trees and Alex licked her lips nervously. In the front Merlin and Morgana glanced at each other and Alex's hand slipped into her bag, closing around the hilt of her dagger.

"You still doing okay, Timothy?" Alex asked.

"Yes," the small voice of the Brownie answered.

Leaning forward, Alex looked out the front window as three parked RVs came into view. The campsite was otherwise empty and she could see the trail leading up into the hills between two of the RVs. Tucked back in the shade of the trees, the RVs were dark and quiet. Merlin turned the SUV around and carefully positioned them so the nose was towards the road. Good for a quick escape.

"Well, here we are," Morgana said. She turned and looked back at Alex and then out the back window. "If things turn violent, Alex, get back in the SUV."

"I'll leave the keys in the ignition," Merlin said. "Leave if we tell you to."

Alex didn't say anything. She couldn't agree to it but knew better than to say she wouldn't go. Morgana's eyes lingered on her for a moment, but Alex stayed silent. Then the older mage sighed and opened her door. Climbing out, Alex looked towards the collection of RVs parked in the small camping area. Nothing about them looked odd or out of place except being out a bit earlier in spring than usual. They were still, but Alex could hear voices even across the campground. The leaves of the trees surrounding them rustled in the wind but provided a spotty patch of shade.

Alex opened the front pocket of her bag and offered her hand to help Timothy. The Brownie scrambled out and onto her palm before racing up her arm to settle on her shoulder. Suppressing a shiver, Alex glanced towards Merlin and Morgana, waiting for guidance. The two elder mages were shoulder to shoulder and eyeing the RVs with frowns.

The slam of another set of car doors behind them reminded Alex that Lance and Jenny were here as well. Turning to look over her shoulder, she found them with the sheathed swords in their hands and standing in front of Lance's truck. Jenny offered her a real if uneasy smile. Alex nodded to them, silently thanking them for coming along.

The door of the first RV opened with a squeal that made Alex shiver. Sídhe descendants, who were almost the same height as her, stepped out first. Smaller creatures jumped down the metal folding stairs of the RV around them. The rest of the RVs opened and their occupants filed out. Without any words, they spread out in the shade and studied them curiously. There really were a bunch of different sorts. Alex's eyes jumped between the different types of Faeries as her brain struggled to identify them. There were more Brownies like Timothy and a few other smaller creatures. There were several Sídhe descendants who could pass as pale humans with hoods pulled over their heads.

The Faeries spread out in the shade, forming a line of alien creatures against the spring green of the trees and undergrowth. Alex shifted so that her shadow kept Timothy out of direct sunlight. To her surprise the Brownie leaped off her shoulder and landed in the trod down dirt with a soft thump. Timothy brushed off his pants and went over to join a small group of Brownies near an RV wheel. He hugged one of them and nodded to the others.

"Greetings," Merlin said. His voice rang through the campground, echoing with power as he stood straight and looked at each of the creatures in turn with his dark brown eyes. "I am known as Merlin." There were whispers amongst the Faeries, but none of them moved away.

"I am Morgana." Alex could see Morgana sizing up all the creatures, though her gaze lingered on the Sídhe descendants. "This is Alexandra, the current incarnation of the Iron Soul."

Blinking, Alex tried to keep her surprise off her face. She hadn't expected Merlin and Morgana to be so blunt about who she was. Unsure of what to do when so many violet and black eyes turned to her, Alex nodded in greeting.

In the corner of her eye, Alex saw small shadowy creatures moving amongst the trees. They flickered in and out of her sight, but she was left with an impression of a dog like creature. Turning her head, she stared nervously into the shadows, worried that something else had found them.

"Pookas," Morgana said softly. "Don't try to look at them. Direct sight usually doesn't work."

"Oh." Swallowing, Alex filed that information away and tried not to stare at the different creatures in front of her.

"The two behind us are humans named Jenny and Lance," Morgana added. She gestured to them, almost dismissively. "They are allies of Alexandra."

"We're here to discuss recent events," Merlin said, drawing attention back to himself. "I'm certain that you must have questions. Your people have lived in relative peace in our world for generations. What happened must have come as a shock."

"Timothy says that Scáthbás cast the spell on all of us," one of the small Brownies said. It made an impressive jump up onto the top of one of the RVs. The Brownie looked a lot like Timothy with the same ears and dark eyes, but an older looking face. This one was dressed in what looked like a doll's old military uniform. "That can't possibly be true."

"Scáthbás is a myth!" one Faery shouted.

"She died during the war!" another insisted. "It couldn't be her!"

"Something with power cast that spell." Merlin's voice was patient, though his eyes were not. "And surely you don't believe that we mages ordered you to attack us?"

"You might have," another creature said. This one was taller, almost as tall as them with a misshapen chin and nose. It sneered. "How many of our brothers and sisters did you destroy?" It sniffed at the air and looked at Morgana. "There are stories about the pair of you as well. Parents warn their children to stay away from the mages, but most of all Morgana le Fey." The creature's voice went low and gravely. "Her hatred of any Faery creatures is a legend in of itself. Raised by Scáthbás and then betraying her. Maybe you cast that spell just to have an excuse!'

There were murmurs of agreement and fear in the small crowd. Alex's eyes jumped to Morgana. Anger welled in her chest on Morgana's behalf. Something at the back of her mind flashed hot and bright. There was a girl with her hand in a bowl of blood, screaming in pain. There was an expression of defeat and horror on the face of a younger Morgana as droplets of glowing blood ran across a green hillside.

"There were no options open to us," Morgana snapped. She glared at the creature, smiling slightly when it shuffled back. "The loss of life was regrettable, but they were compelled to kill mages and so we had to defend ourselves. Debating the morality between two groups who lack their freedom of choice is pointless. Any mage will and must fight to protect their lives so that we can safeguard the Iron Realm."

"I don't believe it!" A voice near the back called out. "Dead or myth, it couldn't have been Scáthbás!"

"She survived the war, I fear." Merlin's brow was furrowing and Alex saw him casually lift his right hand. He was ready to summon his magic. Beneath her feet, Alex could feel the hum of the ground and her own magic stirred. "Her essence was trapped in an Iron Gate, and when it eroded, she was released. We believe that she became a wraith of some sort and possessed a human woman. With the artifact she used to ensnare you, she made herself half-Sídhe by killing Sídhe descendants. She has also successfully created another half-mage half-Changeling creature. We have since destroyed the artifact, but her power and influence are still very much a concern."

"If that's true, then Scáthbás pulled one over on you." This time it was a small pale creature, just over three feet high that spoke. It had pointed ears and unusually large purple eyes. "She's part human and part Sídhe like the two of you."

"She is not like us!" Morgana snapped. Rage exploded across her features, but the mage quickly regained control. "Merlin's existence was allowed by the Iron Realm itself and I am loyal to the Iron Realm. Scáthbás took possession of a human body and then bound Sídhe flesh into herself and that of her son."

"Legends say that you were bound with your Changeling form," the pixie-like creature said. Its gaze jumped between Merlin, Morgana, and Alex. "You were made by the Queen, not by the Iron Realm."

"Morgana was also the sister of the first Iron Soul," Merlin offered smoothly. "I have long believed that Arto's faith in her impacted the Iron Realm's acceptance of her."

Morgana said nothing and didn't look at Merlin. Alex wondered if that was true at all or just a nice little story to tell the Faeries in these circumstances. Nonetheless, she felt a stirring of affection for both older mages that briefly overpowered the churning worry. She didn't like the thoughtful expressions on the faces of some of the Faeries. It was too calculating as the fear melted away.

"This is quite the story you came to tell us," the knotted nose Faery said. It was almost smiling; almost looked amused as it peered towards the Pixie down the line. "Convenient."

"Nevertheless, Queen Scáthbás is alive," Merlin said. He was far too calm now and the air around him was too still. The Faeries shifted and looked nervously at each other. Alex caught a few glints of curiosity, but most of their eyes were fearful or dismissive. "I do not know what stories you may have of her amongst your communities, but she was an intelligent and brutal leader of the Sídhe. Most of you are not descendants of her warriors: most of you are descendants of those she enslaved. You are in this world because, as her forces were defeated, your ancestors decided life hiding in a world of iron was better than enslavement. Scáthbás has already proven happy to use you against the Iron Realm, and make no mistake, if she finds another way to use you, she will."

"But you killed them," one of the smaller creatures said. It had twisted legs and tiny nubs on its forehead. Not a Sídhe, but something else. It was glaring right at Alex. "You mages killed dozens of our kind!"

"I'm sorry." Alex meant the words. She heard Morgana make a small noise but ignored it. "But they had orders to kill us. We didn't know what was happening and had to fight for survival."

"Yet now the spell is gone!" the same creature shouted. Alex wanted to ask its name, but the way those dark, little brown eyes were fixed on her made her nervous. "You say that we are free, but are we truly? How do you know?"

"The artifact that was the focus of the spell has been broken." Alex's voice wavered and she scanned the small group of Fae. None looked convinced. "I destroyed it myself using the Iron Hammer created by the Iron Soul Thor. Believe me, I hated that artifact as well, and I smashed it to break its hold. The remains are in our hands now, beyond the power of Scáthbás. Its power cannot be used anymore."

"For now," the creature with the knobs grumbled. "Until the next plot by you mages, the Queen, or the Old Ones!"

There was a rush of noise as the creatures turned and talked to each other. Staying silent, Alex noticed that some were looking at her angrily. Others looked fearful, some curious but worst of all was the resignation in the eyes of some of them. They were all so different. Some of the creatures almost looked human and wouldn't have gotten much attention in a big city. Others were small like the Brownies with a variety of skin tones and eyes colors. The Sídhe descendants hung at the edges of the group. A pair of young-looking ones were holding hands. Their sweatshirts were ragged and hung awkwardly over their thin frames.

Refugees. The word made Alex's heart clench. Her breath fled her and her knees quivered. They were born here and yet... the world itself would never accept them. Always on the edge of society, living together, and just trying to survive. The anger, fear, and resignation made too much sense.

"We're going to keep fighting Scáthbás," Alex said. Morgana made a soft sound of warning, but Alex ignored her. She needed to say something: she couldn't just stand next to Merlin and Morgana like a puppet waiting for its strings to be pulled. "Her... son, Arthur, the creature that Merlin spoke of murdered my parents." Cold rushed through her body; her knees buckled and Alex feared that she'd fall over. In her chest, the knot tightened and her magic rushed to contain the storm of emotions. "You need to understand what he is; what they both are. I'm sorry for what happened to you, I'm sorry about those you lost, but don't let Scáthbás and Arthur use them against you. They don't care about you."

"Neither do you," the Pixie said. Those large purple eyes were fixed on her. Alex opened her mouth to argue that she had basic compassion and of course she cared, but the Pixie wasn't done. "Why is there a protector of the Iron Realm? Why is there an Iron Soul and yet nothing rose up to save our home worlds before they were enslaved?" Many of the Faeries nodded in agreement and called out for an answer.

"I-"

"We are mages of the Iron Realm," Merlin all but shouted. The Faeries quieted once more. "We cannot speak as to why certain things happened or didn't happen on your home worlds. Our power is from this world: our role and our place are here. Consider that maybe there were defenses but that they fell to the Sídhe. I doubt your ancestors just surrendered to slavery. That is your history, not ours." Inhaling slowly, Alex watched as Merlin tensed and shook his head. "I am sorry for the harm done to your ancestors and the realities you face in this world. That sympathy, and the fact that you don't cause trouble, is why Morgana and I have left you alone. Do not change that."

The words hung in the air, icy and still. It was like the lingering ring of a church bell over a graveyard, heavy with a sense of finality. Morgana was staring down some of the Faeries and Alex was at a loss of what to do. She quickly found Timothy amongst the Brownies. He looked sad and disappointed but resigned. Alex wondered who he was disappointed in. Her gaze moved back to the Pixie who was frowning thoughtfully. The creature with the crooked nose was glaring at Merlin while the Faery with the knobbed head was almost smirking. All three expressions nagged at her. This wasn't the end of it.

"If you hear anything that might be of use, send us a message." Morgana's voice cut through the silence. "You can reach me easily enough through the name Morgana Cornwall."

"And I can be reached through the name Ambrose Yates," Merlin added. "Thank you for meeting with us. Do take care." His lighter tone didn't ease the earlier threat. "I hope we will all be able to return to our peaceful lives soon."

Alex's eyes jumped back to the Brownies, suddenly uncertain of if Timothy was coming with them. The familiar small shape hugged one of the Brownies and waved before rushing across the ground to Alex's feet.

"Timothy?" the Pixie called. "You're going with them?"

Timothy stopped and turned back to them. Alex craned her neck a bit looking down for a moment before she knelt. Opening the front pocket of her bag, she said nothing as Timothy shifted between his feet.

"Iron Soul freed me when I almost killed her," Timothy said softly. "I can't help much, but I can take messages back and forth. Brownies hide easily."

"We have phones," the Pixie replied dryly, glaring at Alex now. "You don't have to stay with them."

"I want to help." Timothy sighed and his ears drooped. "Even if only helping care for a home. It's what Brownies do."

There were murmurs from the Faeries, but none of them said anything as Timothy climbed back into Alex's bag. The Pixie was still glaring at her and the crooked nose creature was whispering to another Faery. Alex wanted to ask why they personally hated her so much, but she could guess. They'd lost track of the Faeries that had attacked them. Alex had no idea how many she'd killed herself.

Alex frowned. Her mouth turned and her brows shifted. A teasing voice that sounded like Jenny warned her that she'd get wrinkles. Yet she couldn't stop. Her mind was a mess of the whispers and a hundred different thoughts that all pulled in different directions. There was guilt yes, absolutely there was guilt, but there was also a bitter sense of resignation that she didn't like.

This was war. That thought solidified all too easily.

21

Making Plans

464 B.C.E. Cashel, Ireland

Frustration radiated from Flaitheas as they rode. While her horse wasn't moving quickly, there was a deliberation in its pace that matched that of its mistress. Leugio found himself watching her with worry. A look back at Aodh and Nyle riding behind them assured him that they were just as concerned.

"Flaitheas?" Leugio urged his horse closer to hers. "Are you alright?"

"I'm fine," she snapped. Then she sighed and shook her head a little. "I'm sorry, Leugio. I'm just frustrated."

"We were able to stop the Sídhe in the area," Leugio reminded her. "Hopefully those people will be safe for a time."

"Yes, the Sídhe have retreated into their mound," Flaitheas agreed. "But for how long? Part of me thinks we should gather an army and go into their mounds to finish this, once and for all."

"No!" Leugio shouted the word before he even thought about it. Flaitheas looked at him quickly. "I don't think that's a good idea, Flaitheas."

"But we can't do this forever, Leugio," Flaitheas said. She sighed again and tightened her grip on the reins of her horse. "The Sídhe are scattered across the land in different kingdoms and are uniting under some mysterious lord. How long do we wait? I know going into their mounds, into their territory is dangerous, but isn't it worse to just wait around?"

"We don't know enough yet," Leugio said. "They've been peaceful for so long. Maybe some are still peaceful. Besides, a full war against them would hurt all of us as well."

"Maybe. But I want to know who this lord of theirs is and how to stop him." She peered at him sternly. "Do you think your magic can help?"

"I don't know," Leugio admitted. "I've never used it for much. It's strongest around the Sídhe."

"There, you see." Flaitheas looked at him triumphantly. "That means that you have magic for fighting them. Just like the old stories said."

"Yes, but I don't know much about how my magic works," Leugio said. "I'll practice of course and see if it can help me learn more about the Sídhe and what they are doing, but we need to be careful." He tried to smile for her even as a knot formed in his gut. "I am only one mage."

Flaitheas just smiled softly at him. The triumph had faded and there was a hint of understanding in her eyes. He wasn't sure how to interpret it. His chest tightened and he was aware of his own sweaty palms. It was completely ridiculous.

"I have faith in you," Flaitheas finally said. She looked ahead of them at the rolling hills once more. "Even before you knew you had magic; you were willing to enter a Sídhe mound for your sister."

"She's my sister," Leugio replied quickly. "Of course, I'd fight for her."

"I envy you that." Flaitheas glanced his way again. "I always wanted a sibling, but both my brothers died and after mother passed..." She trailed off and shook her head. "Well, I'm afraid it's just me and Father. I suppose that's why he's so eager for me to have children. He worries about what will happen after he dies."

"I'm sure your father has many years left."

"I hope so, but these Sídhe attacks are worrying him greatly. Even the ones in the other areas that don't concern his subjects have him troubled. Another king could try to take advantage."

That was a possibility that hadn't occurred to Leugio. He was a shepherd in his own mind despite his magic. He didn't like the idea of waiting for there to be attacks in other areas, but at the same time, he didn't want to lose family and friends to another series of raids. Swallowing, he pushed the idea aside. The best thing he could do right now was focus on the Sídhe threat, but if they were active in other areas, what was he supposed to do?

"Are the attacks bad in other areas?" It was hard to ask the question.

"No worse than here," Flaitheas replied. "Some kidnappings and a few outright attacks, but nothing too bad. The other kings are sending troops around like my father is. Though as far as I know our kingdom is the only one to have a mage."

Leugio didn't know what to say to that. On one hand, it pleased him. He was the only mage: the only one who could do magic. On the other hand, he felt guilty for even the brief flicker of pleasure that had given him. The Sídhe were turning dangerous once more. They weren't content to just occasionally cause trouble now. They were actively taking steps that could lead to a war, and he was the only mage. All those other areas lacked magic to help them.

"Flaitheas…" he trailed off and tried to find the right words. "If things get bad someplace else… I'd feel like I needed to go. Even if it is outside your father's kingdom." The words hung in the air, suffocating him as Flaitheas remained silent.

Then she nodded and sighed a little. "I understand," she said. "And in that case, I'd suggest to Father that I go with you. If he argued with that, then I'd understand you needing to slip away." Relief hit Leugio squarely in the chest as Flaitheas gave him a smile. "You're a good man, Leugio, and while I won't claim to fully understand the responsibilities of being a mage, but if someone has to have the power then I'm glad it is you."

Leugio wanted to say something in response to her words. He felt like he should, but his tongue was too heavy and his chest was too tight. Instead, he smiled at her and nodded gratefully. At least she would understand that he wasn't seeking to help another king or anything political like that.

Night was falling around them and Aodh stopped long enough to pull forth some torches. It wasn't easy to keep the horses moving in the twilight, but they managed. As the last shadows vanished with the sun, Leugio became all too aware that they had entered the time of the Sídhe. Every burst of wind or creaking of a tree made his heart jump and him look around nervously.

Then he noticed it. Magic was building in his chest. It was a slight increase, but the spark was stronger than before. Leugio looked down at his hands and flexed his fingers. White sparks appeared around the fingertips of his right hand. He urged the sparks to come together and to his surprise, they formed an orb that seemed solid in his hand. A white glow surrounded him.

"Leugio?"

"Flaitheas, I think there are Sídhe nearby."

At his words, the others drew their weapons with the smooth slide of metal against leather. He glanced over his shoulder. Aodh and Nyle were ready and scanning the hills around them. Leugio wanted more light and began to raise his hand, but the orb floated out of his hand and over his head.

The light might have helped the Sídhe find them or they may have already been close. Moments later a group of Sídhe dressed in their leather armor and swinging their bronze weapons came charging over the crest of a nearby hill. In the light of the orb, their violet eyes flashed, and Leugio could see just how pale their skin and hair were. One came straight for him, squinting its eyes against the glow of the light orb hanging over his group.

Leugio scrambled off the horse frantically. The horse reared up sharply as soon as his feet hit the ground. The Sid didn't have time to move before the hoofs of the horse hit its chest. Leugio grimaced in sympathy as the horse's fearful cries blended with a howl of pain, but he didn't linger. The magic rushed to his soft call, flooding down his arms and gathering in both of his hands.

Two Sídhe watched him, their bronze swords at the ready. He met their gaze as calmly as he could and debated attacking directly. Behind him he could hear his horse pawing at the ground and was fairly certain that the Sid who'd tried a frontal assault was dead. Magical being or no, being shredded by the hooves of a frightened horse was deadly.

There were more of them now. The Sídhe were closing in around their small group. Aodh shouted something and swung his axe down at the head of one of the creatures. It hissed and dodged, slashing towards Aodh with its bronze sword. Shifting his axe, Aodh easily stopped the blow. With a shout the tall man twisted his axe to force away the blade. He hit the Síd in the face with the iron axe blade. There was only a brief splatter of silver blood before the body had dissolved and the blood vanished.

"Watch yourself, Leugio!" Aodh shouted.

Leugio look to his right to find another Síd charging him. Magic flashed off his hands as he instinctively brought them up. A bolt struck the Síd, sending it collapsing to the ground. Leugio fumbled to draw his iron sword as the Síd struggled to stand. He jumped forward and smashed the sword down onto the Síd's head, missing the neck. There was a moment of resistance, but silver blood poured out and the Síd's body began to vanish.

Turning around, Leugio switched his sword to his left hand and called on more magic. It was easier now and he quickly moved his eyes between the pair of Sídhe who were watching him. They looked ready to run and he wished they would, but both stayed in place. He brought up his hand and pushed on the magic. A wave of white rolled through the air. They both crumbled to the ground. One began to vanish while the other grunted and climbed onto its feet.

Leugio told the magic to make a bolt. It blasted the Síd and made it fall apart into dust, but another one came rushing through the collapsing body. Leugio gasped, barely twisting out of the way as a bronze sword sailed towards him. Then another one came at him from the right.

The world had narrowed. Leugio saw nothing other than the twin swords trying to catch him. He brought up his sword and blocked one blow. His right hand opened and white sparks surged around the other Síd. Blood pounded in his ears. Leugio danced back as the sword moved again. His magic destroyed one, but another came at him. He shouted. Fear clawed at his chest and the white sparks twisted around him wildly. He didn't know what to tell them. A Síd moved in the corner of his eye and there was a flash of bronze. A white bolt destroyed it, but something slashed at his arm.

Leugio's magic formed another orb in his hand and he threw it at the nearest Síd. It screamed and fell back. He just managed to avoid another blow. His lungs were beginning to burn and the spark in his chest was beginning to hurt. The sense of power was fading. A Síd stepped in front of him, sword raised overhead. Suddenly, a sword burst out of the chest of the Síd, slicing through its leather armor. Blinking up in surprise, Leugio was silent as the Síd groaned in pain. Silvery blood glittered on the sword but began to fade away as the Síd's body dissolved into golden sparks. Then it was gone and he was looking up at Flaitheas. Her long brown hair was a mess with one of her braids hanging in her face. She was panting, but there was a pleased smile on her face.

"Thanks," Leugio managed to say. He swallowed, embarrassed at how weak his voice sounded. "Good thrust."

"You looked like you needed some help," Flaitheas replied. Then her expression turned serious. "Almost all of them went straight for you."

"How many were there?" Leugio asked. He glanced around to make sure that they were all gone. His left arm was bleeding a little, but it wasn't deep. Aodh was cradling his right arm as Nyle began to bandage it. "I lost track."

"I'm not sure. Some started to run when you began to use magic," Flaitheas said. She stepped closer to him and touched his left arm gently. "Let's get that bandaged and keep moving. I don't want to stay out in the open any longer than necessary."

Flaitheas worked with fast and purposeful motions. She wrapped the wound after rinsing it with water. Aodh was a bit shaky on his feet but proved himself able to stay in the saddle. Above them the orb of light was dimmer, but was still providing enough illumination that they could retrieve their fallen gear. Thankfully the horses hadn't run too far.

No one spoke as they moved on. The orb of light followed them, and Leugio found himself looking up at it in surprise. In his chest, the spark continued to ache a little, but he didn't think he was pulling on more magic. The orb didn't last much longer before flickering away. They pulled forth torches and kept the horses moving.

"There," Flaitheas said as they came up a hill.

Sighing in relief, Leugio almost fell out of his saddle. The fortified village of Eochu Finn was in sight, and even from here he could see the torches along the wall. It was a welcome sight and made him hope that he'd be home soon. Two encounters with Sídhe warriors had left him nervous about the state of his own home village. If the Sídhe everywhere were turning so violent, then his home was far too close to a mound.

No one spoke as they urged their horses towards the village. Exhaustion hung heavy in the air and Leugio desperately wanted to sleep. His eyelids were heavy and his eyes were beginning to burn with the effort of staying open. Thankfully their horses seemed to know that the end was in sight and sped up.

The guards let them pass and two men helped Aodh out of the saddle. Nyle nodded to them both before quickly following Aodh into one of the roundhouses. Leugio dismounted and lingered near Flaitheas, unsure of what to do now.

"Flaitheas?" he called softly. "Are you going to speak with your father?"

"No, he's already asleep!" Flaitheas snapped. Then she sighed. "I'm sorry. I'm just... frustrated, I suppose. We're on the edge of something; it could be horrible or nothing, and I just can't tell yet." She rubbed her eyes. "And Father..." She shook her head. "He's not happy with me wanting to check on these things myself."

Leugio nodded in understanding. "We don't know yet what is going to happen," Leugio said carefully. "But I'll help you however I can." He paused and debated with himself a moment before he spoke again. "I think there may be a way to get some information."

"How?"

"When my sister was taken, I bartered a cruit to a Síd for information."

"I remember." Flaitheas smiled a little at the reminder of his story. Then a look of understanding took over her face. "You think that it might barter with you again?"

"Maybe," Leugio said. "Iúdás and I spoke briefly and he was quick to stress that he had no power in other mounds. I wonder if he already knew that another Sídhe was gaining power." He ignored the way that Flaitheas' eyes widened at the revelation that he knew a Síd by name.

"I'm not impressed with their loyalty."

"No, but maybe that's the key. If some Síd is taking power then I doubt they are all in agreement. If we're lucky, maybe we can find a dissenter who will share information in exchange for goods or something else."

"We can't give them any children," Flaitheas said firmly. "Just so we're clear."

"Of course not," Leugio agreed in a rush. "I wouldn't consider it, but we need information about what is happening."

"So should we go to the mound near your home or somewhere else?"

"We?"

"I want to know what is happening," Flaitheas replied. "Besides; you travel to my home all the time. Maybe I should return the favor." Her smile softened and there was a faint rush of color on her cheeks. "You've met my father, but I've never met your mother or the sister you brought from the mound. Keelia was down there even longer than you were. Maybe she would have some insight."

Leugio tried not to smile. There was a fluttering in his stomach. Flaitheas wanted to meet his family. Of course, they had a mission and a plan, but she'd actually mentioned meeting his family. Did that mean something? He wasn't sure.

Then Flaitheas smiled at him. The color on her cheeks brightened and she leaned forward. His eyes widened, but he was frozen in place. Warm lips brushed against his own and her nose bumped his. It was strange, a touch awkward and it made his heart constrict painfully. Flaitheas pulled back, looking a touch nervous and Leugio realized that he hadn't moved at all. He smiled at her and Flaitheas' expression instantly softened. She giggled softly and Leugio let himself laugh. Then he leaned forward to kiss her cheek.

"So, we'll discuss the plan in the morning?" he asked.

"Yes," Flaitheas agreed. "Father won't be happy I'm leaving again." She paused and gave him a teasing look. "But I suppose we could tell him that I'm just going to meet your family. He'd be pleased with that explanation." Then her smile faded away a bit. "Go and get your arm seen to, Leugio."

With that Flaitheas vanished into the roundhouse. Leugio released the breath he'd been holding. Her parting words finally reached him and he looked down at his arm. Oddly, he hadn't even noticed it hurting. He smiled a little and turned on his heel. Something about Flaitheas put him at ease. It was like he'd known her forever. His smile somehow widened further.

22

Life Marches On

Life had to go on, despite whatever the Sídhe were doing and Arthur and his mother were planning. School wasn't very high on the priority list anymore, but she was still going. It was almost a waste. Alex eyed her textbook with distaste. Somewhere along the line, studying literature had stopped being fun. Probably about the time that she'd become a character in an overly complicated fantasy story that had her dealing with invading magical species and the reincarnation of an old enemy. Plus, it had left her personal life a mess.

"Alex?" Bran asked. "You okay?"

Blinking, Alex straightened up in her chair. They were at the library in one of the study rooms. It was a bit too hot as they'd shut the door, and bags of chips and a plastic bag of homemade cookies sat open on the table amongst their water bottles. Bran was looking at her from his place beside her with a small frown. His own textbooks were stacked in front of him with his physics book open to a page full of equations.

Bran's question had made the others look up. Nicki was seated across from her and gave Alex a searching look. Jenny tucked a strand of dark hair that had escaped her braid behind her ear while studying Alex. Lance and Aiden were at the far end of the table and both looked her way.

"Fine," Alex said quickly. "Just zoned out I guess." Shaking her head, she looked down at her book and sighed. "Anyone else just done with school?"

"For the year or in general?" Aiden asked. "Because I am so ready for summer. With everything that's happened this year I'd rather not have to worry about doing homework around magic duties."

"Here here!" Nicki said. "Hard to believe that we're almost to the halfway point."

Bran chuckled at her remark. "Well, so long as all of us finish in four years," Bran reminded her. "That's not exactly guaranteed." He looked back at Alex. "Studied out?"

"I guess," Alex replied. "I've been reading the same page forever."

"Well then you're still doing better than Nicki," Jenny said. She looked over at Nicki's tablet. "Nicki isn't even looking at school stuff."

"I'm resting my brain," Nicki protested. "Besides, it's news. I'm an anthropology major. I need to stay up to date with the real world too. I can't just worry about school and magic."

"So, anything interesting in the news?" Lance asked.

"Sure, but nothing surprising," Nicki said. She moved her fingers across the tablet. "Another hurricane building in the south that they expect to land."

"God rolled a critical failure again," Aiden muttered. Leaning on his hand, he peered out the window and ignored the look that Jenny was giving him. "Uh, sorry. Old inside joke from a game a few years back."

Nicki laughed and Jenny just shook her head. "It's fine," Jenny said. "All things considered it doesn't really matter." Jenny reached for the bag of cookies. "If we're taking a break, then enjoy the sugar."

Bran reached into his backpack and pulled out a square cloth bag. Alex snorted a little when he opened it to reveal the cheap tarot card deck

Nicki had gotten him in Paris. Raising an eyebrow, Alex rested her chin in her hand and watched as Bran gently shuffled the cards and began to cut them.

"You're still using those?" Aiden asked. "Really?"

"Figured it couldn't hurt." Bran shrugged and then gave them all a knowing smile. "And it isn't like this group is the image of productive studying at the moment."

Alex didn't want to touch the cards but said nothing as Bran held them out to her. She quickly shuffled them and handed them back to Bran, who focused on them intently. He checked outside through the window in the room, but there was no one else in sight. Then his yellow magic spread from his fingertips and created an aura around the deck. Alex raised an eyebrow and wondered if giving the cards some extra magic would actually help. Bran divided the cards up into three piles and then held them out to Alex one at a time. She pulled a single card from each deck and placed them on the table in front of Bran.

"The past." Bran flipped over a card and visibly grimaced.

Alex merely raised an eyebrow at the image of a figure collapsed on the ground with ten swords sticking out of them. "I'm going to guess betrayal," Alex said dryly. "Well, I'll give your cards credit: they nailed that particular event."

"Yes," Bran agreed. "The Ten of Swords does represent a betrayal in your past. And the present is…" Bran dramatically flipped over the next card. This one had the image of a woman holding a globe, but it was upside down. "The World." He paused thoughtfully, frowning slightly. "It's reversed, which is supposed to mean a lack of completion." His green eyes bored into Alex's. "Or a lack of closure."

"What of the future?" Alex asked in what she hoped was a calm voice. "What does our oracle see?"

Bran hesitated, apparently his thought that this was a good idea was waning. Alex started to reach for the card, unwilling to let it frighten her, but Bran moved and turned it over first. A figure of a man was hanging upside down from a tree.

"Huh," Alex said. "That looks pleasant." Chuckling, Alex shook her head and leaned back in her chair. "No offense, Bran, but I'm not sure what you think that tells us."

"It could mean several things, including letting go." Bran held her gaze for a moment in a silent challenge, but Alex stayed quiet. She only relaxed a little when he added, "And frankly I keep hoping that using the cards will trigger a vision of something useful. It would be nice to have a way to control those."

"Is scrying not working?" Nicki asked.

Bran shook his head. "Not using the mirror. I keep trying to look into them, but I just can't focus and get it to work unless I know what I'm looking for. It's just not the right medium for me." He gestured at the cards. "Hopefully this or something else will work better."

"It would be nice to have some warning," Alex agreed. "But with the way our lives work, we can probably assume that there's always something coming." Her tone turned bitter and Alex tried to smile. "We hardly need a bad omen to know that."

"I don't even want to know what a bad omen would be to mages," Lance said. He offered Alex a slight smile, probably picking up on her own discomfort. "I mean, what would you find weird in this town?"

"Being swarmed with a flock of ravens," Alex suggested with a shrug. "For a place called Ravenslake, there really aren't a lot of ravens here."

"There have never been a lot here," Aiden said. "But the first settlers apparently saw a raven land on the first building frame they put up or something. I don't actually remember the story." Then he glanced towards Alex, "And a group of ravens is actually an unkindness of ravens," Aiden informed her with a smile. "Not a flock."

"And a group of crows is a murder," Nicki added. "A group of owls is a parliament."

"How do you know these things?" Alex demanded around a smile. The tension in the room had been successfully broken.

"My brain," Nicki said dismissively. "It stores what it thinks is interesting and rejects everything else. Bit annoying, especially when I'm trying to study for finals."

"Your brain has always been strange," Aiden said. "That's just you."

"You're being mean, Aiden," Nicki pouted.

"I think the others know you well enough at this point that they know you have a strange brain." Aiden shrugged. "Always has been. The day you become normal is the day I know a pod person has replaced you and we're dealing with aliens of another kind."

Nicki frowned at Aiden. "Is this about Christine?" Nicki asked. "You're not still sore about that, are you?"

Alex blinked, wondering just what she'd missed lately. Who was Christine? Aiden blushed and glanced around the table. They were all watching with curiosity now. Apparently, she wasn't the only one who had missed something.

"I don't need you setting me up with girls." Aiden glared at Nicki and Alex watched with growing amusement. "I'm not that rusty."

"You and Sarah dated for a long time," Nicki reminded him. "She's pretty much the only girl you ever dated."

"Not the only girl," Aiden huffed. "And you kept trying to steal my girlfriends, so the fact that it's a short list is completely your fault!"

"It's not my fault you're still bitter about losing that bet." Nicki was smiling like a cat that had the bird firmly under its paw. "I just was known to be a better kisser."

"Seriously? You're bringing that up now?" Aiden raised an eyebrow at her. "Anyway, it wasn't a fair bet," Aiden grumbled.

"You shouldn't have bet me who would kiss a girl first."

"I still want to know who," Aiden said. "There were only two other lesbians in our school so who was the third?"

"I'll never tell." Nicki laughed out loud, toying with the end of her red braid. "Best twenty bucks I've ever received."

Bran laughed and shook his head. "We've officially devolved into the Aiden and Nicki show."

"You mean Nicki and Aiden show," Nicki corrected quickly.

"I don't think we're going to get much done," Bran finished. His eyes were almost twinkling in amusement. "Shall we call it a night?"

Alex didn't have to be told twice. Closing her book, she reached down for her backpack and began putting everything away. The others chatted as they packed up and Alex let their voices wash over her. It was reassuring and helped ease the knot. Stretching out her arms, Alex groaned slightly at the tension in her back. Everything was tight and a bit painful, but she wasn't sure why.

Suddenly, it hit her. There was no warning. The wave of magic crashed over her and Alex's own power flared in her chest. Gripping the edge of the table, Alex struggled to stay upright. It was crawling over her. A dark sense of familiarity and terror blurred together. Someone grabbed her arm and called her name, but Alex struggled to form any words.

"I've got you," Bran said. "Try to breathe."

"Something is coming," Alex choked. "At the lake."

"What is it?" Aiden asked calmly. Glancing up, she saw that his phone was in his hand. "Can you tell?"

She didn't want to, but Alex focused on the lingering sensation. It tingled all over her body. Like being watched combined with a cold drizzle down the neck. She could breathe easier now, but it stuck to her skin like a bad odor. It took her only a moment to realize where she'd sensed this presence before. There was a vague memory of a dark place and a blue glow. Her mind provided the name: Brekszta.

Without even thinking about it, Alex began to release her magic, letting it roll out around them. There was something in the air. A vibration coming from the lake that taunted her and teased her magic with its own twisted variation.

"Old One," Alex said. "I can feel it releasing its own energy."

"So, it's like Chernobog," Aiden grumbled. "Wonderful."

"Is it Brekszta?" Nicki asked.

"I think so."

"Our cars are at the dorms," Bran pointed out. "It'll take us a few minutes to cross campus."

Alex shivered and rubbed her arms. Bran was clearly worried and Alex didn't even try to reassure him before she took off. The others were behind her as she rushed down the stairs and out the main door. Her backpack made it difficult to run and she considered just dumping it. But there were other students heading into the library. They were chatting and laughing as finals were their biggest problems. Narrowing her eyes at them, Alex was aware of her magic twisting in her chest. One of the voices suddenly grew louder, but she recognized it as Cuthbert. Alex pointedly ignored him, wanting nothing to do with the slave ship captain's view of the world.

It was still light outside, though the sun was beginning to sink to the west of town behind the mountains. Pale golden light poured across the campus, but Alex couldn't even be bothered to appreciate how it illuminated the green trees and the various flower beds scattered around the walkways. Her eyes were scanning the area as she tried to see the lake. Cars drove past them as the group reached one of the roads. There was an itch at the back of Alex's neck that urged her to stop and take one, but instead, she hurried across the street with the others on her heels.

"Alex," Nicki called. "Slow down!"

"We have to get to Brekszta!" Alex shouted.

"We've texted Morgana," Nicki replied. "She and Merlin are on their way. Try to calm down."

Something in Nicki's voice tugged at her. Nicki was worried. Alex could understand that, but her own worry was getting knotted up with her other emotions and she couldn't deal with Nicki's right now. The lights of the dorms were on now as the sun's light started to fade. Most people had headed indoors, but there was one group on the lawn who were walking towards town.

Bran started to move towards the parking lot of the dorm, but Alex stopped in place. Her eyes moved back to the lake and she stretched out her magic. Around her the world was hazy and someone caught her shoulder. Distantly, she heard someone call to Bran. They were all waiting for her. Alex pushed out more magic, letting it wash over her skin.

The being had moved around the lake while they'd been crossing campus. Panting a little, Alex looked towards the lake. Alex could somehow see a figure through the trees of the campus arboretum. She knew she shouldn't be able to, but it was there. Her magic was humming and spreading out further, closing around the figure.

"Alex?" Nicki called.

Breaking into a run, Alex ignored the cold shivers taking over her body. The others would sense it soon. Alex followed the path through the arboretum, glancing around to make sure that there were no students hanging around. The lampposts were flickering on around her as the last rays of the sun vanished. She knew that Old Ones didn't have the same problems with bright lights that the Sídhe did, but it would have been nice to fight in the daylight.

Following the path down towards the shore, Alex finally had to stop at the edge of the pavement. Just down the hill was the pebbled shore of Ravens Lake. The others caught up with her, but no one said anything. Alex wanted to tell Lance and Jenny to leave, but the words were stuck in her throat. Hopefully they'd at least stay back. Alex could see the figure clearly now. She was short with long brown hair pulled up in a ponytail. There were no weapons in her hands. Alex's magic brushed against the figure. It was not human. Energy pushed back against her own and Alex swallowed.

The Old One turned to look at them. Brekszta looked human, but her face was too thin and pale to pass as healthy. Vacant brown eyes rolled like a doll's as she shifted her head towards Alex. Then her worm-thin lips curved into a smile and a spark appeared in those dull eyes. Alex forced herself to stay still even as her heart pounded. Brekszta wore a red sundress beneath a leather coat but had no shoes on. She took a step towards them, unbothered by the gravel of the beach.

"So, the little mages came," Brekszta said. Her smile widened. "Excellent."

23

Goddess of Twilight

There was a moment when no one moved. Alex and her fellow students took in the odd figure. She looked harmless enough: almost childlike with dimples, but Alex's stomach turned as the strange energy of the being brushed against her magic. It was wrong. Wrong in a way that Sif wasn't. A cold chill was creeping up her spine. Brekszta giggled at the silence, bringing a pale hand up to cover her mouth. Her dimples deepened and her eyes glinted with mirth. Alex almost wanted them vacant once more.

"So many mages!" Brekszta clapped her hands together, folding them as if praying. "Oh, and two more on the way. How lovely for the Iron Soul; so many to share the burden." Her eyes fixed on Alex. "And a pretty girl form this time. Tall and blonde. Are you Norse again?" Brekszta looked at her expectantly.

Alex blinked, suddenly at a loss of how to deal with this. "Uh, yes," Alex finally answered. "Not completely though."

"And pretty gray eyes, like a storm," Brekszta said. "Or a stone. Like a lifeless statue with nothing to move for. Oh, or like iron. It's probably like iron, isn't it, Iron Soul?"

"Why are you in Ravenslake?" Bran asked from beside her. "Do you come with a message?"

"I've been sending my messages." Brekszta's playful tone changed, suddenly becoming serious. "But no one is listening."

Crazy was the word that Alex was thinking, but at the moment this Old One wasn't trying to kill them. Alex's magic was still pulsing through her at the ready and she held up a hand to keep the others back. Thankfully, they understood the gesture. Brekszta just kept watching her and Alex took a small step forward. The bottoms of her shoes shifted the gravel and mud of the beach. In her chest, that knot was tightening at the memory of the nightmares.

A truck bearing down on her parents' car flashed in front of her eyes. The knot tightened. Her foot started to slip and Brekszta smiled once again. Regaining her footing, Alex glared at the Old One. The voices suddenly grew louder. Alex flinched.

Brekszta raised her hands, waving her fingers in an almost friendly manner. But then her body shimmered. It rippled like a hologram in a movie. Her smile widened and Alex took an instinctive step back, bringing up her own hands. Flares of dark blue magic spun around Brekszta's hands, swirling out of her physical form. With a shrill laugh, Brekszta shoved them forward towards the group.

The glittering dark blue magic filled the air like a dense fog, curling around them and sweeping through the trees. Fire flashed in the corner of Alex's eyes. Aiden and Bran were both unleashing streams of flame from their hands to hold back the waves of magic. It swirled up in a shimmer of dark blue and purple, twisting like an ice cream cone before crashing down as a wave.

"Lance! Jenny! Go back to the dorm!" Alex shouted. "Merlin and Morgana need to know where we are!"

She didn't turn around to make sure they obeyed. Alex hoped they would. One of the voices quieted at her words, eased and relieved at their safety. Moving towards the lake, Alex tried to track Brekszta's movements. The Old One was drawing back and Alex heard a splash in the water. Rushing forward, she stopped and looked around frantically at the edge of the lake. There was nothing in front of her. The dark magic was spinning through the air but giving her a wide berth as if she was in the eye of a storm.

"Peekaboo."

Spinning around, water splashed around Alex's feet as she stumbled back in surprise. Brekszta was between Alex and the others. The dark blue magic was spinning around them like a tornado, but there were flashes of red, yellow, and a lighter blue in the storm. It wasn't much of a reassurance that the others were okay, but it was enough. Brekszta just kept staring at Alex with brown eyes that were strangely beginning to turn a dark blue color, like the night was falling within her iris. Alex let the dark gray sparks dance around her fingertips in warning. Yet the Old One's smile remained firmly in place,

Alex's fingers twitched. She longed for the Sword or the Hammer. The voices in her mind were clamoring for weapons, but all she had was a dagger. Sadly, the Hammer was too heavy and large to just keep with her. Brekszta's eyes dropped for a moment to Alex's hand and she giggled.

"No Iron Treasures, Iron Soul?" Brekszta met her gaze once more and pouted. "Disappointing. There's so many of them. Bright little balls of power in a dull world. Scattered in history and myth."

"I still have my magic," Alex said. Her voice was remarkably even and she kept her eyes locked on Brekszta's unnerving ones. "You said you've been sending messages, but all I've had is nightmares."

"Poor little, Iron Soul," Brekszta cooed. She shifted a little closer, moving like a drunken student. "So many nightmares."

"Yes, I know," Alex hissed. "You did that, but why?"

"So many memories: so many horrors all jangling around in your head." Brekszta giggled, the sound high-pitched and echoing around them. "I can hear the voices and it isn't even my head. Oh dear, how do you manage?" Before Alex could jump back, Brekszta's hand lashed out and caught Alex's chin, forcing her to look down at the Old One. Despite being taller, Alex felt much smaller as the dark gaze began to twinkle with tiny lights. There were stars, the endless void of space, in her eyes. "You're lost, aren't you? Lost in the voices? After all, what is one life to so many?"

"Why are you in Ravenslake?" Alex demanded. In the corner of her eye, she could see the fog spreading up the hill. The sounds of the others were muted now. "What is it that you want, Brekszta?"

"Oh, the Iron Soul wants to talk!" Brekszta giggled again, the sound grating on Alex's nerves. "Should I be honored? Or should I be offended?"

"You aren't well, Brekszta, let us assist you."

"You'll just put me back to sleep and shove me in water!" Brekszta's smile fell away and she glared, releasing Alex's chin. "I don't want to sleep. My sisters are gone now. Everyone is gone, but I can see it all now." Brekszta backed away and waved her hands, rolling her head back to look up at the sky. "The Tree, Iron Soul! The Tree is sick. Has been for so long, withering and dying. It will all die! Tick tock, tick tock, and then only darkness and dreams." Brekszta paused and frowned. "But who will dream? That's the question, isn't it? I don't think any of us will like the answer."

"So, you showed me that dead world."

"Dead, very dead, and abandoned, but not forgotten," Brekszta said. She rocked back and forth on her bare feet now. "Running, run, run away, but sooner or later there'll be nowhere to run."

"Look," Alex begged. "Stop this fog and we'll talk. You can talk to Merlin and Morgana and we'll figure this out. Stop attacking the others."

"Attacking?" Brekszta frowned, sticking her lower lip far out. "I'm not attacking them. Just keeping them busy."

"Don't hurt them," Alex said. "Or put them into nightmares."

"Nightmares..." Brekszta shook her head.

The eye collapsed. The magic rushed in. A scream tore out of Alex's mouth. She shifted her hands defensively in front of her and the magic jumped wildly. Brekszta just laughed. Pushing her magic forward, Alex grimaced as it crashed against a wall. Alex's magic frantically twisted and pushed back. In her panic, Alex almost forgot to reach for Brekszta's magic.

Brekszta's power was creeping over her. Dancing across her skin, it tugged sharply at the knot keeping her grief contained. Exhaling, Alex reached for Brekszta's magic. Their magics began to blur together and Alex's vision cleared enough for her to see a surprised look on Brekszta's face, but then the Old One smiled. Pleasure replaced the shock and more magic hit Alex in the chest.

"No!" Alex shouted. "Let me go!"

Alex pulled on the attacking magic, twisting her own magic around the dark lines of power. Push and pull. Brekszta fought back even as wisps of her magic turned gray. The Old One's thin lips all but vanished as she snarled.

"You. Will. See!"

Brekszta screamed, the sound like nails on a chalkboard. It reverberated through Alex's bones. Her focus broke and Brekszta's magic surged forth. Crashing over Alex, it crushed her beneath its power. She was being pulled under. A weight settled in her chest, chaining itself to the knot of magic and emotion she carried beneath her heart. Alex pushed with her magic, but the world was slipping away and the voices were louder. They were too loud. She struggled, but her body was too heavy. The alien magic was pushing its way in, twisting around her magic to contain it. Something buckled. The knot in her chest expanded and the magic rushed in. It was so cold.

They were drenched. Rain was pouring down in a curtain of water around them. Beneath their feet the road was muddy and they sank with each step. It stung their skin, lashing their already sensitive flesh. But they didn't stop moving. The storm was building ahead of them. Lightning flashed in the sky and the winds howled. They could feel it. Magic building in the air, but it wasn't like theirs. It was different: alien and sharp. It stung their body and hung too heavy in the air.

"Find Shiva!" a voice shouted. "The demons! The demons are stronger now. My homeland is in danger. Find the Trishula and protect my home-land!"

More magic seeped in, pulling them deeper and deeper.

The dark figure rose above them with bright green eyes. Chernobog. They didn't understand. How could they understand? They had to fight, but they were no warrior. There were others. In the corner of their eye, they saw more figures: more Old Ones ready to fight.

"I didn't want it. Any of it," another voice screamed in frustration. "This wasn't my world. Why me? I'm just a farmer!"

The voices fought. They blurred together in a mess of noise. It was them. There was only them.

Beneath them, the ship rose sharply on the waves. The female slaves on the deck screamed and clutched their children closer. There was moaning from below. The men in the hold were too loud now and they bit back a snarl. Storm or no storm, they would not have disorder on their ship. Their crew dashed about and they eyed the sails as they were being lowered. The storm wasn't the worst they'd seen. Not even close. Their eyes swept over the female slaves again. They were valuable, but an annoyance to transport. Maybe the next voyage, they'd outright skip the females.

"Power. You have power," Cuthbert's voice hissed. "Use it. Gather it and master the world. I couldn't. I didn't understand what I could do, but you do."

It came too fast. There were so many flashes. It was all true, but it didn't fit together. Technology changed. Their hands and reflections changed. Those around them changed, but it was all true. All of them. How? They couldn't think. There were only the memories and the voices. Nothing stayed long. It was there and then gone in a flash. It was heavy and hard and then hot and fast and then airy and kind.

Hands grabbed her upper arms and pulled her back. Brekszta screamed something just before Alex crashed back into the icy water of Ravens Lake. The air rushed out of her lungs at the sudden chill all through her legs and arms. Alex's awareness returned. The visions were fading and the voices quieting. There were flickers of resistance, but her own mind filled her body. She was aware of everything; every sensation, every puff of air, even the cold that she didn't want to deal with.

"Alex!" This voice was other. It wasn't them. Yet it was familiar. "Alex, it's Sif! Can you hear me?"

That name meant something. Alex brought a hand up and brushed her fingers against Sif's face. It was smooth and soft, triggering other memories. Only one voice spoke now and Alex was able to push it back. Her jeans were soaked: she was sitting in the shallows of the lake with Sif right behind her. The Old One was holding her tightly and kneeling in the water with her.

"What?" Alex struggled to remember what had happened.

Blue magic flared in the corner of her eyes and she gasped. Straightening up, Alex pulled away from Sif's grip and surged to her feet. Brekszta was on the shore with a wall of dark blue magic between her and the other mages. There were flashes of silver and green now, confirming that Merlin and Morgana were present. Alex's heart skipped a beat as Brekszta turned towards her. The Old One's feet were covered in mud, but she seemed otherwise undisturbed. She frowned at Alex and her eyes jumped to Sif.

"You shouldn't have done that," Brekszta said.

"Leave this place," Sif ordered sternly.

"No," Brekszta replied. Narrowing her eyes on Alex, she shook her head. "What will be left, Iron Soul, when all the rest are gone? Or what will happen when all the rest take control? The lie must die."

"I don't know what you're trying to do," Alex growled. Her voice was too low and sharp with a hint of some strange accent. "Cease talking in riddles or I'll make you."

Sif stood, the water sloshing around them both and the Old One stepped up beside her. "Leave now, Brekszta. Chernobog was recently destroyed here. There is no need to repeat that."

"As was Cyrridven," Brekszta said. "I will not be ordered about, not even by you, Sif. You were a mate to the Iron Soul once, but no longer."

Brekszta flicked her hand. A bolt of dark blue magic shot through the air. Sif gasped, clutching her chest. Golden light flared around her hand. Rage erupted. Alex's vision narrowed on Brekszta. She screamed and threw forward her hands. Dark silver light flashed through the air and grabbed the expanding cloud of dark blue magic. Brekszta's eyes widened in shock as Alex ripped away control of the magic. The energy resisted her, but Alex's power washed over it. Inch by inch it turned dark gray and spun towards Alex.

"Stay away from her!" Alex shouted. "Sif, fall back!"

The blonde Old One gaped at her but shifted away from the water. In the corner of her eyes, Alex saw the other mages moving on the shore. They were rushing down to join her. Water lapped around her calves, but she didn't notice the chill. Dark silver magic filled the air, consuming Brekszta's power. Alex's vision darkened. There was movement to her right.

A figure dressed in jeans and a purple shirt rushed over. It was a young woman her age of Indian descent with long black hair bound back in a braid. Her brown eyes were wide and her mouth dropped open as she looked up at the spinning swirl of dark gray. Brekszta shrieked and rushed at Alex. The dark silver cloud began to crash down but Brekszta ignored it even as the power rushed at her.

"Look out!" the new woman shouted in an accented voice.

Dark blue magic was spinning around Brekszta's fist. The Old One leapt into the air and sailed towards Alex. A blast of red magic hit the Old One, followed by a bolt of yellow. There was chanting from the accented voice and a golden glow lit up the hillside. Alex adjusted her hand, calling on the magic filling the air. Her heart raced, but she focused on her task. The magic curled back, drawing dark silver patterns in the air. Rushing to her, the magic formed a shimmering half dome in front of her.

Brekszta hit the shield and narrowed her eyes at Alex before darting to the side. Alex's own magic reached her as the shield vanished, gathering into an orb. Turning, Alex prepared to unleash the magic on Brekszta. The Old One turned and began to run. Brekszta dove into the water and vanished from view before Alex could blink.

Sif rushed into the water and dropped to her knees. Grabbing her arm, Alex kept her from going deeper. The water shimmered and swelled for a moment, but then gentled to the usual soft ripple from the wind. Sif looked up at her with bright and confused green eyes. Too many emotions hit Alex all at once. Worry and relief were dominant and her hand moved to Sif's face before she thought about it.

"Are you alright?"

"I'm fine, Alex," Sif replied gently. Her tone was soft and she touched Alex's cheek in return. "I'm alright; it was just a distortion attack. Meant to distract and cause some pain, but not enough to destroy."

"But but she could have..." Alex shivered and shook her head. "She tried, and..." There was a dull pain gathering between her eyes. She blinked and tried to dispel it. "And..."

"Alex?" Morgana's voice called behind her. "Alex? Are you alright?"

Alex ignored her, focusing on Sif, who was staring at her in shock. "I can't watch you get hurt, Sif," Alex said firmly. "Not ever."

"Alex, I think you need to rest," Morgana said. She was right next to Alex in the water. "Come on." Morgana began to pull her away. "Come with me."

"But-"

"Alex," Sif said as she began to follow. Her expression was still stunned, but she was recovering. "I brought a new friend for you to meet."

"A new friend?" Alex repeated.

"Yes," Sif agreed. "So please, calm down. You wouldn't want to be rude."

"No." Alex blinked again: the pain was getting worse. "I wouldn't want... where are my tweezers, Sif?"

"Your tweezers?" Sif repeated. "Why do you want them?"

"I'm not ready to meet someone," Alex protested. "And I need to trim my beard. I can't remember the last time I..." She trailed off and frowned. Sif's mouth was hanging open and her green eyes were watery with tears. "What's wrong?"

"Alex-" Morgana called. "Alex? Focus on my voice. Focus on where you are!"

"Thor," Sif whispered. Alex's eyes jumped back to her. "Please... go with Morgana. You need to go with Morgana. I'm fine and quite safe, but you may be hurt. Please, let her help you."

"I'm fine," Alex insisted. A flare of indignation rose in her chest, but the knot tightened. There was a truck bearing down, a ship full of slaves, and an Iron Gate forming over a hole in the world. Then everything went dark and the pain was blissfully gone.

24

Return to the Mound

4 64 B.C.E. The Golden Vale

Most people never travel far from where they were born. Leugio knew that was certainly true with everyone he'd grown up with. There were stories that in the past when bronze had been used, people would travel far to trade it, but those days were long gone. Trade was limited and usually only within the domain of the king now with rare exceptions.

Now he found himself a rarity. He'd not only left the village he was born in but been all over the area to check on reports of the Sídhe. Yet he was now also aware of just how much he hadn't seen. There were messages from other kings to Eochu Finn about Sídhe raids. Rumors were growing about some new Sídhe army. His magic had made him the one the rumormongers were all interested in, but through all his travels and all the messages, he'd never heard rumors of another mage.

Coming home was odd. He rode into the village atop a fine horse with Flaitheas riding beside him. People stopped and looked his way. Rather than rushing to greet him, they hesitated and eyed the guards who were accompanying them. He didn't think that he'd changed that much. True, he now wore a finer tunic and had leather armor to protect his chest, but he'd forgone any fancy jewelry even though he was in service to the king. Instead, he still wore only the iron brooch from his father.

Leugio scanned the people in search of his mother or his sister, but he didn't see either of them. Galvyn was coming up the pathway through the village and stopped upon seeing them. A wide grin appeared on his old friend's face.

"Leugio!" Galvyn cheered. "You're back!"

"Galvyn," Leugio greeted. He swung himself off the horse, noting with pleasure that he was getting better at it. "Good to see you."

Galvyn moved forward and eagerly met Leugio next to the horses with a hug. Leugio noted that his friend's beard had filled in a great deal since he had last seen him. Galvyn was studying him as well, but thankfully he didn't seem concerned with any of the changes. Thankfully his clothing covered the scar he now had on his right arm from the Síd blade two weeks ago. The pair laughed and hugged. The pressure in Leugio's chest eased at the friendly greeting.

Flaitheas dismounted and came to stand next to him. She gave him an expectant look and Leugio quickly caught on. "Flaitheas, this is Galvyn, an old friend of mine. Galvyn, this is Flaitheas, the daughter of King Eochu Finn."

"Wow," Galvyn said. Then he blushed and grimaced at his greeting. "Sorry. It's very nice to meet you. Our village is humble but if you require anything, just say the word."

"Thank you. Nice to meet you as well, Galvyn," Flaitheas replied kindly. She was smiling a little and then looked around the village. "Your village is a bit smaller than I was expecting."

"Yes," Leugio said. "With traveling to other villages, I'm realizing just how small we are."

"You've been away longer this time," Galvyn said. His expression darkened slightly. "Is everything alright?"

"Forgive me," Leugio replied quickly. "We meant to come here over a month ago, but there were more reports that needed to be investigated."

"Nothing here though, right?" Galvyn pressed. He glanced around nervously and then checked the sun's position. "After what happened with Keelia, everything has been calm and quiet!"

"Speaking of my sister, where is she?"

"Oh, she's in the pasture," Galvyn said. "She's taken over watching the sheep."

"Thank you. What of my mother?"

"I'm not sure where Sabe is," Galvyn replied. "Some of the women went out to the forest to gather roots. I think she might have gone with them. I could show you-"

"That's alright," Flaitheas interrupted. "We have other business to see to."

"Business," Galvyn repeated. His eyes widened and he looked at Leugio. "You aren't going back to the mound, are you?"

"I'll be fine, Galvyn," Leugio promised.

To prove it, he held out his right hand and pulled on the spark of magic below his heart. His hand began to glow and a shimmering white orb took form in his palm. His friend's eyes widened further and next to him, Flaitheas smiled in pleasure.

"You... wow!" Galvyn reached out towards the orb only to pull his hand back. His eyes darted between Leugio, Flaitheas, and their escort. "Do you need any help?"

"No, but if you'd keep an eye out for my mother and sister, I'd appreciate it." Leugio glanced out towards the sheep pasture in the distance. "Especially Keelia: I don't want her trying to come after me."

"Well, alright then," Galvyn replied uneasily. He looked at the guards again. "If you're sure. You know I'm not warrior material."

"I know, but we'll be fine. I'm hoping just to talk to them. Hopefully, the nearby mound isn't involved in any of the raids."

Galvyn paled at the words and nodded eagerly. Around them the others were whispering to each other and looking his way nervously. Holding back a sigh, Leugio mounted his horse once more and peered off into the distance. Flaitheas gave him a supportive look and the familiar smile that made his heart beat faster. He knew that he would blush soon and urged the horse forward.

"Don't you wish to see your mother and sister?" Flaitheas asked.

"Later, after we speak with Iúdás." He tried not to squirm in the saddle. "Mother will worry if she knows where we are going."

Flaitheas nodded her understanding and swung up onto her own horse, still far more gracefully than he could. The villagers drew back, eyeing him as though he were a madman. Perhaps he was. Still, this wasn't the time to worry about it. They headed out of the village and hurried towards the Sídhe's home.

The mound loomed ahead of them. It wasn't as large as Leugio remembered or as frightening. Maybe it was being on a horse with three warriors behind him, or maybe it was just his understanding. He knew that he could stop at least a few Sídhe on his own thanks to his magic. The sounds of the countryside washed over him. There was the baaing of the sheep and the wind in the trees of the forest up the hill. There were the smells of the village lingering in the air even as the scent of the crops grew stronger. It was all very much the same and yet different.

A familiar figure was tucked back in the shadow of the mound entrance, though its feet were almost in the sun as it lounged on a smooth stone. Violet eyes looked up at them, but the figure did not move. Leugio relaxed on his horse in an attempt to appear calm. As they got closer, he recognized that the figure was definitely Iúdás by the cruit he held. He dismounted his horse as they stopped just shy of the entrance, though the others remained mounted.

"Ah, the young mage returns once again," Iúdás greeted. "It has been some time since you last came here." Its violet eyes took in the group. "And I do not think you mean to storm the mound with only five."

"Indeed not," Leugio agreed. He paused and considered how to proceed for a moment. "I seek information from you, Iúdás."

"Do you indeed, Leugio?" Iúdás' expression brightened and he plucked a string of the cruit, producing a sweet sound. "I thought as much." There was a pause as Iúdás seemed to think. Then he nodded. "Ask your question."

"Do you know anything about a new leader of the Sídhe?" Leugio asked, finally voicing the real question. "One who is organizing the mounds to work together?"

"I know some things," Iúdás said. His fingers finally stopped playing and he studied Leugio with sharp violet eyes. "It is a fool's attempt. The magic of the Iron Realm will rise up to stop any real threat our kind may pose, and there is no love lost between the mound dwellers and the other Faery creatures. Our former slaves will fight us back if we break the peace."

"What slaves?"

"The Faeries, creatures who are not Sídhe, but live in your world."

"Like Pookas?"

"Yes. My ancestors had a powerful empire. I suppose that the others still might, but when they sought to take over Earth they were defeated by mages. Many of those they had enslaved used it as a chance to flee in the chaos. A barrier was created between this world and that of the empire, trapping many of us here."

"I'm not sure that I understand," Leugio admitted.

"No." Iúdás studied him and then nodded. "I suppose not. You are alone, little mage of the Iron Realm. I am not sure why. Perhaps we are not such a great threat after all if even the Grand Mages have not returned to this island."

"The Grand Mages?"

"There are stories of two mages who have been alive for centuries," Iúdás explained. "Ever since the great war that banished our ancestors here. My people teach their children of them. We are to run and hide from them should they come, but they have not."

"You speak in riddles," Flaitheas snapped. "Answer the questions!"

"No, I speak plainly. You just do not understand," Iúdás said. He only glanced her way for a moment. "You are not a mage nor a Sídhe. I doubt you could ever understand."

"Who are these Grand Mages?" Leugio asked. He didn't like Iúdás speaking with Flaitheas.

"One is Merlin and the other Morgana. They are ageless mages who have lived from the time of the first war. There are many stories of them and I do not know which to believe, but they have not returned to these shores in a long time, and it is a large world. Even if they detect your magic, it will take them time to find you, unless they throw themselves into the water."

Those words made no sense to Leugio. He wasn't sure if relief or anger was the proper reaction. The aid of others would have been welcome, but they sounded like terrifying beings. He reached up and touched his brooch, which hummed beneath his fingers. Magic was shimmering just beneath his skin, with a strange impulse urging him forward into the tunnel. Thankfully his memory of how many Sídhe there were below was enough to keep him still.

"Never mind the Grand Mages then," Leugio said. He shook his head slightly, noting that Iúdás was still looking at his brooch. "Something about my brooch fascinates you, Iúdás? I doubt you wish to trade information for it; the metal is iron."

"No," Iúdás agreed. "I would not touch that for the world." He leaned forward and sniffed slightly, nostrils flaring. "You wore it when you first came here."

"Yes; I've had it since I was a boy," Leugio replied. "What about it?"

Iúdás didn't answer. He just looked at the brooch, and Leugio risked a glance down at it. The old knot design was worn down a bit and the edges were smooth from his fingers. It was nothing special. He only wore it all the time because of the sentimental value.

"So, this lord?" Leugio coughed lightly to draw Iúdás' attention back to him. "What can you tell me about them? Who is organizing the Sídhe against the humans?"

"I fear the consequences of another attempted conquest. Humans… they are built to fight. Born to fight." Iúdás shook his head and stood from his position. "There is a lord seeking power. He sends messengers between the mounds, but not all follow him. He promises things he cannot deliver. They have had a few small successes: gained a few human slaves and forced some of the other Fae Folk to serve them. Nothing grand, but it is enough to have gained him some followers."

"Where is this lord?" Flaitheas asked. "We can stop him."

"This one can," Iúdás agreed, pointing at Leugio. "While untrained in his magic, he carries power and is forming himself a weapon."

"A weapon?"

"That brooch," Iúdás said. "We have only met thrice, and each time you have been grasping it. Iron is the metal of this realm. You carry it in your blood and build your world with it. That is why it burns us. Your magic lives within it, and with every touch some of your power enters that brooch. It is not too strong, but I can sense the power settling into it. For what purpose, I do not know."

"Purpose?" Leugio's mind was spinning and confusion was taking over. "I don't understand. Do you mean I've made it magical? Like in the legends?"

"Yes," Iúdás said plainly. "Though what exactly you have wrought I do not know. Perhaps it comforts, perhaps it protects, or perhaps it will make you stronger. It depends on what you have thought about as you poured in the magic."

"It can't be that simple, can it?" Leugio argued. "If it was then surely there would be many magical items."

Iúdás was studying him closely now. Then the Síd nodded. "You're not wrong, but many items carry a spark of magic. The question is, will that magic endure, or will it be used up for a purpose? You are placing magic in that iron, but in a time of need you may use it all. Or it may endure beyond your lifespan. I cannot say for certain."

Pulling off the brooch, Leugio ran his thumb over the worn pattern. Now that he was paying attention, he noticed a faint warmth from the iron and saw a glimmer of magic in the metal. It was almost enough to make him drop it. Flaitheas had moved her horse and was looking down at the brooch curiously.

"I'm afraid that I can be of little help to you," Iúdás said. "But I have heard that Teàrlach is aware that there is a mage in the land. I suspect that he will seek you out soon enough." The name Teàrlach rang through Leugio's head. "I have been able to gain full control over this mound and have forbidden my own from aiding him. I wish you well, Leugio. May you defeat Teàrlach before his actions draw the attention of the Grand Mages."

"Wouldn't it be better to have their help?" Leugio asked.

"Death follows those two," Iúdás replied. "They have lived for generations. Death does not take them, but it takes those around them." Shaking his head, Iúdás looked almost pleadingly at him. "And their arrival on these shores would signal a far greater threat than either of us would wish for. For all our sakes, let us hope that they do not feel a call leading them here."

With that, Iúdás turned and vanished into the darkness of the tunnel. Leugio was left holding his brooch and weighing the words. Something about the way Iúdás spoke of Merlin and Morgana frightened him. Flaitheas made a sound of irritation, but Leugio shook his head and pinned his brooch on his cloak. Once he was sure that Iúdás was gone, he swung himself up onto his horse once more.

"Well, that wasn't very helpful," Flaitheas said. She was glowering at him, but Leugio didn't let it bother him. "All we learned was a name."

"No," Leugio disagreed. "I learned several things."

Flaitheas gave him an expectant look, but Leugio had no idea of where to even begin. He wasn't sure what to make of the reality that the Sídhe weren't all on the same side. In one respect it was reassuring, but it made everything more complicated. Touching his brooch again, Leugio pushed a little bit of magic into the metal, and to his surprise he saw a white spark flash off his fingertip and sink into it. The hum became stronger and he smiled.

"And I have some thoughts on how to help us defend ourselves from the Sídhe," he added. "Now that I know I can put magic into iron."

That earned him a smile from Flaitheas. Her shoulders relaxed and her posture eased. She reached over to touch his arm and squeezed it for a moment. Leugio could feel his face heating up and Flaitheas' smile widened. Their escorts thankfully stayed silent.

"Come on," Flaitheas said. "It's about time I met your family, don't you think? What with us being engaged?"

A blush exploded across Leugio's face. "That was your father's idea."

"You didn't object," Flaitheas countered. Her smile softened though it retained a teasing edge. "Unless you do mind."

"No," he said quickly. "No, I don't mind." His throat was a little too tight at the smile she gave him, and his mouth a touch too dry. "Uh, come on then, Mother will be thrilled to meet you."

25

The Magician

Seeing Alex still and silent was becoming an uncomfortably familiar sight. Lance had never really associated the athletic blonde girl with fainting and lying unconscious in a bed. When he'd first met her Alex had been bright and cheerful, even if she wasn't the most outgoing person in the world. And now knowing that she was a mage and the latest incarnation of some great magic warrior just made the sight even more jarring.

He and Jenny had obeyed Alex, despite Jenny's protests, and gone up near the dorms. Merlin and Morgana had arrived shortly after and charged into the fight. Lance wasn't sure if Alex had cast some spell, but none of the other students had seemed to notice anything. Lance had an odd itch to be somewhere else as dark blue clouds swirled around the area. Then it had cleared, and Brekszta had fled.

"Do you think Alex will be alright?" Jenny asked, drawing him back into the present.

He was standing near the doorway of Morgana's house. Alex was being carefully floated back to the guest room and Lance knew that she wouldn't be happy to wake up there once again. Nodding to Jenny, he looked back outside where Sif was speaking with the strange young woman who had turned up. Morgana hadn't been happy when she'd stepped forward to help, but Sif had caught her and said something that calmed her down.

"Are you staying?" the newcomer asked Sif. She sounded a touch distressed and had an accented voice.

"I... I don't think it's wise for me to be around Alex right now," Sif replied.

Lance frowned at the statement. Next to him, Jenny's brow furrowed in confusion and she too frowned. The newcomer blinked in confusion, but stepped back from Sif and nodded. She bowed slightly.

"As you wish. Thank you for bringing me here, milady."

"You don't need to be so formal, and don't worry," Sif replied. "They're good people, and they'll listen to what you need to tell them." Sif glanced towards the house and smiled when she caught sight of him and Jenny "Things are more complicated than I was aware of. I'll be in touch."

"Will you remain in the area?"

"Yes, for the night at least," Sif promised. "In case I am needed."

Then Sif turned and began to walk down the drive. Lance stepped outside and called after her, "Do you need a ride?"

"Oh, no thank you," Sif answered. She turned back to him and smiled. "I'll be just fine, but thank you."

Unsure of what to say or do, Lance lingered on Morgana's porch. Then the newcomer looked up at him. He noted for the first time that she had a backpack on and looked as uncertain as he felt. Nodding to her, he held open the door of the house and waited. She climbed up the stairs and tentatively went inside.

Lance followed her inside, giving himself a moment to study the newcomer. She was a little taller than Jenny with a slim build and black hair tied out of her face. He hated to guess, but judging from her skin tone he thought she was probably Indian. At first glance she looked like any other college student: she was about their age, wearing jeans, black boots, and a flowy purple shirt. Then, before he could say anything stupid, Merlin called for them to come to the living room.

Merlin's eyes were on the newcomer the instant they walked into the living room. The eldest mage's brown eyes were tired and worried, but he forced a smile. There was already a tea set on the coffee table and Aiden and Nicki were on the couch.

"Where's Bran?" Lance asked.

"Here," Bran replied. He and Morgana came down the hallway from the bedroom. "Alex is asleep," Bran offered. "Seems to be peaceful now."

Lance didn't like what that insinuated about earlier, but sat down in one of the chairs by the window. Jenny took the seat beside him and reached across the table between them to take his hand. Squeezing it, Lance focused on the newcomer, who was still standing and looking around the room nervously.

"I take it Sif is already gone," Merlin said.

"Yes... she didn't think she should be nearby at this time," the newcomer said.

"So, where did she bring you from?" Morgana asked. She gracefully sat down in her armchair and took in the newcomer with careful consideration

"My name is Avani Desai," she said calmly. Her brown eyes scanned across the room, meeting each of their gazes for a heartbeat before moving on. "I'm from Mumbai, India, and was sent to find the current Iron Soul by Shiva after Sif came to meet with him."

"Shiva is awake then?" Merlin asked. He exhaled slowly and looked towards Morgana with worry in his eyes. "What's your connection to him?"

"The Desai family are descendants of the Iron Soul incarnation Lokpal," Avani answered. Her gaze jumped towards the hallway leading to the guest bedroom. Jenny gasped softly in surprise. "We maintain some contact with Shiva and an alliance with the Old Ones, helping them in times of need as much as we can."

"Wait, sorry," Nicki said. "Are you a mage?"

"No, I'm only a magician I'm afraid." Avani looked a touch embarrassed now. "My family and I have rituals that we can use to gather a little bit of the realm's magic. I can't control it like you can."

"So that chanting we heard earlier?" Nicki pressed. "That was you?"

"Yes," Avani agreed. "I was preparing a spell, but the fight was over too quickly." She smiled a bit sheepishly. "Sadly, that's the reality of being only a magician. You have to call the magic to you with rituals; it isn't just there like it is for mages."

"And you're related to one of Alex's other lives," Bran said. Avani nodded again. "That's unexpected. Not the descendants thing; that makes sense, but that you know about magic. That's different."

"Magical ritual traditions are rare in the modern world, but not completely gone," Avani replied. Her posture was becoming a little more relaxed. "As I said, my family has maintained contact with the Trimurti, but especially Shiva."

"I'm sorry," Jenny said. She blushed a little but gave Avani an apologetic smile. "I'm not very aware of Indian culture, but the name Shiva is familiar."

It was Morgana who explained. "Hinduism is one of the primary religious belief systems in India. The Trimurti is the trinity of supreme power in Hinduism that embodies the cycle of creation, maintenance, and destruction. They are three powerful Old Ones that we have a peaceful alliance with. Shiva, the destroyer, more so than most. He was very close to the Iron Soul Lokpal, who entrusted Shiva with the Iron Artifact he created, the Trishula."

"Yes," Avani agreed. She finally sat down at the far end of the couch. "That's correct. As my family uses magic to a limited extent and are Lokpal's descendants, Shiva makes a point of checking in on us whenever he is awake. I'll be honest: we aren't the best Hindus, as we know which figures are real and which aren't, but we do honor those like Shiva who help protect humanity."

"Awake?" Lance asked.

"The three Old Ones: Shiva, Brahma, and Vishnu take turns staying awake," Avani explained to him. "The other two stay in the waters to keep themselves from being corrupted by the energies of our world. That way none of them become a threat to humanity."

"Similar to what Cyrridven did and the Norse were doing," Merlin added.

"Exactly, and whoever is awake usually wakes Shiva if things become too magical in the area, as he is the best warrior. Hence, the title of Destroyer," Avani said. "Sadly, that is the case now. Things in India are troubling."

"Indeed," Merlin said. "Avani, what can you tell us about the situation in India? Why would Shiva send you here with Sif?"

"I can't tell you much I'm afraid," Avani admitted. "As you may know Demons and the gods are large parts of Hindu life. Our subcontinent is home to several large conclaves of Demons who originally came from another world. That was before the Iron Gates were created."

"Like the Sídhe," Morgana said. She kept glancing towards the hallway. "And like the Sídhe they created small colonies in our world."

"Yes." Avani nodded and seemed to become more nervous. "Originally there wasn't too much trouble with these beings as they kept to themselves. According to the stories, before the Iron Gates were created, they'd come and go between our world and their own. They didn't take slaves like the Sídhe, which we believe is why the Iron Soul first incarnated in Europe. The first Old Ones in India often helped to fight them back to keep them from harming people, which formed the foundation of the Hindu religion. However, when the Iron Gates were created in the British Isles and their magic spread across the world, it locked many of them here in our world."

"The situation became very violent in the Vedic Period," Merlin said. He gave Avani a warm smile. "Roughly 650 B.C.E, if I remember correctly. Morgana and I went to India after receiving a warning from Cyrridven that a bad situation was growing there. Long story short the Demons in our world had united under a leader and the Old One Shiva was going mad." Merlin shuddered and shook his head. "It wasn't the best situation, but it was resolved with Shiva becoming a staunch ally. Later other Old Ones joined Shiva in protecting the area and keeping the Demon population in check."

"Hence why we haven't had many problems with Demons spreading across the world," Morgana said. "They've always been contained to the area. So, what is happening now?"

"It's difficult to say for certain," Avani admitted. "Shiva has woken and taken charge once again, but the Demon population..." Avani shook her head and seemed lost. "They aren't always violent of course; in fact, many live amongst humans without much difficulty and have spread throughout Asia. Lately something seems to be wrong with them."

"Could the Queen have affected them as well?" Lance asked.

Avani frowned and looked around at the group. "Sif told us a bit about what happened, but I'm not sure if she would have been able to affect the Demons. Not to mention, I'm not sure if she'd even know about them. While they were both active in ancient times, they came from different branches and invaded very far apart. They didn't have any contact and are very distinct species."

"That's a fair point," Merlin agreed. Then he groaned slightly. "This is not what we needed right now. The situation with Arthur and the Queen is complex enough. And Alex-" he cut himself off and shared a look with Morgana.

"Something is coming though," Alex's voice said.

Lance jumped up first and looked over into the hallway. Alex was standing there with a completely neutral expression. Her lips were pressed tightly together, there were dark circles under her eyes and she looked too pale. Yet there she was, and Lance could only wonder how long Alex had been standing there. Her gray eyes scanned the room as Morgana stood up and rushed over to her. The professor took her arm, silently giving Alex some support.

"Where's Sif?" Alex asked quietly. But as everyone else had gone still and silent, they could all hear her. "She's alright, isn't she?"

"Sif is fine," Morgana promised. "How are you, Alex?" Morgana stressed Alex's name and Lance frowned in confusion, wondering what he'd missed. "You should return to bed."

"I'm fine," Alex said. She yawned a little, covering her mouth with her hand. "I'd rather sleep through the night at this point."

"Yes, well, that will be soon," Merlin said. He stood from his chair and smiled at Alex. "We were just catching up with this young woman."

"Avani," Alex said.

She stepped away from Morgana and crossed the living room. Avani all but jumped out of her chair, shifting nervously for a moment before relaxing into almost parade rest. Alex stopped right in front of her. She was only about an inch taller than Avani and the two were like day and night beside each other. Then, to Lance's surprise, Alex reached out and pushed a strand of dark hair behind Avani's ear.

"You're one of mine," Alex said softly. She was smiling. "Avani, it's nice to meet you."

"It's a great pleasure, Iron Soul," Avani replied. Dropping her chin, she bowed slightly to Alex, who shook her head.

"Please, you don't need to do that. We don't bother much with formality here," Alex replied. "So, you're... Lokpal's grandchild."

"Many generations removed," Avani said. "But yes, I am. The eldest children of the family have kept magical traditions strong and held onto our history." Avani studied Alex with intense brown eyes as the rest of them just watched. "Forgive me; I was not aware that you retained any awareness. That was never recorded."

"I carry an.... awareness of the others, as you called it." Alex's eyes widened a little and her smile tightened. "Anyway, how bad are things in India?"

"It's mostly just pranks right now and some protection rackets," Avani said. "Packs of Demons causing trouble, but nothing Shiva is doing is stopping them. There are always more of them. It's like the population has tripled all of a sudden. Recently Shiva got information from one of the pack leaders that revealed there is some sort of Demon king rising."

"A king," Alex repeated. She frowned slightly. "This seems familiar...."

"Well in ancient times when Lokpal was alive something similar happened," Morgana offered.

"I don't think that's what I was thinking of," Alex said slowly. She didn't look distressed, just quizzical. "But maybe it was."

"Shiva was hoping that you could come and help," Avani said. "While he has the Trishula, there are limits to what he can do as an Old One without causing massive damage."

"And where is the worst of it?" Alex asked.

"It seems centered around Mumbai," Avani answered quickly. "We think it's because the Old Ones slumber in the waters near there. Though they are staying clear of Elephanta Island so far. Uh, that's where Shiva's cave temples are located."

"Well, sounds like India is now a priority," Alex said. She was smiling a little again.

"But Alex, we have the Sídhe returning here and Arthur to worry about," Merlin protested. "Are you sure you're up to it?"

"Not yet," Alex admitted. Her shoulders slumped and Lance sighed in relief. "You're right: we need to get some more Iron Gates built here to reinforce the area. Fighting on three fronts is too dangerous." Alex looked back at Avani. "How urgent would you say the situation is?"

"It can wait a little while," Avani said quickly. "I can call my father to let him know what is happening here. I'm not sure how much Sif told Shiva during their meeting."

"That's a meeting I would have liked to sit in on." Aiden chuckled a little and grinned when Avani looked over at him with a frown. "Come on; those are mythological pantheons that don't exactly interact often."

"I suppose not." Avani almost smiled at him and then looked back at Alex. "I can serve as a liaison between you and India for the time being while you defend your position here. I fear I don't know much about the Sídhe: they've never really broken through into Asia, thankfully, but I'll help any way that I can."

"I'm sorry that we can't go straight to India," Alex said gently. She reached out and touched Avani's shoulder in a comforting gesture. "But we'll stay aware of the situation, and once I'm sure that the northwest United States isn't in immediate threat of invasion, I'll go with you to see Shiva."

"Thank you," Avani replied. She bowed her head again. "I'm sorry we did not give you more warning. When Sif offered to bring me through the water tunnel it was too convenient an opportunity to pass up."

"We'll make it work," Alex said. Lance just stared at her. What had happened? This was not the reaction he'd been expecting. He caught Jenny's eye and she shook her head in confusion. At least it wasn't just him. Morgana was frowning slightly and Merlin was outright staring. "Do you have a place to stay?" Alex asked.

"I was just going to get a hotel," Avani answered.

Frowning, Alex turned towards Morgana with an expectant look. Morgana just kept staring at Alex until Alex widened her eyes and nodded towards Avani. Blinking, Morgana shook her head a little and forced a smile.

"Uh yes, Avani, why don't you stay here? I have a guest room. Nothing fancy, but the house does have defenses."

"Yes, thank you," Avani replied. She was looking between Alex and Morgana. "You're Morgana le Fey, are you not?"

"Morgana Cornwall, if you please," Morgana said. "But yes, I am."

"You were sister to the first incarnation of the Iron Soul?"

"Yes, I was," Morgana replied. Her tone and smile were tight. "And he's Merlin, but be sure to call him Professor Yates or Ambrose in public."

"I'm Nicki Russell." Nicki jumped off the couch and offered Avani her hand. "Nice to meet you. I'm sorry to say that you've caught us at a strange time, Avani. We're usually better organized than this."

"Pleasure to meet you," Avani replied with a small smile.

Lance and Jenny stood up as did Aiden and Bran. Everyone introduced themselves to Avani and she thankfully seemed to get more comfortable. It had been a strange night, and Lance kept glancing towards Alex. Her gray eyes were bright and yet distant. Every so often, she tilted her head as if listening to something else. Still, she didn't seem distressed or injured from what had happened with Brekszta. That made him frown: why weren't they talking about what had happened with Brekszta?

"Grab your things from the guest room," Merlin told Alex. "I'll get you home."

"Good idea, it's late," Alex agreed. "Come on, Avani, I'll show you the guest room." Alex held her hand out to the newcomer, who took it tentatively. "Be right back."

Then they were gone down the hall. Morgana moved over to Merlin and spoke with him in a low and urgent voice. Lance looked at Jenny, who shrugged helplessly.

"Dibs," Nicki said in a low voice.

Lance blinked at her in confusion. "I'm sorry, Nicki. What?"

"I'm calling dibs," Nicki repeated.

Next to her, Aiden groaned. "Really, Nicki? Is this the time?"

"She's gorgeous," Nicki sighed. The redhead tilted her head with a dopey smile. "Tall, pretty eyes, beautiful skin, and gorgeous dark hair. Plus, she knows about magic already so I'm calling dibs."

"I think you might be jumping ahead of yourself," Aiden said. "There's no reason to assume that she's bisexual or gay."

"But she might be," Nicki said. "And I can work with a might be. She's the one, I know it!"

Lance looked over at Aiden completely stunned. He knew that Nicki had a dramatic side, but this was a bit different. Aiden didn't look surprised at all and chuckled softly. That reaction allowed Lance to relax a little and he allowed himself a slight smile. If nothing else, Nicki's reaction to the newcomer had distracted him from his worry for Alex for a few moments, and he'd take that.

26

Lost to Memories

Morning found Alex sitting on a bench looking out over the lake. There was a slight chill in the air and Alex zipped up her fleece jacket, but kept her eyes fixed on the ripples of the water. Around her the leaves of the arboretum trees rustled in the breeze and muffled the sounds of the rest of the world. For a few moments, she was able to forget everything.

"Alex?" a familiar voice called.

Turning her head, Alex sat up straighter on reflex. Sif stood a few feet away with a nervous sort of smile on her face. The Old One was still dressed in modern clothes, but for a moment Alex could imagine her clearly in a long gown trimmed with gold and a cloak.

"Sif." The name itself tried to catch in her throat. "Uh, good morning."

"Would you like me to leave?" Sif asked. She twisted her hands in front of her. "I don't want to make things worse, Alex."

Alex tried to remember what had happened that would make Sif so uneasy. She remembered saying something last night, but it was blurry. "I doubt anything could make it worse at this point, Sif," Alex said. The name was light on her tongue, almost too easy to say. Shifting over on the bench, she smiled. "Take a seat. I'm glad to see that you're alright."

"Brekszta fled quickly," Sif replied. She sat down next to Alex and tossed her long golden braid over her shoulder. The action was familiar and made one of the voices, she guessed Thor's, grow louder. "It was odd: she really didn't seem interested in fighting. While that... cloud she released surrounded the other mages, it didn't hurt them."

"She said something odd," Alex admitted. "She said that she was trying to help me. I didn't believe her, but..."

"But?"

"Well, she's been making me dream of my other lives," Alex admitted. The words were easier to say than she thought they'd be. Looking at Sif, she found the Old One's face wonderfully blank of any emotion or judgment. "Did Thor die of old age?"

Sif blinked at the question but then nodded. "Yes, he did. It bothered him of course: he'd always assumed that he'd die in battle. It was one of his arguments for us having a relationship. He didn't think he'd live long enough to die an old man."

"You were with him when he died." It was a statement, not a question.

"Of course," Sif answered. "I loved Thor. He was an arrogant and hardheaded idiot." Her voice quivered for a moment. "But he had a good heart and was surprisingly clever at times. I never regretted our time together."

"I'm sorry to bring it up."

"Don't be sorry," Sif said. "I hope that you don't feel like you can't talk about Thor with me. I don't mind, I just worry about you."

"Thanks for that, I guess." Alex turned her gaze away from Sif. For a time neither of them spoke nor moved. Alex found herself half wishing that Sif would leave even as Thor's rough voice disagreed. "So... did Thor have red hair like in the stories?"

"Yes; his hair was naturally red," Sif agreed. "But like most people in that area, he bleached his hair."

"Really?"

"It was too cold during the winter to even consider a bath," Sif replied. "The Norse were a very clean people. They all had grooming tools and it was very important to them to have neatly trimmed beards." Sif paused as if she expected Alex to say something, but Alex stayed silent. "Bleaching kept lice and other unpleasant pests from taking hold when they couldn't wash their hair."

Alex had the strangest image of several men sitting in a longhouse trimming their beards and washing their faces. It was vivid with the smell of lye filling her nose. "They used lye?" Alex asked. Vaguely she remembered something about tweezers: asking Sif for tweezers last night.

"Yes," Sif replied carefully. "A special soap. Thor used to hate it when the red of his hair showed. I imagine he'd be a bit irritated to know that he's remembered with red hair."

"I'm not sure remembered is the right word," Alex said. "You have to go and actually read the myths to learn that."

"True enough, I suppose," Sif agreed. "But the later Norse who worshiped him wouldn't have imagined that he could be infected with lice."

"I wonder where the story of him needing a belt and gloves to use Mjǫllnir came from," Alex remarked. "Seems a bit odd."

"The Norse allowed their gods to be far more human than many other cultures," Sif said. "It's a fact I've always appreciated about them. Perhaps the legends of the Hammer were too unbelievable so they gave it a limiting factor. Something that would bind it to Thor. After all, they didn't know about the Iron Soul."

"I guess."

There was a group of geese at the edge of the lake, a couple of adults and a bunch of small goslings. It made Alex smile as she watched them paddle across the surface. She struggled with the reality that only last night she'd been facing Brekszta on that same shore. Some of the worst events of her life had unfolded here. It seemed appropriate that Brekszta would make her relive the other horrible events here as well. The truck flashed through her memory and Alex couldn't help but shiver.

"Alex?" Sif asked.

"I'm alright," Alex said. "Just a dark thought. Something Brekszta brought to the surface." Straightening up, Alex rolled her shoulder and smiled for Sif. "I'm working my way through it."

The knot in her chest quivered at the lie and Alex pushed a little more magic into it. In response, the bundle thrummed in silent warning. What would happen when the knot came untied, Alex didn't know. She couldn't bring herself to care.

"You said that Brekszta is making you dream of your other lives," Sif said carefully. "And that she thought she was helping you? Any idea why she might think that?"

"I suppose she might think that this whole memory wipe thing is a bad system," Alex suggested. "And I sort of agree with her. There are times when I wish I just knew what the other Iron Souls knew. Things might be easier that way." The voices grew louder, but they were too mixed up to understand.

"Don't lose Alex," Sif said softly. "Hold onto her: fight for her."

"Why?" Alex asked. She hadn't meant to voice the question and looked at Sif. "Surely the memories would help. You spoke with Shiva and brought Avani here. You know that things just keep getting worse." A sad chuckle escaped Alex and she looked out over the lake. "I remember thinking when we helped Arthur create that Gate that everything was going to get better. I thought we were in control of the situation and that the worst was over." Shaking her head, Alex reached up and tucked a strand of blonde hair behind her ear. "Seems like years ago; decades even, but it wasn't."

"Alex, last night…"

"I was Thor, wasn't I?" Alex asked. She looked at Sif and frowned. "I sort of remember, but it's foggy."

"Yes." Sif's voice was tight and pained. "You were, but you're Alex. You can't be Thor. No matter how much…" Sif trailed off and turned to look out at the lake.

"I'm sorry," Alex said softly. Standing up, she debated if she should say more. One of the voices was angry and hurt, urging her to say more, but offered no suggestions. "Please take care, Sif," Alex finally added. "I'm sorry if I hurt you."

"Alex!" Nicki's voice rang through the arboretum and Alex released a sigh. She wasn't sure if she was grateful for Nicki's timing or not. Alex nodded to Sif and headed up the slope of the hill towards Nicki. "There you are!" The relief was clear in her roommate's voice.

"Just needed some fresh air," Alex said. Then she gestured over to the bench where Sif was still sitting. "I was having a chat with Sif."

"Is everything alright?" Nicki asked. She couldn't hide her worry.

"Sure." Alex tugged another strand of blonde hair out of her face. "I'm a bit restless so I'm going to head over to Merlin's and work on some iron."

"Do you need some help?"

"No, I'll be fine." Alex rocked on the balls of her feet for a moment. "Just restless from last night. Figure I might as well put it to good use."

It was obvious that Nicki wanted to say or ask something, but wasn't sure how. Alex didn't want to know what would make Nicki so nervous. Instead, she stepped past her roommate and briefly knocked their shoulders.

"I'll be home later," Alex promised.

"Just make sure you get your homework done," Nicki said. "We're in the final stretch."

"Yes, ma'am!"

Nicki didn't stop her as she walked away. Alex hoped that Nicki didn't try to talk with Sif– that idea made her stomach twist uncomfortably. Reaching into her bag, Alex pulled out her keys and ran a finger over the leather sheath of her iron dagger. It didn't take her long to find her car and start heading for Merlin's house. She turned on the radio and allowed herself to hum along with a song she sort of knew during the short drive across the river.

Professor Ambrose's house was a welcome and calming sight to Alex as she pulled up. His hedges were overgrown and rough from lack of care, but the gargoyles on either side of his doorway were the same as ever. Looking towards the house, Alex searched for any signs that Merlin was home. His SUV wasn't in front of the one-story house and there were no visible lights on. While it was a Sunday, with the school year wrapping up Alex supposed that he was probably at his office on campus. That was better for her.

She walked up to the gate leading to Merlin's yard and opened it quickly. Nothing had changed. Alex ran a finger over the back of one of the wrought iron chairs on his patio. Her magic hummed in response to the smoothness of the cool iron against her skin.

The workshop was locked, but that was solved with a bit of magic. Alex stepped into the dark workshop and hit the light switch. With a soft buzz, the lights around the walls lit up. Alex set her bag down on the nearest worktable next to a half-finished iron candelabra. With her magic, she stoked up a fire in the nearest furnace. Pulling over a rolling tool rack, Alex collected some of the spare iron bars Merlin kept on hand.

Her eyes traveled to the safe in the workshop floor. Stopping in place, Alex closed her eyes and exhaled slowly. Her magic crept through her limbs and with a gentle push, Alex spread it through the room. It hung in the air like a fine mist, too soft and subtle for anyone to see, but as Alex focused, she could see through it. All the iron in the workshop gleamed to her, and there was an outline of all the tools, tables, and the two forges.

And she could see the safe. Merlin had poured a layer of iron dust across the top of the steel door. Yet despite the security between her and the contents, Alex could sense the hum of magic from both the Iron Chalice and Mjǫllnir. Both called to her. There was an urgency to it that she'd never noticed before and Alex took a step towards the safe. Two voices in her head were louder now. She could somewhat recognize the deeper voice of Thor and his sharp tones. The other one was softer and more worried, but she figured it had to be Gofiben.

"Enough," Alex said out loud. She shook her head. "I have work to do."

She opened her eyes. The magic snapped back like a rubber band, rushing into her chest, and making her dizzy. It passed quickly and Alex marched over to the furnace, determined to get to work. Keeping tight control of her magic, Alex forced it through the hammer and into the hot pieces of metal. One by one, she pounded magic into the iron pieces until they gleamed with her own power. Dark silver sparks danced beneath the surface as she found a rhythm.

Merlin's modern furnace fell away. She could see another furnace; this one was much smaller and rougher. It was sunken into the ground to help keep in the heat, but the flames danced over the coals in the same way. The smell of smoke and hot metal was familiar. The tongs pulling out the pieces of iron were different and the hands were too large. Yet the actions were the same.

It changed again. This furnace was in a small building with long benches along the walls. There was a large pile of wood just waiting for use and iron axe heads and swords spread out on the benches. A strand of blonde hair fell into their face, but they didn't bother with it. Familiar movements: pulling the iron from the heat and forming it into shape. Magic flared from their fingertips and through their Hammer. This time they were aware of a hum from the Hammer itself.

Another forge, another place and another time, but always the familiar actions. Their fingers knew the way even when weaker muscles protested. The magic followed their commands and settled into the heart of the iron. It pulsed with life and waited for its time. They made a Sword, a Chalice, and a Hammer. There were more items. They saw an odd iron container, like an urn or a jar. There was a Chain that was not forged by their hands but held too often with power hungry intentions. The magic followed the intentions and settled into it anyway. There was a Brooch that shimmered with power after too many touches.

The sound of a door opening pulled her back. Alex blinked and looked up sharply. Her heart pounded as the urge to fight took over. Merlin was standing in the doorway, frowning as he took in the pile of finished iron bars. Exhaling, Alex felt the fatigue in her muscles and wondered how long she'd been working. She quickly looked back down to the fire where another piece of iron was heating up.

"Alex?" Merlin called. "What are you doing here?"

"Working on iron for the next Gate," Alex replied. She didn't bother looking up. There was a layer of sweat across her skin and she suddenly wished that she'd brought some clothes to change into when she was done. "With the situation in India, I want to be able to leave soon."

"You still have finals to worry about."

"I suppose," Alex said. Those didn't really matter that much, but it was a fight she wouldn't win. "Still, if we can secure Ravenslake, at least for a little while, then we can go to India and see what is happening there."

"Alex, there is time. You can let Morgana and I worry about that," Merlin said kindly. "It's our job."

"No," Alex said. Looking at him, Alex met his surprised gaze. "It's my job. I'm the Iron Soul. It's my job more than anyone else's."

"That's not true," Merlin protested. "Morgana and I have more experience. We've been helping in this fight for years. I appreciate that you are taking it all so seriously, but you still have a life, Alex." Alex did another round of hammering. He didn't speak again until the metal had started to cool and Alex paused to mop up some sweat from her face. "Your growing awareness of your other lives has Morgana and I concerned, Alex. Lately you've been saying things and-"

"You don't understand." Alex shoved the iron bar back into the coals and watched the sharp orange light flicker across the black surface of the coals. "I'm not just aware of them, Merlin. I hear them. All the time now. Just this constant dull drone at the back of my skull. Someone is always talking, someone always has something to say, but most of the time they all talk at once." She looked over at Merlin with a raised eyebrow. "Even now, they're all chiming in on this decision to tell you."

"Alex?" Merlin's mouth was opening and shutting as he sputtered for something to say.

Chuckling, Alex shook her head and picked up the tongs. "Wild, huh?" She dug through the coals and found the iron bar. Pulling it out,

Alex smiled at the gleaming red-hot metal and laid it across the anvil. "Even today: I keep getting flashes of insight on how to be a better smith. Don't get me wrong, I could do it before, but now I have all these other little ideas of how to be better at it. Ways to improve. Of course, right now I'm just preparing for another Iron Gate and not trying to make anything fancy."

"You're sure?" Merlin finally managed to ask. "You're positive? It isn't just... occasionally?"

"No," Alex answered. She picked up one of the larger hammers. "Not just occasionally." Bringing the hammer down, Alex relished the sharp metallic ring and the way that the hot iron bar bent beneath the blow. "Sometimes someone is louder than the others. Thor was loudest last night, and then when I was with Avani I think Lokpal pushed through more." She didn't give him a chance to reply and hit the metal again. "It comes and goes."

"But that's..." Merlin stayed across the room and just watched Alex.

She didn't look at him. Alex kept pulling on her magic and struck the metal once again. There was a shimmer of dark silver just beneath the surface. There was a tug in Alex's gut towards the iron. It was enough for this one. Holding it with the tongs, Alex lowered it into the water and listened as the hot metal hissed. The sound was delicious in a way she'd never appreciated before, and it sent a pleasant shiver up her spine.

"What do you want me to say?" Merlin asked. He was collapsed against a work table, his eyes dark with sadness. "This is unexpected, Alex. I knew, of course, that things were slipping through. You'd said things that..." Shaking his head, Merlin lowered his gaze from Alex.

"There's nothing to say," Alex replied. "I didn't say anything because I know you can't do anything about it. At this point, it doesn't matter." Alex gave him a smile when he stared at her in shock. "Besides, I don't want to be one of those depressing, annoying heroes who whines too much. This isn't something that needs fixing. It's a bit weird right now, but the others might be able to help me. This makes more sense for a reincarnation."

"But Alex.... This is..." Merlin was struggling and sputtering again. "It isn't fair to you. There's so many of them and you're..."

"Oh, Merlin," Alex said. "Me, you, and Morgana, all the creatures caught in our world from Timothy to Emrys and all those Sídhe and even the Demons... we're all cursed. All of us are cursed in different ways by the power of iron." Shaking her head, Alex used the tongs to pick up the next iron bar. "The Iron Cursed. It isn't fair or easy: we just have to live with it. And that's what I'm going to do. Live with it."

27

To the Walls

64 B.C.E. Cashel, Ireland

Thunder crashed far overhead as Leugio settled down on his bed. He could hear the raindrops hitting the thatch roof and smell the thick earthy musk of the wet ground. In the hearth the fire continued to burn bravely, and the sight of the flames soothed him. Picking up the cruit next to his bed, Leugio plucked a few strings and began to play.

The rain made him homesick. His house here was comfortable and well-supplied thanks to the king, but until he married Flaitheas, he lived alone. In truth he was almost certain that Eochu Finn would merely have him move into the king's roundhouse. The thought of his coming marriage made his chest tighten. His mother had been thrilled but sad, as it meant he would likely never return to his home village permanently. Keelia had liked Flaitheas a great deal and was far more than just accepting; even hinting that she might relocate.

Another roll of thunder made Leugio groan and he looked up in time to see a flash of light through the smoke hole. The flames flickered as some water dripped down through the opening and made strange shadows appear in his home. It was too much like the nights he'd spent snuggled up against Keelia and his mother while she told them stories.

Sabe knew many of the old tales of mages, the Sídhe, and gods, but now Leugio had to wonder which ones might be true.

It wasn't a comforting thought. He again wondered about the Grand Mages and if Iúdás was right about it being better that they weren't here. Teàrlach was still a mystery and one that Leugio couldn't be certain would ever be solved. Would he have to defeat the Sídhe in combat? Would he be able to if it came to that? His eyes jumped to the iron sword at the foot of his bed. While he was improving, his skill was still limited. He was a shepherd.

An odd flutter in his gut that spread up around his heart made him pause. Beneath his skin, there was a warmth spreading through his limbs. It took Leugio only a moment to realize that his magic was becoming stronger. The small flicker was growing. Standing up, he flexed his fingers and swallowed when white sparks jumped around his hand. There was a moment of stunned silence, but then he leapt into action. Leugio bent down to scoop up his sword and rushed outside.

Instantly the curtains of water began to soak him through, but the intensity of the magic in the air kept him from turning around. His eyes searched the roads through the village frantically before he realized that he was alone, apart from the guards who were outside. The Sídhe weren't inside yet. He yelled a warning and ran towards the walls. The torches lining the walls were struggling to stay lit, with roughly half of them already out. Cauldrons with fires set in them were scattered about but burning low as water gathered inside them.

Leugio stopped just long enough to conjure a glowing orb which illuminated everything around him. He pushed a bit more magic into it and lifted it into the air. For a moment he kept his hand close to his body, but the orb obediently floated above him just as he'd desired. The act of controlling his magic, even though it was a small thing, made him feel better. Another flash of lightning spurred him forward and he turned his attention to the wall. Guards were standing on high platforms a few feet apart, wrapped up in cloaks and shivering. One of the nearest guards looked down at him, and his eyes widened in surprise at the sight of the magical floating orb.

"What can you see?" Leugio called up. He strapped his sword firmly to his back.

"Uh, oh!" the man stuttered. "Uh, nothing, sir!" the young man called down.

Leugio grabbed the ladder and began to climb up onto the platform while the young man stuttered again. It quivered slightly at the additional weight but allowed him to see over the wooden wall. The wind howled around them and his companion on the platform shivered once more. The torch fixed to the side of the platform flickered and steam curled up into the air. Leugio doubted it would remain lit for long. Looking out into the blackness, Leugio grit his teeth and waited for something, anything, to give him a clue.

Hurling the glowing orb out into the rain, Leugio pushed a little more magic forward and wished for it to go further. The orb changed in a sputter of white and flew far further than he could have thrown it. Then the light poured over moving figures and Leugio willed it to stop. The orb froze in midair, illuminating the terrain below despite the onslaught of rain.

Sídhe were marching towards them. A few were on horseback while others were on foot. There were three rows of pale skin, white hair, and leather armor. Leugio's eyes scanned over them, trying to count their numbers, but struggled to distinguish them in the low light. Down the wall, he heard shouting as the alarm was raised.

Leugio stared at them. They were marching up the steep pathway that led up the high rocky base of the village. The steepness was slowing them down, but Leugio knew it wouldn't stop them. Waving his hands, he formed more glowing orbs for light and threw them out into the darkness. At his silent command, they stopped and hung in the air, but Leugio had no time to be pleased.

Some of the Sídhe were covering their eyes as others pulled hoods further over their faces. Leugio's eyes widened and he conjured another light orb, which he threw out directly above the group. They spread out away from it and continued to advance towards the wall. Amongst the Sídhe, torches were being lit. Leugio's chest tightened and he rushed back down the ladder. His right foot slipped on one of the rungs and he almost fell.

"What are you doing?" the guard called down.

"We can't let them light the walls on fire!" Leugio shouted up.

There were more shouts of alarm. The whole village was waking. Men were rushing towards the gate as orders were called down from the platforms. Leugio joined the ten armed men who were at the front as the doors opened. They poured out of the village towards the Sídhe, swinging iron weapons at the nearest ones. Scanning the ranks of the Sídhe, Leugio tried once more to count them, but there seemed to be dozens now. His orbs continued to hang in the air above them, illuminating the rocky terrain and puddles of water.

Arrows were raining down from the wall, killing a few Sídhe here and there. Pulling on his magic, the ground beneath Leugio hummed in response. The spark in his lower chest flared to life and spread power all through his limbs. He took a risk and closed his eyes, trying to visualize more of the magic striking the Sídhe. Stopping them. The hum of the magic grew louder, sparks were hot against his hands and he pushed the light forward. Beams erupted from all his fingers, shooting into the night and tearing through the first row of Sídhe.

It seemed to trigger something. There was a roar both behind him from the men and one from the Sídhe before him. Everyone charged and began to fight. Above them, two orbs provided steady illumination between flashes of lightning and crashes of thunder. Bringing up his hand, Leugio pushed the magic. It flared in his chest. There was a sharp jolt through his feet. The thick smell of earth from the rain intensified, filling his nose, throat, and chest. For a moment Leugio was almost dizzy, but then the magic released. A wave of white light exploded around him. Several Sídhe ducked down while others threw themselves out of the way. One of the riders fell off his brown horse, which turned and ran off the battlefield. There were cries of pain from the Sídhe. Some were staggering back, clutching at their faces in pain and others who he'd caught in the chests were dissolving.

That didn't end it. A man next to him fell to the ground, blood spilling out across the earth. Another man a few feet away began to scream before his throat was brutally torn out. Chaos engulfed them, but a quick, worried glance confirmed that the gate was closed behind them and that the walls were still secure. Violet eyes glared at him and Leugio thrust his left hand forward to release a bolt of white magic. Then he swung the sword with his right, catching a Síd in the arm. His ears pounded with his own heartbeat and the screaming.

Long brown hair caught his eye and his chest tightened at the sight of Flaitheas swinging a sword to force a Síd away from a fallen warrior. On instinct, Leugio stepped towards her. A Síd grabbed his left arm and twisted. A hiss of pain escaped him, coloring his mind red and purple. He pushed through it as long claws cut into his skin. His magic was wild; like an animal trying to burst forth, but not sure where to go. Swinging his left hand around, Leugio let the magic fly. Sparks shot off in different directions, but it was enough for the Síd to release its grip. The next bolt caught it in the chest, dissolving its body in moments.

Another Síd charged him. Behind it was another figure on horseback riding into the fight. The Síd brought its sword up with a sharp cry. There was a clash of metal against metal and Leugio frantically tried to focus on calling more magic while defending himself. White sparks escaped from his fingertips, flashing off in different directions, but he couldn't focus them. The horse was closer now and Leugio braced himself to jump. The Síd swung again. There was a shout, and the horse ran past as its rider kicked the Síd down instead of him.

Leugio didn't wait. The Síd was sprawled and dazed. He slammed the tip of his blade down through its neck. The iron sliced through the flesh like a knife through warm fat and his stomach tightened. He glanced up towards the rider, who was dressed in a long heavy cloak and carried a smoldering torch. The rider was swinging a sword at another Síd that had gotten too close to Flaitheas.

Panic. He raised a hand and grasped at the magic. A white bolt shot through the air and struck the Síd. A low cry escaped the creature, but it was already turning to dust. Leugio's knees trembled. There was an ache in his chest; a strange and sharp burn that made it difficult to breathe. The hooded rider who had saved him was rushing towards him. The rider's wet torch was barely giving off any light, even as the rain finally began to ease.

The guards were swarming forth and the Sídhe were retreating down the hill. One of the men had grabbed the reins of a horse while two others pulled down the Síd rider. More of the Sídhe were falling back. One was tackled by Nyle, who shoved a dagger through its eye. Leugio pulled on the magic once more, letting it gather in his palm. Then he blasted it forward as a bolt to catch a Síd in the arm. It fell over, and with a shout Flaitheas put a sword through its skull.

Finally, the last of the Síd had fled. Leugio panted and looked around. His orbs illuminated the landscape. Four human bodies were on the ground dead, and two more men were wounded. There were no Sídhe bodies, all them having dissolved, and only red blood was on the ground. Leugio's legs quivered and he locked his knees to stay upright. Two horses had been captured and were already being led towards the gate. At the walls, there was cheering and some crying at the sight of the bodies.

Then the stranger dismounted his horse and walked closer to Leugio. His hood was low enough that the light of the magical orbs still only revealed the lower half of his face. Tightening his grip on the hilt of his sword, Leugio braced himself nervously. The man had used no magic, but he couldn't help but wonder if this was a Grand Mage.

The man pulled back the soaked hood to reveal a face a little older than his own. He had a square jawline, strong shoulders, and a scar across one cheek that almost connected with his brown eyes. Leugio and the man both panted and stared at each other. Thankfully, the man made no move to harm him.

"Hello," Leugio greeted. His voice was somewhat lost on the wind. "Who are you?"

"Conn!" he answered, almost shouting. "I've been tracking those Síd-he after they stole the horses of my king!"

Leugio hesitated, but the others were coming closer. Flaitheas ran towards him, her brown hair clinging to her skin and her dress splattered with mud. He was certain that he didn't look any better. At least Conn had a cloak on. The stranger lowered his head in deference and adjusted his grip on the sword. Nyle stepped forward and took the weapon without a fight from Conn.

"Who are you?" Flaitheas had her dagger at the ready, and Leugio's lips twitched into a smile. "Why are you here?"

"Please forgive me," Conn said. "I've been trying to catch this group of Sídhe off guard for several days."

"But they don't go out during the day," she said suspiciously.

"Indeed: I've been riding at night by torchlight and sleeping during the day. They've been moving from mound to mound. I've been trying to figure out a way to deal with them on my own. It was a much larger group than my king originally believed.

"I see," Leugio said. "We're grateful for the help."

"You're a fair warrior," Flaitheas observed with a glint in her eye.

Conn smiled slightly at the remark. "I was rewarded for my service with some land and livestock. I was not willing to allow the Sídhe to endanger the good graces of my lord." He turned and looked out into the darkness and then up at the light orbs. "I had heard rumors that there was a mage here, but to see magic with my own eyes... amazing."

Leugio waved a hand and one of the orbs vanished. Flaitheas smiled proudly when Conn's eyes widened again. Then she turned and looked towards the fallen warriors. Her smile vanished and Leugio squeezed her hand gently.

"Conn," Flaitheas said. "I respect that you serve another king, but the Sídhe are becoming more and more active under one named Teàrlach, who seeks to conquer us all." Conn's eyes widened and Leugio looked at Flaitheas in surprise. "I am the daughter of Eochu Finn. I grant you safe slumber here tonight, and of course the horses that were recovered, but I wonder if you might consider staying and helping. We can send a messenger to your king and discuss an alliance."

There was something in Conn's expression that Leugio didn't like, but he wasn't sure what it was. The other man studied him and then glanced up at the light orb once more. Around them, people had come out to tend to the dead as the last of the rain finally stopped. Then Conn nodded in agreement and smiled a little at Flaitheas.

28

Level of Frequency

Lance wanted finals week to be over. He had one more exam and a paper to turn in and dearly wished it could just be over with. But no, Professor Hartman followed the official schedule. He didn't care if his test wasn't until Friday; he was going to follow the schedule. Jenny grabbed his hand and squeezed it as they sat down in Merlin's living room. Across from them Avani was sitting next to Nicki on the sofa. The newcomer was in jeans and a hoodie with her long hair braided over her right shoulder.

The living room was a little too small for the increasing number of people, so Merlin had brought in some folding chairs. Lance wondered why they weren't at Morgana's house. Her place was at least a bit larger. Merlin and Morgana were standing close together, almost shoulder to shoulder in some act of solidarity. Lance wasn't sure what to make of it. Alex, on the other hand, was sitting on the sofa with a glass of water held loosely in her hand. In contrast to Merlin and Morgana, she seemed completely calm and unconcerned. He couldn't figure it out. There were moments when she was normal and then moments that it just seemed like something had been switched off.

"So, what's the plan?" Nicki asked. "When will we be heading to India?" Her excitement was clear and made them all smile. Avani's eyes brightened at the question and she looked at Alex eagerly.

"Soon," Alex said. "The goal is to secure Ravenslake a bit more from the Sídhe. With the Chain broken, hopefully Arthur will keep his distance for a bit." Alex straightened up and looked towards Avani. "Once that's done, we'll head for Mumbai and meet with Shiva."

"So, making more Gates?" Aiden raised an eyebrow and tapped his fingers on his knee. "Do you know where yet?"

"Not yet," Merlin said, clearing his throat. "We'll work on determining locations while you finish the semester."

"Do you need us in the forge around classes?" Bran asked.

"We have enough iron to make two Gates at least," Merlin said. His eyes jumped over to Alex, but she just sipped her water and didn't look at him. There was tension in her shoulders, but otherwise she still just seemed detached. "So that isn't the problem. The issue is where to put another Gate. We usually don't put them in place before we find a tunnel."

"Well, maybe Alex can find the next weak point," Bran suggested. "With her being able to sense through her magic, maybe she could find a good location."

"That's not a bad thought," Alex replied. Her face brightened. "I might need some magical help from you guys, but it sounds doable."

"I suppose that could work," Morgana agreed. She didn't sound convinced, but she did sound curious. "You'd need to be careful though, Alex. We still don't know much about that ability of yours."

"It's clairvoyance," Alex offered with a smile. Glancing over at Aiden and Nicki, she smiled and winked. "Inspired by their magic books."

Avani looked confused, but before she could say anything there was a popping sound outside. Jumping up, Lance pulled back the curtain and looked outside. The last rays of the sun were vanishing behind the mountains, but the purple sky overhead still provided enough light for him to see the small gray creatures running between their cars. Several tires were punctured already and his own truck was balanced on rims. Lance groaned as he caught sight of the bright red hats.

"Red Caps!" he snapped.

"Oh lovely," Morgana growled. She strode towards the door. "Mages outside; stay in pairs at least."

"Timothy," Merlin called towards the kitchen. "Stay inside the house." He paused at the door as the mages followed him with Alex at the lead. "Swords are in the cabinet."

Lance kept his arm around Jenny while the mages filed out. There was a flash of silver through the air that rolled past the large window. Then Jenny shook her head and slipped out of his grasp. Walking past Avani, she offered the newcomer a smile and opened the cabinet. Inside as promised were several swords in leather sheaths. Jenny pulled one out and handed it to Avani.

"Do you know how to use this?" Jenny asked.

"I'm more familiar with a scimitar style of blade, but I should be alright." Avani accepted the sword and wrapped her hand around the hilt. "Thank you."

"Of course." Jenny walked back to him and handed him one. "Let's hope they don't break the roof again."

Lance wanted to chuckle, but the reminder that it could happen made it very unfunny. He pulled the sword out of the sheath and tossed the leather covering onto a nearby table. The blade gleamed in the light of the lamps and he considered turning them off as a bolt of lightning blasted past the window. A car alarm began to go off and he heard Nicki curse. Then it went silent, whether by damage or magic he wasn't sure.

"At least they can fix the cars," Jenny murmured next to him. "I'd hate to see the body work bill."

"Not to mention the questions it would get."

"Is this a frequent problem?" Avani asked. Her brown eyes were wide, but she didn't look frightened. In fact, she looked more curious than anything as she joined them near the window. "Red Caps attacking?"

"Frequent? Uh, probably not frequent," Lance managed to say.

"But often enough," Jenny said with bite in her voice. "And they've slashed the tires. We aren't going anywhere."

"And so, you just wait inside?" Avani questioned. She was looking at them carefully. "Forgive me if I'm rude, but I'm not completely up to speed on everything going on here. You two are the reincarnations of Lancelot and Guinevere, correct?"

Next to him, Jenny blushed and lowered her eyes for a moment, but she rallied quickly. "Those weren't their names," she said. "But close enough. We were the wife and friend of the original Iron Soul."

A Red Cap flew past the window in a rush of yellow magic from Bran. Then there was a shower of flaming sparks, but the magic flared blue. Lance thought that was probably Nicki. Avani's eyebrows went up.

"And you keep being reborn?" Avani asked. "Over and over?"

"We aren't in every life," Lance said. Then he realized that Avani would be aware of that. "Just sometimes... but this time it's different."

"Yes," Jenny agreed. She nodded eagerly and then grimaced at the sight of a group of floating Red Caps being enveloped in green magic and turning to dust. "There was never a romantic relationship between Alex and I, and Lance and I are together and working things out."

"I'm glad that you've made peace with your reincarnations," Avani said calmly. "But why do you stay in this town if it is so dangerous?" She gestured towards the window. "Surely Arthur will make you targets."

Lance paused. He'd never had to try and explain things to someone who hadn't been around for at least part of it. "Well, we're loyal to Alex. I suppose on some level we're trying to make up for things. While we may not have magical powers, there are still times when they need us."

"Magic isn't everything," Jenny said. She eyed the door and then the sword in her hands. "Besides, I'm not half bad with this thing."

"That's good," Avani said. Then she tapped the hilt of the sword and twisted her lips thoughtfully. "Though I suppose I could teach you a bit of the rituals I use to do magic." They both turned to look at her and Avani smiled. "If you like. You can't do big things like mages, but it can be useful from time to time." She nodded out the window where another bolt of lightning was flashing past. Three Red Caps were suddenly tossed past their view and shouted some gibberish. "It's not as impressive as mages obviously but being able to pick a lock or do some basic repairs can be a nice talent to have."

"How does it work?" Jenny asked. A blast of red light outside that made several Red Caps scream lit up her face. "You can't just make something happen like the mages can, right?"

"No, we actually use what you'd think of as spells," Avani explained. "We gather up magical energy and use spells to direct the magic. Create a set pathway for the magic, if you like." Her smile widened and she giggled. "To my parents' annoyance, I use a bunch of spells from books and movies. They stay in my mind better and I can get the magic to know what I mean."

"Books and movies," Jenny repeated. She laughed, only stopping when a Red Cap hit the window. It slid down a second later. "Uh, are you a geek then?"

"Bit of one," Avani replied with her accent thickening a touch. "Fantasy is a great source for inspiration. The family magical tomes are useful, but with all the modern technology you need to be creative in how to interact with it."

"Oh no, not another one!" Jenny sniggered at Avani's curious look. "Uh, most of the mages are pretty serious geeks. I think you'll like them."

"What about you?"

"Me?" Jenny shook her head. "No, I'm more of a social and shopping sort."

"That's fun too," Avani agreed. "I'm a bit worried about staying in a town this size too long." She tossed her long black hair over her shoulder. "Where's the best place to restock on makeup around here?"

"Oh, I'm afraid that Ravenslake doesn't have a lot of good options on that front," Jenny said with a grimace. "I order most of my makeup and hair supplies online. There are some good boutiques on Main Street at least."

"I was afraid you were going to say that." Avani sighed and looked at her braid. "I barely brought enough stuff for three days."

"Well let me know what you need and I'll check my stuff," Jenny said.

A crash outside made them jump as another car alarm started going off. Lance raised the sword and shifted over to the front door as a scraping sound moved across the wood. He barely made it there before the door gave way. Jumping to the side, he managed to avoid Nicki's body crumbling inside. A Red Cap was on her chest. She groaned and started to move. There was blood on her chest. Swinging the sword, Lance caught the Red Cap in the upper torso. It screamed. There was a bit of silvery blood and its body began to dissolve as it was thrown back.

"Oh god!" Jenny cried. "Nicki!"

Lance stepped forward to block the doorway with the sword at the ready. There was still a dozen or so Red Caps running around. With sharp claws and small knives, they kept lashing at the ankles of the mages. Merlin kicked one against the house and Morgana destroyed it with a bolt of silver magic. Bran waved his hands and swept up three of them in a small cyclone of yellow magic. Alex unleashed a bolt of lightning into the group to kill them before having to kick away one trying to cut her tendon.

"Nicki!" Aiden shouted, looking towards the door.

"We've got her!" Lance called back. "Stay focused!" He risked a glance over his shoulder. Jenny and Avani had pulled open Nicki's shirt and were applying pressure to the wound. There was a lot of blood and both women looked worried. "We need the Chalice!"

Aiden shoved a hand forward and sent waves of red sparks rolling down along the ground that glittered like embers. Then he took off around the side of the house towards the workshop. Merlin called after him, but Aiden didn't stop. Merlin gathered a green orb of magic and threw it at the ground. Blades of grass sprang up, entwining around the legs of the Red Caps, who hacked at the grass with their knives. Merlin took off after Aiden.

Morgana used the Red Caps' distraction, and with several quick bolts of bright silver more were dead. There were only two left that he could see, and they were both scurrying towards the forest. Alex snarled at them, her gray eyes bright with anger. Dark silver magic twisted around her hands and then two lightning bolts flashed off her fingertips. They caught each of the Red Caps, who vanished in a burst of ash. Then everything went quiet. Bran came rushing to the doorway, looking over Lance's shoulder.

Stepping out of the way, Lance let Bran and Alex through and both knelt next to Nicki. He watched Alex's face. There was a flicker of something in her eyes and then she grit her teeth. Her expression smoothed out and she took Nicki's hand. Lance wasn't sure if her calm was good or bad. Jenny kept talking softly to Nicki and brushed strands of red hair out of her face.

Aiden and Merlin came in through the back. There was the brief sound of the faucet in the kitchen running and then Aiden was kneeling next to Nicki, calling her name. Avani moved back to give him space. The Iron Chalice shimmered in Aiden's hand as he handed it to Alex. Magic glowed around her hands and the metal of the Chalice lit up. With a soft apology, Aiden lifted Nicki's head as she groaned and whimpered. Then Alex put the Chalice against Nicki's lips and tilted it.

"Easy," Morgana cautioned from the front doorway. "You don't want her to choke."

The warning wasn't necessary. Lance averted his eyes to give Nicki privacy, settling for watching Aiden's face. There was a long moment of silence. No one moved. Then relief filled Aiden's face and Lance relaxed. Nicki was already sitting up and he caught sight of the pinkish, but intact skin across her upper chest. Then Nicki realized that half of her shirt was torn and sat up with a bright red blush staining her cheeks. Lance began to take off his sweatshirt, but Avani unzipped her hoodie and handed it to Nicki with a small smile.

"Here," she said.

"Thanks," Nicki replied. If anything, her blush worsened and she quickly pulled on the hoodie. Holding back a laugh, Lance remembered Nicki's dibs. "I appreciate it."

"Oh, please don't worry about it," Avani replied. "Let's get you up."

Everyone backed away to give Nicki room to stand up. Merlin glanced towards Morgana and headed outside. There were flashes of green light and Lance really hoped it meant that he was repairing tires and vehicle damage. Morgana lingered by the doorway and the wooden pieces of the front door glowed silver. Lance watched as the pieces of wood flew back into the doorway and fit themselves together like a puzzle.

Lance helped Nicki over to the couch. Despite being healed, she swayed a little and sank onto the sofa with a sigh of relief. Aiden sat down next to her, wrapping an arm around her shoulder while Bran gave her a glass of water to drink. Merlin came back inside a few moments later, panting slightly, but he waved Morgana off.

"I'm okay," Nicki finally said. "That was..." she trailed off and shook her head. "Never mind. I'm fine. Thanks for the quick response."

"We need to start carrying the Chalice with us," Alex said. "Needing Merlin to open the safe and keeping it here is too much of a risk." She sat down in an armchair and drummed her fingers against the arms.

"Probably a good idea," Nicki said. She shuddered. "I just... I'm not even sure what happened. Suddenly it jumped off the car hood and-"

"Hey, don't worry about it." Aiden tightened his grip around her. "You're okay. I know it can be scary, but just remind yourself that you're okay."

Alex was staring off into space again. Frowning, Lance studied her face, but Alex's head was tilted. Again, it was like she was listening to something that they couldn't hear.

"Alex?" Bran called. "Alex? You're not... having a flashback, are you?"

"Alex?" Morgana called. She crossed the room quickly and put a hand on her shoulder. "Alex?"

"What?" Alex blinked. "What's wrong?"

"Alex, you weren't having a panic attack, were you?" Morgana asked. "You haven't had any lately, but with your parents and seeing Nicki hurt-"

"I'm fine, Morgana!" Alex snapped. Her gray eyes were bright and almost flared in the light. "For the ancestor's sake stop acting like you're Mother!"

Morgana tensed at the words, hissing softly. Then she gripped Alex's arm and pulled her out of the chair. Merlin made a worried noise and met Morgana's eyes. They nodded and Morgana led Alex towards the door with Merlin on their heels.

"That's our protagonist, guys," Nicki said. Her eyebrows were up and she shook her head slightly. The levity in her voice quickly fell apart and Nicki frowned. "I'm worried."

"She's getting better," Aiden replied. He kissed Nicki's forehead gently. "And her genre savviness is improving. That's a victory right there."

"What do you mean?" Avani asked. Lance tried not to laugh, grateful for the subject change.

"Oh; Alex was never really interested in magic to the same extent as us," Aiden explained. "We've had to educate her a bit, but she'd coming along."

"Please tell me that she'd at least read Harry Potter," Avani said. She looked worried, but happy for the distraction like the rest of them.

Nicki grinned with stars in her eyes. "Nothing that bad," Nicki assured her. She shifted a little closer to Avani and smiled. "She knew the mainstream stuff but needed a brush up on her knowledge."

"In her defense, I don't think she had cable growing up," Bran said.

"I'm sure she's doing her best." Avani gave them a small smile and tucked a strand of dark hair behind her ear. Nicki just kept grinning at her. Lance felt a little embarrassed for her even as he was very amused. "She seems nice enough though, just a bit... distracted, or hyper maybe."

"Alex lost her parents recently," Jenny explained softly. "It's affected her more than she wants to admit."

"Oh." Avani frowned, biting her lower lip. "Sif didn't mention that. So... is she always like this?"

"No," Bran answered. He looked out the window. They could just see Alex speaking with Merlin and Morgana. "She's been a bit... uneven lately."

"I see," Avani said.

Lance didn't know what to say or do as he watched Alex through the window. Then Jenny leaned against his shoulder and he wrapped an arm around her. He rather doubted that Avani did see, but appreciated her trying to be nice about the situation she'd now found herself in. It was obvious that Merlin and Morgana had no idea how to deal with whatever was going on with Alex, and he had no ideas himself.

"She'll be alright, won't she?" Jenny asked him softly.

"Yeah," Lance said. Kissing Jenny's forehead, he smiled and nodded towards the window. "Alex will be alright. She's got us to help her out." No one looked very convinced.

29

Among Friends

Alex was aware of the tension among her friends. She wasn't so far removed from them that she couldn't see it. Caring about it just didn't seem important. They could worry and talk, but it didn't change anything. She felt lighter having told Merlin and Morgana, though it was clear that they hadn't disclosed what was going on to the others. Alex didn't know if it was because they didn't want to admit that they had no clue, if they were trying to avoid scaring the others, or if they thought that she cared about them knowing. In truth, it didn't matter. She'd keep her chin up and do her job.

She'd turned in her final paper to Professor Yates that morning and had only one more exam in a history class. Then she was done for the year, but she wasn't worried about the finals. It all just seemed so small in comparison to what was at stake. Still, there was the day-to-day stuff to get through. It was with a strange sense of relief that she joined the others at Merlin's house; at least it meant that they were getting back to work.

Smiling at Bran, Alex eased herself down on the grass of Merlin's back yard. It was short and tickled, and she vaguely wondered when Merlin found the time to keep it cut. Maybe he used magic. Probably, but this wasn't the time for a mental wander.

"Let's talk through it," Bran said as he sat down. "We'll try this with just me first."

"Since you and I have done this before," Alex replied.

"Something similar at least," Bran agreed. "Do you want me to try reaching out as well like I'm scrying, or just have you try this time?"

Alex considered the question for a moment. One of the voices was reacting strongly to Bran, but she wasn't sure if it was Gofiben or someone else. It was distracting and she lowered her eyes away from his so she could think.

"Let's start with just me," Alex finally said. "I need to know if I can locate the weak points on my own."

"Okay, fair enough."

"This is so exciting," Avani whispered. She was holding a spiral notebook in her hand and was poised to write in it. "Finding weak points in the world's defenses." Looking over at Morgana, she asked. "I've never heard of this, have you tried it before?"

"No," Morgana answered patiently. Then she looked at Avani and smiled a little. "This crop of mages is always coming up with interesting new ideas."

"RPG books, baby," Nicki added. When Avani looked her way, Nicki smiled, but blushed a little.

Avani raised an eyebrow in response and Alex felt an odd little flash of irritation alongside one of amusement. Pushing them aside, she offered Bran her hands as he sat across from her. He rolled his shoulders and exhaled. Yellow sparks appeared across the skin of his hands and Alex could see small flickers of yellow further up his arms.

"So, what exactly are they doing?" she heard Avani ask softly.

"Alex has the ability to transform the magic of others into her own magic," Morgana explained. "Convert the energy, if you will."

"Really?" Alex smiled at the awe in Avani's voice. "How fascinating."

Then Alex had to stop listening because pulling Bran's magic away from him was a process she needed focus for. Her own dark silver magic brushed across the sparks of yellow. His magic swept across her skin, sending small vibrations up and down her arms. It was similar to her own, but different enough. Not as sharp and cold as Chernobog's, but then again, she hadn't cared about hurting Chernobog. Alex coaxed the magic gently and let her own magic wash over the ripples of power Bran was releasing.

It began to change colors and she vaguely heard Avani say something else. Closing her eyes, Alex released the magic around them slowly. It shimmered through the air, encircling objects and brushing against the energy radiating out of the ground. She could see through it now. The world was dark and lit by strange colors, but Alex could identify everything. There were lines of yellow around Bran and Alex pulled on them, gathering them together. She didn't allow the magic to stay together though. Instead of forming an orb like usual, Alex pushed it out into the world.

The magic spread further and further. There was Merlin's house and then the rest of the houses on the road. Alex waited. Sweat began to cling to her brow. So far nothing drew her attention. There was the lake, the campus which was already at lower than the usual population as people fled for the summer, and the forests surrounding Ravenslake. Cars on the highway zipped through her awareness and sent a shiver down her spine.

Then she felt something. There was a dark spot. A void almost, where the magic of the world didn't seem to be touching anything. Pushing more magic that direction, Alex's body quivered, but she kept going. Her magic circled the void, a hole of nothing. It wasn't very large, but it was there. She was pulling back when it occurred to her that she needed an actual location. Shifting the magic, Alex sensed it twist against her, but it obeyed the strange command to find some sort of signage. She found a mile marker sign a moment later and tried to memorize the slope of the hill. Sweat dripped into her eyes and stung, pulling her back towards physical awareness.

Alex eased her grip on the magic. It swirled around her and she tried to coax it back. Some snapped back into her chest, causing her to gasp while the rest dissipated through the air. Opening her eyes, Alex found Morgana kneeling next to her with a handkerchief at the ready. Alex took it with a grateful smile and cleaned up the sweat on her face. The back of her shirt was a bit sticky, but there was nothing to do about that.

"I found something," Alex said. She rambled off the mile marker and the direction as best she could, hearing the scratch of Avani's pencil as she wrote it down. "Let's go."

"Are you up to it?" Merlin asked.

"I'm fine," Alex promised. "I pulled a lot of a magic back so I actually feel a bit hyper." Frowning a little, she looked at Bran. "What about you, Bran?"

"Bit tired magically," Bran admitted. "But not physically, and I'm not exhausted. I'll be fine."

Alex saw Merlin and Morgana exchange a look, but they raised no further objections. Glances at the others told Alex that they were a little surprised at her just wanting to jump into it but hoped it could be dismissed as wanting to be secure. Bran stood up and extended a hand to her. Alex took it with a smile and climbed to her feet.

"I'll get the iron then," Merlin said. His eyes lingered on her for a moment, but Alex didn't let it bother her. "We can take my SUV."

"And my truck," Aiden offered.

Nodding, Alex wiped off the back of her neck and tightened her ponytail. Morgana was still watching her.

"What did you see?" Nicki asked.

"A void in the magic." Alex paused and shifted her lips quizzically "It's hard to explain, but it was a like a black hole that my magic didn't touch right. There might not be a tunnel opened there yet, but there's definitely something wrong there."

"Fascinating," Morgana said. Her intense stare almost made Alex look away. "Your abilities are certainly proving useful."

"The others might have been able to do it," Alex said. Shrugging, Alex folded up the used handkerchief and shoved it into the back pocket of her jeans. "But I'm just the one who stumbled on it."

They loaded up the cars in relative silence, though Alex caught Nicki talking with Avani, who was very interested in what it had been like to be healed by the Iron Chalice. At least Nicki seemed in good spirits. Her near-death experience didn't seem to have shaken her, but then again Alex hadn't really examined the wounds. It was possible that they hadn't been that deep and the Chalice had just prevented scarring. Merlin called her name and Alex climbed into his SUV with him and Morgana. To her relief, Nicki and Avani climbed into the back seat with her, leaving the boys to take Aiden's truck.

"I hope you don't mind me coming along," Avani said to her.

"No, I don't mind."

"But Lance and Jenny are not here."

"Lance and Jenny help with brainstorming and research," Alex replied. She noted that Avani had added a few more braids to her hair today. "We don't take them with us when we make Gates, just in case." Alex paused and shifted her bag around, digging out her dagger. She handed it to Avani. "I know you have some magic but hold onto this just in case."

Nodding solemnly, Avani took the dagger and examined it curiously. Amused, Alex watched the newcomer for a moment before turning her attention to the mile markers as they made their way out of town. Nicki turned in the back seat and looked out the rear window to confirm that Aiden's truck was behind them. Catching Alex's eye, Nicki gave her a soft smile and Alex's chest tightened for a moment. She was grateful, she realized a moment later, that Nicki had come with her and the Professors. If nothing else, Merlin and Morgana would hesitate to start an awkward conversation in front of her. They were very careful about not undermining the Iron Soul in front of other mages.

They pulled off about fifteen minutes later onto a small trailhead parking lot. It was close to the area that Alex had seen, but they'd still need to hike a bit. Aiden pulled up next to them, effectively filling the small turn out. Climbing out, Alex opened the back of Merlin's SUV and grabbed the red backpack. It was heavy, but the hum of the iron infused with her magic was comforting. Nestled at the top was the Iron Chalice which she hoped they wouldn't need. Avani grabbed a pack and didn't make a sound as she pulled it on with a determined expression.

"Alright." Morgana was looking down at an unfolded map in her hands. "This trail heads up into the hills." Her green eyes met Alex's. "We're going to need you to guide us once we get closer."

"No problem," Alex said. "We'll find it." She reached up and tightened her ponytail, giving Avani a reassuring smile. "Hope you're up for a hike."

"I hike a lot on Elephanta Island," Avani replied. "And walk around Mumbai a lot."

"Elephanta Island," Alex repeated in confusion. "Is it near your home?"

"It's an island in Mumbai Harbor," Avani explained. "Sorry, you probably wouldn't know it by that name and I'm not sure what you called it in ancient times. It's an island with a lot of sacred caves and shrines to Shiva."

"Ah, I see." Alex heard one of the voices whispering louder and silently urged Lokpal to calm down. "Well then, let's find this weak spot and seal it up. The sooner we do, the sooner I'll be comfortable leaving Ravenslake."

They fell into a line with Morgana in the lead and Alex right behind her. Avani and Nicki followed her with Aiden, Bran, and Merlin at the back. The trail was narrow and a bit overgrown, making it a bit harder to navigate. Alex kept her eyes open for any sign of tracks that didn't belong, but the trail thankfully only showed signs of deer and birds.

"So Avani," Nicki said. "Tell us a bit about yourself. We haven't really had any time to just talk and get to know you."

Alex glanced over her shoulder as a sudden rush of curiosity took hold of her. It was a nagging and almost desperate sensation that she didn't know how to shake off. Reminding herself that Lokpal lived long ago didn't help any. There was another jolt of longing and a few names echoed through her head. Gottfried was wondering about the fate of his family, but that was a can of worms Alex was afraid to open. Cologne had been in western Germany, so his wife and daughters had probably survived the war and stayed away from the Eastern Bloc, but his sons... Shaking her head, Alex kept moving and focused on Avani's words.

"Well, as I said my family are descendants of Lokpal. We've stayed connected to the Old Ones due to our magical tradition, but it is strongest in my branch of the family."

"Do you have a large family?" Bran asked.

"Huge by western standards," Avani replied. She chuckled lightly. "I have three uncles and their families, and my two aunts and their families. Over fifteen cousins in total."

"Wow," Nicki gasped. "That must be a huge family reunion! Are they all magical?"

"No," Avani answered. "While magic can be taught, some people don't have a talent for it. Unlike math or writing, they won't ever be able to do anything with it. Besides, my family is a bit paranoid about spreading knowledge of magic too far, so my cousins are only told about it if they show the right personality traits."

"Sounds strict," Aiden said.

"A bit, yes," Avani agreed. "But children with magical spells have the potential to cause a lot of problems."

"Fair point," Aiden conceded.

"So do you use magic in English or in Hindi?" Bran asked from the back.

"Actually, my native language is Marathi so I use that the most," Avani answered. "I also speak Hindi and English fluently."

"How old are you?" Nicki asked, changing the subject so suddenly that Alex had to hold back a laugh.

"Twenty-two."

"Oh." Nicki sounded very surprised. "You're older than us. That's surprising."

"Am I?"

"Yeah, most of us are twenty," Nicki replied. "So not much older." Alex actually turned around to look at Nicki. She was blushing and stammering a little. It was enough to make Alex smile. "Is that why they sent you? Cause you would blend in better?"

"No; I'm the best with magic in my generation," Avani said. "Better than even my grandfather. They even thought that I might be a mage when I was young, but sadly that wasn't the case."

"Or maybe that was good," Bran suggested. "While having the powers is nice, life has been more than a little insane since we learned we were mages."

"You would have all had Connections when you met though, correct?"

"Yeah," Alex said. "And some of us worried we were going crazy."

Aiden laughed behind her and Alex smiled. It was strange to remember those first days. They seemed so long ago, but it was just two short years. Not even a full two years. That sobered Alex up, and she focused on their surroundings. Nothing was very familiar yet, but there was a slight tickle at the edge of her senses. They were heading the right way at least.

The tickle grew stronger the longer they walked. Ignoring the conversations behind them, Alex directed Morgana onto a small game trail off the main path. Beneath her feet, the soft pulse of magic rose through her body. It was getting ready to defend, she realized with a slight smirk. A sharp sense of satisfaction sang through her. Alex reached out for the magic.

It rustled in the leaves and around their bodies. The energy, the magic, whatever you wanted to call it, was so obvious now. And yet, Alex could remember being so unaware of it. So blind. She'd doubted it even after forming Connections with the others. Her lips twitched into a smile and the voices became louder. Memories of other Connections zinged across her mind, thankfully fast enough that Alex didn't lose sight of the living world. Several were familiar: she knew them to be Merlin and Morgana. They'd truly been there many times.

"Up ahead," Alex said suddenly. "I sense something."

Morgana glanced over her shoulder and nodded. Alex tugged on her magic and felt it flow into her. She stopped on the trail with a quick gesture to Nicki and exhaled slowly. The magic rippled outward, spreading through the air, and brushing against the trees and bushes like a fine mist. Alex detached. Once again, the awareness of her body faded away and became the hum of magic. It filled her ears, with her eyes she saw strange colors around the shapes, and she tasted a sweetness in the air.

Then she found the void. It was dark and sudden and close. Her magic twisted around it like a ship skimming around rocks. There was another hum there that she hadn't felt before. It was bitter on her tongue but familiar. Alex could almost hear the Sídhe below the ground, pushing their way through. Magic against magic as two universes clashed and struggled for which would be dominant. She scowled only to have that strange dead world flash through her mind. Ash filled her mouth and Alex pulled back the magic sharply.

Everyone was watching her. Alex pulled out her water bottle and rinsed her mouth. Nicki frowned at the action and Alex didn't try to explain. It didn't help: the taste of ash lingered even as Alex decided it was all in her head. She took another drink and started walking again as the void beckoned.

There wasn't much in the area. As the Sídhe hadn't broken through yet, the hillside seemed completely normal. Yet there was a hint of something wrong with the vegetation and Alex didn't see any birds when she searched the tops of the trees with her eyes. She had the feeling that they'd arrived just in time.

Alex said little as everyone unloaded their bags but did ask Merlin to open a hole in the hillside. He gave her a brief searching look but obeyed while Morgana assured the others that it wasn't going to allow the Sídhe through. Physical versus metaphysical. Alex didn't really understand it, but she felt it in her gut.

The false peace was broken by the sudden chirping of a phone. Alex glowered only to realize that it was her phone. Digging it out, she blinked in surprise at the name Matt. She'd been expecting Jenny or Lance. Everyone else who still texted her regularly at this point was with her. Reading the message, the knot in Alex's chest tightened harshly.

"Okay, let's get this Gate made," Alex said as she slipped her phone back into her pocket. "My brothers are coming down for a visit. They want to have dinner tonight."

Nicki smiled and said that would be nice. Bran and Aiden nodded in agreement while Avani stayed silent. Alex struggled to ignore the sudden tightening of the knot. Pushing more magic into it, Alex felt it quiver and threaten to burst, but thankfully it stilled after another moment. Clapping her hands together, Alex looked at the waiting pile of iron and forced a smile.

30

March of the Sídhe

4 63 B.C.E. Cashel, Ireland

Soft hands moved through Leugio's hair. He was lounging on the bed with one of the local healers gently packing his latest wound. His head was pillowed on Flaitheas' lap as she made soft soothing sounds. Shifting slightly, Leugio looked down at the thin red slice in his skin. It made him a bit faint, but he kept still. Instead, he focused on the closeness of his wife.

"I don't understand why you don't heal them," Flaitheas said. She brought her other hand up and touched a long scar on his arm. "You said that you healed your family pet once."

"Yes, but it left me weak," Leugio confessed. He shook his head. "It's difficult to explain, but when I think back on it… I worry that I wouldn't wake up from the attempt. I'm not even sure if I can heal myself, to be honest."

The healer glanced up at him curiously. At this point it was well known that he had magic. In the past season he'd used it often in the village, attempting to understand what he was doing. Leugio ignored the curious look. It wasn't worth trying to explain; he'd learned that much. The woman stood and nodded to Flaitheas before showing herself out of the roundhouse. As she pulled back the pelt door, a cold burst of air rushed into the roundhouse. Flaitheas tried to move, but Leugio groaned in protest.

"I need to put some more wood on the fire! You don't want to freeze do you?"

"I won't," Leugio insisted. "There are furs on the bed and the pelt is sealing things up again now."

"Not that much," Flaitheas corrected. "You're just comfortable."

"Yes, I am." He smiled up at her, admiring the way her brown eyes glittered in the light of the fire. "Please, for the hero."

Flaitheas' expression softened but turned sad. "I'm worried, Leugio. Another attack last night. Just enough to distract us and kill a few more warriors. Does this Teàrlach have a large army or not? What is his plan? Why haven't we heard anything lately? Ours seems to be the only village under attack now."

"I don't know," Leugio admitted. With a sigh and a soft groan, he slowly sat up on the bed. His bare chest was cold despite the fire. He glanced up through the smoke hole, but there was no snow currently falling. "I suppose… if I was trying to take over the land, I would want to kill the only mage."

"Then why not send a larger force against us?" Flaitheas touched the muscles of his back and gently ran a finger down another scar. "I know you've been injured a few times, but nothing too life threatening." She leaned forward and pressed a kiss between his shoulder blades. "In fact, you can take more injuries than any other warrior, even Conn."

"Maybe that is part of the magic," Leugio offered. He meant it more as a joke, but now that he considered it there was a ring of truth to all of it. "Maybe Teàrlach is just testing us, or maybe he doesn't have as much support as we feared."

"That seems too convenient." He turned to find Flaitheas frowning and staring into the fire. "Maybe it is to lure us into believing that they aren't very powerful. I hate to say it, but since they attack at night and with the slope of the hill, many of them always escape. If Teàrlach is willing to sacrifice a small number in these attacks, then he could still be massing large numbers. After all, they must move at night. You remember what Conn told us when he came."

"Of course," Leugio said. "And so far, the mounds still don't seem to be connected underground."

"At least not yet, maybe that's what they're doing. We need to find out what is going on, Leugio!"

"I know," the words came out more sharply than he meant for them to. "But it isn't that simple, Flaitheas. You know that. Last time we visited my home village there was no sign of Iúdás, and we don't have the force to invade a mound. While Iúdás may not want to be part of this war, the guards will protect their home."

"How can you be sure that Iúdás is still alive?"

"I can't be. He was our only source of information, and either he's avoiding the surface now or he's dead. Either way, there isn't a way to get more information." Standing up, Leugio grabbed his tunic and carefully pulled it on so he didn't disturb the bandages. "I don't know what else we can do, Flaitheas."

His wife's shoulders slumped and she lowered her eyes. "I know," she said. "I'm sorry, Leugio. You're doing the best you can and more than the rest of us. I shouldn't be taking my frustration out on you."

"It's alright," he said gently. "We're all worried, and this weather isn't helping."

"I've never liked winter," Flaitheas agreed. She glared at the doorway. "Cold and poor weather for riding." That remark made Leugio smile and he leaned over to kiss her forehead. Then he grabbed his cloak and pulled it on, securing it with his iron pin. "Where are you going?"

"For a walk around the village," Leugio said. "I need to clear my head and think."

"I'm sorry, Leugio," Flaitheas said quickly. She sat up on her knees, looking worried and nervous.

"Oh, I'm not angry," he promised. "I just need some fresh air and a chance to think. I might go outside the wall. Maybe it will help me form a new plan. Ideally, we should have something in place for spring. Some new strategy."

His statement earned another smile from his wife and she nodded in agreement. "If you need to talk it out-"

"You'll be the first I come to."

"And Conn might be able to help as well."

"Of that, I have no doubt," Leugio agreed. Something shifted in his stomach, but he wasn't sure what it was. Flaitheas was smiling now at the mention of their new friend. "I'll be back soon."

"Just be careful and don't slip in the snow." Flaitheas paused. "And take a sword if you're going outside the wall."

Nodding his head, Leugio headed for the door and grabbed the fur wrap waiting on a small rack. He slung it over his shoulders and pulled up the hood of his cloak. Then, with a smile towards Flaitheas, he collected his sword and secured it to his belt. Under the cloak and fur, it wouldn't be easy to draw, but he'd have it. Flaitheas nodded in approval to him before he stepped out of the roundhouse.

A wave of cold hit him and he shuddered. Quickly dropping the pelt back into place, Leugio looked around and noted that there were only a few people outside their homes. The sun was already sinking in the sky and most had finished for the day. He already missed the warmth of summer. At least they were approaching the longest night. Things would get a bit easier once the days started getting longer again.

His side ached a little, but the cold seemed to help as he headed towards the gate. Smoke was curling up from every home and he caught the smell of cooking from several. He moved faster and adjusted his cloak to keep his hands tucked inside. Men were placed on the wall platforms with weapons at the ready, though all of them were huddled by the fire cauldrons. One of them gave him a shocked look as he headed for the gate. However, Conn was at the gate and speaking with one of the guards, his sword at his waist and a scowl on his face.

"Conn," Leugio called. "Everything alright?"

"Caught one of the guards sneaking off," Conn grumbled. He shook his head, making his long brown braid swing around his neck. "Disgraceful. Guards need to be loyal and take things seriously."

"Careful, Conn, or Eochu Finn will make you the leader of his guards. I thought you didn't want that kind of position here?"

"I don't," Conn protested. He looked a touch embarrassed now. "You know my interest is stopping whatever the Sídhe have planned." Conn gestured to the guard at the gate, who nodded quickly and jumped back to his post. "Besides, he likes you far more."

"I'm not sure about that," Leugio said.

"Oh, come now, he must like you. After all, from what Flaitheas told me, he all but ordered the pair of you to marry so you'd become king." Conn shook his head a little, resting his arm lazily on the hilt of his sword. "Surely that says something about his regard."

"I know," Leugio said. His cheeks flushed. "But even now, I'm still never sure what to say to Eochu Finn." Shaking his head, Leugio struggled for the right words. "Even now, I still feel like a shepherd boy."

Conn's grin softened slightly and he studied Leugio for a moment. "You said that your father was a warrior? Did he not teach you?"

"He was, but I was just a child. He never had a chance to teach me, and Mother... well, she always wanted me to stay close to her and Keelia. One of the reasons I fight so much more with magic is that it is truly easier for me. I just flail with a sword."

"Well, you do a decent job regardless," Conn said. "I suppose your mother's reaction is understandable, but it is a great thing to fight in the service of a king!" Conn's tone was almost gleeful and he folded his large arms over his chest. Just standing beside him always made Leugio feel too small and thin. "Though I never expected to fight with the men of Eochu Finn. I suppose that a great threat brings unusual changes."

"Do you miss your home?"

"Sometimes." Conn shrugged and glanced towards Leugio's house. "I had a small farm, but my wife passed in childbirth two summers ago and it hasn't felt right since." Then he laughed a little. "Maybe that's why I let myself get so worked up over the Sídhe taking a few horses." He shook his head. "My brother and his family lived with me. I'm sure they are handling things just fine: my brother has probably forgotten that he isn't the true master of that land."

"Well, I'm grateful that you agreed to stay," Leugio said. He reached up and clapped a hand on Conn's shoulder. "You've been a great asset to us."

"Not as useful as magic, but I'm pleased to hear that I've been of help."

"You have been."

Leugio wasn't sure what else to say, but thankfully Conn seemed to understand. The warrior nodded to him and strode away from the gate. The guard sighed in relief and relaxed a little until Leugio gestured for the gate to be opened. He received a worried look, but the guard didn't protest.

The snow crunched beneath his boots as he walked carefully away from the gate. Once he was off the worn trail the ground was more treacherous. While the snow wasn't deep, it did a good job of hiding the roughness of the hill. He peered out across the white landscape. There were patches of dark trees and dots of livestock around them, but the air was still and quiet. Winter always seemed like the world was bracing itself to him. As a child, he'd enjoyed the evenings that promised stories by the fire and long nights of sleep, but now he was all too aware that these long nights benefited the Sídhe.

There was so much he didn't understand about his enemy. He'd been in one mound, and while he wanted more information, he dared not enter another. Breathing in the cold air, Leugio hoped for inspiration, but nothing came. This was a war where the territory of the enemy was too dangerous to go into. He couldn't in good conscience lead people there. It was a puzzle. As much as Iúdás' words about the Grand Mages frightened him, he couldn't help but wish there was someone around with more information.

Looking up, Leugio noted that the sun had set. The world was colder now and he tightened his cloak around him before bringing a hand up to touch his brooch. It hummed beneath his fingers and he looked out into the darkness. Something was shimmering in the distance: an odd dull light that was growing brighter and brighter. Shifting closer to the edge of the rocky terrain, Leugio heard murmuring up on the wall behind him.

"Any idea what it is, sir?" a guard called down.

"No," Leugio replied. "I'm not sure."

It was sharp and orange: for a moment he feared that something had caught fire. Then he caught the smell of snow on the air and frowned in confusion. There was no smoke on the air. It couldn't be a fire in the fields. Beneath his feet and in the air around him, Leugio sensed the magic swirling. Whatever the odd color meant, it was stirring a reaction from the world itself. His stomach tightened fearfully.

Then he heard the drumming and the voices. An unnatural rhythm began to echo up off the plains toward him. It rang around the rocks and filled his ears. Even the sound of his own heartbeat became muted. Footfalls echoed up towards them. Behind him, the stillness of the village was gone. There was shouting, screaming, and the clanging of metal. Pulling out his sword awkwardly, Leugio heard the gate open but didn't turn around. Conn was at his side moments later.

"Is it them?"

"My magic is reacting to something," Leugio said.

"Sounds like a lot of them." Conn's sword gleamed in the light from the torch he was carrying. "Why now? The solstice is in two days: why not attack then, during the longest night?"

"Maybe they can't, or maybe there is somewhere else they want to attack," Leugio replied. He glanced up at the torches many of the men were carrying. "Just brace yourself."

The line of Sídhe marched up the hill. There were over a dozen rows of seven wide. All were in leather armor and armed with bronze weapons. His own point of reassurance was knowing that they had the stronger weapons. Over his heart, the Iron Brooch warmed further. He and all the men around him were still, bracing themselves for whatever was coming. Then the Sídhe stopped and one stepped forward, looking right at him.

"Surrender," a Síd said. "Your lives will be spared. The mage will be executed and the rest made slaves."

"No," Conn said before Leugio could say anything.

"Lord Teàrlach will destroy all of you," the Síd hissed. "This island will serve as our new homeland. All will gather here and we will have a new home! You cannot win. Humanity is too fragmented."

"You already have the mounds," Leugio said. He kept his voice calm, though a nervous twitch was rising through his arms. Conn shifted closer to him. "Surely we can reach a peaceful arrangement?"

"You are a mage; your kind destroys us!"

"No," Leugio protested. "If that was true then none of you would even be here. You would have been destroyed in the past. I do not wish for war."

The Síd curled its lips and raised its hand. Conn moved before Leugio could. A strong arm pulled him out of the way, but the arrow caught in Conn's shoulder. There was a long groan, but Conn kept moving him. Staring at the arrow in horror, Leugio realized that it would have hit his chest. Ice filled his veins. The Sídhe began to rush forward with a war cry. In the distance he could still see the light, and suddenly realized what it was. A mound: a new mound right beyond their walls. He had no time. The Sídhe were upon them. Swinging the sword in his right hand, Leugio frantically released as much magic as he could with his left.

The world shuddered. Everything turned white and the Sídhe screamed. His heart trembled and burned as magic rushed through it. Too fast, too much, but he kept pushing. Magic was crashing outward. It tore through the first line of soldiers. The one who'd spoken vanished with his mouth open in a scream. The second row hissed and their flesh began to melt while the third-row unleashed arrows into the air.

Humans scattered. Conn was groaning on his knees beside him. As the magic eased and the darkness took over once more, Leugio risked a glance towards him. Should he stop and help him? Conn climbed to his feet and pulled the arrow from his shoulder with a pained huff. There was a rush of brown hair and Flaitheas was suddenly at Conn's side, supporting his weight and touching his face tenderly.

Something twisted. A thought tried to form, but it couldn't. Instead, there was relief as his wife helped Conn away. Around him men were firing bows into the mass of Sídhe. He opened his hand and pulled on more magic. An orb of light formed and he threw it into the sky. Light cascaded around the Sídhe, forcing many to lower their eyes and guards. Raising his sword, he rushed into the fray.

31

Family Meal

It wasn't that Alex hated Central Diner; it just contained memories that she hated. She and Arthur had made it a regular date location thanks to its wonderful burgers and fries. Even now, sitting at the table alone, it was difficult not to think about him. Everything was loud and noisy but familiar in the worst way. There were too many triggers for emotions, and her chest was tightening. Alex gripped at the end of the table for a moment and took a long slow breath. She wasn't going to have a panic attack, she told herself. She was beyond that.

Finally, the tightness eased and Alex scanned the dining room quickly. There were a couple more people, but no one was paying any attention to her. The retro diner wasn't as busy as usual as many students were already gone, but there were several local families. Toying with the straw of her soda, Alex kept glancing around the room. She'd arrived first and managed to get a booth in the corner where she could see most of the diner.

Still no sign of her brothers. Alex held back a sigh. She should have met them at their hotel and come with them in the car. No, she corrected quickly. Public was better. They couldn't go into too many details in public. Of course, Matt had wanted public too. Maybe he was worried about how she'd react or what she'd do.

Rolling her shoulders, Alex groaned a little at the lingering ache in her muscles. They'd made the Gate without any incident. No Sídhe, no Fae creatures, and nothing going wrong. That hadn't stopped them all from being braced for an attack. As the Gate had hammered itself into the ground, the alien magic sputtered and flickered out. Extinguishing like a candle while her magic swept into the void and filled it with the warm, glistening magic of the Iron Realm.

She knew she should be happy with their success. They'd stopped more Sídhe from entering the Iron Realm and trying to capture more slaves. Yet there was no sense of victory, no thrill of having pulled off a fancy new trick in finding the weak points first, and no glow of achievement. There was just another day. There'd be more attacks and they'd build more Gates. She'd need to enchant more iron just in case before they headed to India.

India. There was a sense of excitement that wasn't just her own, and yet she was aware of some fear. Lokpal was worried about seeing his homeland again so far into the future, nervous about Shiva and the other Old Ones, and concerned about his family. It was all right there, and Alex took another sip of her drink as she silently tried to reassure him that it would be okay. They had to go. They had a duty to fulfill as the Iron Soul and couldn't let their emotions get in the way.

The front door opened and Alex straightened as her brothers walked in. Matt looked tired and Ed just looked bored. Her eyes met Matt's and she couldn't help but notice him tense up. He touched Ed's elbow and nodded towards her. Alex made herself smile as her brothers approached.

"Hi, Matt," Alex greeted quickly. Keeping the smile on her face, she bounced out of the booth and opened her arms to hug her brother. "Good to see you."

Matt returned the hug, holding her tight and making the knot quiver. He smelled the same. A bit musky with a layer of books to round it out. It hurt. The knot tightened and was suddenly too small. Something fluttered and twisted out of shape. She was grateful when he released her. Tears were trying to gather in her eyes.

Eddy stepped forward and hugged her even tighter. It was worse now as Ed's scent of dryer sheets and banana shampoo hit her hard. For a moment, she could see them all in the living room of the house, laughing at a stupid movie Mom had picked up. They were playing with action figures on the floor of the living room and building whole Lego cities over the furniture in Matt's bedroom.

"Hi, Ed," she choked out.

Then he let her go, and Alex let her features settle into a slight smile. They sat down in the booth with the boys on one side and her on the other. It wasn't much distance, but she could breathe easier now. Taking a long sip of her soda to distract herself, Alex prayed that the waitress would come over quickly.

"How are you, Alex?" Matt asked.

"I'm fine," Alex replied quickly. "Uh, I've made a new... friend," she offered. Alex couldn't remember how conversations were supposed to go anymore. What was she supposed to talk about? "Her name is Avani; she's from Mumbai in India."

"Is she an international student?" Matt asked politely.

"Not exactly," Alex admitted. "She's here to seek our help with an issue in India."

"So, she's a mage?" Ed asked, perking up in curiosity. "I thought you were all from around here."

"No, she's not a mage," Alex answered in a softer voice. "She's- you know what, never mind." Shaking her head, Alex grinned at Matt. "How are you two? I can at least distract myself in Ravenslake, but you two are still in the house. How are you?"

"It's hard," Matt answered. His features tightened and there was a slight shine of tears in his eyes. "I've gotten everything arranged to finish law school locally so Ed doesn't have to change schools."

"I wouldn't care," Ed grumbled. He was looking down at his phone with a deep frown. "Moving wouldn't be so bad."

"Let's try it another year," Matt said carefully. They'd had this conversation before apparently. "If it isn't working in a year then we can go someplace else."

"Are you still in your room?" Alex asked carefully. "Or have you moved into-"

"No," Matt said quickly. "Mom and Dad's room is still closed up. This summer... we'll pack things up a bit and donate their clothes, but not yet." Matt coughed a bit. "It isn't a priority."

"Okay."

Their waitress came and, in a few moments, they'd all ordered burgers and the boys had drinks on the way. It didn't get easier. Alex wasn't sure what to talk about and there were no helpful suggestions from her other selves. She talked about her classes a bit and confirmed the plan to get a house for the mages next year away from the campus. While Alex wasn't thrilled with the idea of driving in everyday, it would be easier to keep things a secret. There were only so many times that people could write off weird events, even in a college town. Still, it wasn't enough to save the conversation.

Matt ended up talking about some things he needed Alex to do. There were papers to sign since she was a legal adult in order to finish with the estate. Ed made a noise and Alex struggled to focus on Matt's words. They all sounded important and she kept nodding until their food came.

Nothing tasted right. It was all too bitter. Ed only ate half of his burger while Alex ate hers at rapid speed. She was still hungry, at least she thought that was a case, but the hole in her gut may have been something else. Matt tossed his napkin to the side but ate a couple more fries. Silence surrounded the table without them even having the excuse of their meals. It made the rest of the diner seem all the noisier.

"You didn't need to surprise me by coming down," Alex said. "You could have called."

"I called three times this week: you ignored all of them," Matt reminded her. "No texts, no emails from you, Alex. I was worried."

"I'm fine as you can see. I've just been busy."

"You've shut down," Matt snapped. "Why won't you talk to your own brothers?" Alex hated his tone of voice. Her reaction only made Matt's anger grow and he hissed at her. "Damn it, Alex, don't you care at all?"

"Of course, I care," Alex said. The knot tightened. "But crying isn't going to change anything! Staying focused on my job might just keep Arthur from killing more people!"

"No," Ed said slowly. He was looking at her and shook his head. "That's not it. Maybe you want it to be it, but it isn't."

"You need to be a bit clearer than that, Eddy," Alex teased.

"You want protecting people to be your reason, but that's not true," Ed explained. He was looking up at her with sad, disappointed eyes. "You just... don't want to care."

"Look, what happened to Mom and Dad... it was awful," Alex said quickly. "It shouldn't have happened and I'm sorry." Her chest thrummed as her heart beat faster. Alex didn't understand it. The voices were getting louder. There were faces at the back of her memory pushing forward. "I'm so sorry. I hoped that the blood spell would be enough and it wasn't. The horseshoes only protected the house and… it just wasn't enough. I'm sorry."

Ed stood up and stormed towards the door. Several people looked at him, but no one moved to stop him. A few people glanced their way, but Alex glared at them. The voices were louder now, all shouting and saying different things. It was too much and nothing was clear. Across from her, Matt sighed and lowered his face into his hands. Then he raised his head and motioned to the waitress. Alex wanted to offer to get the check so he could go after Eddy, but the waitress brought it over and Matt handed her several bills. He told her to keep the change and stood up.

Holding his hand out to Alex, Matt waited for her to stand and take it. Alex blinked at the outstretched hand for a moment, but slowly stood and let Matt lead her outside. Eddy wasn't in front of the diner and Alex grimaced. She scanned the nearby neon signs and windowsills for Red Caps. It was still daylight, but she couldn't help but eye the shadows suspiciously.

"I see him," Matt said. He pulled her down the sidewalk.

"I think that's enough for tonight." Alex pulled her hand free and forced a smile.

"We have to leave first thing," Matt argued.

Giving her a dark look and frowning, he grabbed her arm and hauled her down towards the alley. Ed was leaning against the wall and looked up as they came around the corner. His gaze was cool and uninterested. Matt sighed and looked at him.

"Don't run off like that."

"I'm not a little kid."

"No, but there are… things around here," Matt said. "You know that."

"Car's right there," Ed countered. He nodded towards the blue car that was parked just a few feet away. "I don't have keys."

"Fine." Matt pulled out his keys and tossed them to Ed. "Say goodnight to Alex: we won't have time to see her tomorrow."

Ed glanced her way. Alex stayed still and waited for him. Ed glanced at Matt who gave him an expectant look. Keeping his eyes down, Ed gave her another long lingering hug that reassured Alex of his affection. Then he let go and raced to the car. As soon as the door slammed shut and Ed looked down at his phone again, Matt whirled back towards her.

"Really?" He asked. "Alex-"

"What do you want from me?"

"I want-" Matt suddenly stopped and grit his teeth, struggling to control his voice. "I want to believe that you care, Alex. I want you to pick up the phone when I call or email back when I'm trying to check in on you. I want you to stop just going through the motions. Mom and Dad are dead!"

"I know," Alex replied. "I was there."

"Yes, fine, you were at the funeral, but you were checked out. Have you cried at all?"

"It doesn't matter. You grieve in your way and I'll grieve in mine."

"Alex, just…. Talk to me. Help me believe that you're okay."

"I'm not your concern. You've got Ed to worry about: you're his legal guardian now."

"Exactly! I've got law school and a grieving teenager to worry about: I can't be terrified of what is happening to my sister. I need you to talk to me. Check in at least, but you've been completely silent for weeks now! Ed's almost done with school for the year, but you haven't told us anything about your plans."

"I'm not coming back to Spokane," Alex answered bluntly. "Better that I stay here." She paused and licked her lips. "Besides, I'm needed elsewhere right now. I'm sorry; this isn't what I wanted. It's just how things have turned out."

"Why?"

Gaping at Matt, Alex wasn't sure what he was referring to. The knot was too tight, it was hard to breathe and the voices were too loud.

"Arthur wanted to hurt me. And I couldn't stop him."

Silence filled the alley. An absence of sound so loud that it smothered the noise of the town trying to intrude. Alex dropped her eyes, unable to watch the tightening of Matt's jaw. She wanted to say more, but there just weren't any right words. A few tried to gather on her tongue, but they weren't English and weren't really hers, so she swallowed them down and waited.

"Alex, you have no idea how much I want to yell at you right now," Matt growled. His eyes were dark and shining with tears. "You have no idea how tempting it is. But I'd regret it."

"Maybe you should," Alex said. She met his gaze, letting more magic twist around the bundle of contained grief. "You should be angry at me. You're not wrong."

"You didn't kill them," Matt said. "I'm not even sure if I believe that Arthur did."

"He did."

"It was a car crash, what makes you so sure-"

"I told you!" Alex snapped, more emotion slipping out then she meant to allow. "I was there."

She saw the moment when realization filled Matt's eyes. He still looked confused, but there it was. He understood, at least in part. Somehow, it didn't make her feel any better. It made her feel worse. It would have been better for him to think that their parents died in a normal crash. Maybe they would have felt safer.

"Is Ed safe?"

"I don't know," Alex said. "Probably not."

"Is this why you're keeping your distance from us?" Matt stepped closer to her; the anger gone from his voice. His hands gripped her arms, sending a shiver up Alex's spine and making the bundle throb. The voices were suddenly quiet, and the world was still. "Alex, I don't think pushing us away will help."

"No," Alex agreed. "It never works in the stories." Then she shook her head. "I've just been busy, Matt. There's a lot going on and I need to focus on it."

"We're your brothers," Matt protested, hurt flashing in his eyes. "Alex, I need your support. I'm not sure what to do with Ed right now. His teachers are giving him a pass for the semester given what happened, but he's not talking much and doesn't want to do anything. He just stays in his room all the time."

"I'm sorry, Matt. I don't know how to help."

"And I don't know how to help you," Matt answered.

They stared at each other. Ed tapped on the car window and Alex flinched, realizing how long they must had been standing there. A deep sigh escaped Matt and he rubbed his jaw. Alex opened her arms and tried to smile. Matt didn't look like he believed it, snorting slightly, but he did step forward to hug her. Then he let go of her. Matt dropped a quick kiss to her forehead and walked towards the car. He paused and turned back to her as he balanced on the curb.

"If you want to talk, Alex, just call. We're still your family."

The knot throbbed, but the voices were back and the sound of them was soothing. Matt climbed into the car and Ed, thankfully, gave her a small wave. It was probably at Matt's insistence. She held up a hand and waved back.

Alex watched the car until it turned off Central and vanished around a corner. Then she started walking. Her legs were heavy and weighed down, almost like the Iron Chain was wrapped around her ankles. Around her, the streets of Ravenslake were unusually quiet. Too many students had already left. The sunlight poured down around her and a breeze ruffled her hair, but Alex didn't notice any of it. Instead, she sped up her pace and headed back towards campus.

32

Dreaming in Ravenslake

Mumbai. The name didn't mean anything to Alex. None of the voices reacted to it and there was no rush of emotion in connection with it. Alex found the reason for that quickly enough. The original name was Bombay, or at least that was the more recent former name. Holding back a sigh, Alex kept skimming through the article and waiting for something to jump out. One of the voices was curious and the caves on the island near the city stirred a blurry memory, but that was it.

In her chest, the knot twisted and Alex pulled her hands away from the keyboard of her laptop before she hit something. Her dorm room was too still and quiet. Twilight was falling outside and while it wasn't too late, the noise that would have normally been present was all but gone. Tomorrow was Thursday: only a few students still remained. Matt would be rushing Eddy back for school and they would be gone from town. She could pack up her things and stash them at Morgana's until they had a place of their own.

Still, that didn't dispel the discomfort. Alex pushed herself away from her desk and looked around for something to distract her. On her pillow, the old stuffed dog Galahad was looking at her. The knot tightened and

Alex couldn't breathe. Tears filled her eyes and she gripped the edge of her desk.

"Don't look at me like that," Alex said. "It... it doesn't matter."

Galahad. The name was ironic now. There hadn't actually been a Galahad like in the stories, but there had been a Galath. A loyal brother who had hidden the Iron Chalice; even from Merlin and Morgana, who he had never forgiven for his brother Gofiben death. Scenes of Galath danced across her vision; his smile and his laugh. He'd been a happy man until the mages had come into his life, but he'd followed them. Even when Merlin and Morgana left to reclaim the sword, he had stayed loyal to Gofiben.

Collapsing on the bed, Alex picked up Galahad and squeezed him against her chest. The stuffed dog couldn't return the hug, and she desperately missed Anne. Her family's golden retriever would have licked her face, whimpered a little, and snuggled up against her. Alex realized with a jolt that she hadn't thought about how their dog was taking the absence of their parents. Was Anne crying at the door waiting for them, or had she begun to settle with just having the boys? Wiping her tears on Galahad's fur, Alex fought down the sobs building in her chest. The knot shuddered. Threads of magic were beginning to unravel.

"No," Alex whispered. "No, I'm not doing this. It won't help." The words didn't help either and she pulled Galahad away to look at him. "I wonder if I did name you after Galath. I don't remember why I gave you that name; it was so long ago." Alex shivered and shook her head. "I don't want Matt and Eddy to turn out the same way. They need their own lives." Those words helped a bit: they sounded good at least, and almost released the bubble of fear growing in Alex's chest.

Whatever else Alex might have said to Galahad was cut off when a chill rolled down her spine. Magic rushed up her limbs, warming them and urging her to move. The voices exploded into a rush of noise. She jumped up and shoved her feet into her sneakers. It was only thanks to habit that she grabbed her keycard as she rushed out the door. There was a sound of surprise from Nicki's room, but Alex didn't stop.

Outside the air was still warm, but the twilight was fading into true darkness. Stars were visible even over the light of the streetlights that lined the parking lot. University Drive was empty and the noise on campus was somehow even quieter. Alex stepped away from her dorm and crossed the lawn, looking around for any sign of anything out of place. Rhodes Hall loomed ahead of her and Alex focused on the small coffee shop that had been built into the ground floor. It wasn't very good coffee, but it was close by. As she approached, Alex spotted a man coming out with a tall cup of coffee. He glanced her way with glassy eyes and headed towards the campus only to slump against the building. Grateful for the distraction, Alex took a step towards him and glanced into the small coffee shop. There were some people asleep at the tables with books in front of them. The man stumbled again.

"Hey," Alex called. The man was about her age and swaying dangerously now towards the road. "You okay?"

Catching his arm, Alex sniffed, but there wasn't any smell of alcohol. His eyes kept sliding shut and he looked ready to fall over. Alex grunted as more of his weight fell onto her, but maneuvered him over to the nearby wall. He slid down it to the ground and yawned.

"Hey, wake up," Alex ordered. Kneeling, she studied him carefully. There was a dopey expression on his face. He didn't even seem to realize where he was. "You're on the sidewalk!" Alex shouted. "Come on, this isn't the place to sleep!"

A snore was her only answer. Alex stood up and rushed back to the windows of the small campus coffee shop. More of the people were sleeping now, pillowing their heads on their arms with contented smiles. A few others were stumbling toward chairs and promptly falling into them. Shaking her head, Alex looked around the main quad as a bubble of worry expanded in her chest. There was another brush of magic across her skin.

Spinning around, Alex scanned the nearby area. People were still moving around, but there was a faint haze spreading through the campus like a mist. Closing her eyes, Alex pulled on her magic roughly and pushed it outward. It clashed. The mist pushed back, sending shivers through Alex's limbs. It was sharp and bitter, alien, and very familiar. Brekszta.

It was spreading. Things were going quiet, though Alex could just make out the low noise of the city beyond the edge of the campus. Spotting a couple of students who were in a daze, Alex watched as they stumbled around and giggled. Any other day she would have dismissed them as drunk, but sparks of magic were circling around them. The young woman laughed and began to fall over, dragging her partner to the ground. Alex ran over to the young woman who had slumped against a wall and searched for her pulse.

Sleeping; she was just sleeping. Alex checked the next person, but it was the same. Matt and Ed's faces pushed forward to the front of her brain. Her eyes darted around the area. There was no sign of them. Of course, there wasn't. They'd be back at their hotel by now. Safe in their room, where if they felt groggy they could just lay down. If the spell even went beyond campus. They had no reason to be on campus. Her soft reassurances didn't help and the knot somersaulted.

Alex ordered herself to calm down and focus on the magic. The fine mist was spreading, but there were threads of magic between each person who was asleep. Reaching for the nearest thread of magic, Alex tugged on it. The cold magic fought back for a moment, but twisted around her fingers and began to turn dark gray. She looked down at the woman she'd pulled it from, but there was a shimmering cloud of blue around her chest and head.

Extending her hand, Alex hesitated and watched the magic flutter around the woman. Alex closed her eyes and focused on how the magic reacted. It was twisting around the woman's heart and brain, sinking beneath the skin, and fear gripped Alex tightly. She pulled her hand back sharply and just watched the dark blue magic dance in the air. Almost like it was mocking her. Could she risk pulling it out and changing it? This was a human that Brekszta had connected to. It wasn't like the Fae; well, it was a bit, but not emotionally.

Taking her eyes off the woman, Alex blinked several times until the view of the lines of magic eased. The colors of the normal world seeped back into her vision only for her to freeze in place. There were ghostly figures appearing out of the thinning mist. They shimmered with magic, but it stung against Alex's senses. None of them moved towards the sleeping people, they just lingered. No move to attack or capture her. Alex didn't understand.

She took a step forward, her sneakers thudding against the pavement. The ghostly figures just kept walking. They passed through objects like they weren't there. Yet they didn't radiate magic. Alex could only see flickers of it around their forms. The reality of what was happening settled across her shoulders. Brekszta was attacking Ravenslake, and while it didn't seem hostile, Brekszta was definitely affecting the nonmages with magic. Pulling out her phone, Alex quickly called Merlin and looked around nervously. The ghosts seemed to have noticed her or sensed her, because they were all now moving in her direction. Odd sounds began to fill the air, echoing through the street and coming from the ghosts.

"Hello, Alex? What is it? Is everything alright with your brothers?" Merlin still sounded a bit tired from helping with the Gate earlier, but they didn't have time for that.

"Merlin, there's trouble on campus. I need you to bring me the Hammer," Alex said in a rush. "I can stop the flow of magic one at a time, but it leaves something behind and I'm not sure it's safe to pull out."

Around her, the strange sounds were clearer now. Words, human words, but many she didn't understand. Yet some of the voices did. They began talking and shouting all at once. A groan escaped Alex; her vision threatened to go blurry and her magic flickered wildly in her chest.

"Alex? What is happening? Are you alright?!"

The voices around her were louder, calling familiar and unfamiliar names. They were coming closer. Figures were reaching for her, their images flickering in and out in the low lamplights. More and more of the campus lights were turning on and illuminating the sidewalks, but the figures were still there. Alex tried to back away, but they were all around. Merlin was saying something, but the noise was too much.

"The Hammer!" Alex shouted into the phone. "Merlin, bring me the Hammer! And be ready to erase a lot of memories!" She noted a nearby collapsed person. "And bring the Chalice too."

Looking around, Alex blinked as one of the faces of the figures almost came into focus. They were blurry, like looking through an old-fashioned window in the rain. She could sort of see eyes, the mouth, and a vague skin tone, but no details. Some were pale and others were dark. There were indistinct flashes of color in the eyes and around their forms, but nothing stayed long enough. More magic was gathering around them and nervous energy built in Alex's chest. She sent a quick text to the others and then tried to call Jenny.

There was no answer from Jenny. Alex told the phone to call Lance, but again after a few rings, there was no answer. Slipping the phone back into her pocket, Alex struggled to catch her breath and looked behind her. The figures were walking towards her, arms outstretched and faces becoming clearer with every passing moment. Backing away, Alex almost tripped over one of the prone humans.

"Arto," one of them called. A stone dropped into her gut.

'Mother,' Arto's voice whispered in return.

"Leugio," another said. This face had a bright smile, freckles, and soft eyes.

'Keelia,' another voice answered.

"Gofiben."

"Cuthbert."

"Lokpal."

"Gottfried."

"Dobiemir."

There were more names, but they blended together. The voices all tried to answer, some happy and some sad or disgusted. Hands reached for her. Magic pulsed in her veins, but Alex was frozen. The eyes looking at her were sad, imploring, and called her. They gathered around her tightly, some shorter than her and others looming over her. There was a soft giggle here and a warm chuckle there. She heard grumbling, more names, and pleas that all called to her.

Then she couldn't hear anything. The voices were too loud. Alex couldn't move. Tears rolled down her cheeks. Everything hurt. Her heart was sluggish and her limbs too heavy. The ghosts or illusions or echoes or whatever they were closed in. Alex didn't move. Cold brushed over the exposed skin of her arms and the world blurred. She could see the shimmer of magic but didn't care. Too many faces. Too many memories pushing forward, but they weren't hers.

A sob escaped her. The voices in her head blended, blurred, and everything else became background noise. They couldn't think. Another ghost was reaching for their face. There were too many tears now to see it clearly. Their chest tightened. The magic around the knot shuddered and began to unravel. More grief. Pain and a truck crashing down.

Shuddering, they took a step back. There was a looming wall behind her and their fingers brushed against rough brick. Something was flaring in the corner of their eye. It was yellow and warm and familiar. Turning to look, they saw a figure running down the street towards them. Magic filled their vision and bolts of yellow blasted through the nearest figures.

Their chest tightened. Protests sprang to their lips, but thoughts cleared and voices eased. Alex blinked and gasped for air. Another round of yellow bolts hit the ghostly figures like arrows raining down. They drew back, moaning and shouting more names. The voices in her head answered, calling to them by name.

Alex moved back, all but curling into a corner where the wall and a decorative pillar met. The air was sharp with energy. Magic danced across her tongue, but it was bitter and foul. Wrong; too wrong and not hers. Shuddering, Alex twisted away from the magic. Her own flickered, but she couldn't- it wouldn't form properly. She couldn't focus. It just slipped through her, past her, and wouldn't settle in her hands.

"Alex!" Bran was running towards her, his glowing hands up and ready. "Are you okay?"

She didn't answer. All her focus was on making her lungs expand and take in oxygen. Even her heart didn't seem to want to work without her urging it forward. Bran caught her arm to hold her steady. The magic still wouldn't come. The voices were arguing. Ghostly figures called to them-her from down the street. Alex struggled while the others fought.

"Easy, just breathe," Bran said gently. Bran started to guide her away, but Alex couldn't move. He struggled for a moment before giving up and gripping her other arm. "That's it, inhale and then exhale. Inhale.... Exhale." His voice was gentle, and despite the undercurrent of worry and fear, it soothed her. She focused on that voice.

Following Bran's instructions, Alex held her breath for a moment and sensation began to return to her body. Magic flowed through her limbs and she could move again. Closing her eyes, Alex grimaced as the bright lines of magic cut into the darkness. She didn't want to see it right now, but it was too bright and vivid to be ignored. There was no escape. A groan escaped her and Bran made a sound of worry.

"Alex, are you injured?"

"No."

"Then what-" Bran cut himself off and Alex opened her eyes to see him shake his head. "Did you alert Merlin and Morgana?"

"Merlin," Alex forced out. Words were hard. "Told him to bring Hammer and Chalice."

"The Hammer?" Bran frowned and looked away from her. His eyes jumped between the sleeping humans and he made a move to let her go but changed his mind. "There's just one spell," he said with growing horror. "And the Hammer... yeah, good call."

Groaning echoed through the air, and Alex looked up once more. The figures were back, coming towards them with extended hands. Bran shifted, keeping one hand supporting her and keeping the other up. Yellow magic flared around his fingertips. He snapped and a wall of fire sprang up in front of them in a semi-circle, sheltering them against the wall.

"Are you with me, Alex?" Bran asked quickly.

Her mouth was too dry to answer. The faces on the ghosts were becoming clearer again. Arto's mother was there, with her long brown braids and features so like Morgana's. Taking a step towards her, Alex barely noticed Bran's grip tightening. He said something, but the words were lost to her. Another figure came forward. This one was tall and male with graying brown hair hanging to his shoulders. Gofiben became louder.

A fireball crashed through the air and exploded across the pavement. Gasping, Alex tried to shout as the ghostly figures flickered and vanished. The knot twisted and the voices screamed in protest. Sad brown eyes locked with hers before vanishing and Gofiben roared in agony. Arto made a whimper of protest and the other voices shouted as the figures dispersed.

"Are you guys okay?" Nicki's voice asked.

Bran's hands kept her from turning on her friend. The knot tightened. Her magic flared, but Bran's voice kept telling her to breathe. Somehow it cut through the haze. She could hear Gofiben speaking in time with him in an accented voice. His anger was somehow suddenly gone at the sound of Bran. Alex knew that meant something, but couldn't remember. Nicki was next to them. Her face was pale, making her faint freckles stand out sharply. Bran squeezed her arm again and shifted between her and Nicki.

"We're okay, considering," Bran replied. "What about you?"

"I'm fine," Nicki replied. She was dressed in what Alex recognized as her sleeping pants and a t-shirt. "You could have gotten me, Alex," Nicki said.

"Sorry," Alex apologized. "I didn't think... I just came outside."

"Hey!" Aiden's voice called from behind them. "Everyone okay?" Alex looked over her shoulder to find Aiden running up.

"We're fine," Nicki said. There was still irritation in her voice, but her relief at seeing Aiden was clear. "What about you?"

"I'm fine, but I was in the campus late store for a sugar run when the cashier fell asleep."

"So, what is happening?" Nicki asked. She nodded towards the ghostly figures that were beginning to reappear. "Is this an invasion from some sort of ghost world?"

"No," Alex answered. Her voice was soft to her own ears. It sounded strange and too high pitched. "It's Brekszta: I think they're some sort of manifestations due to her magic. I can see her power around them." Indeed, as the figures moved closer there was a faint blue aura around them.

"Manifestations of what?" Nicki asked. "They barely look human to me."

Frowning, Alex looked sharply at Bran and Nicki, but their faces were both neutral. "You don't see them?" Alex whispered. "Oh... I guess not."

"Who are they, Alex?" Bran asked, stressing her name.

"People that... I've known," Alex answered. "In my various lives." She tried to smile, but it wasn't worth the effort.

"Oh." Nicki looked embarrassed.

"I see," Bran said carefully. He was barely hiding his horror at the idea. "So, it's Brekszta. Any idea of where she is?"

The question was answered by a flash of light above the lawn behind them. Alex turned first and found Brekszta standing on the retaining wall of the landscaping. She looked the same as before and raised a hand to wave in greeting.

33

The Iron Brooch

463 B.C.E. Cashel, Ireland

There was too much going on. Warriors were hacking at Sídhe frantically as they swarmed forward. Red and silver blood was spurting across the snow, though the silver vanished in a few moments. The white snow was becoming a mess of mud and blood with each charge. Around Leugio people were shouting, but he focused only on the beat of his heart and the pulse of his magic. He gathered the magic in his hand and released another flash of light. It gave the humans the chance to knock over and kill three more Sídhe.

Gritting his teeth, Leugio released another wave of magic. It jolted and zinged amongst the Sídhe, killing those it hit in the chest or head and knocking others to the ground. He paused in his efforts to form two more light orbs that he threw into the sky. They glowed brilliantly and cheers erupted behind him. A Síd climbed to its feet and charged him. An arrow struck it in the eye and it began to dissolve. Another blast of magic left his hand as the humans rushed forward.

Blurs of bodies and iron surrounded him. Sídhe were knocked over again, but their ranks were reforming as they gathered together once more. There was a shout for him to do something. He pulled on more magic. A sharp pain exploded beneath his heart. That didn't stop him. He tried to focus on the magic only harming the Sídhe and released another series of bolts. They were weaker this time. His stomach muscles tightened reflexively at the throb the action sent through his body. His magic was slipping away. He could still feel it, but it was sluggish. Still, it was enough to break the Sídhe ranks for a few moments.

No time to celebrate. Leugio's chest throbbed. It was too hot; even the winter chill did nothing against the burning in his body. The paths that the magic followed through his flesh were raw. He didn't understand what it meant, but every tug on the magic around him only made it worse. Yet, he couldn't stop. There were more Sídhe. As many questions as he had, this was one thing about being a mage that he was sure about. He had to fight them. He couldn't let them just take over; couldn't let them have the surface.

The mound gleamed in the darkness. There was a line of torches set up, providing low light to the Sídhe and a marker for him. Magic was thrumming against his skin, urging him on. Fear tried to tug him back, but he focused on the Sídhe. They had broken ranks, giving him and the other warriors a chance to catch their breath. Leugio's eyes swept over the area. There were fallen bodies scattered about in bloody snow. Arrows were sailing overhead from the wall, but he wondered if it was enough.

Above his head, the orb flickered. His blood kept heating up. Everything hurt, but he kept moving. The battle still raged, but his awareness was narrowing onto the mound. Leugio brought up his sword to block another strike from a Síd. His body moved on its own, slash, strike, and sidestep, but every step ached. His muscles quivered, trying to pull away from his bones. The Síd's weaker bronze blade bent at the force of the clash. Leugio threw his weight forward to unbalance the Síd. It slipped in the snow and fell to the ground. Without hesitation he swung his sword down and sliced the blade into the Síd's neck. It began to dissolve and he moved further down the slope of the great stone hill.

More Sídhe closed in around him. He swung his sword, catching one in the chest. It stumbled back and another warrior took off its head. Another Síd came low, knocking him back several steps. It pulled a dagger and moved to stab him. Leugio's eyes widened at the sudden reminder that he had no armor on. His armor was in his house. Human hands grabbed at the Síd and pulled it off of him. Then in a flurry of iron blades, it began to dissolve.

Leugio gasped for air and looked over his shoulder. Conn was visible at the far side of the battle. His arm was bound to his chest, but he was swinging his sword with his left hand. Flaitheas was next to him, slashing at the nearest Sídhe with her mouth open in a shout. Part of the wooden wall of the village was on fire, and the sounds of people screaming echoed down the hillside. He forced himself to move, releasing another wave of white magic. The effort nearly knocked him to his knees. Bright lights danced across his vision, but only for a moment until blackness began to swirl along the edges of his eyes.

They needed more. Needed some kind of plan. There were still rows of Sídhe. At least thirty more, and while they'd killed plenty, the Sídhe just kept coming. His eyes jumped to the new mound. Maybe there were more there. So far, this Teàrlach hadn't appeared. He needed to... he wasn't sure, but he had to get closer to the mound.

A hole opened in the Sídhe's ranks. They were shifting to face a mass of soldiers. Conn was barking orders. Leugio looked back to see Flaitheas sending arrow after arrow into the surge of Sídhe warriors. There was a look of determination on her face. His heart tightened. He went to the left and a rock started to give under his foot.

Leugio's eyes were drawn to the mound once more. It wasn't too far away, but each step hurt. He sent a bolt of magic to kill a Síd that had suddenly noticed him and broken off from the others. His head was pounding. Reaching up with his free hand, Leugio gripped the Iron Brooch and kept moving. He pushed through the battlefield, doing his best to twist around fighting figures.

The rear of the Sídhe force was exposed. Excitement, relief, and nervousness all warred in his chest. Above the fight, his three light orbs were still in place. Closing his eyes, Leugio breathed slowly. The pain eased slightly. His grip on his sword tightened and he bit his lip. Pushing through the pain, he called more magic. It came, but it set his nerves on fire. There'd never been a warning against this. Some instinct warned him to stop now, but he couldn't. Tears gathered in his eyes, a whimper was torn from his throat, but he didn't stop.

More magic collected in his chest, twisting around his heart and inflaming the muscles. It gathered in his left hand, hot and too bright. This time sparks flew off wildly and his very skin glowed. His hand trembled. There was shouting behind him, snarls, and footfalls. More were coming. Raising his hand, Leugio opened his palm and screamed. The magic blasted forward, a burning star against the dark sky. It eclipsed the orbs as it approached. Then it exploded. Dozens of tiny lights showered down. They all zipped through the air and shot straight through the chests of the Sídhe. A deafening roar of pained screams and excited cheers echoed down the hillside.

His legs gave out. The burn consumed everything. The blackness sank in all around him. Then rough hands grabbed him. There was cold as he was dragged through the snow. More shouting. Leugio realized that his eyes were closed. Forcing them open, he looked towards the shouting. Humans were running towards him, but a small group of Sídhe was moving to block them. Some were still alive. How? The mound, his mind provided. He'd dropped his sword somewhere.

A groan escaped him. His leg hit a rock. He tried to move, but only managed a soft whimper and a slight shudder. There were two Sídhe dragging him. It was too hard to focus: his head fell back, sending a sharp jolt down his spine. There was more light now, but it wasn't his own white, warm glow. It was the red glow of fire. He was turned around and dropped in the snow on his stomach.

He looked up. There was a line of torches in front of a rough earthen mound. It rose up sharply from the ground, bare stone and pounded down earth around a stone arch. Leugio wasn't sure how tall it was, but it was at least the height of a man with room to spare. Nothing grew on it. A faint shimmer moved over the mound. Was it magic or just a trick of the light? Had this been made of magic or created by hand in one massive push by a determined workforce?

His body protested. It didn't move right, it hurt too much, but he forced himself up onto his knees. The fire in his veins suppressed the awful cold. Somehow, he managed to stand, and look at the figure before him. The Síd was dressed in leather armor like the rest, but gold had been inlaid in elegant designs across the breastplate. There was a scar through the Síd's right eye, making it milky white. It was waiting at the entrance of the new mound, just watching him. Struggling to catch his breath, Leugio locked his knees and straightened his back

"The mage."

"I'm guessing that you are Teàrlach." His voice was too thin and weak.

"I am," Teàrlach said. "You are dying."

"Not yet."

"You have used too much magic: your body is decaying. I can smell death on you." Teàrlach's tone left no room for debate. "You have killed much of my army. It will take years to regroup, but we will. My people will not suffer this indignity any longer!" His one violet eye narrowed. "I will at least watch you die."

Numbness settled on his shoulders. The instinct to fight for his life flickered out like the last embers of a fire. He inhaled deeply, but the scent of the world around him was gone. Sounds were dull, and the darkness on the edges of his vision was creeping in. Magic had brought him here, but he'd never thought that there might be a price beyond the war. If his chest hadn't burned so, he might have laughed bitterly.

By old habit, his hand came up to touch his brooch. Teàrlach took a step back, eye widening uncertainly. The brooch burned hot beneath Leugio's fingers, but there was no pain, only warmth. Magic was pulsing through the iron. It was comforting. The smell of his home surrounded him. All of the aches eased. His vision cleared and he found his eyes fixed on the mound, then shifting back to Teàrlach. He couldn't destroy all the Sídhe; that was beyond him, but this enemy was right here.

The worn symbol suddenly brightened. Pulling it off his cloak, Leugio brought it up where he could see. It was a triskelion, worn and battered, but now bright in the darkness. His eyes widened and Leugio tightened his fingers around it. The metal threatened to cut into his skin, but he didn't care. Beneath his skin, the magic reached and pulled. Magic. There was more magic in this. Iúdás' words suddenly made more sense.

Everything fell away. His thumb brushed over the symbol. The glow was spreading through the rest of the iron. White sparks flew off like embers from a fire, but instead of floating away, they all swirled in front of him. He couldn't hear anything now. He couldn't feel the cold or the ache in his bones. There was only the soft flow of magic from the brooch into the air. Its warmth washed over his skin and his eyes slid closed.

He was in the roundhouse with his family. Leaning against his mother's knee by the fire, his father was picking up his sword from beside the bed. Small Keelia was cooing in her little bundle of fabric. Reaching towards his father with his small hands, Leugio tried to speak, but nothing came forth. His father knelt next to him, offering a warm smile. Then his father removed an iron brooch from his cloak and fastened it to Leugio's own tunic. There was a large hand on his head, and he reached up to touch the metal in an action he would repeat for years. There was magic beneath his fingers. Leugio pulled on it, begging it to help him, pleading for whatever power it held to help him.

Magic hit his chest. Stumbling back, Leugio sucked air in greedily. His chest was expanding. The dull pained muscles were suddenly thrumming with energy. The Sídhe nearby all froze and stared at him. Sheer panic took over Teàrlach's face. He screamed for them to stop him, but then Leugio released the first crashing wave of magic. It exploded around him. His own skin burned; his hands blackened as the heat flared back against him. Three Sídhe died screaming and Teàrlach dove into the snow as the wave crashed into him. Leugio's body swayed, but he saw the leather armor crumble and long lines of burning flesh appear on Teàrlach's exposed back.

There was more magic. His heart was racing too quickly, but Leugio kept pulling. Teàrlach was dragging his broken body through the snow towards the entrance, calling orders. Sídhe were running, retreating into the new mound. The entrance was small: too small for all of them. New, just formed by whatever power they had. How long had they been digging? There'd be no answers.

Pushing the magic forward, Leugio sent it twisting all around the mound entrance. Inside the Sídhe were screaming; they protested and ran, but it didn't stop. In his hand the Iron Brooch began to crack.

More flashes of magic exploded into the air and shot towards the mound. Teàrlach shifted his body and looked back at him. His eyes were wide and fearful. There was no rush of pleasure, no satisfaction in Leugio: just a cold acceptance.

The magic hit the mound. Earth flew into the air. He heard stone crack. The ground trembled. His ears rang and flashes of magic lit up the night sky. Torches fell out of the quivering ground and hissed as they hit the snow. There was screaming from up the hill. More magic flashed, splitting open the ground and making dirt and snow pour into the hole. Gone was the mound: all the raised earth crashed into the remains of the tunnels. In a shimmer of gold Teàrlach vanished, and a few remaining warriors took off running into the night. The Brooch crumbled to dust in Leugio's hand.

Collapsing forward, Leugio grimaced as snow compressed beneath his cheek. Cold was spreading, but he couldn't move. The ache was gone. Now there was only the dull burn. Where he'd once had magic there was only emptiness. There was nothing left.

It was beginning to snow. Fat flakes fell onto his cheeks and his eyelashes, making it harder to see. He could hear people, but they were muted. Leugio's eyes began to slide closed. Exhaustion weighed down on him. There was no more magic. He had nothing left. In his right hand, the last of the dust from his Brooch slipped from his fingertips. A tear gathered in his eye, but it couldn't fall. His chest shuddered with a sob, but turned into a painful shiver against the cold.

Fear, grief, and disbelief. Was this what it meant to be a mage? Was this always how the story was going to end? He saved Keelia and came here. He'd done as the king wanted, done what he thought was right, and now he was here in the snow after his magic deserted him. There were voices behind him. Someone touched his shoulder, but he hissed in pain. A droplet of water hit his cheek. Hands carefully turned him over. He was looking up into a thick black sky, though there was the glow of a torch next to him.

"Leugio," Flaitheas' voice called. "Can you hear me?" Her voice was distant; too soft and thick with emotion. He couldn't nod. "I'm here," she said. Then she leaned over him, her brown eyes suddenly meeting his own. Tears were running down her cheeks.

He wanted to smile for her– wanted to say something. His mouth didn't work. In his chest, his heart slowed. It was like drifting off to sleep, there was a vague awareness of something creeping up over you. There was no fear, just a distant sense of regret. He'd never learned what he had wanted to about magic, never really become comfortable with the life the king had given him, and hadn't seen his mother and sister for over a season.

Regret. It tasted bitter and filled his mouth, but it was too late. Flaitheas took his hand and squeezed, only enhancing his pain for a moment. Then the sudden flash faded. The burn in his chest dulled. He couldn't sense any magic anymore. It wasn't just out of reach: it was gone. Letting his eyes slide closed, he exhaled the last of his breath.

34

Herald of the Lie

Alex couldn't move. There was something so wrong about the sight of Brekszta just standing on the retaining wall. Behind her feet was a small flower bed that separated the wall from the lawn. The Old One just giggled and kept waving at them. It went on too long and Alex's body was tensed, preparing to fight.

Then Brekszta dropped her hand and her smile fell away. A cloud of glittering dark blue magic surrounded Brekszta like a nebula of stars. At another time it would have been beautiful. Alex could understand ancient humans thinking she was a Goddess of the Night.

There was a hungry, desperate look on the Old One's face. She took a small step forward on the retaining wall, barely balancing on the edge. Brekszta curled her lips thoughtfully and held out her hands. The magic behind her swept forward, curling around her body and creeping towards them. Around them, the lights flickered. The scents of the grass and coffee faded.

"What are you doing, Brekszta?" Alex demanded.

"I have something of yours," Brekszta announced. Giggling again, the Old One's eyes widened gleefully and she waved her hand.

The dark cloud of magic rolled back. It had been covering something, hiding something, Alex realized with a nervous turn of her stomach. Two figures appeared, and as the light of the nearest street lamp hit them Alex couldn't hold in her gasp. Her brothers were collapsed on the ground, both of them in sweatpants and old t-shirts. Brekszta had grabbed them out of their hotel room. Only the steady rise and fall of their chests reassured Alex that they were alive.

Her heart beat. Her lungs kept working and Alex's muscles eased. For a moment the voices quieted under the weight of her own shock. For a moment she was alone in her terror. The Old One had her brothers. Brekszta's face went from amused to completely blank. Alex could feel the heavy gaze on her as Brekszta watched her reaction. Alex walked towards Brekszta, not daring to look at her brothers and fighting back the fear.

"Isn't this a bit much?" Alex asked.

"Maybe this time you'll listen," Brekszta said. "You have to listen."

"Fine," Alex said shortly. The voices were growing louder again. All around her the magic was thickening. "I'm listening. What's your message?"

"The lie has to die," Brekszta said. "The lie has to end!"

"What lie?" Alex asked. Trembling with anger, she fought to stay calm. "What are you talking about? What is this lie?"

"You," Brekszta replied.

She didn't have time to ponder what the Old One meant by that. Dark blue magic in the sky rained down like a meteor storm. Alex's vision lit up with the streaks of energy and she threw her hands up reflexively. A sharp tug of fear in her gut spurred her into action and she released a wave of her own dark gray magic. It pushed away the bolts of dark blue and she glanced at the others. They'd managed the same, and there was even a shimmering bubble of sorts around Nicki.

Yellow magic streamed past. Bran's magic swept around her brothers and lifted both off the ground, bringing them back towards him. There were no signs of injury. Relief and suspicion hit Alex at once and she sniffed at the air. She could smell ozone, but it was light and barely there. Brekszta was just testing them. Or toying with them, and Alex didn't like either option. Dark blue clouds hung around her brothers' chests, and there were sparkling dark blue lines of magic leading into both of their heads.

"I'll get your brothers further away," Bran said softly.

Barely nodding, Alex didn't dare look at him. Her heart was pounding in her chest. The voices were loud, but now they were mostly saying the same thing. There were remarks of caution, bits of advice on how to fight an Old One, and urgings for her to stop Brekszta. Shifting her fingers, Alex released more dark gray sparks. There were only a few moments of calm while Brekszta glared at them. But then the figures appeared. They were moving across the lawn and along the sidewalks towards her, stretching out their hands as their figures became clearer.

"Ghosts are back," Nicki muttered. "Alex, you alright?"

"I'm fine," Alex replied.

Nonetheless, her eyes jumped between the figures. She knew all of their faces and the voices provided names. Even Cuthbert was drawn towards one, but she kept her feet firmly on the ground. Magic rose up from the Earth and rushed up through her legs making her stronger, but it also made the voices louder. Shivering, Alex shook her head.

"Shut up," she whispered. "Shut up."

They didn't quiet. As the figures came closer, the voices only grew louder. They buzzed like insects burrowing to escape. A wild, high pitched flurry of sounds that no longer meant anything. Alex bit her lip. The figures were getting closer. A flash of red behind her rippled outwards to force some of the ghosts back and was followed by blue bolts. The voices protested.

Brekszta was watching her with narrowed, calculating eyes. She was waiting for something, but Alex didn't know what. Dark silver magic flared around Alex's fingertips, thrumming in the air, and she glanced towards the figures. Her fingers twitched to attack, but the voices were too loud in their protests. Brekszta tilted her head and seemed to be listening to something. Then she shook her head and smashed a foot down on the narrow wall.

"No, no, no! You aren't listening!"

"Look, end the spell and we'll talk!" Alex shouted. "Humans seeing magic is dangerous!"

Her words seemed to surprise Brekszta, and there was a flicker of something in the Old One's eyes. Shaking her head, she made a sound of frustration and tangled her long fingers in her loose dark hair. There were soft pained sounds coming from her, but Alex couldn't understand anything she was saying. Brekszta looked up at her suddenly, her eyes wild and the dark blue magic shuddered all around her. With a scream, Brekszta waved her hands and the magic rose above them like a tidal wave.

Throwing up her hands, Alex released a blast of dark silver magic. It and the incoming wave collided and the air crackled with energy. There was an explosion of sound around them and Alex's ears rang. Grimacing, she sucked in a sharp breath and tried to coax Brekszta's magic towards her. It pushed back. Then it gave and Alex's magic swept forward. Panting, Alex's legs shuddered. All of her energy was drawn out of her and into the swirling magical storm.

Thankfully, she was able to pull some back. Her knees locked. Dark silver spun around her, surrounding Alex in a shimmering dark wave before spinning together into a large orb. Brekszta shrieked, but there was still blue magic surrounding her. For a moment, they just stared at each other. Alex licked her too dry lips and struggled to take another breath. Everything was hurting now. Her muscles were on fire, too hot and too tight.

The tornado of magic calmed and Brekszta smiled. Her magic stretched out, linking once more to the thin strands spread across town. Like the web of a spider, each one was latched to a victim. Looking into the coffee shop, Alex's stomach tightened as she scanned the people slumped over. Over her head the strands were stretching out at least across campus, but maybe further.

Swallowing, Alex reached for the stray wisps of magic in the air. She dared not touch the strands. The flickers of dark blue magic turned the color of iron, swirling together into Alex's hands. Brekszta made an odd sound of irritation. The orb of magic was the size of a grapefruit and pulsing softly as it floated beside Alex.

"No, you're not doing this right!" Brekszta snapped. "Listen to me! Listen! Listen!" Her frantic tone was back. Her eyes were too wide, too dark, and glittered with something that made Alex and all the voices retreat.

More magic flowed into Alex's orb as Brekszta glared. With a shriek, Brekszta threw more magic at them. With a shout, Alex brought up her hands and pushed out a wave of her magic, catching Brekszta's attacks. Bolts of red and blue shot past Alex. Lightning arched off Alex's hands, striking Brekszta in the chest and knocking her back several feet.

"Alex!" Nicki called. "What do you want us to do?! Do you want us to attack her?!"

The question made her pause. They couldn't see the strands. They could see the attacks, maybe see the cloud of magic around her, but they wouldn't be able to see the traces of her spell. Nodding, Alex didn't dare speak again. It was enough, Nicki and Aiden both stepped forward. A ring of fire appeared around them, expanding outwards and forcing back the ghosts. Nicki punched the air and a wave of pressure hit Brekszta, who screamed in frustration.

There was a squeal of tires in the nearby parking lot. Alex tensed as thoughts of a student seeing the light show hit her. They'd pull out a cellphone and... a familiar magic brushed against hers. Relief flooded Alex's system just before a bolt of leaf green magic blasted towards Brekszta. The stone retaining wall shuddered beneath her and a shout of surprise escaped Brekszta. She jumped back only for a layer of earth to rise up and mold around her feet.

"Not fair!" Brekszta screamed. "Cheating!"

Alex spun around. Merlin was behind them with a bag over his shoulder and Mjǫllnir in his right hand. He was panting and his cheeks were red. One of the voices was amused, but it quickly faded. Another voice shouted in joy when her eyes fell on the Hammer while another all but withdrew. Merlin nodded to her, but his eyes jumped past her to Brekszta. Alex held out her hand for Mjǫllnir and Merlin began to move towards her.

"No!" Brekszta shouted.

Alex sensed the magic before she saw it. The air filled with the sharp smell of Brekszta's magic, like a cold night with a hint of decay. Strands of magic were stretching out further into the city. Alex's mind provided visions of cars crashing and people falling into the street, or into running machines. Dark blue magic rained down around them and the figures flickered. Their pale forms shifted to dark blue and the faces vanished, replaced with empty vacant faces without eyes or mouths. They turned as one towards Merlin.

"Merlin!" Alex shouted. "Throw me the Hammer!"

With his left hand, Merlin released a wave of green magic. Silver magic rippled out from the parking lot. Alex could see Morgana running towards them. Bolts of silver ripped through the figures. Merlin raised the Hammer up with his right hand. Grunting, he threw his weight forward and released the Hammer. The world slowed down.

Alex threw out a hand, sending threads of dark silver magic towards the Hammer. Mjǫllnir sailed through the air, twisting unnaturally as her gray magic wrapped around it. Holding out a hand, Alex called back the magic. The spark in the ancient iron metal flared to life. The triskelion on the side flashed and then the handle was in her hands. All around Alex the glimmer of the magical threads twinkled, but she hesitated.

"Alex!" Aiden shouted.

Looking up, Alex gasped. Brekszta had vanished into a whirling cloud of dark blue magic. It was lashing out all around them like a twister, ripping apart the ground. Her hair whipped around her face and the glass window of the coffee shop shattered. The magic crawled over her skin. Alex's eyes jumped to the nearest of the ghostly figures as it reached for Merlin. The other mage slammed his foot on the ground and a massive rock spike rose up to impale the ghostly figure. It only stopped for a moment.

Gripping the Hammer, Alex focused on the pulsing strands of magic passing by her. She swung Mjǫllnir, crashing the Hammer through the stream of magic. Dark gray magic rippled outward, cutting through the stream and several others. The released magic sparked in the air. Alex pulled on it, reaching out with her left hand. Her own magic rushed out and swooped around like a scoop to gather it up. Brekszta shouted something, but Alex didn't stop to listen. She swung the Hammer again and broke through more of the strands, desperately hoping it wouldn't hurt anyone. This had to stop. Distantly she heard voices calling to her.

One of the figures touched her cheek. It was cold and not solid. Instead, it was like walking into mist. She looked without meaning to. Ilse was looking right at her. There were tears slipping from the familiar blue eyes. There were more lines around her face than Alex remembered, but her heart faltered for a moment. Gottfried was sobbing, begging her to do something, and sick with fear.

"Alex!" Aiden shouted. "Alex!" A bolt of red shot through Ilse's chest and the ghostly figure staggered. The features blurred and Alex tore her eyes away from the haunting blue ones. "You okay?!"

She didn't try to answer. More magic was gathering. Alex swung Mjǫllnir through another set of magical threads and watched them snap with satisfaction before quickly gathering the magic. She waved her left hand. The orb was larger now and shimmered like a snowball in the sun. Brekszta's eyes met hers, she opened her mouth to say something, but Alex didn't want to hear anything more. With a squint of her eye, she sent the orb hurtling towards her enemy.

The orb dropped on Brekszta. There was a short scream, but the energy swirled and rippled around her. All of the magic rushed into her body, making the Old One's eyes glow the color of iron. Beneath her skin a dark gray color took over and spread further and further. It was familiar to Alex, that sight of magic spreading beneath the skin, but she couldn't place it. Brekszta took a shaky step towards her. Around them, all the ghosts vanished.

Alex swung Mjǫllnir once more, this time hitting Brekszta in the middle of her chest. Lightning flashed off of the metal and an explosion shook the air. The rest of the magical threads vanished. Alex's feet slid back across the sidewalk while Brekszta stumbled back.

"You don't understand," Brekszta groaned. She wrapped her arms around her body as if that could keep it from falling apart. "I was trying to help! You are... we're all going to... was trying to help."

"Help?" Alex sneered at the being. Anger filled her chest as every nightmare replayed in a flash before her eyes. Every time she'd seen that truck bear down, every face that had haunted her, and every death she'd relived. Every moment that she'd been afraid to sleep in case more memories came forth. "How was driving me crazy helping?"

"The lies have to die," Brekszta whispered. Her voice was fading away. "Or we all die. The lie has to end."

"You were going to destroy me," Alex said. "I was losing myself to all the others!"

"You are the lie," Brekszta answered.

Their eyes met and Alex was silent as the Old One flickered. Brekszta's image was fading faster now. She could see the energy breaking off. There was nothing to hold it there. Brekszta couldn't control her own form anymore. Then Brekszta laughed, but there was no sound. The Old One reached towards her one last time. Alex didn't move as sparks of energy brushed over her. There was no flesh anymore, no matter or substance, but she still felt something.

A dying world. The image of that dead world flashed through her head again. Then there was another, this one unfamiliar but just as barren and dark as the first, with a blue star shining above it. Then Brekszta was gone. Alex exhaled slowly and scanned the area. There were faint traces of energy, but they were dissipating through the air, leaving only a lingering scent of ozone. It was like there had been a thunderstorm, and nothing more.

The lie. Alex shivered and turned around. Bran wasn't far away, a yellow dome surrounding him and her brothers. She walked towards him and he dropped the protective spell. The lie. Brekszta's last words echoed in her mind. She didn't want to think about them, didn't want to give them any power over her. And yet, those dying worlds pulled at something in her chest.

Kneeling beside her brothers, Alex gently reached out to brush back a strand of hair from Ed's face. They were still asleep. There were faint flickers of magic in their bodies, but it was fading away. They and everyone else would wake soon. Sighing in relief, Alex became aware of the others gathering around her and looked up. The ghosts were gone. A wave of grief made her throat tighten. She looked back at her brothers. Someday, that's what they'd be. In another fight, in another life, they'd be the ghosts just like Galath, Ilse, and Eigyr.

You are the lie. The words echoed again and Alex forced a smile for the others. Bran helped her up and Morgana quickly offered suggestions on how to clean up the area quickly. Merlin left to deal with the cameras and Morgana offered to take her brothers back to the hotel. Nicki and Aiden had already broken off and begun to repair the windows of the coffee shop and the retaining wall. Alex just nodded in agreement at their suggestions and kept her hand wrapped tightly around Mjǫllnir.

35

Concerning Family

One of the worst things about the day after magical combat was the way the world just kept going. The sun was already high in the sky when they gathered the next day at Merlin's house. There was a soft breeze keeping the summer heat at bay, and it carried hints of pine with it. Nothing had changed. Merlin's house was as cozy as ever. Across the river students were heading off to their finals and turning in projects and papers. Hopefully no one failed to finish a final paper due to the unplanned nap.

Yet Alex couldn't shake the sense of wrongness. The knot in her chest still hurt, but the dull ache was easier to live with. Brekszta's spell hadn't truly spread that far, and in a lucky twist of fate no one had died. Alex had expected something. Someone to fall down the stairs, some car to crash on University Drive or someone who fell asleep in a dorm kitchen to start a fire. No one had. This event was simply an oddity that people could move on from.

Looking down at her own steaming cup of coffee, Alex tried to sort out the wild and odd thoughts in her head. The others were moving around Merlin's house calmly. Nicki and Avani were talking in one of the corners. There was a foolish expression on Nicki's face and Alex smiled a touch at the sight.

"We were lucky," Merlin declared. "There weren't many students present, and with it being finals week most seem happy to believe that they just dozed off."

"What about the security feeds?" Alex asked. "Were you able to access them?"

"Yes," Merlin assured her. "Though Ravenslake isn't exactly the most watched campus in the world. I did go over all the camera feeds just to make sure that there was nothing strange recorded. That was a bit more difficult for the lawn feed, so I just made that all static."

"That's good," Alex said carefully. She hesitated to call it a victory just yet. "What else do we need to do?"

"I'm not sure; honestly we need to just stay aware and make sure that no one saw anything. There shouldn't have been any other cameras turned towards the lawn, but we'll keep an ear out for any rumors."

"So, what now?" Aiden asked. "Today is the last day of finals."

"You are all done, correct?" Morgana asked.

"I am," Alex said. Her words were followed by agreements from Nicki, Aiden, and Bran.

"Then we can seriously consider Avani's request for you to head to India," Morgana said.

"Well, this weekend if we build another Gate, I'll consider Ravenslake secure, at least for the time being," Alex said. She took another sip of her drink as Avani's face lit up with relief. "If you and Merlin stay here then I'm comfortable with us investigating India."

"Just like that?" Morgana pressed. There was a hint of suspicion in the older mage's voice. "Do you think that's enough?"

"Brekszta is dead and the Sídhe are locked up for a little while. I doubt that Arthur and the Queen will give us much time, so we need to move while things are quiet."

"And the Red Caps?"

"There's a limit to what we can do about the Fae who aren't happy with the current state of things," Alex replied. "We aren't going to just change their minds. Not that easily."

"I'm sorry," Avani offered. "I know this isn't a good time."

"There's never a good time." Alex chuckled a little and inhaled the smell of her coffee. "There's just the best opportunity."

Morgana's frown deepened, furrowing her brow and making her eyes darken. Alex ignored her and took another sip. Bran was watching her with a hint of worry while Aiden and Nicki seemed excited. There was a flutter of excitement in her own chest at the idea of going to India.

"That's a fair point, I suppose," Merlin said carefully. "Are you comfortable going without us? Perhaps the others could stay here and we could go with you."

A thunderous expression appeared on Nicki's face and Aiden frowned. Bran pressed his lips together tightly at their reactions. Alex straightened up and set down her coffee.

"I understand what you're saying, but they don't have any history with Shiva, good or bad. Bran's scrying ability means I want him to go, and we've proven with the Chalice and the Hammer that we make a good team."

"What about Lance and Jenny?" Morgana asked. "Are you taking them?"

The question made Alex pause. Part of her said yes, but another part of her wanted to say no. She carefully considered it. "I'll talk to them. I don't want to put them in danger, but they've been helpful in the past. They bring an outside perspective."

"They'd be more than welcome," Avani promised. "My family home has more than enough space to accommodate all of you."

"Thank you," Alex replied. She ignored the fact they'd be staying with Lokpal's descendants for the time being. That was a can of worms for another day.

There was more conversation, but Alex didn't give it much of her attention. Instead, she focused on the soft voices whispering to her. They were quieter today; all of them more subdued. There was a hint of sorrow and regret that seeped into Alex. It was an odd feeling, a sense of smallness and resignation.

"Alex?" Aiden called. He was on his feet and looking at her curiously. "You okay?"

The others were on their feet too. Smiling in embarrassment, Alex put down her coffee and stood up. She was suddenly unsure what she'd missed but was confident that she'd be informed of any plans.

"I'll come over this afternoon to work on some more iron," Alex told Merlin.

"Very well. I'll have the workshop ready," Merlin agreed. "Finish packing up your dorms. Morgana is checking out a house for you this week so hopefully, we can move you in quickly."

Nodding in agreement, Alex let the others file out ahead of her. She lingered by the doorway for a moment as Merlin said a few words to Morgana. She didn't understand them, but the words echoed in her head and slowly made sense. Arto, Alex realized with a jolt of surprise. That was new. Shaking her head, she went outside and turned over the translated words.

They were worried about her. Nothing surprising there. Alex walked towards her car parked next to Morgana's. Behind her the door opened and Morgana stepped outside. The older mage hesitated on the porch when she spotted Alex, but forced a smile and started for her own car.

Alex gathered her thoughts and took a deep breath. Now or never. Matt and Eddy were on the road back to Spokane with no idea that anything strange had happened. There was a flicker of regret in her chest that she hadn't had the chance to hug them again or challenge them to one last game of Yahtzee, but it was too late now.

"Morgana," Alex said. The older mage stopped and turned back to her. Alex schooled her features into a calm expression. "I need you to take care of something for me while we're gone. You and Merlin."

"What is that?" Morgana asked. There was a hint of worry in her voice that Alex dismissed, though Arto didn't. "Is there something you didn't tell us earlier?"

"I need you to make my brothers forget about me," Alex replied.

Stunned was too simple a word. All of Morgana's usually collected features fell away, her mouth went slack, and utter shock filled her eyes. For an instant, Morgana stuttered. Under other circumstances, Alex would have been proud of herself as vague memories of Morgana in shock throughout their long history played through her mind.

"What?" Morgana asked carefully.

"They aren't safe." Alex's voice was too calm. Yet she didn't experience the fear that she knew should be filling her chest. "I need you to make them forget about magic and me. Alter their memories and court records. I have my part of the insurance payout already so that's not an issue. If you can, arrange a new life for them away from me so even Arthur can't find them."

"Alex, that's madness." Horror filled Morgana's face.

"No, it isn't," Alex said firmly. "Madness is pretending that Arthur isn't going to go after them. Madness is pretending that I can protect them and the Iron Realm at the same time."

"Alex, that's... you told them the truth about magic so they'd understand!"

"Yes, but they've lost their parents. I don't want them living with the fear that they are next. I want them to be able to move on. Believe their parents' death really was just an accident." Alex shook her head sadly and looked north towards Spokane. She wondered if she spread out her magic far enough if she'd be able to find her brothers. "I'd do it myself, but I have no experience with changing memories. I hate the idea of harming them, but this isn't working. Matt and Eddy can't handle this."

"I'm not sure they're the ones who can't handle it," Morgana said. Her green eyes were dark with worry and she began to reach for Alex.

"This isn't grief." Alex shifted away from Morgana's hand. "I'm about to go to India for who knows how long. Then what happens? Maybe I finish a semester without a crisis, but school at this point is secondary. I'm the Iron Soul... I'm on call for the rest of my life."

"Alex, as we told your parents, there is no reason why you can't live a long, happy and peaceful life when all this passes."

"Do you think it is going to pass?" Alex demanded. "Really? I remember parts of my other lives now, Morgana. There was sometimes, and only sometimes, one threat. But now there are Old Ones waking, Demons acting up, a Dragon in Wales, a Sídhe invasion, and a hybrid made with my own power all at once. We're juggling at best and fighting a war on multiple fronts at worst. This isn't like the other lives. I'm not like other lives."

They stared at each other. Alex didn't turn away from Morgana's sharp searching gaze. The knot ached, but it was dull and distant. This was just one more little hurt to be contained, one more distraction to be kept at bay.

"Just try to make it smooth," Alex said. "I know I'm asking for a lot in the age of digital records, but Arthur won't leave them alone. In his position, I'd hurt them or take them hostage."

There was a long pause. There were questions glittering in Morgana's eyes. Alex heard the others driving off and waited. Behind them the door of Merlin's house opened. Alex glanced back to find him watching them and gave him a little wave. Merlin looked like he wanted to say something, but went back into the house.

"Is this really just about Arthur, or something else?" Morgana asked finally.

"It's a lot of things," Alex admitted. "Those ghostly figures... they had the faces of people I've cared about. I saw Ilse and our mother last night. It... hurt."

"Our mother?" Morgana repeated, in confusion. "You mean Elizabeth?"

"No, our mother," Alex said, stressing the our. Morgana made a soft pained sound. "At this point, I probably remember her face more clearly than you do," Alex said. She didn't mean for the words to be sharp, but they were. "I see them now. There are glimpses of memories, faces that play in my mind when I sleep. I carry them with me, Morgana. And I'll carry Matt and Ed with me. But I don't want to bury them." The knot twisted. Tears pricked at Alex's eyes, but she did not let them fall. "There's already so much pain to live with. I can't add them to it. I don't want them dead because they wouldn't abandon me."

Morgana reached for her and Alex didn't pull away. Catching a strand of blonde hair, Morgana tucked it behind Alex's ear and stared at her sadly. In her head, Arto apologized for the sorrow they were causing her, but Alex didn't voice it.

"I can't change your mind, can I?" Morgana's shoulders slumped in defeat. She pulled her hand back, letting it drop to her side. "I'll try to make sure that it is possible to make them remember," Morgana finally said. "So that when you change your mind-"

"I'm not going to change my mind," Alex insisted. "They'll have to live with losing their parents, no matter the new story you give them: that will remain just by their absence. At least they won't have to be afraid of being next, and worry about or resent their sister. They'll be able to move on."

"And what about you?"

The answer came too quickly, too easily, and for a moment Alex felt a twinge of worry for herself. Nonetheless, she said it anyway, "I'll live this life, die, and be reborn without that burden. It doesn't matter. Not really; not in the grand scheme of things."

"Not everything is about the grand scheme, Alex."

"No, but my existence is."

"This isn't a good idea," Morgana pleaded. "I don't want this for you."

Smiling softly, Alex leaned down and kissed Morgana's forehead. Something settled in her chest and the knot eased. This was hard, this hurt, but she'd still have Morgana. Somehow that was comforting. Stepping back, Alex almost said something more but settled for smiling.

"I'll speak with Merlin," Morgana sighed. "He won't like it, but we'll do it. While you're in India, we'll see what we can do."

"Thank you."

Alex turned to her car and pulled out her keys. She was grateful that she'd come here by herself this morning. Opening the door, Alex slid into her driver's seat and released a slow breath. That had gone better than she had expected. Rather than feeling sad or worried, there was relief. It would be done. She'd miss her brothers, but this was for the best. The engine turned on and Alex pulled away from the curb.

Humming softly, Alex looked in the rearview mirror to see Morgana heading back into Merlin's house. Her fingers drummed on the steering wheel and she quickly headed back to the university. The parking lot was almost empty and she got a spot close to Gallagher Hall. Alex caught sight of Aiden and Bran heading inside, though Nicki was nowhere to be seen. She waited a few moments before climbing out of her car to give the boys a chance to get inside before she went to her own room.

They'd packed up most of the kitchen stuff and the living room had a stack of boxes waiting for Nicki to take back to her grandmother's. Some of her things were in the corner waiting to be loaded. Alex paused and looked at the sofa. Then she shook her head. She'd be glad to see the last of this dorm room. There were too many memories of Arthur here. Using her keycard, she unlocked her bedroom door and stepped into her room, closing it behind her with a grateful sigh. Against the wall were a few cardboard boxes waiting for the last of her things.

Sitting down at her desk, Alex rolled her shoulders and opened the photos folder on her computer. She was able to look through the first couple of them with a soft smile. She, her parents, and her brothers were all together by a lake and smiling. Reaching out, Alex touched the screen and allowed a few tears to slip from her eyes. The knot eased and began to unravel. She staggered out of her chair to the bed, collapsing on it with a muffled sob.

It was time to say goodbye. In a few days she'd be in Mumbai, confronting yet another past life and another species. Demons and Shiva were her future. Arthur was still out there, along with his mother, and sooner or later they'd need to deal with the violent Fae who didn't want peace. Galahad was still on her pillow, and Alex scooped up the little dog as she finally allowed herself to cry.

www.ingramcontent.com/pod-product-compliance
Lightning Source LLC
Chambersburg PA
CBHW060933120726
47910CB00002B/305